DATE DUE

Demco, Inc. 38-293

MARKUS ZUSAK

UndeR DoGS

• THREE NOVELS •

ARTHUR A. LEVINE BOOKS
AN IMPRINT OF SCHOLASTIC INC.

ISBN 978-0-545-35442-4

10 9 8 7 6 5 4 3 2 1   11 12 13 14 15

Printed in the U.S.A. 23

Book design by Steve Scott and Elizabeth B. Parisi

First omnibus edition, August 2011

• TABLE OF CONTENTS •

AUTHOR'S NOTE

I guess there aren't too many writers who can say their career started with a horror trip to the dentist — but if there's one thing I've learned over the years, it's that you take your good luck however you get it. For me, it was a trigger-happy dental surgeon. It was several fillings, hundreds of dollars paid in cash, and one small thought of revenge: What if two brothers tried to rob the dentist?

That's how I became a writer.

Of course, I'm not telling the whole truth. I left out my first embarrassing attempt at a book when I was sixteen (all eight pages of it), and the seven years of failed attempts that followed. For the better part of a decade, I'd been trying to write something very serious, but suddenly I knew what my next project would be. It was those brothers and their farcical holdup. They would use a baseball bat and a cricket bat as their weapons. They would get there and be immediately bewitched by the beautiful dental nurse behind the desk . . . and they would end up getting checkups instead — the beginning of *The Underdog*.

Originally, it was supposed to be a short story, but I discovered very quickly that Cameron and Ruben Wolfe were a pair of boys I knew without question. The voice of Cameron was me. The spirit of Ruben was my brother. The only difference was that Rube spoke more in one minute than my brother usually did in a year . . . but finally I had what I needed. Writing became a joy; I was like a kid in a sandpit.

All up, *The Underdog* took me a few months to write and edit. When I thought about publication, I held little hope. After all, three other manuscripts had already been rejected over the last seven years, and this was the one I had worked on least.

Around this period was also the first time I ever went overseas. I left the manuscript under my bed with fifty dollars attached, for my brother to mail for me while I was away. When I rang to ask him to send it off, he did what any self-respecting older brother would do. He paid the eight dollars to mail it and kept the forty-two dollars change — and I started waiting for the rejection that never came.

To this day, I remember it very clearly.

I was woken at 2:20 A.M. in Vienna, where I was staying with my dad's best friend. The phone was ring-ing, and strange as it sounds, I knew. It was the book. They were going to publish the book. I never went back to bed after that.

Upon hearing the news from my father, I immedi-ately called my two sisters, the first of whom told me she nearly hit the ceiling when she heard. The second one cried and told me she was so proud of me.

Then I called my brother.

After ten minutes of this-and-that, I said, "So, you heard about my book?"

My brother, in typical fashion, said, "Yeah. Pretty good."

This, to be fair, was most people's version of screaming congratulations from a rooftop. It's about as animated as my brother gets, and I knew he was happy.

Since then, twelve years have passed, and it's a real thrill for me that *The Underdog* is being released in America for the first time as part of this omnibus. When I think about these three books, I realize that the first one was my great fluke. The second was a slightly steadier step in the direction of where I wanted to go. The third brought with it the realization that it was time to move on again and rise to newer writing challenges.

In the end, it's like finding an old photo of yourself; you hope for as little embarrassment as possible. Of course, there are so many things I'd love to change, but I also look back with a lot of happiness. After twelve years, the doubts and fears subside — they loom larger over the work I'm doing now. For Cameron and Ruben, twelve years is enough time to just let them be, I think.

Lastly, I have to confess that I haven't reread a single word of these books to write this note. You didn't think I'd be reckless enough to bring the old demons out of the cupboard, did you? No, I'm going on memory alone. I remember a pair of dirty boys. I remember their sister on the couch, their overachieving eldest brother, and parents who, in my view, were the real heroes in these stories. I even remember Miffy — the infernal Pomeranian — and I know that I'm a little more alive for having written these books, and I hope the same thing happens for you, in the reading.

All my best,
Markus
Sydney, Australia
September 2010

THE
UNDERDOG

for my family

CHAPTER 1

We were watching the telly when we decided to rob the dentist.

"The dentist?" I asked my brother.

"Sure, why not?" was his reply. "Do you know how much money goes through a dental surgery in a day? It's obscene. If the prime minister was a dentist, the country wouldn't be in the state it's in right now, I can tell you. There'd be no unemployment, no racism, no sexism. Just money."

"Yeah."

I agreed with my brother Ruben only to keep him happy. The truth was that he was just grandstanding again. It was one of his worst habits.

That was the first truth, of two.

The second was that even though we had decided to knock over our local dentist, we were never going to do it. So far this year we'd promised to rob the bakery, the fruit shop, the hardware, the fish 'n' chip shop, and the optometrist. It never happened.

"And this time I'm serious." Rube sat forward on the couch. He must have been seeing what I was thinking.

We weren't robbing anything.

We were hopeless.

Hopeless, pitiful, and a shake-your-head kind of pathetic.

I myself had a job twice a week delivering newspapers but I got sacked after I broke some guy's kitchen window. It wasn't even a hard throw. It just happened. The window was there half open, I threw the paper, and *Smack!* It went through the glass. The bloke came running out and went berserk and hurled abuse at me as I stood there with a pile of ridiculous tears in my eyes. The job was gone — cursed from the start.

My name's Cameron Wolfe.

I live in the city.

I go to school.

I'm not popular with the girls.

I have a little bit of sense.

I don't have much sense.

I have thick, furry hair that isn't long but always looks messy and always sticks up, no matter how hard I try keeping it down.

My older brother Ruben gets me into plenty of trouble.

I get Rube into as much trouble as he gets me into.

I have another brother named Steve who's the oldest and is the winner of the family. He's had quite a few girls and has a good job and he's the one a lot of people like. He's also some kind of good footballer on top of it.

I have a sister named Sarah who sits on the couch with her boyfriend and has him stick his tongue down her throat whenever possible. Sarah's second oldest.

I have a father who constantly tells Rube and me to wash ourselves because he reckons we look filthy and stink like jungle animals crawling out of the mud.

("I don't bloody stink!" I argue with him. "And I have a shower quite bloody regularly!"

"Well have you heard of soap? . . . I was once your age myself y' know, and I know how filthy guys your age are."

"Is that right?"

"Of course it is. I wouldn't say it otherwise."

No point arguing on.)

I have a mother who says very little but is the toughest thing in our house.

I have a family, yes, that doesn't really function without tomato sauce.

I like winter.

That's me.

Oh, and yeah, at the point in time I'm talking about, I had never, not even once, robbed a single thing in my life. I just talked about it with Rube, exactly like that day in the lounge room.

"Oi."

Rube slapped Sarah on the arm as she kissed that boyfriend on our couch.

"Oi — we're gonna rob the dentist."

Sarah stopped.

"Hey?" she enquired.

"Ah, forget it." Rube looked away. "Is this a useless house or isn't it? There are ignorant people everywhere, too busy with 'emselves to care."

"Ah, stop whingein'," I told him.

He looked at me. That was all he did, as Sarah got back down to business.

I switched off the TV then and we left. We left to check out the dentist's surgery we were going to "hit," as Rube put it. (The real reason we went there was just to get out of the house, because Sarah and her boyfriend were going insane in the lounge room and our mother was cooking mushrooms in the kitchen, which stank out the whole place.)

"Bloody mushrooms again," I said as we walked out onto the street.

"Yeah," Rube smirked. "Just drown 'em in tomato sauce again so you can't taste 'em."

"Bloody oath."

What whingers.

"And there she is." Rube smiled as we walked onto Main Street in the darkening air of June and winter. "Doctor Thomas G. Edmunds. Bachelor of Dental Surgery. Beautiful."

We started making a plan.

Plan-making between my brother and me consisted of me asking questions and Rube answering them. It went like this:

"Won't we need a gun or somethin'? Or a knife? That fake gun we had got lost."

"It isn't lost. It's behind the couch."

"Y' sure?"

"Yes. I'm sure . . . and in any case, we don't need it. All we need is the cricket bat and we'll get next-door's baseball bat, right?" He laughed, very sarcastically. "We swing those babies a few times and they can't possibly say no."

"Okay."

Okay.

Yeah, right.

We scheduled everything for the next afternoon. We got the bats, we went over everything we had to remember, and we knew we weren't going to do it. Even Rube knew.

We went to the dentist next day anyway, and for the first time ever in one of our heists, we actually went inside.

What greeted us was a shock, because behind the counter was the most brilliant dental nurse you've ever seen. I'm serious. She was writing something with her pen and I couldn't take my eyes off her. Never mind about the baseball bat I was holding. I forgot all about it. There was no robbery. We just stood there, Rube and I.

Rube and I, and the dental nurse, in the room, together.

"Be with y' in a sec," she said politely, without looking up. God almighty she was beautiful. Absolutely. Brilliant.

"Oi," Rube whispered to her, really quiet. He was

making sure only I could hear him. "Oi . . . This is a holdup."

She didn't hear.

"Stupid bloody cow." He looked at me and shook his head. "Y' can't even hold up a dentist anymore. Sheez. What's the world comin' to?"

"Now." She finally looked up. "What can I do for you fellas?"

"Ah . . ." I was uneasy, but what else was I meant to say? Rube said nothing. There was silence. I had to break it. I smiled and fell apart. "Ah, we just came to get a checkup."

She smiled back. "When would you like it?"

"Aah, tomorrow?"

"Four o'clock okay?"

"Yep." I was nodding, wondering.

She looked into me. Right in. Waiting. Helpful. "So what are your names?"

"Oh yeah," I responded, laughing pretty stupidly. "Cameron and Ruben Wolfe."

She wrote it down, smiled again, and then spotted the cricket and baseball bats.

"Just been puttin' in some practice." I lifted the baseball bat.

"In the middle of winter?"

"We can't afford a football," Rube interrupted us. We had a football and a soccer ball somewhere in our backyard. He pushed me toward the door. "We'll be back tomorrow."

She grinned her happy-I'm-here-to-help smile. She said, "Okay, bye-ee."

I stayed a second and said, "Bye."

Bye.

Could I think of nothing better?

"Y' bloody spastic," Rube told me, once we were back outside. "Checkups," he whined. "The old man wants us smellin' like roses, sure enough, but he's not interested in us havin' clean teeth. He couldn't give a bloody toss about our teeth!"

"Well, who got us in there to begin with, ay? Whose great idea was it to rob the dentist? Not bloody mine, mate!"

"Okay, okay." Rube leaned against the wall. Traffic limped past us.

"And what the hell was all that whisperin' about?"

I'd decided by now that while I had him against the wall I'd go in for the kill. "The only thing you forgot to say was *please*. Maybe she'd have heard y' then. *Oi, this is a holdup*," I imitated him with a whisper. "Absolutely pathetic."

Rube snapped. "All right! I blew it. . . . Still, I didn't exactly see you swingin' that baseball bat." This was better now for Rube, since we were back on what I did wrong as opposed to what he did. "You didn't swing a thing, mate. . . . You were too busy lookin' in Blondie's big blue eyes and starin' at her, her breasts."

"I was *not*!"

Breasts.

Who was he kidding?

Talking like that.

"Oh yeah." Rube kept laughing. "I seen you, y' dirty little bastard."

"Ah, that's lies." But it wasn't. Walking down Main Street, I knew I was in love with the beautiful blond dental nurse. I was already fantasizing about lying in the dentist chair with her over the top of me, on my lap, asking, "Are y' comfortable, Cameron? Y' feeling nice?"

"Great," I'd reply. "Great."

"Oi."

"*Oi!*" Rube shoved me. "Are you still listenin'?"

I turned back to him. He continued talking.

"So why don't y' tell me where the hell we're gonna get the money for these checkups, ay?" He thought about it for a minute as we started up walking again and quickened the pace for home. "Nah, we're better off canceling."

"No," I answered. "No way, Rube."

"Dirty boy" was his retort. "Forget the nurse. She's prob'ly doin' it with Mister Doctor Dentist as we speak."

"Don't you talk about her like that," I warned him.

Rube stopped walking again.

Then he stared.

Then he said, "You're pitiful, y' know that?"

"I know." I could only agree. "I guess you're right."

"As always."

We walked on. Again. Tail between the legs.

Oh, and by the way, we didn't cancel.

We considered asking our folks for the cash but they'd have wanted to know just why we went down there to begin with, and a discussion of that nature wasn't exactly high on our list. I myself got the money I needed by taking it out from my stash under the wrecked corner of carpet in our room.

We went back.

I tried like hell to keep my hair down. For the nurse.

We went back there the next day.

It didn't work — with the hair.

We went back there next day and there was a kind of beastly dental nurse there of about forty years of age.

"Now *there's* someone in your range," Rube whispered at me in the waiting room. He was grinning like the dirty juvenile he had always been. He disgusted me, but then again, quite often, I disgusted myself.

"Hey," I told him and waved a finger. "I think you've got somethin' stuck in your teeth there."

"Where?" He panicked. "Here?" He opened his mouth and grimaced a wide smile. "Is it gone?"

"Nah — further right. That way." There was nothing there, of course, and when he looked at his reflection in the dental surgery fish tank and found out, he returned and slapped me across the back of the head.

"Huh." He kept going with his original line. "Y' dirty boy." He chuckled. "I'll admit it, though. She was good. She was fully great."

"Mmm."

"Not like middle-aged fat woman here, ay?"

I laughed. Boys like us — boys in general — would have to be the scum of the earth. Most of the time, anyway. I swear it, we spend most of our time being inhumane.

We need a good kick in the pants, as my old man always says (and gives us).

He's right.

The nurse came in. "Right, who's first?"

All quiet.

Then, "Me."

I stood up. I decided it would be best to get this over with quickly.

In the end, it wasn't too bad. There was just this fluoride treatment stuff that tasted pretty ordinary and some scratching around inside from the big man. There was no drill. Not for us. There is no justice in the world.

Or maybe there is . . .

The dentist ended up robbing *us*. He was pretty pricey, even for the little bit he did for us.

"All that money," I said after we'd walked out again.

"Still," Rube was finally the one not doing the complaining, "no drill." He punched my shoulder. "I s'pose. No chocolate biscuits at our joint. It's good for somethin', ay. Good for the fangs . . . We've got a genius for a mother."

I disagreed. "Nah, she's just tight."

We laughed, but we knew Mum was brilliant. It was just Dad that was a worry.

Back home, not much was going on. We could smell leftover mushrooms heating on the stove and Sarah was going at it on the couch again. No point going in.

I went into Rube's and my room and looked at the city that spread its filthy breath across the horizon. The sun was pale yellow behind it and the buildings were like the feet of huge black beasts lying down.

Yeah, it was around the middle of June at this time, and the weather was really starting to bite.

I guess things happened in my life that winter, but nothing too out of the ordinary. I failed in getting my old job back. My father gave me a chance. My elder brother Steve screwed up his ankle, insulted the hell out of me, and eventually came to realize something. My mother held a boxing exhibition in our school welfare office and went berserk one night, throwing the compost at my feet in the kitchen. My sister, Sarah, got jilted. Rube started growing a beard and eventually woke up to himself a bit. Greg, a guy who was once my best friend, asked me for three hundred bucks to save his life. I met a girl and fell in love with her (but then, I could fall in love with anything that showed an interest). I dreamed a whole lot of weird, sick, perverted, sometimes beautiful dreams. And I survived.

Nothing much happened really.

It was all pretty normal.

First dream:

It's late afternoon and I'm walking to the dental surgery when I see someone standing on the roof. As I move closer I realize it's the dentist. I can tell from the white coat and the mustache. He's right on the edge, looking prepared to throw himself off.

I stop beneath him and yell, "Oi! What the hell are you doing?"

"What's it look like?"

At that, I'm speechless.

All I can do now is run into the arcade building where the dental surgery is situated and go through and tell the beautiful dental nurse.

"What!" is her reply.

My God, she looks so great that I almost tell her, "To hell with Mister Dentist, let's go down the beach or something." I don't say anything else, though. I just run to the end of a corridor, open the door, and take some stairs up to the roof.

For some reason, when I make it to the edge, the dental nurse hasn't come with me.

When I stand next to the brooding, mustached dentist and look over the edge, she's standing at the bottom, trying to tell him to come down.

"What are you doing down there?" I call down to her.

"I'm not going up there!" she shouts back up. "I'm scared of heights!"

I accept her statement, because, quite frankly, I'm happy enough because I can see her legs and body, and my stomach tightens under my skin.

"Come on, Tom!" She tries to negotiate with the dentist. "Come back down. Please!"

"Say, what are you doin' up here anyway?" I ask him. He turns to face me.

Candid.

Then he says, "It's because of you."

"Me! What the hell did I do?"

"I overcharged you."

"Geez, mate, that wasn't very nice," and suddenly, sadistically, I urge him on. "Go on, jump, then — you deserve it, you bloody cheat."

Even the beautiful dental nurse wants him to jump now. She calls out, "Come on, Tom — I'll catch you!"

It happens.

Down.

Down.

He jumps and falls down, and the beautiful dental nurse catches him, kisses his mouth, and places him gently on the ground. She even holds him, touching bodies with him. Oh, that white uniform, rubbing on him. It drives me wild, and instantly, when she calls for me to jump as well, I do it and fall. . . .

In bed, waking up, I'm lying there with the taste of blood in my mouth, and with the memory of footpath and impact in my head.

CHAPTER 2

Since the whole dentist incident drained my money situation, I pretty much went and begged for my old job back. The guy in the newsagent's wasn't impressed.

He said, "Sorry, Mr. Wolfe. You're just too much of a risk. You're dangerous."

Have a listen to the bloke. You'd think I was walking around with a sawn-off shotgun or something. Bloody hell, I was just a paper boy.

"C'mon, Max," I pleaded with him. "I'm older now. More responsible."

"How old are y' anyway?"

"Fifteen."

"Well . . ." He thought hard. He stopped — drew the line. "No." He shook his head. "No. No." But I had him, surely. There was too much hesitation in him. He was thinking too hard. "Fifteen's too old now, anyway."

Too old!

Mate, it didn't feel too good to be a washed-up, redundant paper boy, I can tell you.

"Please?" I drooled. It was sickening. All this for a lousy paper run, while other guys my age were raking it in at Maccas and Kentucky Fried bloody Chickens. It was a disgrace. "C'mon, Max." I had an idea. "If y' don't employ me again I'll come here wearin' these clothes

I'm wearin' right now" (I was wearing crummy track-suit pants, old shoes, and a dirty old spray jacket) "and I'll bring my brother and his mates along and we'll treat the place like a library. We won't cause trouble, mind you. We'll just hang round. A few of 'em might steal, but I doubt it. Maybe just one or two . . ."

Max stepped closer.

"Are you threatenin' me, y' little grot?"

"Yes, sir, I am." I smiled. I thought things were going along fine.

I was wrong.

I was wrong because my old boss Max took me by the collar of my jacket and removed me from his property.

"And don't come back in here again," he ordered me.

I stood.

I shook my head.

At myself.

A grot. A grot!

It was true.

My game plan for getting the job back had backfired miserably. The pulse in my neck felt really heavy, and I felt like I could taste last night's blood in the bottom of my throat.

"Y' grot," I called myself. I looked at myself in the bakery shop window next door and imagined I was wearing a brand-new light blue suit with a black tie, black shoes, nice hair. The reality, though, was that I was wearing peasants' clothes and my hair was sticking up worse than ever. I looked at myself in that window, oblivious to all the people around me, and I stared and smiled that particular smile. You know that smile that seems to knock you and tell you how pathetic you are? That's the smile I was smiling.

"Yeah," I said to myself. "Yeah."

I looked in the local paper — I had to get Rube to go in the newsagent's and buy it for me — for another job, but nothing was going. Things were skinny. Jobs. People. Values. No one was on the lookout for anyone or anything new. It got to the point where I considered doing the unthinkable — asking my father if I could work with him on Saturdays.

"No way," he said, when I approached him. "I'm a plumber, not a circus clown, or a zookeeper." He was eating his dinner. He raised his knife. "Now, if I was —"

"Ah, c'mon, Dad. I can help."

Mum put in her opinion.

"Come on, Cliff, give the boy a chance."

He sighed, almost moaned.

A decision: "Okay," although he waved his fork under my nose. "But all it'll take is one screwup, one smart-mouth remark, one act of stupidity, and you'll be out."

"Okay."

I smiled.

I smiled to Mum but she was eating her dinner.

I smiled to Mum and Rube and Sarah and even to Steve, but they were all eating their dinner because the matter was over and the whole thing didn't really excite any of them. Only me.

Even at work on Saturday my father didn't seem too enthusiastic about me being there. The first thing he made me do was stick my hand down some old lady's toilet and pull all the blockage out. It's true, I nearly vomited into the bowl right there and then.

"Oh, blood–y *hell*!" I screeched under my breath, and my father just smiled.

He said, "Welcome to the world, my boy," and it was the last time he smiled at me all day. The rest of the time he made me do all the sap jobs like getting pipes off the roof of his panel van, digging a trench under a house, turning the mains off and on, and collecting and tidying his tools. At the end of the day he gave me twenty bucks and actually said thanks.

He said, "Thanks for your help, boy."

It shocked me.

Happy.

"Even though you *are* a bit slow." He cut me down right after. "And make sure you have a shower when we get home. . . ."

During lunch it was funny because we sat on these two buckets at Dad's van and he made me read the paper. He took the Weekend Extra part out of the inside and threw the rest of it over to me.

"Read," he told me.

"Why?"

"Because you don't learn anything unless you can find the patience to read. TV takes that away from you. It robs you from your mind."

No need to say that I stuck my head in that paper and read it. I could easily have been sacked for not reading the paper when I was told to.

The most important thing was that I survived the day and I had another twenty dollars to my name.

"Next Saturday?" I asked Dad when we got back out at home.

He nodded.

The thing is, I had no idea that this working Saturdays was going to lead me to the feet of a girl who was even better than the dental nurse. It was a few weeks away yet, but when it came I felt something shift inside me.

On that first Saturday night, though, I walked in our front door feeling quite proud of myself. I went down to the basement because it's Steve's room and Steve always goes out on Saturday nights, and I turned up his old stereo and moved around to it a bit. I sang along like all poor saps do in their own company, and I danced like a complete klutz. You don't care when there's no one around to look.

Then Rube came in, without me knowing.

He looked.

"Pitiful." His voice shocked me.

I stopped.

"Pitiful," he repeated, shutting the door and taking slow, deliberate paces down the old, worn steps.

He was followed in by Dad saying, "I've got four things to say to you blokes. One, dinner's ready. Two, have showers. Three" — and he looked directly at Rube for this one — "you — shave." I looked briefly at Rube and saw patches of beard growing on his face. It was just becoming kind of thick and consistent. "And four, we're watchin' *The Good, The Bad and The Ugly* tonight and if either one of you wants to watch something else, tough luck — the TV's booked."

"We don't care," Rube assured him.

"Just so there's no complaints."

"Just so there *are* no complaints," I corrected the man. Big mistake.

"Are you tryin' to start something?" He pointed as he came farther in.

"Not at all."

He backed away. "Well, good. Anyway, come to dinner," and as we walked toward him, he mentioned, "Don't forget your old man can still give you a good kick in the pants for bein' smart." He was laughing, though. I was glad.

At the door, I said, "Maybe I'll save to get a stereo, like Steve's. A better one, maybe."

Dad nodded. "Not a bad idea." No matter how harsh the man could be, I guess he liked it that I never just asked for things. He saw that I wanted to earn them.

I did.

I wanted nothing for free.

Nothing came for free at our place anyway.

Rube spoke.

He asked, "Why would you want a stereo for, boy? So you can dance up in our room as pitifully as *that*?"

Dad only stopped, looked back at him, and clipped him on the ear.

He said, "At least the boy wants to work, which is more than I can say for you." He turned away again and said, "Now come for the dinner."

We followed our father back up and I had to get Sarah out of her room for dinner. She was in there with the boyfriend getting it off with him against the wardrobe.

It's a movie scene in which I have a noose around my neck, waiting to be hanged. I'm sitting on a horse. The rope is attached to a heavy tree branch. My father is on a horse in the distance, waiting with a gun.

I know that there has been a price on my head for quite some time, and my father and I have a plan going where he turns me in, collects the reward, then shoots the rope as I'm about to be hanged. Somehow I will then get away and we will continue the process in towns all over the countryside.

I'm sitting there with that rope around my neck in a whole lot of outrageous cowboy gear. The sheriff or lawman or whoever he is is reading me the death sentence and all these tobacco-chewing country folk are cheering because they know I'm about to die.

"Any last words?" they ask me, but at first, I only laugh.

Then I say, still laughing, "Good luck," and with sarcasm, "God bless."

The shot should come any moment now.

It doesn't.

I get nervous.

I twitch.

I look around, and see him.

The horse is slapped, to make it take off, and next thing, I'm hanging there, choking to death.

My hands are tied in front of me and I reach them up to keep the rope off my neck. It isn't working. I gasp, horribly, saying, "Come on! Come on."

Finally.

The shot comes.

Nothing.

"I'm still choking!" I hiss, but now my father is riding toward the mob. He fires again, and this time the rope is broken and I fall.

I hit the ground.

I suck.

Air.

Lovely.

Bullets fly all around me.

I reach for my father's hand and he lifts me onto his horse on the run.

Wide shot (camera shot).

New scene.

All is now calm and Dad holds about a dozen hundred-dollar notes in his hand. He gives me one.

"One!"

"That's right."

"You know," I reason, "I really think I should get more than just this — after all, it's my neck hangin' up there."

Dad smiles and throws away a cigar, chewed.

He speaks.

"Yeah, but it's me who shoots you down."

With desert all around me, I realize how sore my back is from falling down.

Dad is gone, and alone, I kiss the note and say, "Damn you, my friend." I begin walking somewhere, waiting for next time, hoping that I will live that long.

CHAPTER 3

I'd forgotten they were there.

I'd forgotten they were there until the next day when I was lying in bed with an incredible pain in my back from the trenches I'd dug the day before. I don't know why I remembered. I just did. The pictures. The pictures.

They were hiding under my bed.

"The pictures," I said to myself, and without even thinking, I got out of bed in the dark but slowly lightening room and got out the pictures. They were pictures of all these women I'd found in a swimwear magazine catalog thing that came through the mail last Christmas. I'd kept it.

Back in bed I looked at the pictures of all the women with their arched backs and their smiles and their hair and lips and hips and legs and everything.

I saw the dental nurse in it — not really, of course. I just imagined her there. She would have fitted.

"God almighty," I said when I saw one of the women. I stared, and I felt really ashamed in my bed because . . . I don't know. It just seemed like a low thing to be doing — gawking at women first thing in the morning while everyone else in the house was still asleep. In a Christmas catalog no less. Christmas was just under six months ago. Still, though, I stared and thumbed through the issue. Rube was still snoring his head off on the other side of the room.

The funny thing is that looking at those women is supposed to make a kid like me feel pretty good, but all it did was make me angry. I was angry that I could be so weak and stare like some sick degenerate at women who could eat me for breakfast. I thought too, but only for a second, about how a girl my age would feel looking at this stuff. It would probably make her angrier than me, because while all I wanted was to touch these women, the girl was supposed to *be* the women. This was what she was meant to aspire to. That had to be a lot of pressure.

I fell back, hopeless, to bed.

Hopeless.

"Dirty boy," I heard Rube saying from the other day at the dentist.

"Yeah, dirty," I agreed out loud again, and I knew that when I got older I didn't want to be one of those sicko animal guys who had naked women from *Playboy* magazines hanging on the garage wall. I didn't want it. Right then, I didn't, so I pulled the catalog from under my pillow and tore it in half, then quarters, and so on, knowing I would regret it. I would regret it the next time I wanted a look.

Hopeless.

When I got up I threw the pieces of women in amongst the recycling pile. I guessed they'd be back again next Christmas in a new catalog. Glued back together. It was inevitable.

Another thing that was inevitable was that since today was Sunday I'd be going down to Lumsden Oval to watch Rube and Steve play football. Steve's side was one of the best sides around, while Rube's was one of the worst sides you would ever see in your life. Rube and his mates got flogged every week and it was always pretty brutal to watch. Rube himself wasn't too bad — him and a few others. The rest were completely useless.

Eating breakfast later on in front of *Sportsworld*, he asked me, "So what's the bet on today's scoreline? Seventy–nil? Eighty–nil?"

"I d'know."

"Maybe we'll finally crack the triple figures."

"Maybe."

We munched.

We munched as Steve came up from the basement and laid out five bananas for himself to eat. He did it every Sunday, and he ate them while grunting at Rube and me.

At the ground, Rube ended up being not too far wrong. He lost, 76–2. The other side was massive. Bigger, stronger, hairier. Rube's side only got their two points at the end of the game when the ref gave them a mercy penalty. They took the shot at goal just to get on the board. There was no sand boy or anything so the goal-kicker took his boot off, put the ball in it, and kicked the goal in just his socks. By comparison, Steve's side won a pretty good game, 24–10, and Steve, as usual, had a blinder.

All up, there were really only two halfway-interesting things about the whole day.

The first was that I saw Greg Fienni, a guy who had been my best friend until not too long ago. The thing was that we just stopped being best friends. There was no incident, no fight, no anything. We just slowly stopped being best mates. It was probably because Greg became interested in skating and he joined another gang of friends. In all honesty, he even tried to get me into the group with him, but I wasn't interested. I liked Greg a lot, but I wasn't going to follow him. He was into the skateboard culture now and I was into, well, I'm not sure what I was into. I was into roaming around on my own, and I enjoyed it.

At the ground, when I arrived, Rube's game had already started, and there was a pack of boys sitting up in the top corner, watching. When I walked past it, a voice called out to me. I knew it was Greg.

"Cam!" he called. "Cameron Wolfe!"

"Hey." I turned. "How's it goin', Greg." (I should have put a question mark there, but what I said wasn't really a question. It was a greeting.)

Next thing, Greg came out from his mates and walked over to me.

It was brief.

He asked, "You wanna know the score?"

"Yeah, I'm a bit late, ay." I looked strangely at his bleached, knotted hair. "What is it?"

"Twenty–nil."

The other side went in to score.

We laughed.

"Twenny–four."

"Ay, sit 'own," someone from in the group yelled out. "Or get out of the way!"

"Okay." I shrugged, and I raised my head to Greg. I looked at his mates for a moment, then said, "I'll see y' later, ay." Some girls had just showed up at the group now as well. I think there were about five of them, and pretty. A couple of them were school beauty queen pretty while a few were that more real-looking type. A realer kind of pretty. *Real girls*, I thought, *who might, if I'm lucky, talk to me someday.*

"Okay." Greg returned to his mates. "Catch y' later." About a month later, as it turned out.

Funny, I thought as I walked on, around the rope that made the field an enclosure. *Best friends once, and now we have almost nothing to say to each other.* It was interesting, how he had joined those guys and I just stayed on my own. I didn't like it or dislike it. It was just funny that things had turned out that way.

The second interesting thing was that back home, toward evening, I was sitting on our front porch watching traffic go by when Sarah and her boyfriend came walking up our street. His car was outside our house but they'd decided just to go out for a walk. The car was his pride and joy. It was a red Ford that had plenty of guts under the hood. Some people are heavily into cars, but to me they seemed pretty stupid. When you looked out my window you could see the whole city crouched under a blanket of car smog. Also, there are guys who tear up and down our street till all hours of the night and think they're absolutely brilliant.

Frankly, I think they're tossers.

Yet, who am I to say?

The first thing I do when I get up on a Sunday morning is look at pictures of half-naked women.

So.

From way down the street, I watched them: Sarah and the boyfriend. I could tell it was them because I could see Sarah's pale jeans that she wore quite often. Maybe she had a couple of pairs.

What I remember best is the way she and the boyfriend, whose name, by the way, was Bruce, were holding hands as they walked. It was nice to look at.

Even a dirty boy like me could see that.

I could.

I admitted to myself on our tiny front porch that beauty was my sister and Bruce Patterson walking up the street like that, and I honestly don't care what you call me for saying so.

In reality, that was what I wanted — what my sister and Bruce had.

Sure, I wanted those women I'd seen in that catalog, but they were just . . . not real. They were temporary.

They would be like that every time — just something to pull out and then pack away.

"How's it goin'?"

"Okay."

Sarah and Bruce came onto the front porch and went inside.

Right now I still remember them walking up the road like that. I still see it.

The worst thing about it was that it didn't take a whole lot longer for Bruce to ditch Sarah for someone else. I do meet the replacement girl, later in these pages, but I only get a short look at her. Short words. Short words at a front door . . .

She seemed okay but I don't know.

I don't know anything, not really.

I —

Maybe all I know is that on that day on our front porch, when I watched Sarah and Bruce, I felt something and vowed that if I ever got a girl I would treat her right and never be bad or dirty to her or hurt her, ever. I vowed it and had all the confidence in the world that I would keep the vow.

"I'd treat her right," I said.

"I would."

"I would."

"— I would."

I'm at the one-day cricket with a large group of guys behind me. It's raining lightly and the players are off the field, so everyone is miserable. The guys behind me have been screaming all day, abusing the opposition, each other, and anyone else they can find.

Earlier on, they yelled out to this guy named Harris.

"Oi, Harris! Show us y' bald spot!"

"Harris, y' dirty boy!"

I'm down at the fence, quiet.

When our mob was fielding, they gave our own players a good mouthful as well, yelling, "Hey, Lehmann — you're lucky to be in the side — give us a wave!" He didn't, but they didn't stop. "Hey, Lehmann, y' ignorant bloody — give us a wave or you'll get my beer on your head!"

After a while the guy waved and everyone cheered, but now in the rain delay, it's all getting a bit much.

The Mexican wave is going around the ground.

People go up, throwing anything they possibly can into the air and booing when it gets to the Members, and they don't go up like everyone else.

When the wave stops, the fellas discover a young security guard maybe twenty meters to our right. He's one of many security guards wearing black pants, black boots, and yellow shirts.

He's kind of big and stupid-looking and he has black greasy hair and huge lamb chop sideburns that go right down to his jawline.

He gets started in on: "Hey, you! Security man! Give us a wave!"

He sees us but there's no response.

"Hey, Elvis, give us a wave!"

"Hey, Bobby Burns, give us a wave!"

He smiles and nods, very cool, and cops a barrage for it. Oohs and aahs and you're an idiot this and that.

Still they keep going.

"Hey, Travolta!"

"Hey, Travolta, give us a wave! A proper one!"

Toward the end of the dream, I suddenly feel weird and I realize that I'm actually naked.

Yes, naked.

"Geez, y' right, mate?" someone asks from behind.

Then the streaking dares start coming.

"C'mon mate, I'll pay your fine if you make it to the other side."

I refuse, and each time I do, another piece of clothing reappears over my skin.

The sick dream ends with me sitting there in my normal clothes again, glad and smiling that I didn't streak or do the pitch invasion I was urged to do.

As the dream suggests, I may be perverted and sick, but I'm not completely stupid.

"You won't catch me without my trousers. Not for long anyway."

No one hears.

The players come back out.

The security guard still cops a good mouthful.

CHAPTER 4

During the next week the weather turned a corner to a more intense kind of cold. The mornings at our place were pretty hectic, as always.

In her room, Sarah put her makeup on for work. Dad and Steve shouted out good-byes. Mum cleaned up all the havoc we'd caused in the kitchen.

On the Wednesday Rube gave me a dead leg and then dragged me into the bathroom so Mum wouldn't see me writhing around in agony on the floor in our room. I laughed and whimpered at the same time as he dragged me.

"Y' don't want Mum hearin' this." He covered my mouth. "Remember — she tells Dad and it won't be just me who gets it. It'll be both of us."

That was the rule at our place. If there was ever any trouble, absolutely everyone in it copped it. The old man would come down the hall with that look on him that said, *I've had one hell of a day and I didn't come home to mess around with you lot.* Then he'd pull out his backhander — either in the ribs or across the ear. There was no mucking around. If Rube got it, I got it. So no matter how bad a fight was, it never went further than us. We were usually in enough pain as it was. The last thing we needed was Dad getting involved.

"Okay, okay." I slashed my voice at Rube once we were in the safety of the bathroom. "Bloody, what was that for, anyway?"

"I d'know."

"I can't believe you." I looked up at the stupid sap. "Ya give me a dead leg for no reason. That's shockin', that is."

"I know." He was grinning, and it made me push him in the bathtub and try to strangle him, but it was no use — Sarah was banging on the door.

"Get outta there!" she thumped.

"All right!"

"Now!"

"All right!"

When we were on our way to school we met some of Rube's mates.

Simon.

Jeff.

Cheese.

They were invited around in the afternoon for a game of what in our household gets called One Punch. It came about because we only have one pair of boxing gloves in our garage, so the game is pretty much a box-ing match where both fighters have only the one glove. One Punch.

We played it that same Wednesday, and we were keen. Very keen. Keen to hit. Keen to get hit. Keen to get away with it, even if it meant not socializing with the rest of the family. I mean, you'd be surprised how well you can hide a bruise in the darker corner of the lounge room.

Rube's left-handed, so he likes to have the left glove. I get the right, which is my good hand. There are three rounds and the winner is declared fairly. Sometimes it's easy to tell who wins. Sometimes not.

This particular afternoon was a pretty bad one for me.

We took the gloves out into the backyard and first up was Rube against me. Rube and I always had the best fights. It was no holds barred. All it would take was one good punch from me and Rube would really try to knock my head off. One good punch from Rube on me would send the sky into my head and the clouds into my lungs. I just always tried to stay up.

So "Ding, ding," went Cheese with no enthusiasm, and the fight was on.

We circled the small backyard, which was half concrete, half grass. It was an urban box, not much bigger than a real boxing ring. Not much room to get out of the way. Hard concrete as well . . .

"C'mon." Rube stepped in and went for my head, faked, and cracked my ribs. He then took a shot at my head for real and just skimmed my ear. That was when I saw him open up so I slammed one right in at his nose. It hit. Brilliant.

"*Yow!*" Simon cheered, but Rube remained focused. He walked in again without fear and didn't worry about my cocky bouncing around. He leaned in and whacked me over the eye. I blocked it and aimed up myself. He swerved me and turned me around and rammed me back against the wall, then pulled me out. He pushed me back. He hauled me onto the grass and crashed his fist into my shoulder. Yes. He hit. Oh, it was okay. It was like an ax had burst open my joint and next thing my head was rocked by his left hand. It flung forward and jammed onto my chin.

Hard.

It happened.

The sky came down.

I breathed in the clouds.

The ground wobbled.

The ground.

The ground.

I swung.

Missed.

Rube laughed, from under that increasing beard of his.

He laughed as soon as I fell down to my knees and got up a little just to crouch there. The count came, with delight. Rube: "One — two — three —"

Once I was up again and the cheers of Simon, Jeff, and Cheese were no longer mere blurs, there were only a few more punches and Round One was over.

I sat in the corner of the yard, in the shade.

Round Two.

It was much the same, only this time Rube went down once as well.

Round Three was a dog fight.

Both of us came out throwing hard and I recall reefing at Rube's ribs close to seven or eight times and copping at least three good shots on my cheekbone. It was brutal. The neighbor on our left kept caged parrots and had a midget dog. The birds screeched from over the fence and the midget dog barked and jumped at the fence while my brother and I fought each other senseless. His fist was this big brown blur that kept driving forward from his long arm, pumping out at me and singing as it pushed my skin into my bones. All was mirrored and shaky and shivery and getting orange-dark and I could feel that metallic taste of blood crawling from my nose to my lip, over my teeth and onto my tongue. Or was I bleeding inside my mouth? I didn't know. I didn't know anything until I was crouched down again and dizzy and feeling like I might throw up.

"One — two —"

The count meant nothing this time.

I ignored it.

All I did this time was sit down against the back fence till I recovered.

"Y' okay?" Rube asked a bit later, his rough hair swinging down into his eyes.

I nodded.

I was.

Back inside, I surveyed the damage and it didn't look too good.

There was no blood in my nose. It did turn out to be

in my mouth, and I had a black eye. A good one. No hiding it. Not today. No point. Mum was going to kill us.

She did.

She took one look at me and said, "And what happened to you?"

"Ah, nothin'."

Then she saw Rube, who had a slightly swollen lip.

"Ah, you boys." She shook her head. "You disgust me, I swear it. Can you not go one week without hurting each other?"

No, we couldn't.

We were always hurting each other, whether it was boxing, or playing football in the lounge room with a rolled-up pair of socks.

"Well, stay apart for a while," she ordered us, and we obeyed the order. We tried hard to listen to our mother because she was tough and she cleaned rich people's houses for a living and she worked hard to let us have an okay house. We didn't like it much when she was disappointed in us.

The disappointment was to continue.

It really got bad throughout the next day because some of my teachers became a bit concerned about the state of my face and the way that every second week it seemed to have a bruise or a scab or a graze on it. They asked me all these weird questions about how things were at home and how I got on with my parents and all that kind of thing. I just told them I got on pretty well with everyone and that things were just as usual at home. Pretty good.

"Are you sure?" they asked. As if I'd lie. Maybe I should have told them I ran into the door or fell down the basement stairs. That would have been a laugh. Mainly I just told them that I did boxing as a recreational sport and that I hadn't really become too good at it yet.

They clearly didn't believe what I told them because on Thursday afternoon my mother got a call from the school, requesting a meeting with the principal and the head of welfare.

She came on Friday at lunch and made sure Rube and I were there as well.

Outside, just before she went into that welfare office, she said, "Wait here and don't move till I say you can come in." We nodded and sat down, and after about ten minutes, she opened the door and said, "Right — in." We got up and went in.

Inside the office, the principal and the welfare officer stared at us with a kind of amused, measured repugnance. So did Mum, for that matter, and the reason for this became quite clear when she reached into her handbag and pulled out our boxing gloves and said happily, "Okay, put them on."

"Ah, c'mon, Mum," Rube protested.

"No no no," insisted Mr. Dennison, the principal. "We're very interested in seeing this."

"Come on, boys," my mother egged us on. "Don't be

ashamed. . . ." But that was the whole point. Embarrass us. Humiliate us. Shame us. It wasn't hard to see what was going on, as each of us put our glove on.

"My sons," my mother said to the principal, and then to us. "My sons."

The look on our mother's face was one of bitter disappointment. She looked ready to cry. The wrinkles around her eyes were dark-dry riverbeds, waiting. No water came. She just looked. Away. Then, with purpose, she looked at us and seemed ready to spit at our shoes and disown us. I didn't blame her.

"So this is what they do," she told them. "I'm sorry about all this, to waste your time like this."

"It's okay," Dennison told her, and she shook hands with both him and the welfare woman.

"I'm sorry," she said again and walked out, not even looking at us again. She left us standing there, wearing those gloves, like two ridiculous beasts in winter.

Don't ask me why, but I'm in Russia, sitting on a bus in Moscow.

It's crowded.

The bus moves slowly.

It's freezing.

The guy next to me has the window seat and he's holding some kind of rodent that hisses at me even if I so much as look at it. The guy nudges me, says something, and laughs. When I ask him if this really is Moscow (because of course I've never been there), he starts having this long drawn-out conversation with me, which is a miracle because I can't even say a word to him on account of not knowing the language.

He's unbelievable.

Talking.

Laughing, and by the end of it, I actually like the guy. I laugh at all his jokes by the lines they make on his face.

"Slow bus," I say, but of course he has no idea.

Russia.

Can you tell me what in God's name I'm doing in Russia?

The bus is freezing as well — did I mention that already? Yeah? Well, trust me, it is, and all the windows are fogged up.

Shiver.

I shiver in my seat until I can take it no longer.

Stand.

I try to get up but I seem pasted down. It's like I've actually been frozen to the seat.

"Get up," I tell myself, but I can't. I can't!

Then I see someone amongst the crowd in the aisle hobbling toward me.

No.

Oh, no.

It's an old woman, and since being in Russia, I've realized that these old women really get into the thick of it. And worse still, she's looking right at me. Right, at me.

"Help me up," I say to the guy next to me. I beg, but he does nothing. He even turns away to sleep, squashing his rodent up against the window. It gags.

She's still coming.

No.

A nightmare.

She grimaces and fixes her eyes on mine, silently telling me to get out of the seat.

Get up! I shriek inside me.

I can't, and she —

Arrives.

"Yah!" she begins, and from there, there is no stopping her. She spits her Russian swearing right in my face and gives me a barrage with her fists. Her tiny ferocious hands try to lift me by my clothes to throw me from the seat.

"I'm sorry!" I wail, but this old lady is like fury personified, sending flurries all over me.

Later, I'm sitting down in the aisle, with the seat of my pants still stuck on the seat. A middle-aged man who speaks English tells me, "Shouldn't offend the lady, old boy."

"No kidding," I agree, trying to keep my bare skin off the frozen floor.

The old lady smiles down at me, with disgust.

CHAPTER 5

This is an important chapter.

I think so, anyway.

The bruises on my face healed pretty quickly and I spent the next while of my life just hanging around. A happening was looming. It was out there somewhere beyond the regular enclosed life that I had been living. It was out there, not waiting, but existing. Being. Perhaps it was only slightly wondering if I would come to it.

Maybe I'm just talking stupid.

Anyway.

The happening that happened was that I met this girl when I was working with Dad on a Saturday.

She was something, I promise you.

I'd spent the whole morning digging a trench under the house at this job in a district maybe five kilometers away from ours, and I was dead. Dead by lunch.

There was dirt all over me and my neck was straightened and stiffened from bending over and digging. When I came out from underneath, she was there. She was there with her mother and father and she was so real I nearly choked on the nothingness in my mouth. My height, she was, and calm and real in the face. She smiled at me with real lips and her real voice said "Hi" when we met.

I wiped my right hand on my pants and shook all their hands. Mother. Father. Girl.

"My son, Cameron," my dad told them when I crawled out, shaking the dirt from my hair. He even sounded like he remotely liked having me around.

"G'day," I said when I faced up to them, and Dad kind of took the parents on a tour of what we'd done on their property. They were having pretty massive extensions done, which were cramping up the yard a little. It was a nice house, though.

The girl.

"Rebecca," her mother had told me.

When Dad was doing the grand tour I was alone with her.

What was I meant to do?

Talk?

Wait?

Sit down?

All up, all we did was stand there a while and then sit on these deck chair sort of things. I looked away and looked at her and looked away again.

What an animal.

I sure had a way with the ladies, didn't I?

Finally, when it was almost too late and the old fellas were coming back, I said to her in this crazed quiet voice, "I like workin' here," and after the silence, we both laughed a bit and I thought, *What a weird thing to say*. I like working here. I like working here. I Like. Working here. I. Like working here.

As I repeated it over in my head I wondered if she knew what it really meant.

I think she did.

Rebecca.

It was a nice name, and while I liked the calmness in her face, I liked her voice better. I remembered it and let it chant across me. Just that "Hi." Pathetic, I know, but when your experience with women is as minimal as mine, you take whatever you can get.

All afternoon, it lasted. There was even very little pain in the work I did because I had Rebecca now. I had her voice and the realness of it to numb everything. It numbed the blisters forming at the base of my fingers and blunted the blade seeking my spine.

"Hi," she'd said. "Hi," and she'd laughed with me when I said something stupid. I'd been laughed at before by girls, but it was rare for me to laugh *with* one. It was rare to feel okay with a city over my shoulder and a girl's face so close to mine. She had breath and sight and she was real. That was the best thing. She was realer than the dental nurse because she wasn't behind a counter being paid to be friendly. And she was definitely realer than the women in that catalog thing because there was no way I would ever tear this girl up. There was no way I would dare to hurt her or curse her or hide her under my bed.

Eyes. Alive eyes. Light hair falling down her back. A pimple at the side of her face, near her hairline. Nice neck, shoulders. Not a beauty queen. Not one of those. You know the ones.

She was real.

She played music later on and it wasn't anything much that I liked, but that made her realer still. The whole situation even made me smile at Dad when he told me off for digging something in the wrong place.

"I'm sorry, Dad," I said.

"Dig over there."

I wonder if he knew. I doubt it. He didn't seem to catch on when I asked if we'd be back here next week.

"Yeah, we'll be back," he'd answered bluntly.

"Good," but I said it only to me.

A bit later, I asked, "What's these people's last name?"

"Conlon."

Rebecca Conlon.

The thing that hit me most was that I suddenly started praying. I started saying these prayers for Rebecca Conlon and her family. I couldn't stop myself.

"Please bless Rebecca Conlon," I kept saying to God. "Just let her be okay, okay? Let her and her family be okay tonight. That's all I ask. In the name of the Father, the Son, and the Holy Spirit," and I crossed myself like the Catholics do and I'm not even a Catholic. I don't know what I am.

During the next week, I kept praying, and I kept making sure to remember her face, and her voice.

"I'd be good to her," I kept telling God. "I would."

I was actually torn between the love I had for her face and her body and the love I had for her voice.

Her face had character all right. Strength. I loved it. I definitely loved her neck and her throat and her shoulders and her arms and legs. All of it — and then there was the voice.

The voice came from somewhere in her. It came from somewhere that didn't show itself, I hoped, to just anyone.

The question was, *Which part of her was I interested in most?* Was it the look of her, or the inner realness I could sense slipping out?

I started taking walks, just to think of her — just to imagine what she was doing and if by any chance she was thinking of me.

It became torture.

"God, is she thinking of me?" I asked God.

God didn't answer so I just didn't know. All I knew was that I walked parallel to urban traffic that laughed as it went past me. Crowds of people dropped out of buses and trains and ignored me as they went past. I didn't care. I had Rebecca Conlon. Nothing else meant a whole lot. Even back home when I bickered with Rube I didn't worry. I just kept not worrying, because she was somewhere near it all in my thoughts.

Joy.

Is that what I felt?

Sometimes.

At other times I was shouldered by thoughts of doubt and a kind of truth that told me she hadn't thought of me at all. It was possible, because things never work out how they should. It was most likely that a sweet girl like that could do a whole lot better than me. She could do better than a fella who plotted ridiculous robberies with his brother, got thrown out of newsagencies, and humiliated his mother.

Sometimes I thought about her naked, but never for long. I didn't want her only like that. Honestly.

I wanted to find the place where her voice came from. That was what I wanted. I wanted to be nice to her. I wanted to please her, and I begged for it to happen. Begging gets you nowhere, though. I knew that was true, but I did it inside me anyway as I counted the hours till I was going back to her.

Things happened during the week that will follow in the next chapters, but now I should tell you at the end of this one here what happened when Dad and I showed up at the Conlons' the next Saturday.

This is what happened.

My heart beat big.

One of them's back.

Can you believe it?

The nerve of her.

Do you know who I mean? It's one of the women from that swimwear catalog, and she comes to me in our kitchen.

Seductively.

It's musty and half-dark. Sweaty.

"Hello, Cameron." She keeps coming, and she pulls a chair over to sit right opposite me. Our knees touch — that's

how close she comes to me. Her smile is one of definite something. Danger? Lust? Eroticism?

How can I dream this now?

Tonight?

After what's been happening lately?

I've gotta be kidding me.

Is this a test?

Well, whatever it is, she leans closer and licks her lips. Her swimsuit is a bikini and it's yellow and it shows a whole lot of her. Can you believe this? She lets one of her fingers touch my neck and she strokes her way down with it, and her fingernail is just light enough not to scratch. It's smooth, and something tells me to make the most of it, to never let her stop. Then something else screams silently somewhere in my feet that I must tell her to stop. It rises.

She's on me.

Breathing.

I smell her perfume and feel the soft thrill of her hair. Her hands undress me and her mouth takes me.

I feel it.

Gathering.

Pushing.

Against me.

She falls, letting her teeth touch the skin of my throat. She kisses, long, with her tongue touching —

I jump.

"What?"

I'm standing.

"What?" she asks. Ohh . . .

"I can't." I hold her hand to tell her the truth. "I can't. I just can't."

"Why not?"

Her eyes are fire-blue and I almost allow her to go on as she begins stroking my stomach and searching for the rest of me. I stop her, just in time, and I wonder how I do it.

I turn away and answer her.

"I've got someone real. Someone who isn't just —"

"Just what?"

Truth: "Something I only lust for."

"Is that all I am? A thing?"

"Yes," and I see her change. She is ghost-like, and when I reach out to touch her, my hand goes through. "See," I explain, "look at me. A guy like me can't really touch someone like you. It's just the way it is."

When she disappears completely, I understand that my reality isn't the catalog girl or school beauty queen or anyone like that. My reality is the real girl on her left.

On the table, the swimsuit model has left her purse. I go to pick it up, but I don't open it for fear of it blowing up in my face.

The beauty queen, I long for.

The real girl, I long to please.

Dream complete.

CHAPTER 6

Remember when I said how I liked watching Sarah and Bruce come up the street that Sunday night?

Well, during the week that all seemed to change.

There was also another change, because Steve, who normally didn't get home from his office job until about eight at night, was home too. The reason for this was that the previous day at football, he'd turned on his ankle. It was nothing serious, he'd said, but on the Monday morning, his ankle was the size of a shot-put ball. The doctor had ruled him out for six weeks because of ligament damage.

"But I'll be back in a month, you watch."

He sat on the floor with his foot raised on some pillows and his crutches next to him. He would be stranded at home for a fortnight, after his boss gave him half of his holiday early. This drove Steve mad, not only because he would miss some of his holiday in summer, but because he hated just sitting around.

His somber mood sure didn't help things in the lounge room between Sarah and Bruce.

On the couch on Tuesday, rather than going at it like they normally did, they both seemed to be glued down by tension.

"Smell this pillow," Rube instructed me at one point as I watched them while trying not to.

"Why?"

"It stinks."

"I don't feel like smellin' it."

"Go on." His hairy, threatening face came closer and I knew he wouldn't take no for an answer.

He threw the pillow over and I was expected to pick it up and stuff it in my face and tell him if it stank. Rube was always making me do things like that — things that seemed ridiculous and meaningless.

"Go on!"

"All right!"

"Go sniff it," he said, "and tell me it doesn't smell like Steve's pajamas."

"Steve's pajamas?"

"Yeah."

"My pajamas don't stink." Steve glared.

"Mine do," I said. It was a joke. No one laughed. So I turned back to Rube.

"How do *you* know what Steve's pajamas smell like? You go round sniffin' people's pajamas? Are you a bloody pajama-sniffer or somethin'?"

Rube eyed me, unimpressed. "Y' can smell 'em when he walks past. Now *sniff*!"

I did it and conceded that the pillow didn't smell like roses.

"I told ya."

"Great."

I returned it to him and he threw it back where it was. That was Rube. The pillow stank and he knew it stank and was concerned about it. He wanted to talk about it, but one thing was certain — there was no way he would wash it. Back in the corner of the couch, the pillow sat, stinking. I could still smell it now, but only because Rube had brought it up. It was probably my imagination. Thanks, Rube.

What made things even more uncomfortable was the fact that normally, if Bruce and Sarah weren't all over each other, they would at least throw something into the conversation, no matter how stupid we were talking. On that day, however, Bruce said nothing, and Sarah said nothing. They only sat there and watched the movie they'd rented. Not one word.

While all this was going on, I'd better point out that I was praying for Rebecca Conlon and her family. It led me to even start praying for my own family. I prayed that I wouldn't let Mum down anymore and that Dad wouldn't work so hard that he'd kill himself before he hit forty-five. I prayed for Steve's ankle to get better. I prayed that Rube would make something of himself sometime. I prayed that Sarah was okay right there and then and that she and Bruce would be okay. Just be okay. *Be okay.* I said that a lot. I said it as I started praying for the whole stupid human race and for anyone who was hurting or hungry or dying or being raped at that exact moment in time.

Just let 'em be okay, I asked God. *All those people with AIDS and all that stuff as well. Just let 'em be okay right now, and those homeless blokes with beards and rags and cut-up shoes and rotten teeth. Let 'em be okay. . . . But mainly, let Rebecca Conlon be okay.*

It was starting to drive me crazy.

Really.

When Sarah and Bruce weren't aware I was watching them, I stared at them hard and wondered how just days and weeks ago they were all over each other.

I wondered how this could happen.

It scared me.

God, please bless Rebecca Conlon. Let her be okay. . . .

How could things be so different all of a sudden?

Later on, when I was back in Rube's and my room, I could hear the drone of Sarah and Bruce talking behind the wall, in her room. The city was dark except for the building lights that seemed to appear like sores — like Band-Aids had been ripped off to expose the city's skin.

The only thing that seemed never to change was the city at this transition time between afternoon and evening. It always became murky and aloof and ignorant of what was going on. There were thousands of households throughout that city and there was something happening in all of them. There was some kind of story in each, but self-contained. No one else knew. No one else cared. No one else knew about Sarah Wolfe and Bruce Patterson, or cared about Steven Wolfe's ankle. No one else out there prayed for them or prayed repeatedly for Rebecca Conlon. No one.

So I saw that there was only me. There was only me who could worry about what was happening here, inside these walls of my life. Other people had their own worlds to worry about, and in the end, they had to fend for themselves, just like us.

By the time I went to bed, I was going in circles.

Praying.

Worrying about Sarah.

Praying like an incoherent fool.

I could feel the city at the window, but mostly, I remained in my head, hearing every thought — quiet but loud, and true.

The future:

Time to relax.

We're at the edge of the city, right next to it, as if we can reach across and touch the buildings — reach in and turn off the lights that try shining in our eyes to blind us.

We're fishing, Rube and I.

We've never fished before, but we are today, through this whole evening.

Our lines dangle in what is a huge, darkening blue lake with stars dropping up through the water.

The water is still, but alive. We can feel it moving beneath the old beat-up boat we have hired from some con man on the shore. Once in a while it shifts beneath us. We are unafraid, at first, because although nothing has been totally stable, we know where we are, and things aren't moving along too rapidly.

We catch.

Nothing.

Absolutely. Nothing.

"*Bloody hopeless.*" *Rube initiates conversation.*

"*I told y' we shouldn't have gone fishing. Who knows what's in this lake?*"

"*Dead souls from the city.*" *Rube smiles with a kind of sarcastic joy.* "*What'll we do if we get one on the end of our line?*"

"*Jump ship, mate.*"

"*Too bloody right.*"

The water moves again, and slowly, waves start rolling in from somewhere we can't see. They rise up and jump into the boat, and they get higher.

There's a smell.

"*A smell?*"

"*Yeah, can't you smell it?*" *I ask Rube. I say it like an accusation.*

"*I can, yeah, now that you mention it.*"

The water is excessively high now, lifting the boat and us and throwing us back down. A wave hits my face and I get a mouthful. The taste, it's grotesque, burning, and I can tell by the look on Rube's face that he's swallowed some too.

"*It's petrol,*" *he tells me.*

"*Oh God.*"

The waves die a little now, and I turn to a boat that sits closer to the city, right near the shore. There's a guy in it, and a girl. The guy steps out onto the shore with something in his hand.

It — glows.

"No!" I stand and throw my arms out.

He does it. Cigarette.

He does it as I see another person doing laps across the bay, intense. Who is it? I wonder, and in another boat still, a man and a woman are also rowing, middle-aged.

The guy throws his cigarette into the lake.

Red and yellow rolls into my eyes.

Oblivion.

CHAPTER 7

On the Thursday of that week, Rube also conned me into making a new exodus — a journey away from our normal robbery expeditions.

Street signs.

That was the new plan.

It was still afternoon when he thought about it and told me which sign he wanted to get.

"The give-way," he said. "Down Marshall Street." He smiled. "We sneak out, right, say elevenish, with one of Dad's spanners — the one you can adjust by rubbing that thing on the top . . ."

"The wrench?"

"Yeah, that's it. . . . We put our hoods on, walk down there casual as M. E. Waugh in bat, I climb up on your shoulders, and we take the sign."

"What for?"

"What, exactly, do you mean, *what for*?"

"I mean, what's the point?"

"Point?" He was, what's the word? Exasperated. Frustrated. "We don't need a point, son. We're juvenile, we're dirty, we don't have girls, we have noses full of snot, throats sore as hell, we've got scabs on us, we suffer bouts of acne, we've got no girls — did I already say that? — little money, we eat mushrooms mashed next to meat almost every night for dinner and drown 'em in tomato sauce so we can't taste 'em. What more reasons do we need?" My brother threw his head back on his bed and stared desperately at the ceiling. "We don't ask for much, dear God! You know that!"

So that was it.

The next mission.

I swear it, that night, we were like savages, just as Rube had described in his outburst. It shocked me at first that he knew us like that. Like I did. Only, Rube was proud of it.

Maybe we didn't know *who* we were, but we knew *what* we were, and to Rube it made acts of vandalism such as stealing street signs seem like a logical thing to do. He sure didn't feel like considering that we could end up in a police cell without the proper safety-standard bars.

Of course, we knew we couldn't succeed.

The only problem was, we did.

We snuck out the back door of home at about quarter to twelve with our hoods hunching over our heads and footsteps raking us forward. We walked calmly, even toughly, down our street with smoky breath, hands in pockets, and whispers of greatness stuffed down our socks. Our sniffs and breathing scratched us through the air, pulling it apart, and I felt like that Julius Caesar guy going to conquer another empire — and all we were doing was stealing a lousy gray-and-pink triangle that should have been white and red.

Give way.

"More like give *away*," Rube snickered as we arrived at the scene of the sign. He got up, slipped, then got up again on my shoulders.

"Right." He spoke again once he found balance. "Spanner."

"Huh?"

"*Spanner*, you stupid sap." His whisper was harsh and heavily smoked in the cold.

"Oh, right, yeah, I forgot."

I handed him the spanner or wrench or whatever you want to call it and my brother proceeded to unscrew the give-way sign on the junction of Marshall and Carlisle streets.

"Geez, she's a bit bloody stubborn," Rube pointed out. "The bolt's so rusty that all the garbage is gettin' stuck on the nut. Just keep holdin' me up, okay?"

"I'm gettin' tired," I mentioned.

"Well, get through it. The pain barrier. The pain barrier, son. All the greats could always break through the pain barrier."

"The great whats? Sign stealers?"

"No." It was sharp. "Athletes, you yobbo."

Then came the triumph.

"Right," Rube announced, "I've got it." He jumped off my shoulders with the sign just as a light came on in one of the dilapidated flats on the corner.

A woman stepped out onto her balcony and sighed, "Ah, grow up, will y's."

"C'mon." Rube tugged at my sweatshirt. "Go go go!"

We took off, laughing as Rube held the sign up above his head, cheering, "Oh, yes!"

Even when we snuck back into our house, the adrenaline was still crouching in my blood, then springing forward, taking off. It disappeared slowly when we were back in our bedroom. With the light off in our room almost instantly, Rube slid the sign under his bed and said, just for fun, "Tell Mum or Dad about this and I'll see if I can fit this sign down your throat." I laughed a little and soon fell asleep, still hearing the gentle sounds of women sighing at undesirables in the middle of the night. I wondered about Rebecca Conlon before sleep came as well, and I remembered moments when we walked down the street and when we were abducting the sign in which I pretended she was watching me. I wasn't sure if she would like me or think I was a complete idiot. Complete idiot, most likely.

"Ah, well," I whispered to myself under my blanket. "Ah, well," and I started praying for her and everyone else I had prayed for lately. In the night, not long after sleep captured me, my dream came — a bad one. A nightmare. A proper one.

You will see it soon enough. . . .

Next day, in the morning, Rube took the sign out to admire it again in the comfort of our room. I was coming back in from the shower.

"Isn't she beautiful?" he told me.

"Yeah." I didn't sound too keen, though.

"What's with you?"

"Nothin'." It was the nightmare.

"Okay." He put the sign away again and poked his head into the hall. "Aah." He looked back at me. "Y' left the bathroom door open again — do you do that on purpose just to let the cold in before I go in the shower?"

"I forgot."

"Well lift your game."

He left, but I followed him, with my hair wet and sticking up in all directions.

"Where the hell do y' think you're going?"

"I've gotta tell you something."

"Right." He shut me out of the bathroom. I heard the shower go on, the door unlock, the curtain shut, and then a shout came. "Come in!"

I went in and sat on the shut-up toilet.

"Well," he called out to me, "what is it?"

I began talking about the nightmare I'd had, and through the heat in the bathroom, an extra heat seemed to come from out of me, overpowering it. I took a minute or two to explain the dream properly.

When I finished, all Rube said was, "So what?" The steam was getting intense.

"So what should we do?"

The shower stopped.

Rube stuck his head around the curtain.

"Pass me that towel."

I did it.

He dried himself and stepped out, breaking through the steam with, "Well, it's certainly a disturbing dream you speak of, son."

He had no idea how disturbing. It was me who dreamed it. It was me who had believed it when it was in me. It was me who.

End.

End this.

No . . .

It was me who had woken up in the darkness of our triumph with sweat eating my eyes out, and a silent scream pressed down on my lips.

In the bathroom now, I suggested, "We've gotta take the sign back."

Rube had other ideas, at first.

He came closer and said, "We can ring the RTA and tell 'em the sign needs replacing."

"It'll take absolute weeks for *them* to replace it."

Rube paused, then said, "Yeah, good thinkin'." Unhappiness. "The state of our roads down this way is a disgrace to the nation."

"So what do we do?" I asked again. I was genuinely concerned now, for the safety of the public at large, and I also remembered a story I'd seen on the news a year or so back where these guys in America got something like twenty years for stealing a stop sign because it caused a fatal accident. Look it up if you don't believe me. It happened.

"What do we do?" I asked again.

Rube answered by not answering quickly.

He walked out of the bathroom, got dressed, and then held his head in his hands as he sat on my bed.

"What else *can* we do?" he asked, almost pleaded. "We take it back. I s'pose."

"Really?"

Savages, all right.

Savages, frightened.

"Yeah." He was miserable. "Yes. We take it back." It was as if Rube himself had been robbed of something — but what? Why this need to take things? Was it just to feel how it felt to cut up the rules and feel good about being bad? Maybe it was that Rube felt like a failure and he was proving it to himself by trying to steal. Maybe he wanted to be like the hero in the American movies we see on TV. Frankly, I had no idea what was going on in his head and that was that.

Before we went to school, he pulled the sign out and gave it one last sad, adoring stare.

That night, Friday night, we took it back at around eleven and nobody caught us, thank God. It would have been pretty ironic — busted for stealing a sign when we were actually returning it.

"Well," he said when we got home, "we're back, empty-handed. As usual."

"Mm." I couldn't get a word out just then.

One thing I will always remember about that night now is that when we made it back home, Steve was sitting out on the front porch in the cold. His crutches were still next to him, because his ankle was still very screwed up. He sat there, on our old couch, with a mug perched up on the railing.

When we slipped down the side of the house, sort of ignoring him, I heard his voice.

I returned.

I asked.

"What did you just say?" I said it just very normally, like I was interested in what he'd said.

He repeated.

This: "I can't believe we're brothers."

He shook his head.

He spoke again.

"You guys are such losers."

To tell you the truth, it was the vacancy he'd said it with that chewed into me. He said it like we were so far below him that he could barely be bothered. Then, considering what we had just done, I could almost see his point of view. How could Steven Wolfe be of the same blood as Rube and me, and even Sarah for that matter?

All the same, I only stopped slightly before walking off, hearing a high-pitched noise cut open my head, from inside. It whined, as if injured.

Back in our room, I asked Rube where he would have put the sign on the wall in our room. Maybe I asked it to forget what Steve had said to me.

"Here?"

"Nah."

"Here?"

"Nah."

"Here?"

I didn't get an answer for a long time, and that night the light was left on for a while as Rube thought thoughts about things I would never know. All he did was lie on his bed, softly rubbing his beard, as though it was all he had left.

Once settled on top of my own bed, I thought intensely about the next day, working at the Conlons'. Rebecca Conlon. I'd thought the day would never come, but the next day, I was going back. Once I forgot about Rube and Steve, it was beautiful to be alive, conscience free and awaiting a girl who was worth praying for.

After a long while, Rube made a statement.

He said, "Cameron. I wouldn't have put that sign anywhere on our wall."

I turned to look at him. "Why not?"

"You know why not." He continued staring toward the ceiling. Only his mouth moved. "Because the moment Mum saw it, she would have killed me."

There's a car, prowling around the city. It's orange and big, and it makes the heavy, brooding sound cars like that make. It roars around the streets, though it always stops at red lights, stop signs, and all that kind of thing.

Cut to somewhere else —

Rube and I are walking, out of our front gate, supposedly to watch Steve play football, even though it's about two o'clock in the morning. It's cold. You know, that kind of sickly cold. Cold that somehow breathes. It plows into our mouths, blunt and hurtful.

A question.

Rube: "You ever think about beatin' up the old man?"

"Our old man?"

"Sure."

"Why?"

"I don't know — don't you reckon it'd be fun?"

"No, I don't."

At that, we return to silence, walking. Our feet drag over the path as a few stray cars stroll by. Taxis come past and swerve all over the road, a garbage truck struggles past us, overweight. The orange car rolls past, growling.

"Tossers," I say to Rube.

"Definitely."

As he says it, the car takes off and we hear it draw away, then come back on a side street behind us.

Cut to somewhere else —

Rube and I are standing at the corner of Marshall and Carlisle streets. Rube crouches down as the closing statements of a car call closer. He crouches down, holding the give-way sign we stole between his legs. The pole there is empty when I look at it. It's just an empty pole embedded in cement.

Arrival.

The orange car comes up Marshall Street, almost devouring its own speed, gathering it greedily.

When it gets to us it's flying.

No sign.

No sign.

It speeds past us, and as my eyes smash shut, there is an almighty clenching sound of metal wrapping into metal, a shriek, and a delayed downpour of broken glass.

Rube crouches.

I stand, eyes still shut.

Murmuring silence.

It's everywhere.

My eyes open and we walk.

Rube drops the sign, stands, and we walk in a slow, shuddering panic down to the cars that look to have bitten into each other in attack.

Inside, the people look swallowed.

They are dead and bleeding and mangled.

They're dead.

"They're dead!" I call across to Rube, but nothing comes out of my mouth. No sound. No voice.

Then a dead body comes to life.

The eyes in it punch out at me and when the person cries out, the sound in my ears is unbearable. It sends me to the ground, squashing my hands to the side of my head.

CHAPTER 8

When I went to the Conlons' place the next morning with Dad, it's true, my heart beat so hard, or big, as I originally put it, that it kind of hurt. It pumped something into my throat, causing me to salivate, with questions.

What would I say?

How would I act when I saw her?

Nice?

Calm?

Indifferent?

That shy and sensitive style that had never worked for me in the past?

I had no idea.

In the van on the way over, I thought I was going to choke or suffocate or something. Such was the feeling this girl had planted inside me. It grew as we drove closer to her house. It even got to the point where I was hoping the next light would be red so I had more time to think things through. It's funny. I had all week to go over this, to be prepared, and now Saturday had come and I was at a loss. Maybe I'd had too much time to think about it. Maybe I should have spent less time worrying about Sarah and Bruce, and Steve, and stealing and returning road signs with Rube. Maybe then my own game wouldn't have suffered. Maybe then I would have been all right.

If.

Only.

It was no use.

All was lost.

When we arrive there, I thought, *I'd be better off just sticking my head into the ditch and digging a hole for myself.* Girls didn't go for someone like me. What self-respecting girl could even stomach me? Permanently messy hair. Grubby hands and feet. Uneven smile. Uneasy, limping walk. No, this was definitely no good. Not at all.

Let's face it, I even lectured myself inside, *you don't even deserve a girl.* I was right. I didn't. I showed clear signs of dubious morality, at best. I was easily led by my brother. I committed pathetic acts that were petty and done just for some kind of wild pride that was so ridiculous it was hard to comprehend. All I was was a panting desperate mess of a person, scrambling around for something to make me okay. . . .

Then. Suddenly.

In an instant, I thought how strange it was that I never prayed for myself. Was I unable to be saved? Was I so dirty that I didn't deserve a prayer? Perhaps. Maybe.

Yet, *I did get Rube to return the sign*, I managed to rationalize. *So maybe I'm not so bad after all.* That was better — a bit of positive thought, as Dad's panel van rumbled on in the direction of my fate.

When we pulled up at the house, I even started to have some tiny moments of belief that maybe I wasn't the ugly, sick degenerate I'd judged myself to be. I started telling myself that I was probably quite normal. I remembered what I thought that day back in the dental surgery — that all young boys are pretty disgusting, like beasts. Maybe the challenge was to somehow rise above it. Maybe that's what I was looking for with Rebecca Conlon. Just one chance to prove that I could be nice and respectable instead of purely lustful and terrible. I just wanted one shot to treat her right and I knew I wouldn't blow it.

I couldn't.

I wouldn't allow myself.

"I'm not gonna blow it," I whispered to myself as I got out of the van. I took a big breath, like I was walking toward the most important thing in my life. Then I realized. This *was* the most important thing in my life.

"Take this," my father told me, handing me a shovel, and through the morning, I worked hard and waited for Rebecca Conlon to make her appearance. Then I found out in a conversation between Dad and her mother that she wasn't there. She'd slept the night at a friend's place.

"Brilliant," I said, in the gap between my tongue and my throat.

And do you know what the worst part of it was?

It was knowing that if Rebecca Conlon was coming to work at my place, I would have made sure without doubt that I was there to see her. I would have been there. I would have nailed myself to the floor two days earlier if I knew she was coming, just to make sure I wouldn't miss her.

"I would have," I said, agreeing with myself, as I kept working.

I worked myself into a state of numbness. It was awful. Even Dad asked if I was okay. I told him yes, but we both knew I was miserable.

At the end of the day, when the girl still hadn't arrived, Dad gave me an extra ten dollars. He gave it to me and said, "You did well today, boy." Then he walked away and stopped, turned, and said, "I mean, Cameron."

"Thanks," I said, and even though I tried so hard to make it real, the smile I gave my father was one of misery.

"I'd have treated her well," I said to the city outside my window back home, but it was no use. The city didn't care, and in the next room, Sarah and Bruce were arguing.

Rube came in and slumped forward onto his bed. He put his pillow over his head and said, "I think I liked 'em better when they were all over each other."

"Yeah, me too."

I too slumped onto my bed, only I decided to turn on my back and cover my eyes with my hands. Squashing my thumbs in, I made myself see patterns in my darkness.

"What's for dinner?" I asked Rube, dreading the answer.

"Sausages, I think, and leftover mushrooms."

"Ah, beautiful." I turned on my side, in pain. "Just bloody beautiful."

Rube took his pillow off his head then and gravely said, "We're out of tomato sauce as well."

"Even more beautiful."

I stopped speaking then, but I continued moaning inside. After a while I got tired of it and thought, *Don't worry, Cameron. Every dog will have his day.*

Just, not on this day.

(We did eat the mushrooms, by the way. We looked down at them, then up. Then down again. Disgusting. No point backing away. We ate them because we were us and in the end, we ate everything. We always did. We always ate everything. Even if we spewed up our dinner and had it given to us again the next night, Rube and I probably would have eaten that too.)

There's a big crowd, around a fight, and they are all yelling and howling and screaming, as though punches are landing and fists are molding faces. It's a huge crowd, about eight deep, so it is very difficult to push my way through.

I get down on my knees.

I crawl.

I look for gaps and then slip through them, until eventually, I'm there. I'm at the front of the crowd, which is a giant circle, thick.

THE UNDERDOG

"Go!" the guy next to me yells. "Go hard!"

Still, I look at the crowd. I don't watch the fight. Not yet.

There are all kinds of people amongst this crowd. Skinny. Fat. Black. White. Yellow. They all look on and scream into the middle of the ring.

The guy next to me is always shrieking in my ear, drilling right through my skull to my brain. I feel his voice in my lungs. That's how loud he is. Nothing stops him, even the ones behind who throw words at him to make him shut up. It is no use.

I try stopping him myself, by asking him something — a shout over the rest of the crowd. "Who y' going for?" I ask.

He stops his noise. Immediately.

He stares.

At the fight. Then at me.

A few more seconds pass and he says, "I'm goin' for the underdog . . . I have to." He laughs a little, sympathetically. "Gotta go for the underdog."

It is then that I look at the fight, for the first time.

"Hey."

Something is strange.

"Hey," I ask the guy again, because there is only one fighter inside the huge, loud, throbbing circle. A boy. He is throwing punches wildly and moving around and blocking and swinging his arms at nothing. "Hey, how come there's only the one fella fighting?" It is the guy next to me again that I have asked.

He doesn't look at me this time, no. He keeps focused on the boy in the circle, who fights on so intensely that no one can take their eyes off him.

The guy speaks to me.

An answer.

He says, "He's fighting the world." And now, I watch as the underdog in the middle of the circle fights on and stands and falls and returns to his haunches and feet and fights on again. He fights on, no matter how hard he hits the ground. He gets up. Some people cheer him. Others laugh now and rubbish him.

Feeling comes out of me.

I watch.

My eyes swell, and burn.

"Can he win?"

I ask it, and now, I too cannot take my eyes off the boy in the circle.

CHAPTER 9

On the Sunday, Rube copped another hammering on the football paddock, Steve's side lost without him, and I wandered the streets a little bit. I didn't feel like going home that day. Sometimes you just don't. You know. It was time to take stock of things.

At first, I allowed the sullen events of the previous day to cloud my path as I walked. I walked beyond Lumsden Oval, deeper into the city, and I have to tell you that there are so many weirdos in the city that by the time I made it home, I was actually feeling glad I made it back at all.

I was wearing jeans and desert boots and I'd had a shower in the morning and actually washed my hair. As I walked I still felt it sticking up in that uncontrollable way, as if it was out to expose me. Still, I felt okay about being clean.

Maybe the old man's right, I thought to myself. *All that carryin' on he goes on with about us bein' dirty and a disgrace . . . I guess it feels okay to be clean.*

The usual shops crept back from me as I went past. Milk bar places. Fish 'n' chips. I also walked past a barbershop and there was a bald guy in there cutting at a guy's locks with a kind of ferocity that scared me. I always see something like that — some kind of molestation of a human being that can only make me trip or lose my footing with grim surprise. Or fidget with discomfort. That day, I remember it made me try to persuade my hair down, but it was up again right away.

All up, the day and the walk weren't the success or rejuvenation I had been looking for.

I kept walking.

Have you ever done that?

Just walk.

Just walk and have no idea where you're going?

It wasn't a good feeling, but not a bad one either. I felt caged and free at the same time, like it was only myself that wouldn't allow me to feel either great or miserable. As normal, traffic echoed around me, adding to the sense of not belonging anywhere. Nothing was fixed. Everything was moving. Turning into something. Exactly like me.

Since when did I have something for a girl in my gut?

Since when did I care about my sister and what was happening in her life?

Since when did I bother caring about the contents of Rube's mind?

Since when did I listen to Success Story Steve and care about whether he looked down at me or not?

Since when did I walk aimlessly around? Walking, almost prowling, through the streets?

Then it hit me.

I was alone.

I was alone.

No denying it.

I was certain.

See, I was never a guy who had a whole heap of friends to belong to. Besides Greg Fienni, I never really had friends. I kind of stayed on my own. I hated it, but I was proud of it too. Cameron Wolfe needed no one. He didn't need to be amongst a pack. Not all of us roam like that. No, all he needed was his instincts. All he needed was himself, and he could survive backyard boxing matches, robbery missions, and any other shame that came down the alley. So why was I feeling so strange now?

Let's be honest.

It had to be the girl.

It had to.

No.

It was everything.

This was my life.

Getting complicated.

My life, and as I walked along the hurrying street, I saw sky above me. I saw buildings, crummy flats, a grimy cigar shop, another barber, electric wires, rubbish in gutters. A derelict asked me for cash but I had none. There was city all around me, breathing in and out like the lungs of a smoker.

Almost instantly, I stopped walking when I knew that all the good feeling had vanished from me. Maybe it slipped out of me and was given to the derelict. Maybe it disappeared somewhere in my stomach and I didn't even notice. All there was now was this anxiety I couldn't explain. What a sight. What a feeling. This was terrible: a skinny kid standing, alone. That was the bottom line. Alone, and I didn't feel equipped to handle it. Very suddenly. Yes, quite suddenly, I didn't feel like I could handle my feeling of aloneness.

Was this how it was always going to be?

Would I always live with this kind of self-doubt, and doubt for the civilization around me? Would I always feel so small that it hurt and that even the greatest outcry roaring from my throat was, in reality, just a whimper? Would my footsteps always stop so suddenly and sink into the footpath?

Would I always?

Would I?

Would?

This was terrible, but I dug my feet from out of the footpath and continued walking.

Don't think, I told myself. *Think nothingness.* But even nothingness was something. It was a thought. It was a thought, and gutters were still full of the loosened stuffed guts of the city.

I didn't feel like I could cope with this, but I walked on regardless, trying to dig up a new idea that would make things better again.

Can't worry yourself like this, I advised myself a bit later, when I reached Central Station. I hung around in the newsagent's for a while, looking at *Rolling Stone* and all that kind of thing. It was a waste of time, of course, but I did it anyway. If I'd had the money on me I would have got a train to the quay, just to set my eyes on the bridge and the water and the boats there. Maybe there would be a mime there or some other poor sap I couldn't give money to anyway because I had none on me. But then, if I had the money for the train, maybe I would have it too for a humble busker. Maybe I could even have taken a ferry ride over the harbor. Maybe. Maybe . . .

The word *maybe* was beginning to annoy me, because the only thing that was fixed was that *maybe* would be with me forever.

Maybe the girl had something inside her for me.

Maybe Sarah and Bruce would be okay.

Maybe Steve would get back to work and on the paddock as quickly as he wanted. Maybe one day he wouldn't look down at me.

Maybe my old man would be proud of me one day, maybe when we finished off the Conlon job.

Maybe my mother wouldn't have to stand over the stove at night, cooking mushrooms and sausages after working all day.

Maybe *I* could cook.

Maybe Rube would tell me what was going on in his head one night. Or maybe he would grow a beard down to his feet and become some kind of wise man.

Maybe I would end up with a couple of good mates at some point.

Maybe this would all go away tomorrow.

Maybe not.

Maybe I oughta just walk down to Circular Quay, I thought, but decided against it, because one thing that wasn't a maybe was that Mum and Dad would fold me if I came in late.

After fifty times of hearing that guy over the loud-speaker saying, "The train on Platform Seventeen goes to MacArthur" or wherever it was going, I walked home, seeing all my doubt from the other side. Have you ever seen that? Like when you go on holiday. On the way back, everything is the same but it looks a little different than it did on the way. It's because you're seeing it backward.

That's how it felt, and when I made it home, I shut our half-broken, half-hearted small front gate and went in and sat on the couch. Next to that stinking pillow. Across from Steve.

After half an hour of a *Get Smart* repeat and part of the news, Rube entered the room. He sat down, looked at his watch, and said, "Bloody hell, Mum sure is draggin' the chain with dinner."

I looked at him.

Maybe I knew him.

Maybe I didn't.

I knew Steve because he was less complicated. Winners always are. They know exactly what they want and how they're going to get it.

"Just as long as it isn't the usual," I talked over to Rube.

"The what?"

"The usual dinner."

"Oh yeah." He paused. "That's all she cooks, though, isn't it?"

I have to admit right now that all the dinner complaining really shames me now, especially with the way people on the city streets are begging for food. The fact is, the complaining happened.

Still, though, I was over the moon when I found out we weren't having mushrooms that Sunday night.

Maybe things were finally looking up.

Then again, maybe not.

I'm running.

Chasing something that doesn't seem to exist, and time and time again I tell myself that I'm chasing nothing. I tell myself to stop, but I never do.

The city is thrashed around me by broad daylight, but there is no one on the streets. There is no one in the buildings, flats, or houses. There is no one in anything. The trains and buses drive themselves. They know what to do. They breathe out but never seem to breathe in. It's just a steady outpour of non-emotion, and I am alone.

Coca-Cola is spilled down the road. It flows into the drains like blood.

Car horns blow.

Brakes snort and then the cars carry on.

I walk.

No people.

No people.

It's weird, I think, how everything can just carry on without all the people. Maybe it's that the people are there but I just can't see them. Their lives have worn them away from my vision. Perhaps their empty souls have swallowed them.

Voices.

Do I hear voices?

At an intersection, a car pulls up and I feel someone staring at me — but it is emptiness that stares at me. When the car leaves, I hear a voice, but it fades.

I run.

I chase the car, ignoring blaring don't-walk signals that flash their red legs at me and beat at my ears, just in case I'm blind.

Am I blind?

No. I see.

I keep running and the entire city swipes past me like I'm driven by some human-alien force. I bump into invisible people and keep running. I see . . . cars, road, pole, bus, white line, yellow line, crossing, Walk, stutter, Don't Walk, smog, gutter, don't trip, milk bar, gun shop, cheap knives, reggae, disco, live girls, Calvin Klein billboard with woman and man in underwear — enormous. Wires, monorail, green light, orange, red, all three, go, stop, run, run, cross, Turn left anytime with care, Howard Showers, drain, Save East Timor, wall, window, spirit, Gone for lunch, back in five minutes.

No time.

I run, till my pants are torn and my shoes are simply the bottoms of my feet with some material around the ankles. My toes bleed. I splash through Coke and beer. It dribbles up my legs, then down.

No one is there.

Where is everyone?

Where?

No faces, just movement.

I fall. I'm out. Cracked head on gutter. Awaken.

Later.

Things have changed, and now, people are everywhere. They're everywhere they should be, in the buses, trains, on the street.

"Hey," I say to the man in the suit waiting for the walk sign to clock on. He acts like he may have heard something, but walks on when the right sign arrives.

People come right at me, and I swear they are trying to trample me.

Then I realize.

They come right at me because they can't see me.

Now it's me who is invisible.

CHAPTER 10

During the week, I must confess, Rube and I were up to old tricks. Again. We couldn't help ourselves.

Robberies were out.

One Punch. Out.

So what the hell else was there for us to do?

The decision I came to was backyard soccer, or football, or whatever you please to call it.

For starters, we had to.

We did.

I promise.

Maybe I asked Rube if he wanted to get into it because he was still so miserable about the whole street-sign debacle. Admittedly, it was demoralizing, to actually succeed and then find a way to make yourself fail again. It hurt more than Rube could relate. He just sat there every afternoon and rubbed his gruff jawline with an ominous, melancholic hand. His hair was dirty as ever, strewn over his ears and biting at his back.

"C'mon," I tried to get him in.

"Nuh."

It was often like this. Me, being the younger brother, I had always wanted Rube to do things, whether it was a game of Monopoly or a ball game in the backyard. Rube, the older brother, well he was the judge and jury.

If he didn't feel like doing it, we didn't do it. Maybe that's why I was always so willing to go on his robbery missions — simply because he actually wanted me to come along. We'd given up on doing things with Steve years ago.

"C'mon," I kept trying. "I've got the ball pumped up, and the goals are ready. Come have a look. They're chalked onto the fence at both ends."

"The same size?"

"Two meters wide, nearly one and a half high."

"Good, good."

He looked up and gave a slight smile, for the first time in days.

"We on?" I asked again, with far too much eagerness.

"Okay."

We went outside then and it was lovely.

Absolutely lovely.

Rube fell to the cement and got up. Twice. He swore his head off at me when I scored, and it was getting serious. An out-of-control shot at goal went flying to the top of the fence, we held our breath, then let it out when it hit the edge and came back. We even smiled at each other.

It was brilliant mainly because Rube had been down and out with his own form of identity crisis while I was in my typical agony over the whole Rebecca Conlon affair. This was much better. Yes. It was, because all of a sudden we were back to doing the things we did best — throwing ourselves and each other around the backyard and getting dirty and making sure to swear and carry on and, if possible, offend the neighbors. This was better all right. This was a welcome return to the good old days.

The ball thumped into the fence, making next-door's dog bark and the caged parrots over there go wild. I copped a whack in the shins. Rube fell on the concrete again, taking some skin off his hand when he braced himself for the landing. All the while that dog next door kept barking and those parrots were in some kind of frenzy. It was old times all right, and typically, Rube won, 7–6. I didn't care, though, because both of us ended up laughing and not taking things so seriously.

What greeted us on the back step was, however, something very different.

It was Sarah, alone.

First to notice her was Rube. He backhanded me lightly on the arm and motioned over to her with his head.

I looked.

I said very quietly, "Oh, no."

Sarah looked up then because she must have heard me, and I promise you, the way she looked was bad. She was sitting there, all crumpled up, with her knees up to her shoulders and her arms folded, holding them up as if to keep all air inside her. Tears cut down her face.

Awkward.

That's exactly how it was when we walked over to our sister and stood on each side of her, looking at her and feeling things and not knowing what to do.

Eventually, I sat down next to her but I had no idea what to say.

In the end, it was Sarah who broke the silence. The dog next door had settled down, and the neighborhood seemed stunned by this event occurring in our backyard. It was like it could sense it. It could sense some form of tragedy and helplessness being played out, and to tell you the truth, it all surprised me. I was so used to things just going on, oblivious and ignorant to all feeling.

Sarah spoke.

She spoke. "He got someone else."

"Bruce?" I asked, to which Rube looked down at me with an incredulous face on him.

"No," he barked, "the king of bloody Sweden. Who do y' think?"

"Okay, all right!"

Then Sarah leaned away and said, "I think you'd better leave me alone for a while."

"Okay."

As I stood up and left with Rube, the city around us seemed colder than ever again, and I realized that even if it really had sensed something going on, it certainly didn't care. It moved forward again. I could feel it. I could almost hear it laugh and taste it. Close. Watching.

Mocking. And it was cold, so cold, as it watched my sister bleeding at the back of our house.

Inside, Rube was angry.

He said, "Now, you see? This spoils things."

"It was always gonna happen." As I said it, I saw Steve's figure out on the front porch. Away from us.

"Yeah, but why today?"

"Why not?"

From the couch, I looked at an old photo of Steve, Sarah, Rube, and me as very young children, standing in staggered formation for some photographer man. Steve smiled. Sarah smiled. We all did. It was strange to see it, because it was there every day and only now was I really noticing it. Steve's smile. It cared — for us. Sarah's smile. It was beautiful. Rube and I looked clean. All four of us were young and undaunted and our smiles were so strong that it made me smile even then on the couch, with a kind of loss.

Where did that go? I asked inside me. I couldn't even remember the photo being taken. Was it actually real?

At that moment, Sarah was on our back step, crying, and Rube and I were slumped on the couch, powerless to help her. Steve didn't seem to care, for any of us.

Where did it go? I thought again. How could that picture turn into this one?

Had years defeated us?

Had they worn us down?

Had they passed like big white clouds, disintegrating very slowly so that we couldn't notice?

92

In any case, this was pretty awful, and it was to worsen.

It worsened during the night when Sarah went out and didn't come back for hours.

She left with the words "I'm goin' out for a walk," and a lot of time passed while she was gone. The rest of us acted indifferent to it at first, but by just after eleven, we were all worried. Even Steve seemed a bit affected.

"C'mon," our father told us. "We're goin' out lookin'."

No one argued.

Rube and I went out in the panel van with Dad while Mum and Steve stayed home in case Sarah showed up while we were gone. We checked the pubs and all her friends' places. Even Bruce's place. Empty. She was nowhere.

By midnight, when we got home, she still wasn't back, and all we could do now was wait.

We each did it differently.

Mum sat, silent, not looking at anyone.

Dad made coffee after coffee and drank them down like there was no tomorrow.

Steve put a heat pack on and off his ankle and kept it elevated, determined.

Rube mumbled something very quietly, at least five hundred times: "I'm gonna kill that bastard. I'm gonna kill that bastard. I'm gonna get that Bruce Patterson. I'm gonna kill that . . . I'm gonna. I'm gonna . . ."

As for me, I ground my teeth together a bit and leaned forward with my chin resting on the table.

Only Rube went to bed.

The rest of us stayed.

"No sign?" Mum asked when she woke up at one o'clock.

"No." Dad shook his head, and quite soon, we were all falling asleep, under a white, aching kitchen light globe.

Later on, a dream was arriving.

Interruption.

"Cam?"

"Cam?"

I was shaken awake.

I jumped.

"Sarah?"

"Nah, me."

It was Rube.

"Ah, bloody you!"

"Yeah." He grinned. "She's still not here?"

"No. Unless she walked straight past us to bed."

"Nah, she's not in there."

That was when we noticed something else — now Steve was gone as well.

I checked the basement.

"Nup." I looked back up at Rube. So now just the two of us went out on the porch, then out on the street. Where the hell was he?

"Wait." Rube turned around, looking down the road. "There he is."

We saw our brother sitting, propped up against a telegraph pole. We ran down to him. We stopped. Rube asked, "What's goin' on?"

Steve looked up, and I had never seen him afraid like that, or as knotted up. He looked so lanky, and still like a man; he had always seemed to be a man. Always . . . but never like this. Not a vulnerable one.

His crutches were two dead arms, lying there, wooden, next to him.

Slowly, meltingly, our brother said, "I guess." He stopped. Started again. "I just wanted to find her."

We said nothing, but I think when we helped Steve up and helped him walk home, he must have seen what the lives of Rube, Sarah, and me were like. He'd seen what it was to fall down and not know if you could get back up, and it scared him. It scared him because we did get up. We always did. We always.

We took him home.

We —

From there, we all waited in the kitchen again, but only Rube and I were awake. At one point, he whispered something to me. The same thing as before.

He went, "Ay, Cam. We're gonna get that Patterson bloke." He sounded so sure of it. "We'll get him."

I was too tired to say anything but "We will."

Pretty soon, Rube was asleep, like Mum, Dad, and Steve. It didn't take long for my own eyes to feel like cement and I went as well.

All of us, asleep in the kitchen.

I dreamed.

It's coming up.

Not a bad one.

When I woke up again, there was an extra person now, sleeping like the rest of us, at the crowded kitchen table.

I'm standing in an empty goal. The stadium is packed. Perhaps 120,000 people have their eyes glued to me.

They chant.

"Wolf Man! Wolf Man!"

I look around the entire stadium, at all the people willing me on, and I love them, even though they are complete strangers to me. I think they're South Americans or something. Brazilians or something. Maybe Argentinians.

"I won't let you down," I whisper to them, knowing they couldn't hear me even if I screamed to them.

In front of me, there is a line of people, all in the opposition's colors.

They are the people from my story:

Dad, Rube, Mum, Steve, Sarah, Bruce, Bruce's faceless new girlfriend, Greg, the dental nurse, the dentist, Dennison the principal, Welfare Woman, Rube's mates, and Rebecca Conlon.

I'm wearing all the stuff the goalkeeper has to wear: boots, socks pulled up, a green jersey with a diamond pattern on the front, and gloves. It's night and the black air is busted through by huge lights standing like watchtowers, over all of us.

I'm ready.

I slap my hands together and crouch, ready to dive either way for the ball. The goal behind me feels kilometers wide and kilometers deep. The net is a loose cage, swaying and whispering in the breeze.

Dad steps up, places the ball, calls out that this is some kind of cup final penalty shootout, and that everything depends on me. He walks back, props, and runs and drills the ball to my right. I dive but the ball is way out of reach. He looks at me after the ball flies into the corner of the net, and he smiles, as if to say, "Sorry, boy. I had to."

Mum steps up. Then Rube. They both score, Rube with a callous smile. He says, "You've got no hope, sunshine."

The crowd through all of this is always buzzing, like static in my ear. When I am beaten and the ball scores, they roar and then sigh, because they are on my side. They want me to save one because they know how hard I'm fighting. They see my small arms and the will on my lips, and they cannot hear, but feel the smacking of my hands when I ready myself for each penalty kick. They still chant.

My name.

My name.

Yet, no matter how hard I try, I can't save a single goal.

A miserable Sarah even gets through me. Before her shot, she says, "Don't try to help me. It's pointless. All is out of your control."

Steve goes, and Bruce. Rube's mates. Everyone.
Then Rebecca Conlon steps up.
She walks toward me.
Slowly.
Smiling.
She says: "If you save it, I'll love you."
I nod, solemnly, ready.
She goes back, comes in, kicks the ball.

It's up high and I lose it in the lights. I find it and dive, high to the right, and somehow, when the ball hits my wrist, it comes back and hits me hard in the face.

I come down with it.

It pops out when I land and it rolls, so slowly, over the line and into the back of the net.

Oh, I dive for it, but it's no use. I fall short — and quickly, I'm alone, not in the stadium but in our sun-drenched backyard, sitting against the fence with a bloodied nose.

CHAPTER 11

Our plan was to get him quickly. No point letting a week or two pass. If we did, maybe the burning desire to really put it to the guy would fade. There was no way we could afford that.

We found out that this Bruce Patterson had been getting it off with some other girl for about a month, thus leading our sister on by still coming over. It was a slap in the head for all of us that we allowed him into our house when he was into it with some scrubber around the city.

"Should we go bash him?" I asked Rube, but he only looked at me, with ridicule.

"Are you serious? Look at the size of y'. You're like a Chihuahua and Patterson's built like a brick bloody shithouse. Do you have any idea what the guy would do to you?"

"Well, I thought maybe the two of us."

"I'm a weed myself" was Rube's curt response to that one. "Sure, I've got a hell of a beard goin', but Bruce could kill the pair of us."

"Yeah, you're right."

What happened next was unexpected.

There was a knock at the door that was more like scraping, and when I opened it, my former best mate Greg was standing there.

"Can I come in?" he asked me.

"Whatta y' reckon?"

I opened the flyscreen door and he entered the house, just after taking a look over at Steve, who sat grim-faced as ever on the porch.

"Hey, werewolf," Greg greeted Rube inside, to which Rube threatened to throw him out.

"Sorry," he apologized, and I took him into Rube's and my room.

He sat down under the window, against the wall. Silent.

"Well," I asked, sitting on my bed, "if you don't mind my asking, but what the hell brings you here?"

"I need help" was the swift, frank reply. He rummaged his hands through his hair and I could see the 'druff go flying out. Greg always had a bit of a dandruff problem. He enjoyed it, shaking it out on the desk in school.

"Help with what?" I kept probing.

"Money."

"How much?"

"Three hundred."

"*Three hundred!* Bloody hell, what the hell've you been doin' lately?"

"Ah, don't ask. Just . . ." His face flinched a bit. "You got it?"

"Geez, three hundred, I d'know."

I went to my piece of carpet and got out what was stashed under there. Eighty bucks.

"Well, I've got eighty here." I got out my bankbook thing and saw that I had a hundred and thirty in it. "So I've got two-ten all up. That's the best I can do."

"Ah, damn, mate."

I joined him on the floor, against my bed, asking, "Just tell me what it's for, will y'?"

He was reluctant.

"Tell me or I won't give y' the cash." This was a lie and we both knew it. We both knew I was giving Greg my money and I wouldn't even ask for it back. That was all there was to it. But he owed me at least this. He owed it to me to say where my money was going.

"Ah," he gave out. "One of me mates, Dale. You know 'im?"

Dale Perry.

Yeah, I knew him all right. He was exactly the kind of guy I hated because he walked around like he owned the joint no matter where he went, and I hated his guts. In Commerce the previous year (a subject I should never have chosen), he had taken his metal ruler, heated it up on the heater, and then held it up against my ear, burning the absolute hell out of me. That's who Dale Perry was. He was also in that big group chatting with the pretty girls at the football that day.

"Yeah, I know the guy," I stated calmly.

"Yeah, well, a few of his older mates, they needed someone to pick some gear up for 'em. Three hundred bucks' worth."

"Gear?"

Of course, I knew exactly what the gear was, but I thought I'd make this whole thing just a little uncomfortable for Greg. After all, I was giving the guy every cent I had on me. So much for buying myself a stereo or whatever. So much for that hard-earned cash I'd got working the past few weeks with Dad. It was all getting flushed down the toilet because a former best mate of mine came to me because he knew I was the only guy who wouldn't let him down. None of his new mates would help him out, but his original one would.

It's weird.

Don't you think?

It's not so much that the old friend is a better friend. It's just that you know the person better, and you know they don't really care if you're acting like a poor, grovelling idiot. They know you would do the same for them. I knew Greg would do it for me if it was the other way around.

So yes, "Gear?" I asked him. "What are y' talkin' about?"

"You know," he answered.

I let him get away with it. "Yeah, I know."

"Just light stuff," he went on, "but a whole lot of it. There were about ten guys and they all threw in and they were all too lazy to go get it 'emselves." He slipped down against the wall a little further. "I got the stuff no problems, but things got bad when I had to sit on it for a night."

"Aah." I threw my head back and started laughing. I was pretty sure I knew now exactly what had happened.

"Yeah, that's right." Greg nodded. "Me old bloody lady found it under my bed and the old man threw it in the fire. It was like signing my death warrant. . . . I can't believe the old boy chucked it in the fire, ay."

By now, I was in stitches, because I could just see Greg's old man — a tiny, curly-haired, wiry brute of a man swearing his head off and throwing it into the fire. It actually got Greg laughing as well, even though he kept saying, "It's not funny, Cam. It's not funny."

It was, though, and that was what saved him for the money.

It saved him because I told the story to Rube and he shelled out the extra ninety bucks Greg needed, even though he threatened to kill him if he didn't get it back in a fair hurry. The solution ended up being that I would pay Rube back from the money I earned with Dad over the next month or so and everyone was happy. Then Greg would pay the lot back to me.

For Greg, you could see the pressure released from his face. He didn't look so drawn once that cash had found its way into his hand.

In the next room, Sarah was lying on her bed in a hundred pieces.

We walked past her on our way out back, where Rube, Greg, and I took potshots at goal against the fence. We took turns at being goalie. It was my idea (mainly because of the dream I'd had the night before), and I was actually just hoping I wouldn't get a bleeding nose. Although, Rebecca Conlon wasn't in the yard, was she? I thought I was pretty safe.

Of course, next-door's dog started barking and the parrots went berserk.

It was all heightened when Rube phoned his mates. This was the conversation:

"Hello."

"Hello, Simon. Ruben here."

"Ruben. How are you?"

"I'm well. Y' comin' over?"

"Why not indeed. That sounds convenient enough."

"Get Cheese an' Jeff."

"Right."

"Good-bye."

"Good-bye."

When they made it to our place, we got a fully fledged game going.

Over and over, we hammered the ball into the fence, making the most of the time we had before Mum and Dad got home. You should have heard it. *Smash. Smash.* The ball at both ends was killing it and the sound echoed around everywhere, followed by the shrieks and the swearing.

My team was Jeff, Greg, and myself and we were actually winning, even though we were smaller and weaker than Rube's team. It was our hunger.

Four–two it was when next-door's dog stopped barking.

"Stop, stop!" I shouted when I noticed. "You hear that?"

"What?"

"The dog."

"Hey, yeah. It's stopped barkin'."

I climbed up the fence and peeked over, and you won't believe what I saw.

The dog was dead.

"Geez, I think it's dead," I said, looking back at everyone else.

"What!?"

"I'm tellin' y's. Come have a look."

Rube climbed up next to me and could only agree.

"Bloody 'ell, I think he's right," he laughed back down to the others. "I think we've given the poor bloody thing a heart attack."

"Y' sure?"

"Or a stroke."

"Oh no," I said. "What have we done?"

"What sort of dog is it?"

Rube had had enough.

"I don't bloody know!" he yelled down at Cheese. "I think it's a, a —"

"Pomeranian," I answered for him.

"What the hell's a Pomeranian?"

"You know," Cheese explained to the others, "one of those fluffy rodent-lookin' things . . . I guess he just barked till he couldn't take it anymore."

Even the parrots over in the cage were looking morosely down at the dog.

"We've gotta do somethin'," I said to Rube.

"Like what? Give it mouth to mouth?"

"Look, it's shakin'."

"Oh, this is lovely, ay."

I jumped over and took off my flanno shirt and wrapped up the dog. Rube came over and the rest of the fellas looked over the fence as we stroked the fluffy rodent-looking dog, wondering if it really was about to die.

After about fifteen minutes, our next-door neighbor came home — a fifty-year-old fella with a mouth fouler than all of us put together. He showed a lot of restraint, to tell you the truth, as he raced out back, called us a few names, picked up the Pomeranian — whose name was Miffy by the way — and took it to the vet.

"Y' think it'll live?" we asked each other, back at our place.

"Mate, I d'know."

Gradually, everyone left. Greg was last.

"Man." He shook his head on his way out. "I'd forgotten what it's like round here."

"Old times, ay?"

"Yeah," he nodded. "Chaos."

"Absolutely."

It really had been like old times, but I knew it was fruitless to think it would go on. We both knew that the next time he came over would be to pay either some or all of my money back. It was just the way things were.

In the evening, something I knew was coming came. The neighbor.

He came over telling Mum and Dad that they couldn't control Rube and me, and because Rube was the only one out of us with any money left, he was the one who paid the man's vet bill.

Miffy the Pomeranian, by the way, was okay. It was just a very mild heart attack. Poor rodent midget dog.

It was all pretty much the last straw for our mother, though.

She had us sitting at the kitchen table and she circled us, shouting and telling us off like you wouldn't believe. She even held the wooden spoon under our noses, even though she hadn't hit us with it since I was ten. I tell you, she looked ready to wrap it around our heads.

"Why do you keep doing this!?" she screamed at us. "Giving each other black eyes, giving bloody neighbors' dogs heart attacks. It's a disgrace. . . . I'm ashamed of you both. *Again!*"

Even Dad could only sit in the corner, completely silent. He didn't dare to speak himself for fear of being the next to be set upon.

At the end, she really went crazy, getting the compost off the kitchen sink, and instead of taking it outside to put it in her compost bin, she threw it to the floor, picked it up, and threw it down again, this time at my feet.

"You're like animals!" she shouted with even more volume than earlier. Then she said the thing that always seems to hurt the most: *"Grow up!"*

Needless to say, Rube and I cleaned up the mess and took it outside and stayed out there. We didn't dare to go back in.

From her bedroom window, Sarah looked out at us and smiled, shaking her head through her suffering. She was laughing, which made us laugh a bit ourselves. It made Rube find his resolve again and say, "We're still gettin' Patterson. Make no mistake about that."

"We've gotta," I agreed.

After a longer while, I reflected on the day's proceedings, because now I owed Rube half the vet's bill as well. Things had really gone downhill, I promise you.

"Damn that Pomeranian," I suggested.

"Huh," Rube snorted. "Pomeranian with a weak heart. It could only happen to us, ay."

There's a guy in front of me on a dirt road at sunrise.

He looks at me.

I look at him.

We stand, maybe ten meters apart, until finally I decide to break the silence.

I say, "So?"

"So what?" comes his reply. He's wearing a robe and scratches his beard and tries to get a stone out of one of his sandals.

"Well, I don't know," I think to say. "Who the hell are you, for starters?"

He smiles.

Laughs.

Stands.

When he's ready, he repeats the question and answers it: "Who the hell am I?" A brief laugh. "I'm Christ."

"Christ? You actually exist?"

"Of course I bloody do."

I decide to test Him.

"So who am I, then?"

"I'm not interested in who you are," and He walks toward me along the road, still trying to get that pebble out of His sandal. "Bloody sandals." He scuffs, then continues. "Actually, I'm interested in what you are."

"Which is?"

"Miserable."

"Yeah." I shrug in agreement.

"I can help," He goes on, and I'm expecting Him now to give me the usual line all those scripture teachers give us on their annual pilgrimage to our school. He doesn't.

Instead, He hands me a bottle with red liquid in it and motions with hands saying, "Bottoms up" for me to drink it.

"What is it?" I ask.

"Wine."

"Yeah?"

"Actually, no, it's red cordial — you're too young to be drinking."

"*Aah, y' wet blanket.*"

"*Hey, don't blame me. It's not my fault, I'm telling you. It was me old man who wouldn't let me give you the real thing. So you can blame Him.*"

"*Okay, okay . . . What's up with Him anyway?*"

"*Ah, He's been under a lot of pressure lately.*"

"*The Middle East?*"

"*Yeah, they're at it again.*" He comes closer and whispers, "*Just between you and me, He was close to calling the whole thing off last week.*"

"*What? The world?*"

"*Yep.*"

"*Christ almighty!*"

Christ's face looks disappointed at my words.

"*Oh, yeah. Sorry,*" I say. "*That sort of talk's no good, ay.*"

"*No worries. Look.*" Jesus has decided it's time to get down to business. "*I really came to give you this.*"

He pulls something out of a robe pocket and I ask, "*What's that?*"

"*Oh, it's just some ointment.*" He hands it to me. "*For the bleeding nose.*"

"*Oh, great. Thanks very much.*"

CHAPTER 12

If you're wondering if we ever did get our mate Bruce Patterson, well, we didn't. We planned it out and everything, but we just never went through with it. There were more important issues at hand at home, like the frostiness that was afforded to Rube and me by Mum and Dad. They were obviously pretty unhappy about the kind of lives we were leading, and the way we had this knack of embarrassing them. You might also think that this frostiness may have dampened our enthusiasm for somehow getting back at Bruce for Sarah, but it didn't. Not really. Steve told us to let it go as well. He was back to his "I'm better than you people" routine and he told us we were idiots. It all intimidated me just a little, but not Rube. He was as keen as ever, and he truly believed that we weren't responsible for next-door's dog having a heart attack. He explained to me that we couldn't help it if the stupid mutt was weak as water.

"Hell, it's not illegal to play soccer in your own back-yard, is it?" he asked me.

"I guess not."

"You know not."

"I s'pose."

Stewing over it for a few days, Rube finally came into our room and told me what the plan was and what it all meant. He said, "Cam, this is gonna be my last job." You'd think the guy was Al Capone or something. "See, after this last effort, I'm retiring from the robbery, thieving, vandalism game."

"How can you retire if you never even had a career?"

"Ah, shut up, will y'. I admit I've had my ups and downs, but it's gotta stop right here. I can't believe I'm sayin' this, but I've gotta grow up."

I thought for a while, in disbelief, then asked, "So what are we doin'?"

"Simple" was the answer. "Eggs."

"Ah, come on." I turned away. "We can do a lot better than lousy eggs."

"No, we can't," and this was the first time I'd heard Rube speak on this subject with reality in his voice. "The truth, mate, is that we're hopeless."

To this I could only nod. I then said, "All right," and it was decided that we would go to Bruce Patterson's house on Friday night and egg that beautiful red car of his. Maybe his front door and windows too. I was truly glad as well that this was the last time because I was getting sick of it.

Another unavoidable fact also made this whole thing harder than it should have been. It was the fact that I still couldn't get my mind off Rebecca Conlon. I just couldn't, no matter how hard I tried. I thought of her and wondered if she would be there this week, or if she would be off again, having a life without me. It hurt sometimes, while at others I convinced myself that it was all far too risky. *Just look at Bruce and Sarah*, I told myself. *I bet that guy was as obsessed with Sarah as I am with this other girl, and I bet he promised himself never to hurt her, just like I've been doin' — and look what he's done to her. He's left her a crumpled mess, lyin' on her bed all the time.*

When Friday evening came, I think Rube and I were too tired to go through with it. We were sick of ourselves, and with two cartons of eggs sitting in our room, we decided not to go.

"Ah, well, that's it, then." Rube said it. "If you have to think about it so long, it isn't worth doin'."

"Well, what are we gonna do with all these eggs?" I asked.

"Eat 'em, I s'pose."

"What? Twelve each?"

"I guess."

For the time being, we left the eggs under Rube's bed, but I myself still took a trip out to Bruce's place.

I went down there after dinner and walked past his car and imagined myself throwing eggs at it. The thought was ridiculous, to say the least.

It made me laugh as I knocked on the door, though the smile was wiped off my face when a girl I assumed was Sarah's replacement answered. She opened up and stared at me through the flyscreen.

"Bruce around?" I asked her.

She nodded. "You wanna come in?"

"Nah, I'll be right." I waited out on the porch.

When Bruce saw me, he looked pretty confused. It wasn't like he and I had been good mates or anything. It wasn't like we had a pool and he'd thrown me around in it or as if we'd kicked footballs around together. No, we'd barely even talked, and I could see he was afraid that I might be here to give him a serve. I wasn't.

All I did was wait for him to come out of the house so we could talk. Just one question. That was all I had, as we leaned on his front railing, looking onto the street.

I asked it.

"When you first met my sister . . . did you promise yourself never to hurt her?"

There was silence for a while, but then he answered.

He said, "Yeah, I did," and after a few more seconds, I left.

He called out, "Hey, Cameron."

I turned around.

"How is she?"

I smiled, raising my head, resolute. "She's okay. She's good."

He nodded and I told him, "See y' later."

"Yeah, see y' later, mate."

At home, the night wasn't finished. An act not of vandalism but of symbolism was to occur.

At around eight-thirty, Rube walked into our room and something was different. What was it?

His beard was gone.

When he presented his post-animal face to the rest of the family, there were claps and sighs of relief. No more animalistic face. No more animalistic behavior.

I myself kept hearing Bruce Patterson telling me that he had promised to never hurt my sister. It hunted me, even as I sat through an extremely violent movie on TV. I kept hearing his voice, and I wondered if I would ever hurt Rebecca Conlon if she would let me get near her in the first place. I was hunted all night.

It's jungle and I'm with her. I can't see her face, but I know I'm with Rebecca Conlon. I lead her by the hand and we are moving very fast, ducking around twisted trees whose fingers are branches spread like cracked ceiling under gray sky.

"Faster," I tell her.

"Why?" is her reply.

"Because he's coming."

"Who's coming?"

I don't answer her because I don't know. The only thing I am completely sure of is that I can hear footsteps behind us through the jungle. I can hear a hunching forward, coming after us.

"Come on," I say to her again.

We come to a river and plunge in, wading hurriedly across the freezing cold water.

On the other side, I see something upriver and I lead her there. It's a cave that crouches down amongst some heavy trees above the water.

We go in. No words. No "In here."

She smiles, relieved.

I don't see it.

I know it.

We sit down right in the back corner of the cave, and we hear the meditative water of the river outside, climbing down, down. Slow. Real. Knowing.

She falls.

Asleep.

"It's okay," I tell her, and I feel her in my arms. My own eyes try to sleep as well, but they don't. They stay wide awake as time snarls forward and silence drops down, like measured thought. I can't even hear the river anymore.

When.

The figure enters the cave.

He walks in and pauses.

He sees.

Us.

He has a weapon.

He looks.

Smiles.

Even though I can't see his face, I know he smiles.

"What do you want?" I ask, afraid but quiet so I won't wake the girl in my arms.

The figure says nothing. He keeps stepping forward. Slow. Reeling. No.

There's a sound, like a slit, and smoke rises from the weapon the figure is holding. It rises up to his face and wraps itself around it. It tells me that something terrible has happened, and Rebecca Conlon stirs slightly on my lap.

A match is struck.

Light.

I look at her.

Know!

This.

She's hurt, for sure, because I see blood dripping from her heart. Slow. Real.

I look up. The figure holds the lit match and I see his face. His eyes and lips and expression belong to me.

"But you promised," I tell him, and I scream, to try and wake up. I need to wake up and know that I would never ever hurt her.

CHAPTER 13

As usual, Dad and I went to work on Saturday, at the Conlon place.

Rather than keep you in suspense (if you even still care by now), I might as well let you know that this time she was there, and she was as brilliant as ever.

I was still working under the house when she came to me.

"Hey, I missed you last week," I said when she showed, and immediately chastised myself in my head — the statement was so ambiguous. I mean, did it mean *I missed you* as in I just didn't see you (which was the intended message), or did it mean *I was really heartbroken that you weren't here, y' stupid bitch*? I wasn't sure what messages I was sending out. Overall, I could only hope she thought I was saying we just didn't see each other. You can't seem too desperate in a situation like that, even if your heart is annihilating you from the inside.

She said, "Well . . ." God, she said it with that voice that made her real. "I wasn't here on purpose."

What the hell was this?

"What?" I dared to ask.

"You heard." She grinned. "I wasn't here . . ."

"Because of me?"

She nodded.

Was this bad or good?

It sounded bad. Very bad.

But then, it also sounded good, in some sick, twisted way. Was she having me on?

No.

"I didn't wanna be here because I was" — she swallowed — "scared to make a fool out of myself — like last time."

"Last time?" I asked, confused. "Wasn't it me who said something stupid?" It was me all right, who said, "I like workin' here." I remembered it and cringed.

We were both crouched down under the house and these wooden beams hovered over us, warning us that one loss of concentration would leave our heads nice and bruised. I made sure not to stand up straight.

"At least you said *something*." She pushed her argument.

Suddenly, something poured out of me.

I said, "I wouldn't hurt you. Well, at least I'd try like hell not to. I promise."

"Pardon?" She stepped away a bit. "What do you mean?"

"I mean, if . . . Did you have an okay weekend last week?" Drivel. Drivel talk.

"Yeah." She nodded and stayed where she was. "I was at a friend of mine's house." Then she slipped it in. "And then we went over to this guy's place — Dale."

Dale.

Why was that name so familiar?

Oh no.

Oh, great.

"Dale Perry?"

Dale Perry.

Greg's mate.

Typical.

A hero like that.

I could tell she really liked the guy.

More than me.

He was a winner.

People liked him.

Greg did.

Though he could depend on me.

"Yeah, Dale Perry," she replied — confirming my worst fears — nodding and smiling. "You know him, do you?"

"Yeah, I know him." It dawned on me then as well that this Rebecca Conlon was most likely one of the girls in the group at Lumsden Oval, on that day that seemed decades ago now. There were a few girls like her there, I remembered. Same real hair. Same real legs. Same . . . It all made sense. She was local, and pretty, and real.

Dale Perry.

I almost mentioned that he'd nearly burned my ear off just over a year ago but held it back. I didn't want her thinking that I was one of those completely jealous guys who hated everyone who was better than himself — which actually was exactly the kind of guy I was.

"My best friend reckons he likes me, but I don't know. . . ."

She went on talking but I couldn't bring myself to listen. I just couldn't. Why in the hell was she telling me this anyway? Was it because I was just the plumber's son and I went to an old state school while she most likely went to a Saint something-or-other school? Was it because I was the kind of guy who was harmless and couldn't bite?

Well, I came close.

I almost stopped her to say, "Ah, just go away with your Dale Perry," but I didn't. I loved her too much and I wouldn't hurt her, no matter how much I myself was hurting.

Instead, I asked if she knew Greg.

"Greg Fiennes or something?"

"Fienni."

"Yeah, I do. How do you know him?"

And for some reason, all these tears started welling up in my eyes.

"Ah," I said. "He was a friend of mine once," and I turned away, to keep working and to hide my eyes.

"A good friend?"

Damn this girl!

"My best friend," I admitted.

"Oh." She looked through my back. I could feel it.

I wondered if she was getting the picture here. Maybe. Probably. Yes, probably, because she left then with a far too friendly "Okay, bye-ee." Had I heard that before? Of course I had, and it gashed my throat with reality.

The whole altercation didn't drive me through the day like the disappointment of last week had. No, this time I limped through it.

I felt something awful in me.

Limping on.

Dad saw me and gave me a serve for being so slow, but I couldn't pick it up. I tried like you wouldn't believe, but my back was broken. My spirit was crushed.

I had the chance to tell her off.

I could have hurt her.

I didn't.

It was no consolation.

As I worked, I constantly had to pull myself together and it was such a struggle. It was like every step was out to get me. Blisters on my hands started opening up and feeling kept creeping into my eyes. I started sniffing at the air to get enough in my lungs, and when the day was over I struggled out from under the house and stood there, waiting. I really wanted to collapse to the ground, but I held it together.

I felt itchy, dirty, diseased — by simply being me. What was wrong with me?

I felt like the dog that's got rabies in this book I was reading in school, *To Kill a Mockingbird*. The dog, it's limping and slobbering all over the road and the father, Atticus, he surprises his son by shooting it.

I'm walking along top a fence line that seems to stretch for an eternity. Somehow, though, I know that it will stop at some point. I know it will last as long as my life.

"Keep walking," I tell myself.

My arms are out to keep me balanced.

On either side of me, there is air and ground, trying to get me to jump down into it.

Which side do I jump?

It is early, early morning. It's that time when it's still dark but you know the day is coming. Blue is bleeding through black. Stars are dying.

The fence.

Sometimes it's stone, sometimes it's wood, and sometimes it's barbed wire.

I walk it, and still, I am tempted by each side that flanks it.

"Jump," I hear each side whisper. "Jump down here."

Distance.

Out there, somewhere, I can hear dogs barking, although their voices seem human. They bark and when I look all around me I can't see them. I can only hear barking that forms an audience for my journey along this fence.

Purple in the sky.

Pins-and-needles legs.

Shivers down my right side.

Concussion thoughts.
Footsteps.
Alone.
Take one after the other.
Barbed wire now.
Where do I jump?
Who do I listen to?
Daisy sun, maroon sky.
First part of the sun — a frown.
Last part of the sun — a smile.
Dark day.
Thoughts cover the sky.
Thoughts are the sky.
Feet on fence.
One side of the fence is victory. . . .
The . . . other side is defeat.
Walk.
I walk, on.
Deciding.
Sweat reigns.
It lands on me, controlled, and drips down my face.
Victory one side.
Defeat on the other.
Clouds are uncertain.
They throb in the sky like drumbeats, like pulses.
I decide —
I jump.
High. High.

THE UNDERDOG

The wind gets me, and high up, I know that it will throw me down to the side of the fence it wants.

Wherever I land, soon enough, I know I will have to climb back up and keep walking, but for now, I'm still in the air.

CHAPTER 14

Where did I go from there?

What did I do?

How did things turn out?

Well, this is basically the end, so the answers should be in these next few pages. I doubt they will surprise you, but you never know. I don't know how smart or thick you are. You could be Albert Einstein for all I know, or some literary prizewinner, or maybe you're just middle of the road like me.

So we might as well cut to the chase — I will tell you now how things pretty much finished up in this wintry part of my life. The end began like this:

Moping.

I did it for the whole of Sunday, and on Monday at school. Something churned in me, starting in my stomach and rising till it was reaching its arms up to strip my skin from the inside. It burned.

On Wednesday at school, I had a bit of a conversation with Greg, mainly because of the beaten-up look of his face.

"What happened to you?" I asked him when I ran into him in one of the walkways.

"Ah, forget it," he answered me. "Nothin'." But we both knew it was really pretty obvious that the fellas he'd bought the gear for were still unimpressed by his efforts, even after he'd come through with the money.

"They got you anyway, ay?" I asked. I smiled mournfully as I said it and Greg smiled as well.

"Yep, they got me," he nodded. His smile was a knowing, ironic one. "They decided on giving me a hidin' for the inconvenience I'd caused them. . . . The original guy was out of gear so they had to go somewhere else. They weren't impressed."

"Fair enough" was my conclusion.

"I s'pose, yeah."

We parted ways a few moments later, and looking back at him, I looked at Greg and tried praying for him, like all those prayers I had made earlier on in this story, but I couldn't. I just couldn't. Don't ask me why. I hoped that he was okay, but I couldn't summon the strength to pray for it.

What good had my prayers done anyway?

They sure as hell hadn't helped my own cause too much — but remember? I never did get around to praying for myself, did I? Maybe that's what was behind it, though. Myself. Maybe the only reason I'd prayed for others to begin with was to bring myself good fortune. Was that true? Was it? No. No way. It wasn't.

Maybe the prayers did actually work.

It's quite probable when you think about it, because back home, Sarah had started talking on the phone to replace the intense getting-off sessions on the couch,

Steve was starting to walk again, Rube had sorted himself out a bit, Mum and Dad seemed happy enough, and no doubt Rebecca Conlon was happy fantasizing about Dale Perry. . . .

It seemed that everyone was going along just fine.

Except me.

Quite often, I found myself chanting the word *misery*, like the pitiful creature I was.

I whinged inside.

I whined.

I whimpered.

I scratched at my insides.

Then I laughed.

At myself.

It happened when I was out in the evening, after dinner.

The sausages and mushrooms were settling in my stomach and amongst all the anguish I was carrying around, a very weird laughter broke through me. As I lifted my feet over the ground, I smiled and eventually placed my hand on a telegraph pole to rest.

Standing there, I allowed the laughter to come out of me, and people coming past must have thought I was crazy or drugged or something like that. They looked at me as if to say, "What are you laughin' at?" They walked on quickly, though, toward their own lives, as I stood paused amongst mine.

That was when I decided that I had to decide something.

I had to decide what I was going to do, and what I was going to be.

I was standing there, waiting for someone to do something, till I realized the person I was waiting for was myself.

Everything inside me was numb, vaguely alive, almost as if it wasn't daring to move, waiting on my decision.

I breathed out and said, "Okay."

That was all it took.

One word, and sprinting home, I knew that what I was going to do was make it back, clean myself up a bit, and run the five kilometers to Rebecca Conlon's place and ask if she wanted to do something on the weekend. Who cared what anyone thought? I didn't care what Mum or Dad would say, what Rube or Steve would say, what Sarah would say, or what *you* would say. I just knew that this was what I had to do.

"Right now," I emphasized as I ran, forcing my shoulders forward and going like I was after a fake rabbit. Sickness swept over me as I ran, as if food was turning to acid. Still, though, I ran harder and jumped our front gate and into our house to find.

Sarah on the phone.

Phone.

Yes, phone, I thought. *Of course.* Running all the way there and talking to her face-to-face seemed pretty scary by now, so the new plan was to get to a phone box somewhere. I got some change out of my drawer, wrote down the Conlon number on my hand from Dad's work pad, and ran back out for the nearest phone box.

"Oi!" A voice followed me onto the footpath. It was Steve, from the porch. I hadn't even noticed him when I'd come charging into the house. "Where y' goin'?"

I stopped, but I didn't answer his question. I walked back to him quickly, suddenly remembering what he'd said to me the last time he'd spoken from the porch, the night Rube and I returned the give-way sign.

"You guys are such losers." That's what he'd said, and now I walked up our steps and pointed a finger at him as he leaned on the railing and stretched.

I pointed at him and said, "If you ever call me a loser again, I'm gonna smash your face in." I meant it, and I could see from the look on his face that he knew I meant it. He even smiled, like he knew something. "I'm a fighter," I concluded, "not a loser. There's a difference."

My eyes stayed in his for barely another moment. I meant it all right. I meant every word. Steve enjoyed it. I enjoyed it more.

Phone box.

I took off again, obsessed.

The only problem now with the phone box plan was that I couldn't exactly find one. I thought there was one at a particular spot on Elizabeth Street but it had been taken away. I could only keep running, this time in the direction of the Conlon place, until about three kilometers later, I found one. Had I run another two kilometers I could have talked to her in person after all.

"Oh, mate." I stuck my hands on my knees when I made it to the phone. "Mate," and I knew very abruptly that running there had been the easy part. Now I had to dial the number and talk.

My fingers were claws on the ancient dialer as I called up the number, and . . .

Waited.

". . . ing."

It was ringing.

"Noth–ing."

"Noth–ing."

"Noth–ing."

She didn't answer and I had to explain to the person who did exactly who I was.

"Cameron."

"Cameron?"

"Cameron Wolfe, y' silly old cow!" I felt like scream-ing, but I kept myself back. Instead, I said with quiet dignity, "Cameron Wolfe. I work with the plumber." I realized after speaking those words that I was still very much out of breath. I was panting into the tele-phone, even when Rebecca Conlon was finally on the other end.

"Rebecca?"

"Yeah?"

The voice, her voice.

Hers.

I stuttered things out, but not dumbstruck. I con-centrated, and it was all done with purpose, with desire, almost with a severe, serene pride. My voice crawled to her. It asked. Squashing the phone. Go on. Do it. Ask.

"Yeah, I was wonderin' . . ."

My throat hurt.

"Wonderin' if . . ."

Saturday.

That would be the day.

No.

No?

Yes, *no* — you heard me.

Although, Rebecca Conlon didn't say the word *no* when she rejected me for some kind of meeting between us on Saturday. She said, "I can't," and I look back now and wonder if the disappointment in her voice was genuine.

Of course I wonder, because she went on to tell me that she couldn't do anything on Sunday or the next weekend either because of some kind of family thing, or another thing of some description. No point pretending. She was giving herself some good safe ground to keep me at bay. See, I hadn't even asked her about Sunday yet. Or the next weekend! The pain in my ear counted at me. The black sky above me seemed to come down. I felt like I was sucking in the gray clouds that stood above, and very slowly, the phone call faded out.

"Well, maybe some other time." I smiled viciously inside the dirty phone box. My voice was still nice, though, and dignified.

"Yeah, that'd be great, ay." Nice, great voice. The last time I would hear it? Probably, unless she was dumb enough to be at her house on the upcoming weekend when Dad and I would finish the job.

Yes, her voice, and somehow, I couldn't be sure if it was so real to me anymore. It was too far out of reach now to be real.

"Okay, I'll see y' later," I finished, but I wasn't seeing anyone later.

"Okay, bye-ee," adding insult to injury.

Hearing her hang up then was brutal. I listened hard and the sound was something ripping apart my head. Slowly, slowly I dropped the receiver down to leave it hanging there, half-dead.

Caught.

Tried.

Hanged.

I left it hanging there and walked away, home.

The way back wasn't as bad as you might think, because thoughts fighting in my head made the time go past quickly. Every step left an invisible print on the footpath, which only I could smell on my way past in the future. Good luck.

Halfway there I noticed another phone box in a side street, sitting there joking me and laughing.

"Huh" was all I said to myself, as I kept walking and eased an itch on my shoulder blade with a tired hand stretching at the end of a bent, twisting elbow.

This time, I staggered into the front gate, stayed around a while, and went to bed at about ten-thirty.

I didn't sleep.

I sweated, shivering, alone.

I saw things, plastered down onto my eyes.

Thrown into them.

I saw it all. Every detail. From a baseball and cricket bat, fluoride treatment, an empty signpost, dreams, fathers, brothers, mother, sister, Bruce, friend, girl, voice, gone, and into. Me.

My life trampled my bed.

I felt tears like hammers down my face.

I saw myself walking to that phone.

Talking.

Staggering home.

Then, close to one o'clock, I stood up and put my jeans on and walked barefoot out into the backyard.

Out of our room.

Down the hallway.

Out the back door.

Freezing cold night.

Past the cement and onto the grass, till I stood.

I stood there and stared, into the sky and at the city around me. I stood, hands at my side, and I saw what had happened to me and who I was and the way things would always be for me. Truth. There was no more wishing, or wondering. I knew who I was, and what I would always do. I believed it, as my teeth touched and my eyes were overrun.

My mouth opened.

It happened.

Yes, with my head thrown into the sky, I started howling.

Arms stretched out next to me, I howled, and everything came out of me. Visions poured up my throat and past voices surrounded me. The sky listened. The city didn't. I didn't care. All I cared about was that I was howling so that I could hear my voice and so I would remember that the boy had intensity and something to offer. I howled, oh, so loud and desperate, telling a world that I was here and I wouldn't lie down.

Not tonight.

Not ever.

Yes, I howled and without me knowing it, my family stood just beyond the back door, watching me and wondering what I was doing.

At first, all is black and white.

Black on white.

That's where I'm walking, through pages.

These pages.

Sometimes it gets so that I have one foot in the pages and the words, and the other in what they speak of.

Sometimes I'm there again, hatching plans with Rube, fighting him, working with Dad, getting called a wild animal by my mother, watching Sarah's life stumble at the hands of Bruce, and telling Steve I'll smash his face in if he ever calls me a loser again. I even see Greg's bought stash going up through his chimney, drugging the air above his roof. One foot walks me toward Rebecca Conlon's place and working there, and ringing there. One foot stands me in the picture where the strangled public telephone hangs, dead, with only the remains of my voice left inside it.

Sometimes, when I am deep inside the pages, the letters of every word are like the huge buildings of the city. I stand beneath them, looking up.

I run at times.

I crawl.

Through.

Every page.

Dreams cover me sometimes, but at others, they strip the flesh off my soul or take the blanket away from me, leaving me with just myself, cold.

Fingers touch the pages.

They turn me.

I continue on.

I always do.

All is big.

The pages and the words are my world, spread out before your eyes and for your hands to touch. Vaguely, I

can see your face looking down into me, as I look back.
Do you see my eyes?

Still, I walk on, through a dream that takes me
through these pages.

I arrive at the point where I see myself walking out to
the backyard into the freezing cold. I see city and sky, and
I feel the cold. I stand next to myself.

Jeans.

Bare feet.

Bare chest, shivering.

Boys' arms.

They're stretched out, reaching.

A wind picks up and sheets of paper take flight and
fall down around us as we stand there. A howling noise
stumbles despairingly for my ears and I receive it.

I hang on to that desperation, because.

I need it.

I want it.

I smile.

Dogs bark, far away but coming closer.

Next to me, I hear myself howl.

This is a good dream.

Howling. Loud.

Intense.

The last sheets of paper still fall.

I'm alive.

I've never been so —

I look down.

The words are my life.
Howling continues.
I stand with pages strewn at my ankles and with that
howling in my ears.

FIGHTING RUBEN WOLFE

For Scout

CHAPTER 1

The dog we're betting on looks more like a rat.

"But he can run like hell," Rube says. He's all flannelette smiles and twisted shoes. He'll spit, then smile. Spit, then smile. A nice guy, really, my brother. Ruben Wolfe. It's our usual winter of discontent.

We're at the bottom of the open, dusty grandstand.

A girl walks past.

Jesus, I think.

"Jesus," Rube says, and that's the difference, as both of us watch her, longing, breathing, being. Girls like that don't just show up at the dog track. The ones we're used to are either chain-smoking mousy types or pie-eating horsy types. Or beer-drinking slutty types. The one we watch, however, is a rare experience. I'd bet on her if she could run on the track. She's great.

Then there's only the sickness I feel from looking at legs I can't touch, or at lips that don't smile at me. Or hips that don't reach for me. And hearts that don't beat for me.

I slip my hand into my pocket and pull out a ten-buck note. That should distract me. I mean, I like to look at girls a bit, but it always ends up hurting me. I get sore eyes, from the distance. So all I can do is say something like, "So, are we puttin' this money on or what,

Rube?" as I do on this grayish day in this fine lecherous city of home.

"Rube?" I ask again.

Silence.

"Rube?"

Wind. Rolling can. Bloke smoking and coughing close behind. "Rube, are we betting or not?"

I hit him.

A backhander.

To my brother's arm.

He looks at me and smiles again.

He says, "Okay," and we look for someone to con into placing our bet for us. Someone over the age limit. It's never hard around here. Some old bloke with half his crack pouring out the back of his trousers will always put one on for you. He might even ask for a share of the winnings, if the pooch you bet on wins, that is. However, he'll never find you — not that we would leave him out anyway. You have to humor those poor old alcoholic please-don't-let-me-turn-out-like-him sort of fellas. A cut of the winnings isn't going to hurt them. The trick is to win something at all. It hasn't happened yet.

"C'mon." Rube stands up, and as we walk, I can still see that girl's legs in the distance.

Jesus, I think.

"Jesus," Rube says.

At the betting windows we encounter a small problem.

Cops.

What the hell are they doin' here? I wonder.

"What the hell are *they* doin' here?" Rube says.

The thing is, I don't even hate cops. To tell you the truth, I actually feel a little sorry for them. Their hats. Wearing all that ridiculous cowboy gear around their waists. Having to look tough, yet friendly and approachable at the same time. Always having to grow a mustache (whether male, or in some cases, female) to look like they have authority. Doing all those push-ups and sit-ups and chin-ups at the police academy before they get a licence to eat doughnuts again. Telling people that someone in their family just got mangled in a car wreck. . . . The list just goes on and on, so I'd better stop myself.

"Look at the pig with the sausage roll," Rube points out. He clearly doesn't care that these cops are hanging around like a bad smell. No way. It's actually the exact opposite, as Rube walks straight toward the cop with the mustache who is eating a sausage roll with sauce. There are two of them. There's the sausage roll cop and a female cop. A brunette, with her hair tied under her hat. (Only her bangs fall seductively to her eyes.)

We arrive at them and it begins.

Ruben L. Wolfe: "How y' feelin' today, constable?"

Cop, with food: "Not bad, mate, how are you?"

Rube: "Enjoyin' that sausage roll, are y'?"

Cop, devouring food: "Sure bloody am, mate. You enjoyin' watchin'?"

Rube: "Certainly. How much are they?"

Cop, swallowing: "A buck eighty."

Rube, smiling: "You got robbed."

Cop, taking bite: "I know."

Rube, starting to enjoy himself: "You should haul that tuckshop in for that, I reckon."

Cop, with sauce on edge of his lip: "Maybe I should haul you in instead."

Rube, pointing at sauce on lip: "What for?"

Cop, acknowledging sauce on lip and wiping it: "For plain smart aleck behavior."

Rube, scratching his crotch conspicuously and glancing at the female accomplice cop: "Where'd y' pick *her* up?"

Cop, beginning to enjoy himself now as well: "In the canteen."

Rube, glancing at her again and continuing to scratch: "How much?"

Cop, finishing sausage roll: "A buck sixty."

Rube, stopping the scratching: "You got robbed."

Cop, remembering himself: "Hey, you better watch it."

Rube, straightening his ragged flanno shirt and his pants: "Did they charge you for sauce? On the sausage roll, that is."

Cop, shifting on spot: nothing.

Rube, moving closer: "Well?"

Cop, unable to conceal the truth: "Twenty cents."

Rube, staggered: "*Twenty cents!* For sauce?"

Cop, obviously disappointed in himself: "I know."

Rube, earnest and honest, or at least one or the other: "You should have just gone without, out of principle. Don't you have any self-control?"

Cop: "Are you tryin' to start somethin'?"

Rube: "Certainly not."

Cop: "Are y' sure?"

At this point, the accomplice brunette female cop and I exchange looks of embarrassment and I consider her without her uniform. To me, she is only wearing underwear.

Rube, answering the cop's question: "Yes sir, I'm sure. I'm not trying to start anything. My brother and I are just enjoying this wonderfully gray day here in the city and admiring the speedy beasts on their way around the track." A showbag, he is. Full of garbage. "Is that a crime?"

Cop, getting fed up: "Why are you talking to us anyway?"

Female accomplice cop and I look at each other. Again. She has nice underwear. I imagine it.

Rube: "Well, we were just . . ."

Cop, testy: "Just what? What do you want?"

Female cop looks great. Brilliant. She's in a bath. Bubbles. She rises up. She smiles. At me. I shake.

Ruben, grinning loudly: "Well, we were hoping you might put a bet on for us. . . ."

Female cop, from the bath: "Are you kidding?"

Me, smashing my head up through the water: "Are you bloody jokin', Rube?"

Rube, smacking my mouth: "My name's not Rube."

Me, back in reality: "Oh, sorry, James, y' tosser."

Cop, holding scrunched-up sausage roll bag with sauce smothered inside it: "What's a tosser?"

Rube, distressed: "Oh God almighty, this can't be happening! How ridiculously stupid can one man be?"

Cop, curious: "What *is* a tosser?"

Female accomplice cop, who is about five foot nine and uses the police gym I'd say four nights a week: "You look at one every morning in the mirror." She's tall and lean and great. She winks at me.

Me: speechless.

Rube: "That's the way, love."

Female unbelievably sexy cop: "Who you callin' love, lover boy?"

Rube, ignoring her and going back to ignorant don't-even-know-what-a-tosser-is cop: "So will you put a bet on or not?"

Tosser cop: "What?"

Me, to all of them but not loud enough: "This is downright bloody ridiculous." People mill around and past us, to place bets.

Female accomplice cop, to me: "You wanna taste me?"

Me: "Love to." It's my imagination, of course.

Tosser cop: "Okay."

Rube, shocked: *"What?"*

Tosser cop: "I'll put the bet on for y's."

Rube, floundering: "Really?"

Tosser cop, trying to impress: "Yeah, I do it all the time, don't I, Cassy?"

Hundred percent pure female cop, clearly *unimpressed*: "Whatever y' reckon."

Me: "Is that ethical?"

Rube, incredulous, to me: "Are you mentally challenged?" (He's recently become tired of the word *spastic*. He reckons the new way makes him sound more sophisticated. Something like that, anyway.)

Me: "No, I'm not. But —"

All three of them, to me: "Shut up." The bastards.

Tosser cop: "What's the dog's number?"

Rube, happy with himself: "Three."

Tosser cop: "Its name?"

Rube: "You Bastard."

Tosser cop: "Pardon?"

Rube: "I swear it. Here, look at our program."

We all look.

Me: "How'd they get away with a name like that?"

Rube: "It's 'cause today's just a lot of amateur stuff. Anything with four legs'll get a run. It's a wonder there aren't any poodles out there." He glances at me seriously. "Our fella can run but. Take my word for it."

Tosser cop: "Is that the one that looks more like a rat?"

Accomplice gorgeous cop: "But he runs like clappers, they reckon."

In any case, while the tosser cop takes our money, walks away, throws his sausage roll bag in the bin and makes the bet, the following things happen: Rube smiles incessantly to himself, the accomplice cop has her hands on her honey hips, and I, Cameron Wolfe, imagine making love to her in my sister's bed of all places.

It's disagreeable, isn't it?

Yet.

What can you do?

When the cop comes back, he says, "I put ten on 'im myself."

"You won't be disappointed." Rube nods, accepting our ticket. Then he says, "Hey, I think I'm gonna turn you in for this puttin' bets on for minors. It's a dis-grace."

(In all the time I've known him, my brother has never said just simple *disgrace*. He has to say it in two parts. *Dis* and *grace*. "Dis-grace.")

"So what?" the cop says. "And besides . . . who y' gonna tell?"

"The cops," Rube answers, and we all smirk a little, and head for the open grandstand.

We all sit down and wait for the race. "This You Bastard better be good," the cop announces, but no one listens. You can cut the air with a knife, as the trainers, gamblers, thieves, bookies, fat guys, fat girls, chain-smokers, alcos, corrupt cops, and juvenile delinquents all wait, with their scattered thoughts scattering onto the track.

"It *does* look like a rat," I say, when the greyhound we've chosen trots ferret-like and scrawny past us. "And what the hell are clappers, anyway?"

"I don't know," the cop says.

Rube: "We don't know what they are, but we know they're fast."

"Yeah."

The cop and Rube are inseparable now. Best mates. One has a uniform and black, close-cropped hair. The other is in rags, stinks of sweat and No-Name cologne, and has wavy brown-blond hair that staggers toward his shoulders. He has eyes of stomped-out fire, a wet nose that sniffs, and he has bitten claws for fingernails. Needless to say, the second one is my brother. A Wolfe, a dog, through and through.

Then there's the female cop.

Then there's me.

Drooling.

"And they're off!"

It's some tosser, dare I say it, over the loudspeaker, and he's rattling off names of the dogs so fast, I can barely understand him. There's Chewy on a Boot, Dictionary, No Loot, Vicious, and Generic Hound, and they're all in front of You Bastard, who scampers around the back like a rodent with a mousetrap stuck to his arse.

The crowd rises.

They shout.

The female cop looks great.

People scream.

"Go Pictionary! Go Pictionary!"

People correct. "It's *Dictionary!*"

"What?"

"*Dic*tionary!"

"Oh . . . go *Pic*tionary!"

"Ah, forget it!"

People clap and shout.

Great, I tell you. Great, she looks. Brunette.

Then, finally, the rat gets rid of the mousetrap and makes some ground.

Rube and the cop get happy.

They scream, almost sing with joy. "Go You Bastard! Go You Bastard!"

All of the dogs chase the ludicrous rabbit around the track and the crowd is like an escaped convict.

Running.

Hoping.

Knowing that the world is catching up.

Hanging.

Hanging on for dear life to this moment of liberation that is so sad that it can only lurk. It's the deception of something real inside something so obviously empty.

Screaming.

"Go Vicious!"

"Go No Loot!"

Rube and the cop: "Go You Bastard! Go You Bastard!"

We're all watching as the rat comes flying around the outside of the track, clipping first place and losing balance to fall back into fourth.

"Oh, you bastard!" Rube winces, and he isn't calling the dog by its name as he pedals like hell to make it back.

He does.

He runs well, our bastard.

Runs into second, which makes Rube look at our ticket and ask the cop a question. He says, "Did you bet each way or on the nose?"

By the look on his face, we can tell that the cop has bet on the nose. All or nothing.

"Well, you're a bit useless then, aren't y' mate?" Rube laughs, and he slaps the cop on the back.

"Yep," the cop says. He isn't a tosser anymore. He's just a guy who forgot about the world for a few moments when some dogs sprinted around a track. His name is Gary, a bit of a Nancy-boy name, but who cares?

We say our good-byes and I dream one last time about Cassy the cop and compare her with other imagined women in the lecherous soul that is my youth.

I think about her all the way home, where the usual Saturday night awaits us:

Our sister going out. Our brother staying in, staying quiet. Dad reading the paper. Mrs. Wolfe, our mother, going to bed early. Rube and me talking briefly across the room before sleep.

"I liked her," I say on our front porch.

"I know." Rube smiles and he opens the door.

"Hey Rube, are you awake?"

"Whatta y' reckon? I've only been in here two lousy minutes."

"It's been longer than that."

"It hasn't."

"It has, y' miserable idiot. And tell me what do you want, ay? Can y' tell me that? Whatta y' want?"

"I want you to switch the light off."

"No way."

"It's only fair — I was in here first and you're closer to the switch."

"So what? I'm older. You should respect your elders and switch the light off yourself."

"What a load of bloody."

"It stays on then."

It stays on for ten minutes, and then, take a guess. It's me who switches it off.

"You suck," I tell him.

"Thank you."

CHAPTER 2

There's a noise at about three a.m. It's Sarah spewing her hole in the bathroom. I get up to check her out, and there she is, wrapped around the bowl, hugging it, cradling it. Soaking into it.

Her hair is thick, like all of us in the Wolfe family, and as I look at her through my burning, itchy eyes, I notice that there's some vomit caught in one of her tough tufts of flowing hair. I get some toilet paper and fish it out, then wet a towel to get rid of it altogether.

"Dad?"

"Dad?"

She throws her head back, to the toilet rim. "Is that you, Dad?" and my sister begins to cry. She gathers composure and pulls me to my knees and concentrates on me. With her hands on my shoulders, she wails almost silently. Wailing: "I'm sorry, Dad. I'm sorry I —"

"It's me," I tell her. "It's Cameron."

"Don't lie," she responds. "Don't lie, Dad," and saliva falls to the skin above her red top, hitting her through the heart. Her jeans cut into her hips, slicing them up. It surprises me that they don't draw blood. Same with her heels. Her shoes leave bite marks in her ankles. My sister.

"Don't lie," she says one more time, so I stop.

I stop lying and say, "Okay Sarah, it's me, Dad. We're puttin' you into bed." And to my surprise, Sarah manages to stand up and limp to her room. I get her shoes off, just in time before they sever her feet.

She mumbles.

Words tumble from her mouth as I sit down on the floor, against her bed.

"I'm sick," she says, "of gettin' shattered." She goes on and on, until slowly, she falls.

Asleep.

A sleep, I think. *It'll do her good.*

Her last words are, "Thanks Dad . . . I mean, thanks, Cam." Then her hand trips onto my shoulder. It stays. I smile as slightly as a person can smile when they sit, cold, cramped, and crumpled in his sister's room when she's just come home with alcoholic veins, bones, and breath.

Sitting next to Sarah's bed, I think about what's happening with her. I wonder why she's doing this to herself. *Is she lonely?* I ask. *Unhappy? Afraid?* It would be nice if I could say I understand, but that would not be right. No, it wouldn't be, because I just don't know. It would be like asking why Rube and I go down to the dog track. It's not because we're ill-adjusted or we don't fit in or anything like that. It just is. We go to the track. Sarah's getting drunk. She did have a boyfriend once, but he went.

Stop, I tell myself. *Stop thinking about that.* But somehow I can't. Even when I try to think of other things, I just get on to thinking about the other members of my family.

Dad the plumber, who had an accident at work a few months ago and lost all of his jobs. Sure, insurance paid for his injuries, but now he's just plain out of work from it.

Mrs. Wolfe — working hard cleaning people's houses and just got a new job at the hospital.

Steve — working and waiting and dying to leave home.

Then Rube and me — the juveniles.

"Cam?"

Sarah's voice swims to me on a stream of bourbon, Coke, and some other cocktail that drowns the room.

"Cam."

"Cam'ron."

Then sleep.

Then Rube.

He arrives and mutters out a "Huh."

"Can y' flush the toilet?" I ask him. He does it. I hear it, rising and falling like the blowhole down south.

At six, I get up and return to Rube's and my room.

I could kiss Sarah's cheek as I leave, but I don't. Instead, I trounce my hair with my hand, giving up on it in the end — it's bound to stick up. In all directions.

When I get up for real, around seven o'clock, I check on Sarah one last time, just to make sure she hasn't made herself a superstar and choked on her own vomit. She hasn't, but her room's a shocker. The smell is of:

Juice.

Smoke.

Hangover.

And Sarah lying there, caked in it.

Daylight shoots through her window.

I walk.

Out.

Sunday.

I get breakfast, wearing trackies and a T-shirt. I'm barefoot. I watch the end of *Rage* with the volume turned completely down. Then there's a business show that wears a suit and tie and a fake hankie in its pocket.

"Cam."

It's Steve.

"Steve," I nod, and that's about all we'll say to each other for the entire day. Saying each other's name is the way he and I say hello. He always leaves the house early, including on Sundays. He's here but he's not. He'll go to see his friends or go fishing or just disappear. He'll leave the city if he wants. Go down south, where the water's clean and a person passing by will acknowledge you. Not that Steve cares about being acknowledged. He works, he waits. That's all. That's Steve. He offers Mum and Dad to pay more than his board so they can stay ahead, but they won't take it.

Too proud.

Too stubborn.

Dad says we'll manage and that some work is just around the corner. But the corner never ends. It stretches and continues, and Mum drives herself into the ground.

"Thanks."

The day echoes past and that's what Sarah says to me in the evening when I finally see her again. She comes into the lounge room just before dinner.

"I mean it," she tells me softly, and there is something in her eyes that makes me think of *The Old Man and the Sea*, and how the old man's patched sail looks like the flag of permanent defeat. That's what Sarah's eyes look like. The color of defeat chokes her pupils, even though her nod and smile and uncomfortable sitting motion on the couch indicate that she is not finished yet. She will just carry on, like all of us.

Smile stubborn.

Smile with instinct, then lick your wounds in the darkest of dark corners. Trace the scars back to your own fingers and remember them.

At dinner, Rube comes in late, just before Steve.

This is how the Wolfe family looks at the table:

Our mother, eating politely.

Dad, feeding burnt sausage into his mouth but tasting unemployment. His face has healed from the busted pipe that smashed his jaw and ripped open his face. Yes, the injury has healed nicely, at least on the outside of his skin.

Sarah, concentrating on keeping it all down.

Me, watching everyone else.

Rube, swallowing more and more and smiling at something, even though we have an extra dirty piece of business to cater for very soon.

It's Dad who brings it into the foreground.

"Well?" he says when we're done. He looks at Rube and me.

Well what?

"Well what?" Rube asks, but both of us know what we have to do. It's just, we've got an agreement with one of our neighbors that we'll walk his dog for him, twice a week. Sundays and Wednesdays. Let's just say that most of our neighbors think that Rube and me are kind of hoodlums. So to get in the good graces of Keith, the neighbor on our left (who we disturb the most), it was decided that we would walk his dog for him, since he doesn't get much time to do it himself. It was our mother's idea, of course, and we complied. We're many things, Rube and me, but I don't think we're difficult or lazy.

So as the ritual goes, Rube and I grab our jackets and walk out.

The catch is, the dog's a fluffy midget thing called Miffy. Bloody Miffy, for God's sake. What a name. He's a Pomeranian and he's a dead-set embarrassment to walk. So we wait till it gets dark. Then we go next door and Rube hits the highest note in his voice and calls, "Oh Miffy! Miffy!" He grins. "Come to Uncle Rube," and the fluffy embarrassment machine comes prancing toward us like a damned ballerina. I promise you when we're walking that dog and see someone we know, we pull our hoods over our heads and look the other way. I mean, there's only so much guys like us can get away with. Walking a Pomeranian that goes by the name of Miffy is not one of them. Think about it. There's street. Rubbish. Traffic. People yelling at each other over the top of their TVs. Heavy metallers and gang-looking guys slouching past . . . and then there are these two juvenile idiots walking a ball of fluff down the road.

It's out of hand.

That's what it is.

Disgraceful.

"A dis-grace," says Rube.

Even tonight, when Miffy's in a good mood.

Miffy.

Miffy.

The more I say it to myself the more it makes me laugh. The Pomeranian from hell. Watch out, or Miffy'll get you. Well, he's got us all right.

We go out.

We walk him.

We discuss it.

"Slaves are what we are, mate," is Rube's conclusion. We stop. Look at the dog. Carry on. "Look at us. You, me, an' Miffy here, and . . ." His voice trails off.

"What?"

"Nothin'."

"What?"

He gives in easily, because he wanted to all along.

At our gate upon our return, Rube looks me in the eye and says, "I was talkin' to my mate Jeff today and he reckons people're talkin' about Sarah."

"Sayin' what?"

"Sayin' she's been gettin' round. Gettin' drunk and gettin' around a bit."

Did he just say what I thought he said?

Getting around?

He did.

He did, and soon, it will alter the life of my brother Rube. It will put him in a boxing ring.

It'll make a heap of girls notice him.

It'll make him successful.

It will drag me with him, and all it will take to start it all is one incident. It's an incident in which he beats the hell out of a guy in school who calls Sarah something pretty ordinary.

For now, though, we stand at our gate.

Rube, Miffy, and me.

"We're wolves," is the last piece of conversation. "Wolves are up higher on the ladder for sure. They oughta *eat* Pomeranians, not walk 'em."

Yet, we do.

Never agree to walk your neighbor's midget dog. Take my word for it.

You'll be sorry.

"Hey Rube."

"What? The light's off this time."

"You reckon it's true what people are sayin'?"

"Reckon what's true?"

"You know — about Sarah."

"I d'know. But if I hear someone sayin' anything about her, I'm gonna nail 'em. I'm gonna kill 'em."

"Y' think so?"

"I wouldn't say it otherwise."

And sure enough, he nearly does.

CHAPTER 3

Rube smashes the guy, with bloody fists and trampling eyes, but first, this:

Our dad's been out of work now for nearly five months. I realize that I've mentioned it before, but I should really explain exactly how it came to be. What happened is that he was working on a site out in the suburbs, when some guy turned on the water pressure too early. A pipe busted and my dad caught the shrapnel, flush in the face.

Busted head.

Broken jaw.

Lots of stitches.

Plenty of wires.

Sure, he's like all fathers, my dad. My old man.

He's okay.

He's hard.

He's sadistic-like. That is, if he's in the mood. Generally though, he's just a human guy with a dog's last name and I feel for him at the moment. He's half a man, because it seems that when a man can't work and when his wife and kids earn all the money, a man becomes half a man. It's just the way it is. Hands grow pale. Heartbeat gets stale.

One thing I must say again, though, is that Dad wouldn't allow Steve or even Sarah to pay a single bill. Just their usual board. Even as he says his regular "No, no, it's okay," you can see where he's been ripped apart. You can see where the shadow opens the flesh and grabs his spirit by the throat. Often, I remember working with him on Saturdays. He'd tell me off and swear when I screwed something up, but he would tell me I did something decently as well. It would be short, to the point.

We are working people.

Work.

Struggle.

Even laugh about it sometimes.

None of us are winners.

We're survivors.

We are wolves, which are wild dogs, and this is our place in the city. We are small and our house is small on our small urban street. We can see the city and the train line and it's beautiful in its own dangerous way. Dangerous because it's shared and taken and fought for.

That's the best way I can put it, and thinking about it, when I walk past the tiny houses on our street, I wonder about the stories inside them. I wonder hard, because houses must have walls and rooftops for a reason. My only query is the windows. Why do they have windows? Is it to let a glimpse of the world in? Or for us to see out? Our own place is small perhaps, but when your old man is eaten by his own shadow, you realize that maybe in every house, something so savage and sad and brilliant is standing up, without the world even seeing it.

Maybe that's what these pages of words are about.

Bringing the world to the window.

"It's okay," Mum says one night. I hear her from my bed as she and Dad discuss paying the bills. I can picture them at the kitchen table, because many things are fought, won, and lost in the kitchen at our place.

Dad replies, "I don't understand it — I used to have three months' work ahead of me, but since . . ." His voice trails off. I imagine his feet, his jeaned legs, and the scar that angles down the side of his face and onto his throat. His fingers hold each other gently, entwining, making a single fist against the table.

He's wounded.

He's desperate — which makes his next move pretty understandable, even if it can't be condoned.

It's door to door.

Door to dead-set door.

"Well, I've tried advertising in the papers." He raises his voice in the kitchen again. It's the next Saturday. "I've tried everything, so I decided to knock on doors and work cheap. Fix what needs fixin'." While my mother places a chipped mug of coffee in front of him. All she does is stand there, and it's Rube, Sarah, and me that watch.

The next weekend it gets worse, because Rube and I actually see him. We see him as he returns from someone's front gate and we can tell he's copped another rejection. It's strange. Strange to look at him, when just a matter of months ago our father was tough and hard and wouldn't give us an inch. (Not that he does now. It's just a different feeling, that's all.) He was brutal in his fairness. Cruel in his judgments. Harder than necessary for our own good. He had dirty hands and cash in his pocket and sweat in his armpits.

Rube reminds me of something as we stand there by the street, making sure we don't let him see us.

He says, "Remember when we was kids?"

"*Were* kids."

"Shut up, will y'?"

"Okay."

We walk to a trashed, scabby shop on Elizabeth Street that closed down years ago. Rube continues to talk. It's gray sky again, with blue holes shot through the cloud-blankets. We sit, against a wall, under a bolted-up window.

Rube says, "I remember when we were younger and Dad built a new fence, because the old one was collapsing. I was about ten and you were nine, and the old man was out in the yard, from first light to sunset." Rube brings his knees up to his throat. His jeans cushion his chin, and the bullet holes in the sky widen. I look through them, at what Rube speaks of.

I remember that time quite clearly — how at the end of a day, when sun was melting back into horizon, Dad turned to us with some nails in his hand and said, "Fellas, these nails here are magic. They're magic nails." And the next day, we woke to the sound of a pounding hammer and we believed it. We *believed* those nails were magic, and maybe they still are now, because they take us back, to that sound. That pounding sound. They take us back to our father as he was: a vision of tall, bent-over strength, with a tough, hard smile and wire-curly hair. There was the slight stoop of his shoulders and his dirty shirt. Eyes of height . . . There was a contentment to him — an air of control, of all-rightness that sat down and hammered in the wake of a tangerine sky, or in that gradual twilight of slight rain, when water fell like tiny splinters from the clouds. He was our father then, not a human.

"Now he's," I answer Rube, "just too real, y' know?" Not much else to say when you've just seen the man knock on doors.

Real.

Reel from it.

Half a man, but.

Still human.

"The bastard," Rube laughs, and I laugh with him, as it seems like the only logical thing to do. "We're gonna cop a hidin' for this at school, ay."

"You're right."

You must understand that we know he's doing his door-knocking in our own district, which means people in school are getting closer and closer to whipping us with remarks. They'll find out all right, and Rube and I will go down heavily. It's just the way it is.

Dad, doors, shame, and in the meantime, Sarah has been out late again.

Three nights.

Three drunken hazes.

Two throw-ups.

Then it happens.

At school.

"Hey Wolfe. Wolfe!"

"What?"

"Your old man came knockin' at our door on the weekend, lookin' for work. Me mum told him he's too useless to even let him *near* our pipes."

Rube laughs.

"Hey Wolfe, I can get your dad a paper run if you want. He could use the pocket money, ay."

Rube smiles.

"Hey Wolfe, when's your old man gonna get the dole?"

Rube stares.

"Hey Wolfe, you might have to leave school and get a job, boy. Y' family could use the extra money."

Rube rubs his teeth together.

Then.

It happens.

The one comment that does it:

"Hey Wolfe, if your family needs the money so bad, your sister should take up whoring. She gets around a bit anyway, I hear. . . ."

Rube.

Rube.

"Rube!" I shout, running.

Too late.

Far too late, because Rube has the guy.

His fingers get bloody from the guy's teeth. His fist hacks through him. Left hand only at first, but it's over and the guy doesn't have a chance. Hardly anyone sees it. Hardly anyone knows, but Rube is standing there. Punches fall fast from his shoulder and land on the guy's face. When they hit him, they pull him apart. They spread out. His legs buckle. He falls. He hits the concrete.

Rube stands and his eyes tread all over the guy.

I stand next to him.

He speaks.

"I don't like this guy very much." A sigh. "He won't get back up. Not in a hurry." He's standing in the guy's eyes, and the last thing he says is, "No one calls my sister a prostitute, slut, whore, or anything else you please to call it." His hair is lifted by the wind, and sun reflects from his face. His tough, scrawny frame is growing good hard flesh by the second, and he smiles. A handful of people have seen what has happened now, and the word is beginning to travel.

More people show up.

"Who?" they ask. "Ruben Wolfe? But he's just a —"

A what? I wonder.

"I didn't mean to hit him so hard," Rube mentions, and he sucks on his knuckles. "Or that good." I don't know about him, but I get a flashback of the many fights Rube and I have had in our backyard, with just the one boxing glove each. (You do that when you have only one pair of gloves.)

This time it's different.

This time it's real.

"This time I used both hands," Rube smiles, and I know that we've been thinking about the same thing. I wonder how it feels to really hit someone, to make that final commitment of putting your bare fist in his face, for real. Not just some brotherly thing you do in the backyard, for fun, with boxing gloves.

At home that night, we ask Sarah what's been happening.

She says she's done a few stupid things lately.

We ask her to stop.

She says nothing, but gives us a silent nod.

I keep meaning to ask Rube what it was like to really beat the hell out of that guy, but I never do. I always pull out.

Also, in case you're interested, something has started to stink in our room, but we don't know what it is.

"What the hell *is* that?" Rube asks me. A threatening tone. "Is it y' feet?"

"No."

"Y' socks?"

"No way."

"Y' shoes? Undies?"

"It's this conversation," I suggest.

"Now don't get smart."

"All right!"

"Or I'll crush y'."

"All right."

"Y' little —"

"All *right!*"

"Somethin' always stinks in here," interrupts my dad, who has stuck his head into the room. He shakes his head in amazement, and I feel like everything's going to be okay. Or at least half okay anyway.

"Hey Rube."

"You just woke me, you bastard."

"Sorry."

"No, you're not."

"Yeah, you're right. I'm glad I did. You deserve it."

"What is it this time?"

"Can't y' hear 'em?"

"Who?"

"Mum and Dad. They're talkin' again in the kitchen. About the bills and all that."

"Yeah. They can't pay 'em too good."

"It's —"

"Bloody hell! What is that smell? It's a dis-grace, ay. Are you sure it's not y' socks?"

"Yes. I'm sure."

I stop and breathe.

I think a question and speak it. Finally.

"Did it feel good to smash that guy?"

Rube: "A little, but not really."

"Why not?"

"Because . . ." He thinks for a moment. "I knew I'd beat him and I didn't care about him one bit. I cared about Sarah." I sense him staring at the ceiling. "See, Cameron. The only things I care about in this life are me, you, Mum, Dad, Steve, and Sarah. And maybe Miffy. The rest of the world means nothing to me. The rest of the world can rot."

"Am I like that too?"

"You? No way." There's a slight gap in his words. "And that's your problem. You care about everything."

He's right.

I do.

CHAPTER 4

Mum's cooking pea soup now. It'll last us about a week, which is okay. I can think of worse meals.

"Top-notch soup," Rube tells her after it's swallowed on Wednesday night. Miffy night.

"Well, there's more where that came from," Mum answers.

"Yeah," Rube laughs, and everyone else is pretty quiet.

Steve and Dad have just argued about Dad going on the dole. The silence is slippery. It's dangerous, as I go over what was said:

"I won't do it."

"Why not?"

"Because it's below my dignity."

"Like hell it is. You're even knockin' on doors like a pathetic Boy Scout offering vacuuming and dusting for fifty cents apiece." Steve glares. "And it'd be nice to pay our bills on time," which is when Dad's fist comes down on the table.

"No," and that's pretty much it.

Know that my father will not be bent easily. He will die fighting if he has to.

Steve tries a different tactic. "Mum?"

"No," is her response, and now it's final for sure.

No dole.

No deal.

I feel like saying something about it when we walk Miffy later on, but Rube and I are concentrating too hard on not being noticed by anyone to say anything. Even later, there is no conversation in our room. We both sleep hard and wake up without knowing that this is Rube's day — the day that will change everything. Short and sweet.

It's after school.

It waits.

Outside our front gate.

"Can we talk inside?" a rough bloke asks us. He leans on the gate, not realizing it could fall apart any minute (although he doesn't seem like the type of guy who would care). He is unshaven and wears a jeans jacket. He has a tattoo on his hand. He puts the question to us again, with just a "Well?"

Rube and I stare.

At him.

At each other.

"Well, for starters," Rube says in the windy street, "who the hell are y'?"

"Oh, I'm sorry," says the guy in his thick city accent. "I'm a guy who can either change your life or smack it into the ground for bein' smart."

We decide to listen.

Needless to say it.

He continues with, "I've heard a rumor that you can

fight." He is motioning to Rube. "I have sources at my disposal that never lie, and they say that you gave someone a good caning."

"So?"

Straight to the point now. "So I want you to fight for me. Fifty dollars for a win. A decent tip for a loss."

"I think you'd better come inside."

Rube knows.

This could be interesting.

No one else is home so we sit at the kitchen table and I make the guy coffee even though he says he wants a beer. Even if we did have beer, I wouldn't give it to this guy. He's arrogant. He's abrasive, and worst of all, he's likable, which always makes a guy difficult to deal with. See, when someone's strictly an awful person, they're easy to get rid of. It's when they make you like them as well that they're hard to contain. Throw likable in and anything can happen. It's a lethal combination.

"Perry Cole."

That's his name. It sounds familiar, but I shrug it off.

"Ruben Wolfe," says Rube. He points at me. "Cameron Wolfe." Both Rube and I shake hands with Perry Cole. The tatt is of a hawk. Real original.

One thing about the guy is that he doesn't muck around. He talks to you and he isn't afraid to lean close, even if his coffee breath reeks like hell. He explains everything straight out. He talks of steady violence, organized fights, raids from police, and everything else that his business involves.

"See," he explains with that succinct, violent voice of his, "I'm part of an organized boxing racket. All through winter, we have fights every Sunday afternoon at four different places in the city. One's a warehouse out the back of Glebe, which is my home arena. One's a meat factory over at Maroubra. One's a warehouse in Ashfield, and there's a pretty decent ring way down south on some guy's farm at Helensburgh." When he speaks, spit fires from his tongue and sticks to the corner of his mouth. "Like I said — you get fifty dollars if you win a fight. You might get a tip if y' lose. People pay in like you wouldn't believe. I mean, you'd think they'd have better things to do on a Sunday afternoon and evening, but they don't. They're sick of football and all that other garbage. They pay five bucks to get in and see up to six fights into the night. Five rounds each and we've had some good fights. We're a few weeks into this season, but I reckon I've got room for you. . . . If you feel like going to one of the other guys who run a team, you'll get the same deal. If you fight well, we'll give you enough money to scrape by, and I myself get rich off the way you fight. That's how it is. You wanna do it?"

Rube hasn't shaved today so he rubs his spiky beard, in thought. "Well, how the hell do I get to all the fights? How'm I gonna get back from Helensburgh on a Sunday night?"

"I've got a van." Easy. "I got a van and I cram all my fighters in. If you get hurt, I don't take you to a doctor. That's not in the service. If you get killed, your family buries you, not me."

"Ah, stop bein' a tosser," Rube tells him, and all laugh, especially Perry. He likes Rube. I can tell. People like someone who says what they think. "If you die . . ." My brother imitates him.

"One guy came close once," Perry assures him, "but it was a warmer than usual night. It was heat exhaustion and it was only a mild stroke. A heavyweight."

"Oh."

"So," Perry smiles. "You want in?"

"I d'know. I've gotta discuss it with my management."

"Who's your management?" Perry smiles and motions to me with a nod. "It's not this little pansy here, is it?"

"He ain't no pansy." Rube points a finger at him. "He's a cream puff." Then he gets serious. "Actually, he might be a bit skinny, but he can stand up all right, I tell you," which shocks me. Ruben L. Wolfe, my brother, is sticking up for me.

"Is that right?"

"It is. . . . You can check us out if you want. We'll just have us a game of One Punch in the backyard." He looks to me. "We'll just climb over and get Miffy so he doesn't start barking. He likes watching when he's in our yard, doesn't he?"

"He loves it." I can only agree. It's being on the other side of the fence that offends old Miffy. He's gotta be closer to the action, where he can see what's going on. That's when everything's apples. He either watches contentedly or gets bored and goes to sleep.

"Who the hell's Miffy?" Perry asks, confused.

"You'll see."

Rube, Perry, and I stand up and proceed to the backyard. We put the gloves on, Rube climbs the fence and hands Miffy to me over the top, and One Punch is about to happen. By the look on Perry's face, I can tell he'll appreciate it.

We each wear our solitary boxing glove, but Miffy the Pomeranian is demanding attention and pats. We both crouch down and pat the midget dog. Perry watches. He looks like the kind of guy who would drop-kick a dog like this from here to eternity. As it turns out, he isn't.

"The dog's an embarrassment," Rube explains to him, "but we have to look out for 'im."

"Come 'ere, fella." Perry holds out his fingers for the dog to sniff and Miffy likes him immediately. He sits next to him as Rube and I start our game of One Punch.

Perry loves it.

He laughs.

He smiles.

He watches with curiosity when I hit the ground the first time.

He pats Miffy happily when I hit it the second time.

He claps when I get Rube a good one on the jaw. Just a good, solid clip.

After fifteen minutes we stop.

Rube says, "I told you, didn't I?" and Perry nods.

"Show us a bit more," he states calmly, "but swap gloves." He looks like he's thinking hard. Then he watches as Rube and I go at it again.

It's tougher with the other glove. We both miss more, but slowly, we get into a rhythm. We circle the yard. Rube throws out his hand. I duck it. Swerve. Make my way in. I jab. Hit his chin. Shoot one at his ribs. He counterpunches. His breath is stern as he stabs his fist through my cheekbone, then gets me in the throat.

"Sorry."

"Okay."

We resume.

He gets one under my ribs and I can't breathe. A yelp escapes from under my breath.

Rube stands.

So do I, but crooked.

"Finish him off," Perry tells him.

Rube does it.

When I wake up, the first thing I see is Miffy's dog-ugly face pressed into mine. Then I see Perry, smiling. Then I see Rube, worried.

"I'm okay," I tell him.

"Good."

When they get me back up, we all walk back into the kitchen and Rube and Perry sit down. I slump down. I feel like death warmed up. A strip of green flanks my vision. Static reaches through my ears.

Perry motions to the fridge. "Y' sure you don't have a beer?"

"Are you an alcoholic or somethin'?"

"I just like a beer now and then."

"Well." Rube is forthright. "We don't have one." He's a bit upset about knocking me unconscious, I can tell. I remember him saying, *The only things I care about in this life* . . .

Perry decides to get back down to business.

What he says is a shock.

It's this:

"I want both of y's."

Rube sniffs, with surprise, and rubs his nose.

Perry looks now at Rube and says, "You . . ." He smiles. "You can fight, all right. That's a fact." Then he looks at me. "And you've got heart. . . . See, one thing I didn't go into detail about before was the tips. People throw money into the ring corners if they think you've got heart, and . . . it's Cameron, isn't it?"

"Yeah."

"Well, you've got it in spades."

Trying not to, I smile. Damn guys like Perry. You hate them, but they still make you smile.

"So what will happen is this." He looks at Rube. "You're gonna win fights and you'll be popular because

you're fast and young and you've got a rough but somehow attractive head."

I look at my brother now as well. I examine him,
and it's true. He *is* good-looking, but in a strange way.
It's sudden, rough, rugged. A wayward kind of handsome that's more around him than on him. It's more of
a feeling, or an aura.

Perry looks now at me. "And you? You'll most likely
get hammered, but if you keep clean enough and stay
off the ropes, you'll get close to twenty bucks in tips,
'cause people will see your heart."

"Thanks."

"No need for thanking. These are facts." No more
time-wasting. "So do you want in or not?"

"I don't know about my brother," Rube admits to
him, with caution. "He can take a beating in the backyard, but that's different to taking it week in week out
by some guy who wants to kill him."

"He'll fight someone new each week."

"So what?"

"Most of 'em are good fighters but some are dead
average. They're just desperate for the money." He
shrugs. "Y' never know. The kid might win a few."

"What are the other dangers?"

"In general?"

"Yes."

"They're these." He makes the list. "Rough guys watch
the fights and if you back out of a bout they might kill y'.
Some nice girls come along with these guys and if you

touch 'em those guys might kill y'. Last year, some cops were getting close to raiding an old factory we were using in Petersham. If they catch y', they'll kill y'. So if that happens, run." He's pretty happy with himself, especially for the last one: "The biggest danger, though, is leaving *me* in the lurch. If you do it, *I'll* kill y', and that's worse than all the others put together."

"Fair enough."

"You wanna think about it?"

"Yeah."

To me: "How 'bout you?"

"Me too."

"Right," and he stands up, handing us his phone number. It's written on a piece of torn cardboard. "You've got four days. Ring me on Monday night at seven sharp. I'll be home."

Rube has two more questions.

The first: "What if we join and then wanna quit?"

"Up until August, you have to give me two weeks' notice or find someone to take your place. That's all. People quit all the time because it's a rough game. I understand. Just two weeks' notice or three legitimate names of blokes that can fight well. They're everywhere. No one's irreplaceable. If you make it to August, you've gotta finish the season, into September, when the semifinals are on. See, we do a draw, a competition ladder, the lot. We have finals and everything, with more money in 'em."

The second question: "What weight divisions will we fight in?"

"You'll both be in lightweight."

This triggers a question in me.

"Will we ever fight each other?"

"Maybe, but the chance is pretty slight. Once in a while, fighters from the same team have to fight each other. It does happen. You got a problem with that?"

"Not really." It's Rube who says it.

"Me neither."

"Well why'd y' ask?"

"Just curious."

"Any more questions?"

We think.

"No."

"Good," and we see Perry Cole out of our house. On the front porch, he reminds us. "Remember, you've got four days. Ring me Monday night at seven with yes or no. I'll be unhappy if you don't ring — and I'm not someone you want unhappy with you."

"All right."

He leaves.

We watch him get into his car. It's an old Holden, done up well, and it must be worth a bit. He must be rolling in money to have both his van *and* this car. It's money earned off desperates like us.

Once back inside, we hang around with Miffy, feeding him some bacon fat. Nothing. Not yet. Miffy just rolls around and we pat his stomach. I go to our room to try and find out once and for all what stinks in there. It's not going to be pretty.

"Yes, I'm awake."

"How'd y' know I was gonna ask?"

"You always do."

"I found out what the smell was."

"And?"

"Remember when we got that job lot of onions from the fruit shop?"

"What? The ones my mates stole? Last Christmas?"

"Yeah."

"That was six bloody months ago!"

"A few strays must have got out of the bag. They were under my bed, in the corner, all disgusting and rotten."

"Oh, man."

"Damn right. I chucked 'em in the compost, up near the back fence."

"Good idea."

"I was gonna show 'em to y', but they stank so bad, I fully ran out there with 'em."

"Even better idea . . . Where was I?"

"Next door, returnin' Miffy."

"Oh yeah."

Change of topic.

"Are y' thinkin' about it?" I ask. "About that Perry character?"

"Yep."

"You reckon we can do it?"

"Hard to say."

"It sounds . . ."

"What?"

"I d'know — scary."

"It's a chance."

. . . Yes, but a chance at what, I wonder. Our bedroom seems extra dark tonight. Heavy dark.

I think it again. A chance at what?

CHAPTER 5

It's Friday evening and we're watching *Wheel of Fortune*. It's rare for us to watch a lot of TV because we're usually fighting, doing something stupid in the backyard, or hanging around out front. Besides, we hate most of the crap on the telly anyway. The only good thing about it is that sometimes when you watch it, you can get a bright idea. Previous bright ideas we've had in the midst of TV are:

Attempting to rob a dentist.

Moving the small lounge table up onto the couch so we could play football against each other with a rolled-up pair of socks.

Going to the dog track for the first time.

Selling Sarah's busted old hair-dryer to one of our neighbors for fifteen dollars.

Selling Rube's broken tape player to a guy down the street.

Selling the telly.

Obviously, we could never carry out *all* of the good ideas.

The dentist was a disaster (we pulled out, of course). Playing football with the socks resulted in giving Sarah a fat lip when she walked through the lounge room. (I swear it was Rube's elbow and not mine that hit her.)

The dog track was fun (even though we came back twelve bucks poorer than when we left). The hair-dryer was thrown back over the fence with a note attached that said, *Give us back our fifteen bucks or we'll bloody kill you, you cheating bastards.* (We gave the money back the next day.) We couldn't end up finding the tape player (and the guy down the street was pretty tight anyway so I doubt we'd have got much for it). Then, last of all, there was just no way we could ever sell the TV, even though I came up with eleven good reasons why we should give the telly the chop. (They go like this:

One. In ninety-nine percent of shows, the good guys win in the end, which just isn't the truth. I mean, let's face it. In real life, the bastards win. They get all the girls, all the cash, all the everything. Two. Whenever there's a sex scene, everything goes perfectly, when really, the people in the shows should be as scared of it as me. Three. There are a thousand ads. Four. The ads are always much louder than the actual shows. Five. The news is always kind of depressing. Six. The people are all beautiful. Seven. All the best shows get the ax. For example, *Northern Exposure.* Have you heard of it? No? Exactly — it got the ax years ago. Eight. Rich blokes own all the stations. Nine. The rich blokes own beautiful women as well. Ten. The reception can be a bit of a shocker at our place anyway because our aerial's shot. Eleven. They keep showing repeats of a show called *Gladiators.*)

The only question now is, *What's today's idea?* The truth is, it's more of a decision to conclude on last night, as Rube speaks over at me. He starts with an "Oi."

"Oi," he says.

"Yeah?"

"What are your thoughts?"

"On what?"

"You know what. Perry."

"We need the money."

"I know, but Mum and Dad won't let us help pay the bills."

"Yeah, but we can hold our own end up — pay our own food and stuff so everything lasts longer."

"Yeah, I s'pose."

Then Rube says it.

It's decided.

Concluded.

Ended.

He speaks the words, "We're gonna do it."

"Okay."

Only, we know we won't pay our own food. No. We have no intention. We're doing this for some other reason. Some other reason that wants inside us.

Now we have to wait till Monday so we can ring Perry Cole, but already, we have to think — about everything. About other guys' fists. About the danger. About Mum and Dad finding out. About survival. A new world has arrived in our minds and we have to handle it. We have decided and there is no time to stick our tail between our legs and run. We've decided in front of the telly and that means we have to give it a shot. If we succeed, good. If we fail, it's nothing new.

Rube's thinking about it, I can tell.

Personally, I try not to.

I try to focus on the woman's brilliant legs on *Wheel of Fortune*. When she swivels the letters, I can see more of them, just before she turns around and smiles at me. She smiles pretty, and in that split second, I forget. I forget about Perry Cole and all those future punches. It makes me wonder, *Do we spend most of our days trying to remember or forget things?* Do we spend most of our time running toward or away from our lives? I don't know.

"Who y' goin' for?" Rube interrupts my thoughts, looking at the TV.

"I d'know."

"Well?"

"Okay then." I point. "I'll take the dopey one in the middle."

"That's the host, y' idiot."

"Is it? Well, I'll take the blonde one there on the end. She looks the goods."

"I'll take the guy on the other end. The one who looks like he just escaped from Long Bay Jail. His suit's a dead-set outrage. It's a dis-grace."

In the end it's the guy from Long Bay that wins. He gets a vacuum cleaner and has already won a trip to the Great Wall of China, from yesterday apparently.

Not bad. The trip, that is. In the champion round, he misses out on a ridiculous remote control bed. In all honesty, the only thing keeping us watching is to see the woman turning the letters. I like her legs and so does Rube.

We watch.

We forget.

We know.

We know that on Monday we'll be ringing Perry Cole to tell him we're in.

"We better start training then," I tell Rube.

"I know."

Mum comes home. We don't know where Dad is.

Mum takes the compost out to the heap in the backyard.

Upon returning she says, "Something really stinks out there near the back fence. Do either of you know anything about it?"

We look at each other. "No."

"Are you sure?"

"Well," I crack under the pressure. "It was a few onions that were in our room that we forgot about. That's all."

Mum isn't surprised. She never is anymore. I think she actually accepts our stupidity as something she just can't change. Yet she still asks the question. "What were they doing in your room?" However, she walks away. I don't think she really wants to hear the answer.

When Dad arrives, we don't ask where he's been.

Steve comes in and gives us a shock by saying, "How y' goin', lads?"

"All right. You?"

"Good." Even though he still watches Dad with contempt, wishing he'd get the dole or Job Search payments or whatever you please to call it. He soon changes clothes and goes out.

Sarah comes in eating a banana Paddlepop. She smiles and gives us both a bite. We don't ask for one, but she knows. She can see our snouts itching for the gorgeous sickly cold of an iceblock in winter.

Next day, Rube and I begin training.

We get up early and run. It's dark when the alarm goes off and we take a minute or two to get out of bed, but once out, we're okay. We run together in track pants and old football jerseys and the city is awake and smoky-cold and our heartbeats jangle through the streets. We're alive. Our footsteps are folded neatly, one after the other. Rube's curly hair collides with sunlight. The light steps at us between the buildings. The train line is fresh and sweet and the grass in Belmore Park has the echoes of dew still on it. Our hands are cold. Our veins are warm. Our throats suck in the winter breath of the city, and I imagine people still in bed, dreaming. To me, it feels good. Good city. Good world, with two wolves running through it, looking for the fresh meat of their lives. Chasing it. Chasing hard, even though they fear it. They run anyway.

"Y' awake, Rube?"

"Yeah."

"Jeez, I'm a bit sore, ay. This runnin' in the mornings isn't much chop for the ol' legs."

"I know — mine are sore too."

"It felt good but."

"Yeah. It felt great."

"It felt like I'm not sure what. Like we've finally got something. Something to give us — I d'know. I just don't know."

"Purpose."

"What?"

"Purpose," Rube continues. "We've finally got a reason to be here. We've got reason to be out on that street. We're not just out there doin' nothin'."

"That's it. That's exactly how it felt."

"I know."

"But I'm still sore as hell."

"Me too."

"So are we still runnin' again tomorrow?"

"Absolutely."

"Good." And in the darkness of our room, a smile reaches across my lips. I feel it.

CHAPTER 6

"Bloody hell."

The phone's been cut off because we don't have the money to pay the bill. Or really, Mum and Dad don't have the money to pay it. Steve or Sarah could pay, but there's no way. It's not allowed. It isn't even considered.

"Well, up this, then," Steve rips through the kitchen air. "I'm movin' out. Soon as possible."

"Then they miss y' board money," Sarah tells him.

"So what? If they wanna suffer they can do it without me watchin'." It's fair enough.

As well as being fair enough, it's Monday night, and it's close to seven. This is not good. This is *very* not good. Very not good at all.

"Oh no," I say across to Rube. He's warming his hands above the toaster. This means we can't use the phone in Sarah's room to ring Perry. "Hey Rube."

"What?" His toast pops up.

"The phone."

He realizes.

He says, "Bloody typical. Is this house useless or what?" and the toast is forgotten.

We go next door with Perry's number in Rube's pocket. No one home.

We go the other side. The same.

So Rube runs into our house, flogs forty cents out of Steve's wallet, and we take off. It's ten to seven. "You know where there's a public phone?" Rube talks between strides. We pant. This is close to a sprint.

"Trust me," I assure him. I know about phone boxes in this district.

I sniff one out and we find it hunched in the darkness of a side street.

It's bang on seven when we ring.

"You're late," are Perry's first words. "I don't like being kept waiting."

"Calm down," Rube tells him. "Our phone got cut and we just ran close to three Ks to get here. Besides, my watch says seven sharp."

"Okay, okay. Is that y' breathing I can hear?"

"I told you, we just ran nearly."

"All right." Business. "Are you in or out?"

Rube.

Me.

Heartbeat.

Breath.

Heartbeat.

Voice.

"In."

"Both of y's?"

A nod.

"Yeah," Rube states, and we can feel Perry smiling through the phone line.

"Good," he says. "Now listen. Y' first fights won't be this week. They'll be the week after, out at Maroubra. First though, we gotta get some things organized. I'll tell y's what y' need and we've gotta give you some hype. Y' need names. Y' need gloves. We'll talk about it. Can I come over again or do y's wanna meet somewhere else?"

"Central," is Rube's suggestion. "Our old man might be home and that won't be apples."

"Okay. Central it is. Tomorrow, four o'clock. Down at Eddy Avenue, where it leads into Belmore Park."

"Sounds good."

"Good."

It's settled.

"Welcome," is Perry's final word, and the phone runs dead. We're in.

We're in and it's final.

We're in and it's final, because if we back out now, we'll probably end up at the bottom of the harbor. Down near the oil spill, in garbage bags. Well, that's exaggerating, of course, but who knows? Who knows what kind of seedy world we've just entered? Our only knowledge is that we can make money, and maybe some self-respect.

As we walk back, it feels like the city is engulfing us. Adrenaline still pours through our veins. Sparks flow through to our fingers. We've still been running in the mornings, but the city's different then. It's filled with hope and with bristles of winter sunshine. In the evening, it's like it dies, waiting to be born again the next morning. I see a dead starling as we walk. It's next to a beer bottle in the gutter. Both are empty of soul, and we can only walk by in silence, watching people who watch us, ignoring people who ignore us, and Rube growling at people who attempt to force us from the footpath. Our eyes are large and rimmed with awakeness. Our ears detect every opened-up sound. We smell the impact of traffic and humans. Humans and traffic. Back and forth. We taste our moment, swallowing it, knowing it. We feel our nerves twitching inside our stomachs, lunging at our skin from beneath.

When morning slits across the horizon the following day, we have already been running for a while. As we do so, Rube discusses a few things with me. He wants a punching bag. He wants a skipping rope. He wants more speed and another pair of gloves so we can fight properly for practice. He wants headgear so we don't kill each other doing it. He wants.

He wants hard.

He runs and there is purpose in his feet, and there's hunger in his eyes and desire in his voice. I've never seen him like this. Like he wants so savagely to be somebody and to fight for it.

When we get home, sunshine splashes across his face. Again. A collision.

He says, "We're gonna do it, Cam." He is serious and solemn. "We're gonna get there, and for once, we're gonna win. We're not leavin' without winning." He's leaning on the gate. He crouches. He buries his face into the horizontal paling. Fingers in the wire. Then, a shock, because when he turns his head back up to look at me, there's a tear dangling from his eye. It edges down his face and his voice is smothered with his hunger. He says, "We can't accept bein' just us anymore. We've gotta lift. Gotta be more . . . I mean, check Mum out. Killin' herself. Dad down and out. Steve just about moved and gone. Sarah gettin' called a slut." He tightens his fist in the wire and explains it through half-clenched teeth. "So now it's us. It's simple. We've gotta lift. Gotta get our self-bloody-respect back."

"Can we?" I ask.

"We've gotta. We will." He stands and grabs me by the front of my jersey, right at my heart. He says, "I'm Ruben Wolfe," and he says it hard. He throws the words into my face. "And you're Cameron Wolfe. That's gotta start meaning somethin', boy. That's gotta start churnin' inside us, making us wanna be someone for those names, and not be just another couple of guys who amounted to nothin' but what people said we would. No way. We're gettin' out of that. We have to. We're gonna crawl and moan and fight and bite and bark at anything that gets in our way or tries to hunt us down and shoot us. All right?"

"Okay." I nod.

"Good," and to my dismay, Rube leans on my shoulder with his forearm and we stare onto the morning street of black light and glinting cars. I feel that we're together to face whatever falls down around us, and it staggers me for a moment that Rube has grown up (even though he's a year older than me). It staggers me that he wants and aches so hard. His final words are, "If we fail, we're gonna blame *us*."

We walk inside soon after, knowing he's right. The only people we want to blame are ourselves, because it will be ourselves that we rely upon. We're aware of it, and the knowing will always walk beside us, at the edge of each day, on the outskirts of each pulse in each heart-beat. We eat breakfast, but our hunger is not fed. It's growing.

It grows even more when we meet Perry at Eddy Avenue, just like he told us. Four o'clock.

"Lads," he greets us. He carries a small suitcase.

"Perry."

"Hi Perry."

We all walk together to a bench near the middle of the park. The bench has been slapped hard by the pigeons from above, so it's a pretty *dodgy* place to be sitting. Not something you'd eat off. Still, it's safer than some of the others, which the birds seem to recognize as their own public toilets.

"Check the state of this place," Perry smirks. He's the kind of guy who likes to sit in a scummy park and talk business. "It's disgraceful," though his smirk is now a full-blown smile. It's a smile of diseased malice, friendliness, and happiness all rolled into one devastating concoction. He wears a flanno, rough jeans, old boots, and of course, that vicious smile of his. He looks for a place on the table to put the suitcase but settles for the ground.

A pause of silence arrives.

An old man comes to us asking for change.

Perry gives him some, but first he asks the poor old bloke a question.

He says, "Mate, what's the capital of Switzerland, do y' know?"

"Bern," the old man replies, after some thought.

"Very good. However, my point is this." He smiles again. Damn that smile. "In that country, once, they gathered up all the gypsies, whores, and drunken bums such as yourself, and they threw 'em over the border. They got rid of every dirty swine that graced their precious land."

"So?"

"So you're an incredibly lucky drunken bum now, aren't you? You not only get to stay in our fine land, but you also earn a living out of kindhearted people such as myself, and my colleagues here."

"They didn't give me anything."

(We blew our last cash at the dog track the other day.)

"Certainly, but they didn't throw you in the Pacific either now, did they?" He grins, evil. "They didn't chuck you out there and tell you to start swimming." He adds for good measure, "Like they should have."

"You're crazy." The drunk begins to leave.

"Of course I am," Perry calls after him. "I just gave you a dollar of my hard-earned wages."

Yeah, right, I think. *It's money he earns from fighters.*

The old man is already on to the next people — a grungy black-dressed couple with purple hair. They've got earrings stapled across their faces, and Docs on their feet.

"He oughta give *them* the buck now," Rube observes, and I laugh. He's about right, and as the old man lingers around the couple, I watch him. He has turned his life into the pocket scraps of other people. It's sad.

It's sad, but Perry has forgotten all about the man. He's had his pleasure and is now strictly onto business.

"Right." He points at me. "We'll get you out of the way first. Here are your gloves and shorts. I thought about shoes but you're not getting any. Neither of you are worth it, because I don't know how long you'll last. I might get you some later, so wear your gymmies for now."

"Fair enough."

I take my gloves and shorts and like them.

They're cheap, but I like them a lot. Blood-colored gloves and navy-blue shorts.

"Now." Perry lights a cigarette and pulls a warm beer from the suitcase. Smokes and beer cans. He annoys me with that garbage, but I listen on. "We need to get you a name, for when you get introduced to the crowd before your fights. Any ideas?"

"The Wolf Man?" Rube suggests.

I shake my head.

Thinking.

It hits me.

Smiling.

I know. I nod. I say it.

"The Underdog."

I continue to smile as Perry's face lights up and I watch old beggars and weirdos and city pigeons scouring the city floor for the sake of their lives.

Yes, Perry lights up, behind his smoke, and says, "Nice. I like it. Everyone loves an underdog. It appeals to them and even if y' lose they'll send some tips your way." A laugh. "It's better than nice. It's flat-out perfect."

No time-wasting though.

"Now," he moves on. There's a finger pointed at Rube. "You're all sorted out. Here are y' gloves an' shorts." Gray-blue gloves. Cheap. No laces. Just like mine. His shorts are black with gold rims. Nicer than mine. "You wanna know what name you've got?"

"Don't I get a choice?"

"No."

"Why not?"

"Y' sorted out, that's why. Tell y' what, you'll find out when you fight, okay?"

"I s'pose."

"Say yes." Forceful.

"Yes."

"And say thank you, because when I'm done with you, the women'll fall over you like dominoes."

Dominoes.

What a tosser.

Rube obeys him. "Thank you."

"Right."

Perry stands and leaves, suitcase by his side.

He turns.

He says, "Let me remind you fellas that your first fight is next Sunday at Maroubra. I'll take you there in my van. Be here at Eddy Avenue again at three o'clock sharp. Don't make me wait or a bus'll clean me up and I'll clean the pair of *you* up. Okay?"

We nod.

He's gone.

"Thanks for the gear," I call, but Perry Cole is gone.

We sit there.

Gloves.

Shorts.

Park.

City.

Hunger.

Us.

"Damn it."

"What, Rube?"

"It's been annoyin' me all day and night."

"What?"

"I wanted to ask Perry if he could get his hands on a punching bag for us, and some of that other practice gear."

"You don't need a punching bag."

"Why not?"

"You've got me."

"Yeah."

"Y' didn't have to agree."

"I wanted to."

A long pause . . .

"Are y' scared, Rube?"

"No. I was before, but not anymore. Are you?"

"Yeah."

There's no point lying. I'm scared as hell. Scared crazy. I'm asylum scared. Straitjacket scared. Yes, I think it's pretty much decided.

I'm scared.

CHAPTER 7

Time has elapsed and it's the Sunday morning. Fight day, and I'm dying to get into the bathroom. I have to do a nervous one. We've trained hard. Running, push-ups, sit-ups, the lot. Even skipping, with Miffy's leash. We've done One Punch and also fought two-handed with our new gloves, every afternoon. Rube keeps telling me we're ready, but still, I have to go. Desperately.

"Who's *in* there?" I cry through the door. "I'm in agony out here, ay."

A voice booms back. "It's me." Me as in Dad. Me as in the old man. Me as in the guy who may be unemployed but can still give us a good kick in the pants for being smart. "Give me two minutes."

Two minutes!

How am I going to survive two minutes?

When he finally comes out, I feel like I'm going to collapse onto the seat, but the doorway's as far as I get. *Why's that?* you may well ask, but I tell you, if you're anywhere near our bathroom this morning, you'll be tasting the worst smell you've ever swallowed in your whole life. The smell is twisted. It's angry. No, it's downright ropeable.

I breathe and choke and breathe again, turning around, almost running. Now, though, I'm almost howling with laughter as well.

"What?" Rube asks when I make it back to our room.

"Oh, mate."

"What is it?"

"Come 'ere." I tell him, and we walk back toward the bathroom.

The smell hits me again.

It smacks into Rube.

"Whoa." That's all he says, at first.

"Shockin', ay?" I ask.

"Well, it isn't too cheerful, is it, that smell," Rube admits. "What's the old man been eating lately?"

"I've got no idea," I go on, "but I'm tellin' y' right now — that smell's physical."

"Damn right." Rube backs away from it. "It's bloody relentless is what it is. Like a gremlin, a monster, a —" He's lost for words.

I muster up some courage and say, "I'm goin' in."

"Why?"

"I'm dyin' here!"

"Okay, good luck."

"I'll need it."

I'll need more later though, and I feel the nerves, waiting at Eddy Avenue. Fingers of fear and doubt scratch the lining of my stomach. I feel like I'm bleeding

inside, but it's only nerves. I'm sure. Rube, on the other
hand, sits with his legs stretched out. His hands rest
firmly on his hips. His face is awash with his hair, blown
in from the wind. A small smile is forming on his lips.
His mouth opens.

"He's here," my brother says. "Let's go."

The van pulls in — a real heap of a thing. A Kombi.
Four other guys are already in it. We enter it, through
the sliding door.

"Glad y's could make it." Perry grins at us through
the rear vision mirror. He's wearing a suit today.
Bloodred and tough to look at. It's nice.

"I had to cancel my violin recital," Rube tells
him, "but we made it." He sits down and some guy the
size of an outhouse slides the door shut. His name is
Bumper. The lean guy next to him is Leaf. The fatty sort
of bloke is Erroll and the normal-looking one is Ben.
They're all older than us. Daunting. Scarred. Fist-
weathered.

"Rube 'n' Cameron." Perry introduces us, via the
mirror again.

"Hey."

Silence.

Violent eyes.

Broken noses.

Missing teeth.

In my uneasiness, I look to Rube. He doesn't ignore
me, but rather, he closes a fist as if to say, "Stay awake."

Minutes follow.

They're silent minutes. Awake. Moving. On edge, as I concentrate on survival, and hope for this trip to never end. Hope to never get there. . . .

We pull into the meat factory out the back of Maroubra and it's cold and windy and salty.

People hang.

Around us, I can sniff out a savagery in the noisy southern air. It knifes its way into my nose, but I do not bleed blood. It's fear I bleed, and it gushes out over my lip. I wipe it away, in a hurry.

"C'mon." Rube drags me with him. "This way boy, or do y' wanna play with the locals?"

"No way."

Inside, Perry takes us through a small room and into a freezing compartment, where some dead frozen pigs hang like martyrs from the ceiling. It's terrible. I stare at them a moment, with the tightened air and the frightening sight of dead cut meat gouging at my throat.

"It's just like Joe Frazier," I whisper to Rube. "The hangin' meat."

"Yeah," he replies. He knows what I mean.

It makes me wonder what we're doing here. All the other fellas just wait around, even sit, and they smoke, or they drink alcoholic beverages to eat the nerves. To calm the fear. To slow the fists but quicken the courage. That huge bloke, Bumper, he winks at me, enjoying my fear.

He's just sitting there and his quiet voice comes to me, casually.

"The first fight's the toughest." A smile. "Don't worry about winning it. Survive first, then consider it. Okay?"

I nod, but it's Rube who speaks.

He speaks, "Don't worry, mate. My brother knows how to get up."

"Good." He means it. Then, "How 'bout you?"

"Me?" Rube smiles. He's tough and sure and doesn't seem to have any fear. Or at least he won't show it. He only says, "I won't need to get up," and the thing is, he knows he won't. Bumper knows he won't. *I* know he won't. You can smell it on him, like that guy in *Apocalypse Now* that everyone knows won't die. He loves the war too much, and the power. He doesn't even consider death, let alone fear it. And that's exactly how Rube is. He's walking out of here with fifty dollars and a grin. That's it. Nothing more to say about it.

We meet some people.

"So you've got some new blokes, ay?" an ugly old guy smiles at Perry — a smile like a stain. He sums us up and points. "The little one's got no hope, but the older fella looks all right. A bit pretty maybe, but not too bad at all. Can he fight?"

"Yeah," Perry assures him, "and the little one's got heart."

"Good." A scar crawls up and down the old guy's chin. "If he keeps gettin' up, we might just have us a slaughter. We haven't had a slaughter here for weeks." He gets right in my eyes, for power. "We might just hang him up here with the pigs."

"How about you leave, old man?" Rube steps closer. "Or maybe we'll hang you up instead."

The old man.

Rube.

Their eyes are fixed on each other, and the man is dying to have Rube against the wall, I swear it, but something stops him. He only makes a brief statement.

He states, "You all know the rules, lads. Five rounds or until one of y's can't get up. The crowd's restless tonight. They want some blood, so be careful. I've got me some hard fellas myself, and they're keen, just like you. See you out there."

When he leaves, it's Perry who has Rube up against the wall. He warns him. "If you ever do that again, that guy'll kill you. Understand?"

"Okay."

"Say yes."

Rube smiles. "Okay." A shrug. "Yes."

He releases him and straightens his suit. "Good."

Perry then takes us through another hall and into a new room. Through a crack in the door, we see the crowd. There are at least three hundred of them. Probably more, all crammed into the cleared factory floor.

They drink beer.

They smoke.

They talk.

Smile.

Laugh.

Cough.

It's a crowd of stupid men, old and young. Surfers, footballers, rednecks, the lot.

They wear jackets and black jeans and rough coats and some of them have women or girls clinging to them. They're brainless girls, otherwise they wouldn't be seen dead here. They're pretty, with ugly, appealing smiles and conversations we can't hear. They breathe smoke and blow it out, and words drop from their mouths and get crushed to the floor. Or they get discarded, just to glow with warmth for a moment, for someone else to tread on later.

Words.

Just words.

Just sticky-blond words, and when I see the ring all lit up and silent, I can imagine those women cheering later on when I hit the canvas floor, my face all bruised up and bloody.

Yes.

They'll cheer, I reckon.

Cigarette in one hand.

Warm, sweaty hand of a thug in the other.

Screaming, blond, beer-filled mouth.

All of that, and a spinning room.

That's what scares me most.

"Hey Rube, what're we doin' here?"

"Shut up."

"I can't believe we got ourselves into this!"

"Stop whisperin'."

"Why?"

"If y' don't, I'll be forced to trounce you myself."

"Really?"

"You're startin' to aggravate me, y' know that?"

"I'm sorry."

"We're ready."

"Are we?"

"Yes. Don't you feel it?"

I ask myself.

Are y' ready Cameron?

Again.

Are y' ready Cameron?

Time will tell.

It's funny, don't you think, how time seems to do a lot of things? It flies, it tells, and worst of all, it runs out.

CHAPTER 8

It's the sound of my breathing that gets me, pouring down into my lungs and then tripping back up my throat. Perry's just come in and told me. It's time.

"You're up first," he says.

It's time and I'm still sitting there, in my old, too-big-for-me spray jacket. (Rube's got an old hooded jacket of Steve's.) All is numb. My hands, fingers, feet. It's time.

I stand up.

I wait.

Perry's gone back out to the ring, and the next time the door opens, I'll be heading there myself. With no more time to think, it happens. The door is opened and I start walking out. Out into.

The arena.

Aggression quivers inside me. Fear shrouds me. Footsteps take me forward.

Then the crowd.

They lift my spirit, as I'm the first fighter to come out.

They turn and look at me in my spray jacket, and I walk through them. The hood is out and over my head. They cheer. They clap and whistle, and this is just the beginning. They howl and chant, and for a moment, they forget the beer. They don't even feel it pouring down their throats. It's just me, and the fact that violence is near. I'm the messenger. I'm the hands and feet. I bring it to them. I deliver it.

"THE UNDERDOG!"

It's Perry, standing in the ring, holding a microphone.

"Yes, it's Cameron Wolfe, the Underdog!" he shouts through the mike. "Give the boy a hand — our youngest fighter! Our youngest battler! Our youngest brawler! He'll fight to the end, people, and he'll keep getting up!"

The hood of the jacket is still over my head, even though it has no string, no anything to hold it in place. My boxing shorts are comfortable on my legs. My gym boots walk on, through the sharp, thick crowd.

They're alert now.

Awake.

Eager.

They watch me and size me up and they're tough and hard and suddenly respectful.

"Underdog," they murmur, all the way to the ring, till I climb in. Rube's behind me. He'll be in my corner, just like I'll sit in his.

"Breathe," I say to me.

I look.

Around.

I walk.

From one side of the ring to the other.

I crouch.

Down in my corner.

When I'm there, Rube's eyes fire into mine. *Make sure you get up*, they tell me, and I nod, then jump up. The jacket's off. My skin's warm. My wolfish hair sticks up as always, nice and thick. I'm ready now. I'm ready to keep standing up, no matter what, I'm ready to believe that I welcome the pain and that I want it so much that I will look for it. I will seek it out. I'll run to it and throw myself into it. I'll stand in front of it in blind terror and let it beat me down and down till my courage hangs off me in rags. Then it will dismantle me and stand me up naked and beat me some more and my slaughter-blood will fly from my mouth and the pain will drink it, feel it, steal it, and conceal it in the pockets of its gut and it will taste me. It will just keep standing me up, and I won't let it know. I won't tell it that I feel it. I won't give it the satisfaction. No, the pain will have to kill me.

That's what I want right now as I stand in the ring, waiting for the doors to open again. I want the pain to kill me before I give in. . . .

"And now!"

I stare into the canvas floor beneath me.

"You know who it is!"

I close my eyes and lean on the ropes with my gloves.

"Yes!" It's the old ugly guy who yells now. "It's Cagey Carl Ewings! Cagey Carl! Cagey Carl!"

The doors are kicked open and my opponent comes trotting through, and the crowd goes absolutely berserk. Five times louder than when I walked in, that's for sure.

Cagey Carl.

"He looks about thirty years old!" I scream at Rube. He barely hears me.

"Yeah," he replies, "but he's a bit of a runt of a thing."

Nonetheless, however, he's still taller, stronger, and faster-looking than me. He looks like he's been in a hundred fights and had fifty broken noses. Mostly though, he looks hard.

"Nineteen years old!" the old man continues into the mike. "Twenty-eight fights, twenty-four wins," and the big one — "twenty-two by knockout."

"Christ."

It's Rube who speaks this time, and Cagey Carl Ewings has jumped the ropes and circles the ring now like he wants to kill someone. And guess who just happens to be the closest guy around. It's me, of course, thinking, *Twenty-two knockouts. Twenty-two knockouts.* I'm dog's meat. I'm dog's meat, I swear it.

He comes over.

"Hey boy," he says.

"Hey," I answer, although I'm not sure he wants one. I'm just being friendly, really. You can't blame one for trying.

Whatever it is, it seems to work, because he smiles.

Then he states something very clearly.

He states, "I'm gonna kill you."

"Okay."

Did I just say that?

"You're scared." Another statement.

"If you like."

"Oh, I like, mate, but I'll like it even more when they cart you out of here on a stretcher."

"Is that right?"

"Definitely."

In the end, he smiles again and returns to his corner. Frankly, I'm quite sure he'll beat the skin off me. Cagey Carl. What an idiot, and I'd tell him so if I wasn't so afraid of him. Now there's only me and the fear and the furled footsteps I take to center ring. Rube stands behind me.

Now I feel naked, in just my dark blue shorts, my gymmies, and with the gloves on my hands. I feel too skinny, too bare. Like you can read the fear on me. The warm room filters across my back. The cigarette smoke breathes onto my skin. It smells like cancer.

Light is on us.

Blinding.

The crowd is dark.

Hidden.

They're just voices now. No names, no blondes, no beers or anything else. Just voices drawn toward the light, and there's no way to liken them to anything else. They sound like people gathered around a fight. That's all. That's what they are and they like what they are.

Both Carl and I sweat. There's Vaseline above his stare, which grinds its way into my eyes. It dawns on me very quickly that he really *does* want to kill me.

"Fair fight," the referee says, and that's all he says.

Then it's back to the corner.

My legs rage with anticipation.

My heart turns.

My head nods, as Rube gives me two instructions.

The first: "Don't go down."

The second: "If you do go down, be sure to get up."

"Okay."

Okay.

Okay.

What a word, ay? What a word, because you can't always mean it when you say it. Everything's gonna be okay. Yeah, whatever, because it's not. Everything hinges on you yourself, which in this case, is me.

"Okay," I say again, feeling the irony of it, and the bell rings and this is it.

Is it? I ask myself. *Is this it? Really?*

The answer to my question comes not from me, but from Cagey Carl, who has made his intentions excessively clear. He sprints over to me and throws out his left hand. I duck it, swing around, and get out of the corner.

He laughs as he chases me.

All round.

He comes at me, I duck.

He swings and misses and tells me I'm scared.

Toward the end of the round, his left glove finds its way through, echoing onto my jaw. Then his right finds me, and another one. Then the bell.

The round is over and I haven't thrown a single punch.

Rube tells me.

He says, "Just a hint you can't win a fight without throwing any punches."

"I know."

"Well?"

"Well what?"

"Well, start throwin' a few."

"All right." But personally, I'm just glad I survived the first round without being knocked down. I'm ecstatic that I'm still upright.

Second round. Still no punches, but this time, late, I hit the canvas and the crowd roars. Cagey Carl stands over me and says, "Hey boy! Hey boy!" That's all he says as I struggle to my knees and stand. Soon after, the bell rings. Everyone knows I'm scared.

This time Rube abuses me.

"If y' gonna carry on like this there's no point bein' here! Remember what we said that morning? This is our chance. Our *only* chance, and you're gonna blow it because you're scared of a little pain!" His face snarls at me. He barks. "If I was fightin' this guy I'd have dropped 'im in the first round and we both know it. It takes me twenty minutes to beat *you*, so get interested an' pull y' finger out, or go home!"

Yet still, I throw no punches.

Boos emerge from the crowd. No one likes a coward.

Rounds three and four, no punches.

Finally, the last round, the fifth.

What happens?

I walk out, my hammering heart smashing through my ribs. I duck and swerve and Cagey Carl lands a few more good punches. He keeps telling me to stop running, but I don't. I keep running, and I survive my first fight. I lose it, on account of throwing no punches, and the crowd wants to lynch me. On my way out of the ring, they yell in my face, spit at me, and one guy even gives me a nice crack in the ribs. I deserve it.

Back in the room, the other fellas only shake their heads.

Perry ignores me.

Rube can't bring himself to look at me.

Instead, he punches the raw meat that hangs down around us as I take my gloves off, ashamed. There's another fight before Rube goes on. He punches hard and waits and we know. Rube will win. He has that about him now. I don't know where it came from — maybe that fight in the school yard. I'm not sure, but I can smell it, right up to the time when the other fight's over.

When Perry tells him, "It's time," Rube punches one last pig and we go to the doors. Again, we wait, and when Perry's voice comes to us, Rube bursts through the door.

Perry yells again: "And now, I think you'll see something tonight that you'll talk about for the rest of your life! You'll say that you saw him." All quiet. All quiet and Perry's voice lowers. Serious. "You'll say, 'I was there. I was there that first night when Ruben Wolfe fought. I saw Fighting Ruben Wolfe's first fight.' That's what you'll say. . . ."

Fighting Ruben Wolfe.

So that's his name.

Fighting Ruben Wolfe, and what the crowd does see is Rube walking toward the ring, in Steve's jacket. Like everyone else so far, they can smell it. The confidence. They see it in the eyes that peer out from his hood.

His walk is not bouncy or cocky.

He throws no punches to the air.

No step, however, is out of turn.

He is straight ahead, straight out, straight and hard, and ready to fight.

"Hope you're better than your brother," someone calls.

It hurts me. Wounds me.

"I am."

But not as much as that. Not as much as those two words from my own brother's lips, as he walks on, without flinching.

"I'm ready tonight," he talks on, and I am aware that now, he speaks only to himself. The crowd, Perry, me — we're all just out there somewhere, unfocused. Now it's just Rube, the fight, and the win. There is no world around it.

Typically, his opponent jumps into the ring, but that's about it. In the first round, Rube knocks him down twice. The bell saves him. In the break, all I do is give my brother some water as he sits and stares and waits. He waits for the fight with a slight smile, like there's nowhere else he'd rather be. He makes his legs rise and fall very slightly and very fast. He does it over, over, over again, before jumping up and going out, fists raised. Fighting.

The second round's the last round.

Rube catches him with a great right hand.

He punches his lungs out.

Then he goes under his ribs.

Even in the neck.

Shoulder.

Arm.

Anywhere legal and uncovered.

Finally, he goes straight through his face. Three times, until the blood rants and raves on its way out of the other guy's mouth.

"Stop it," Rube says to the ref.

The crowd roars.

"Stop the fight." But the ref has no intention to do so, and Rube is forced to bury one last punch onto the chin of Wizard Walter Brighton, and he falls cold to the canvas.

All is loud and violent.

Beer glasses smash.

People shout.

A drop of extra blood hits the canvas.

Rubes stares.

Then another roar does a lap around the factory floor.

"That's it then," Rube says when he returns to the corner. "I told 'em to stop it but I guess they like the blood. That's what people're payin' for, I s'pose."

He climbs out of the ring and is given instant worship by the crowd. They pour beer on him, shake hands with his glove, and yell out how great he is. Rube reacts to none of them.

At the end of the night, we all file back into Perry's van. Bumper won in five but the other blokes all lost, including me, of course. The ride home is all silent. Only two fighters hold a fifty-dollar note in their hand. The others have a little bit of tip money in their pockets, thrown into their corner at the end of the fight. All of them except me, that is. Like I've said, it's clear that no one likes a coward.

Perry drops everyone else off first and lets Rube and me out at Central.

"Hey Rube," he calls.

"Yeah."

"You can fight, boy. See y' next week."

"Same time?"

"Yeah."

Perry, to me: "Cameron, if you do what you did tonight next week, I'll kill you."

Me: "All right."

My heart falls to my ankles, the van takes off, and Rube and I walk home. I kick my heart along the ground. I feel like crying, but I don't. I wish I was Rube. I wish I was Fighting Ruben Wolfe and not the Underdog. I wish I was my brother.

A train passes above us as we walk through the tunnel and onto Elizabeth Street. The sound is deafening, then gone.

Our feet take over.

Out on the other side, on the street, I can smell the fear again. I can pick up the scent. It's easy to find, and Rube smells it too, I can sense it. But he doesn't know it. He doesn't feel it.

The worst part is the knowing that things have changed. See, Rube and I had always been together. We were both down low. We were both scrap. Both no good.

Now Rube's a winner, and I'm a Wolfe on my own. I'm the Underdog, alone.

On our way through the front gate back home, Rube pats me on the shoulder, twice. His previous anger has calmed, probably on account of his own great victory. We brace ourselves for the questions of why we're so late for dinner. It doesn't happen, as Mum's doing an evening shift at the hospital, and Dad's out walking. The first thing Rube does is hose the blood off his gloves in the backyard.

When he comes into our room, he says, "We'll have dinner and then walk Miffy, right?"

"Yeah."

My own gloves go straight back under my bed. They're spotless. Squeaky clean.

"Rube?"

"Yeah?"

"You've gotta tell me how it felt. Y' gotta tell me how it felt to win."

Quiet.

All quiet.

Voices of Mum and Dad wander down at us from the kitchen. They're talking to Steve, because I hear my brother's voice as well. Sarah sleeps in her own room, I guess.

"How'd it feel?" Rube asks himself. "I don't know exactly, but it made me wanna howl."

CHAPTER 9

"Grab that bag there," Steve tells me. Just like he said he would, he's moving out. All his stuff is cleared from the basement as he prepares to leave home, get a flat with his girl. He will rent for a while, I'd say, and then he'll probably buy something. He's been working a long while now. Good job, just started part-time university. Nice suits. Not bad for a few years out of school. He just says it's time to leave, with Mum and Dad struggling to pay bills, and Dad refusing the dole.

He isn't dramatic.

He doesn't look down into his room with a last nostalgic gaze.

He just smiles, gives Mum a hug, shakes Dad's hand, and walks out.

On the porch, Mum cries. Dad holds up his hand in good-bye. Sarah holds the last remnants of a hug in her arms. A son and brother is gone. Rube and I travel with him, to help him unpack what's left of his stuff. The flat he will live in is only about a kilometer away, but he says he wants to move south.

"Down near the National Park."

"Good idea."

"Fresh air and beaches."

"Sounds good."

We drive off and it's only me who turns around to see the rest of the Wolfe pack on the front porch. They will watch the car till it disappears. Then, one by one, they will go back inside. Behind the flyscreen. Behind the wooden door. Behind the walls. Into the world within the world.

"Bye Steve," we say, when all is unpacked.

"I'm only up the street for now," he says, and I reach for a semblance of recognition in his voice. Anything that sounds like *It's okay, lads. We'll be right. We all will be.* Steve's voice sounds nothing like it though. We all know that Steve will be okay. There's no irony in the word for him. Steven will always be okay. That's just how things are.

None of us embrace.

Steve and Rube shake hands.

Steve and I shake hands.

His last words are, "Make sure Mum's okay, right?"

"Right."

We run home, together, in the nearly-dark of Tuesday evening. Rube is waiting for me as we run. He pushes me. The next fight loiters around, like a thief, waiting to thieve. It's five days away.

Each night, I dream about it.

I nightmare.

I sweat.

In my dreams, I fight Perry. I fight Steve and Rube. Even my mother steps up and beats the hell out of me. The weirdest thing is that every time, my father is in the crowd, just watching. He says nothing. Does nothing. He simply watches everything go by, or reads the classifieds, looking for that elusive job.

On Saturday night, I hardly sleep at all.

All through Sunday, I mope around. I barely eat.

Like last week, Perry picks us up, but he takes us to Glebe this time, way down the end.

All is the same.

Same type of crowd.

Same guys, same blondes, same smell.

Same fear.

The warehouse is old and creaky, and the room we sit in is nearly falling apart.

Before the doors kick open, Rube reminds me.

"Remember. Either the other guy kills you, or Perry does. If I was you, I know who I'd prefer it to be."

I nod.

The doors.

They're open.

Perry shouts again and after a last deep breath, I enter the crowd. My opponent awaits me, but tonight, I don't even look at him. Not at the start. Not at the pre-match talk by the referee. Not ever.

The first time I see him is when he's in my face.

He's taller.

He has a small goatee.

He throws punches that are slow but hard.

I duck and swerve and get out of the way.

No suspense now.

No wondering.

I take one on my shoulder and counterpunch him. I get inside and throw a jab into his face. It misses. I throw another. It misses.

His giant hand seems to shake me first, then land on my chin. I hit him back, in the ribs.

"That's the way, Cam!" I hear Rube call out, and when the round is over, he smiles at me. "Even round," he tells me. "You can drop this clown easy." He even begins to laugh. "Just imagine you're fighting me."

"Good idea."

"You afraid of me?"

"A bit."

"Well, beat him anyway."

He gives me a last drink and I go out for the second.

This time it's the crowd that swerves. Their voices climb through the ropes and wrap around me. When I'm on the canvas, they fall over me like a stream, making me get up.

The third is a nonevent. We both get tangled up and throw punches into the ribs. I hurt him once but he laughs at me.

In the fourth, he tells me something at the start. He says, "Hey, I had y' mother last night. She's pretty lousy, ay. Pretty dirty." That's when I decide that I have to win. There's a picture in my mind of Mum, Mrs. Wolfe, working. Tired to the bone, but still working. For us. I don't lose my mind or go crazy, but I get more intense.

I'm more patient, and when I get my chance, I land three good punches in his face. When the bell rings for the end of the round, I don't stop punching him.

"What the hell happened to you?" Rube laughs in our corner.

I answer, "Got hungry."

"Good."

In the fifth, I go down twice and the guy they call Thunder Joe Ross goes down once. Each time I hit the canvas, the crowd urges me to my feet, and when the bell rings and the decision is announced, they clap, and coins are thrown into my corner. Perry collects them.

I've lost the fight, but I have fought well.

I've risen to my feet.

That's all I had to do.

"There." Perry gives me every cent when we reach the dressing room. "Twenty-two bucks eighty. That's a good tip. Most losers are happy with fifteen or twenty."

"He ain't a loser."

The voice belongs to Rube, who is standing behind me.

"Whatever you say," Perry agrees (not caring if it's true or not), and he's gone.

When it comes to Rube's fight, the crowd is extra sharp. Their eyes are glued to him, watching his every move, every mannerism, every everything that might indicate what they've heard about him. Word has traveled fast that Perry Cole's got a hot new fighter, and everyone wants to see him. They don't see much.

His fight begins with a massive left hook.

The guy hits the ropes and Rube keeps going. He rinses the guy out. Whales him. His hands launch into his ribs. Uppercuts, one after the other. Midway through the round, it's all over.

"Get up!" people shout, but this guy just can't. He can barely move.

Rube stands there.

Above him.

He doesn't smile.

The crowd sees the blood, and they smell it. They look into Rube's fire-stomped eyes. Fighting Ruben Wolfe. It's a name they will come to see here now for a long time.

Again, when he climbs out of the ring, they smother him.

Drunk men.

Horny women.

They all rub up against him. They all try to touch him, and Rube remains as he is. He walks straight through them, smiling out of obligation and thanking them, but never losing the concentration on his face.

Sitting in the room, he says to me, "We did good today, Cam."

"Yeah, we did."

Perry gives him his fifty. "No tip for the winner," he says. "He gets his fifty anyway."

"No worries."

When Rube stands and goes to the toilet, Perry and I have words together.

"They love him," he explains. "Just like I thought." A pause. "You know why?"

"Yep." I nod.

He tells me anyway. "It's because he's tall and he's got looks and he can fight. And he's hungry. That's what they like most." He grins. "The women out there are begging me to tell 'em where I found him. They love fellas like Rube."

"It's to be expected."

Outside, when we leave, there's a blonde thing hanging round.

"Hey Ruben." She tiptoes over. "I like the way you fight."

We walk on and she follows and her arm touches slightly with his. Meanwhile, I look at her. All of her.

Eyes, legs, hair, neck, breath, eyebrows, breasts, ankles, front zipper, shirt, buttons, earrings, arms, fingers, hands, heart, mouth, teeth, and lips.

She's great.

Great, dumb, and stupid.

Next, I'm shocked.

Shocked, because my brother stops and they look at each other. Next thing she has him in her mouth. She's swallowing his lips. They're against the wall. Girl, Rube, wall. Pushed up against each other. Merging. He kisses her hard for a fair while. Open tongue, hands everywhere.

Then he stops and walks away.

Rube walks on and says, "Thanks, love."

"Hey Rube. Y' awake again?"

"As usual. Do you ever shut up of a night?"

"Not lately."

"Well, I guess you've got an excuse this time — you fought real well."

"Where's the next one on at?"

"Ashfield, I think, then Helensburgh."

"Rube?"

"What now?"

"Why haven't y' moved into Steve's room?"

"Why haven't you?"

"Why hasn't Sarah?"

"I think Mum wants to turn it into like an office, for doin' paperwork and that kind of thing. That's what she said, anyway."

I say, "And it wouldn't feel right, I don't reckon."

The basement is Steve's room and it always will be. He's moved on but the rest of the Wolfe family stay as they are. They need to. I feel it in the dusty night air, and I taste it.

I also have another question.

I don't ask it.

I can't bring myself.

It's that girl.

I think about it but I don't ask it.

There are some things you just don't ask.

CHAPTER 10

We train and fight and keep training, and I get my first win up. It's down in Helensburgh, against some lowlife yobbo who keeps calling me cowboy.

"That all y' got, cowboy, huh?"

"You hit like my mother, cowboy."

All that kind of thing.

I put him down once in the third and twice in the fifth. I win it on points. Fifty dollars, but more importantly, a win. A sniff of victory for the Underdog. It feels great, especially at the end, when Rube smiles at me and I smile back.

"I'm proud a' you."

That's what he says afterward, in the dressing room, before concentrating again.

Later, he worries me.

He . . . I don't know.

I notice a deliberate change in my brother. He's harder. He has a switch, and once a fight comes near, he flicks it and he is no longer my brother Rube. He's a machine. He's a Steve, but different. More violent. Steve's a winner because he's always been a winner. Rube's a winner because he wants to beat the loser out of himself. Steve *knows* he's a winner, but I think Rube's still trying to prove it to himself. He's fiercer, more fiery, ready to beat all loss from his vision.

He's Fighting Ruben Wolfe.

Or is he actually *fighting* Ruben Wolfe?

Inside him.

Proving himself.

To himself.

I don't know.

It's in each eye.

The question.

Each breath.

Who's fighting who?

Each hope.

In the ring tonight, he leaves his opponent in pieces. The other guy is barely there, from the very beginning. Rube has something over all of them. His desire is severe, and his fists are fast. Every time the guy goes down, Rube stands over him tonight, and he tells him.

"Get up."

Again.

"Get up."

By the third one, he can't.

This time, Rube screams at him.

"Get up, boy!"

He lays into the padding in the corner and kicks it before climbing back out.

In the dressing room Rube doesn't look at me. He speaks words that are not directed at anyone. He says, "Another one, ay. Two rounds and he's on the deck."

More women like him.

I see them watching him.

They're young and trashy and good-looking. They like tough fellas, even though guys like that are likely to treat them poorly. I guess women are only human too. They're as stupid as us sometimes. They seem to like the bad ones a bit.

But is Rube bad? I ask myself.

It's a good question.

He's my brother.

Maybe that's all I know.

As weeks edge past us, he fights and wins and he doesn't bother shaving. He turns up and wins. Turns up and wins. He only smiles when *I* fight well.

At school, there's a new air about him. People know him. They recognize him. They know he's tough, and people have heard. They know he does fight nights, though none of them know that I do. It's for the best, I s'pose. If they saw me fight, it would only make them laugh. I would be Rube's sidekick. They'd say, *Go watch them Wolfes fight, ay. The younger one, what's his name, he's a joke, but Ruben can fight like there's no tomorrow.*

"It's all rumors," is what Rube tells people. "I don't fight anywhere except in my backyard." He lies well. "Look at the bruises on my brother. We fight all the time at home, but that's it. No more than that."

One Saturday morning, a colder one than normal, but clear, we go out for a run. The sun's barely coming up, and as we run, we see some fellas just coming home. They've been out all night.

"Hey Rubey!" one yells.

It's an old mate of Rube's named Cheese. (Well, at least, his nickname's Cheese, anyway. I don't think anyone knows his real name.) He's standing on the walkway up to Central Station with a giant pumpkin under his arm.

"Hey Cheeser." Rube raises his head. We walk up toward him. "What y' been doin' lately?"

"Ah, nothin' much. Just livin' in a drunken haze, ay. Since I left school, all I do is work and drink."

"Yeah?"

"It's good, mate."

"Enjoyin' it?"

"Lovin' every minute."

"That's what I like to hear." But really, my brother doesn't care. He scratches his two-day growth. "So what's the go with the pumpkin?"

"Been hearin' you're a bit of a gunfighter these days."

"Nah, just in the backyard." Rube recalls something. "You of all people should know that."

"Yeah mate, certainly," because Cheese used to be in our yard sometimes when we got the gloves out. He remembers the pumpkin he's holding. He lifts it back into the conversation. "Found this in an alley, so we're gonna play football with it." His mates arrive, around the three of us.

"About here, Cheese?" they ask.

"Why, certainly," and he gives the pumpkin a good kick down the walkway. Someone chases it then and comes running back with it.

"Belt him!" someone else yells, and it's on. Teams divide quickly, the fella gets belted, and pieces of pumpkin go flying all over the place.

"Rube!" I call for it.

He passes.

I drop it.

"Ah, y' useless bloody turkey!" Cheese laughs. Do people still use that word? It's a word people's grandfathers use. In any case, I erase my disappointment by tackling the next guy into the concrete.

A bag lady walks past, checking things out for breakfast.

Then a few couples get out of the way.

The pumpkin's in half. We continue with one of them, and the other half is squashed against the wall under the money machine.

Rube gets belted.

I get belted.

Everyone does, and all around us, there's the stench of sweat, raw pumpkin, and beer.

"You blokes stink," Rube tells Cheese.

"Why thank you," Cheese responds.

We keep going, until the pumpkin's the size of a golf ball. That's when the cops show up.

They walk up, a man and a woman, smiling.

"Boys," the bloke cop opens with. "How's it going?"

"Tosser Gary!" Rube calls out. "What are *you* doin' here?"

Yes, you've guessed right. The cops are our mates from the dog track. Gary, the corrupt, bet-placing male cop, and Cassy, the brilliant brunette gorgeous cop.

"Ahh, *you!*" the cop laughs. "Been down the track lately?"

"Nah," Rube answers. "Been a bit busy."

Cassy nudges Gary.

He pauses.

Remembers.

His job.

"Now fellas," he begins, and we all know what he'll say. "You know this kind of thing isn't on. There's pumpkin all over the place and when the sun hits it, it's gonna stink like my old man's work boots."

Silence.

Then a few yeahs.

Yeah this, yeah that, and a yeah you're right I s'pose.

But no one understands, not really.

No one cares.

I'm wrong.

I'm wrong because I find myself stepping forward, saying, "Okay Gary, I know what y' mean," and start picking up pieces of pumpkin. Silently, Rube follows. The others, drunk, only watch. Cheese helps a bit, but none of the others do anything. They're too shocked. Too drunk. Too out of breath. Too stoned.

"Thanks a lot," Gary and Cassy say when we're done and our drunken friends are on their way.

"I think I'd love to beat the hell out of some of those fellas," Rube mentions. His words are offhand, but fierce. Like he'd do it if the cops would turn their backs for a minute.

Gary looks at him.

A few times.

He notices.

He says it.

"You've changed mate. What's happened?"

All Rube says is, "I don't know."

Neither do I.

It's a conversation with myself at Central Station. It goes on inside my head as Rube and Gary talk a little further.

It goes like this:

"Hey Cameron?"

"What?"

"Why does he scare you all of a sudden?"

"He's fierce now, and even when he smiles and laughs, he stops it real fast and concentrates again."

"Maybe he just wants to be somebody."

"Maybe he wants to kill somebody."

"Now you're bein' stupid."

"All right."

"Maybe he's just sick of losin' and never wants to feel it again."

"Or maybe he's the one that's afraid."

"Maybe."

"But afraid of what?"

"I don't know. What can a winner be afraid of?"

"Losing?"

"No, it's more than just that. I can tell. . . ."

"All the same, though, Cassy looks great, doesn't she?"

"She sure does. . . ."

"But afraid of what?"

"I told you. I don't know."

CHAPTER 11

I only know that I'm a new kind of afraid.

You know how dogs whine when they're afraid, like when a storm's coming? Well, I feel like doing it right now. I feel like asking questions, in desperation.

When did this happen?

How did it happen?

Why did he change so quickly?

Why aren't I happy for him?

Why does it scare me?

And why can't I put my finger on exactly what it is?

All of those questions swing through me, eroding me a little each time. They swing through me during my brother's next few fights. All knockouts. They swing through me each time he stands over his man, telling him to get up, and when the people touch him to grab a little piece of his greatness. I ask the same questions in the dressing room, among the smell of liniment and gloves and sweat. I ask them the next time I see Rube get it off with a nineteen-year-old uni student behind the Maroubra factory, before he walks away from her (without looking back). Then the next time a different girl. Then the next. I ask the questions at home when we eat our dinner with Mum pouring out the soup, and Sarah eating it politely, and Dad eating more failure with his meal. Putting it in his mouth. Chewing it. Tasting it. Swallowing it. Digesting it. Getting used to it. I ask them when Sarah and I wrestle some washing off the line. ("Damn it!" she yells. "It's raining! Hey Cam! Come help us get the washing off!" Just lovely, the two of us sprinting out back and ripping it all off the line, not caring if it's in shreds, just as long as it's bloody dry.) I even ask the questions when I smell my socks to see if they can go one more day or if I should wash them next shower. I ask them when I go and visit Steve at his new place and he gives me a cup of black coffee and a silent, friendly conversation.

Finally, someone else arrives to help me out a bit.

It's Mrs. Wolfe, who, thankfully, has some questions of her own. The best thing about this is that maybe she can get something out of Rube to help me understand him better. Also, she has chosen a night and a week in which I've won my last fight, so I don't have any bruises on me.

It's a Wednesday night, and Rube and I sit on our front porch with Miffy, patting him after his walk. The little wonder dog laps up the attention on the old lounge. He rolls on his stomach as Rube and I pat him and laugh at his ridiculous little fangs and claws.

"Oh Miffy!" Rube breathes out, and it's the shadow of his former callings for the dog when we used to pick him up. He only laughs now with something inside the voice of his throat.

What is it?

Regret?

Remorse?

Anger?

I don't know, but Mrs. Wolfe, she can sense it as well, and she has joined us now on the front porch, in the cold, dim light.

I love Mrs. Wolfe.

I've gotta tell you that right now.

I love Mrs. Wolfe because she's brilliant and she's a genius even though her cooking's downright oppressive. I love her because she fights like hell. She fights better than Rube. Even Rube will tell you that — though her fight has nothing to do with fists. But it has plenty to do with blood. . . .

Her words tonight are these:

"What's up boys? Why are you always coming home so late on Sundays?" She smiles, alone. "I know that you were going down to the dog track not so long ago. You're aware of that, aren't you?"

I look at her. "How'd y' find that out?"

"Mrs. Craddock," she confesses.

"Bloody Craddock!" I yelp. Mrs. Craddock, a neighbor of ours, was always at the dogs, chewing a hot dog with her false teeth, and sinking Carlton Cold beer like there was no tomorrow. Not to mention smoking Long Beach 25s till the cows came home.

"Forget the dogs," Mum sighs.

She talks.

We listen.

We have to.

When you love and respect someone, you listen.

"Now, I know things are rough at the moment, fellas, but just do me a favor and come home at a decent hour. Try to get here before dark."

I break.

"Okay Mum."

Rube doesn't.

He says, straight and hard, "We've been goin' down to the gym. Sunday afternoons it's cheaper, and you can learn boxing."

Boxing.

Nice one, Rube.

We know how Mum feels about boxing.

"Is that what you want to do?" she asks, and her mild tone is surprising. I think she knows she can't stop us. She knows the only way is to let us find out. She continues and ends with two words. "Boxing? Really?"

"It's safe. All supervised and taken care of. Not like we used to do in the backyard. None of the one-handed rubbish."

Which isn't a lie. Yes, the fights *are* supervised and taken care of, but by whom? It's funny how truth and lies can come in the same clothes. They wear flanno shirts, gym boots, jeans, and Ruben Wolfe's lips.

"Just look after each other."

"We will," and I smile at Mrs. Wolfe because I want her to think that everything's all right. I want her

going to work without worrying about us. She deserves
at least that.

Rube gives her an "Okay."

"Good."

"We'll try to get back quicker," he goes on, before
Mum returns inside. First she pats Miffy for a while,
running her dry fingers through our friend's soft,
fluffy fur.

"Look at this dog," I say once she's gone. Just to say
something. Anything.

"What about him?"

I'm lost, and unsure what to say. "I guess, we've got
to liking him, ay."

"But what does liking do?" Rube looks at the road.
"It doesn't do anything."

"Does hating?"

"What have we got to hate?" He's laughing now.

The truth is, there's a lot to hate, and a lot to love.

Love.

The people.

Hate.

The situation.

Behind us we hear Mum cleaning up the kitchen.
We turn and see the silhouette of our dad helping
her. We see him kiss her on the cheek.

He is unemployed.

He still loves her.

She loves him.

Watching it, I see the handful of fights that Rube and I have had inside the warehouses and factories. They're pale, I decide. Pale in comparison. There's a vision also of Sarah, putting overtime in (as she's been known to do lately), or even just watching TV or reading. There's even a vision of Steve, out there on his own, living. Mainly though, it's Mum and Dad. Mr. and Mrs. Wolfe.

I think about Fighting Ruben Wolfe.

I think about fighting Ruben Wolfe.

From the inside.

I think about finding Ruben Wolfe. . . .

I think about fights you know you'll win, fights you know you'll lose, and the fights you just don't know about. I think about the ones in between.

It's me now who looks at the road.

I speak.

Talk.

Say it.

I say, "Don't lose your heart, Rube."

And very clearly, without moving, my brother answers me.

He says, "I'm not tryin' to lose it, Cam. I'm tryin' to find it."

Tonight, there's nothing.

  There's no "Hey Rube, are you awake?"

  No "Of course I bloody am!"

There's just silence.

Silence, Rube and me.

And the darkness.

He's awake, though. I can sense it. I can feel it, just out of reach from my vision.

There are no voices from the kitchen.

There's no world but this one.

This room.

This air.

This awake-ness.

CHAPTER 12

In the half-consciousness of Saturday morning, I'm dreaming of women, flesh, and fights.

The first fills me with fear.

The second fills me with thrill.

The third fills me with more fear.

My blanket covers me. Only my human snout sticks out the top, allowing me to breathe.

"We goin' for a run?" I ask across to Rube.

Is he still asleep?

"Rube?"

An answer. "Nah, not today."

Good, I think. *This blanket might be full of fear, but it's still pretty warm under here. Besides, I reckon we could use a rest.*

"I wanna do a bit of work later though," Rube continues. "Gotta work on my jab. Can we do some One Punch later in the backyard?"

"I thought we were finished with that. Like you said to Mum."

"Well, we're not. I've changed my mind." He rolls over but still talks. "You could use some work on your own jab too, y' know." He's right.

"Okay."

"So stop whingein'."

"I don't mind." It's the truth. "It'll be fun anyway. Like the old days."

"Damn right."

"Good."

We return to sleep. For me, it's back to the flesh, fighting, and women. *What's it back to for Rube? I wonder.*

Once we're up and the day progresses, Mum, Dad, and Sarah go to Steve's place, to see how he's going. It's our golden opportunity to train. We take it.

As we always do now, we go over and get Miffy.

From our back step, the pooch looks up at us. He licks his lips.

We circle the yard.

Rube hits me, but I hit back. He gets more in than me, but about every second punch Rube gets in, I get one back. He becomes a little frustrated.

When we have a break, he says, "I've gotta be quicker. Quicker once the jab goes out. Quicker to block."

"Yeah, but what happens in your fights," I tell him, "is that you throw a jab or two and follow it with your left. Your left's always quicker than the counterpunch."

"I know, but what if I come up against a real good counterpuncher? Then I'm in trouble."

"I doubt it."

"Do y'?"

From there, we practice more and then swap gloves for a bit of fun. Back to the old days all right. One glove each, circling the backyard, each throwing punches. Smiling at hitting. Smiling at being hit. We don't go all out, because we both have to fight tomorrow, so there are no bruises and no blood. *It's funny*, I think, as we crouch and I watch Rube, who also crouches with that look on his face. Just content. *It's funny when we fight one-handed in our backyard, that's when I feel closest to my brother. That's when it feels strongest that we're brothers and always will be.* I feel it, watching him, and when he gives me a slight Ruben Wolfe grin, Miffy flings himself at him, and Rube mock-fights him, letting Miffy curl around his solitary glove.

"Bloody Miffy," he smirks. There are glimpses.

Later, the tempo changes back to what has become normal.

We're sitting in our room, and Rube pulls open the wretched corner of carpet next to my bed. In one envelope is his money. In the other is mine. Rube's envelope holds three hundred and fifty dollars. Mine holds about one sixty. Rube has won seven fights from seven starts. My own money comes from two wins and the rest of it is tips.

Rube sits on his bed and counts his money.

"All there?" I inquire.

"Why wouldn't it be?"

"I was only bloody askin'!"

He looks at me.

Thinking about it, it's actually the first time in a while that either of us has raised his voice in real anger at the other. We used to do it all the time. It was normal. Almost fun. A regular occurrence. Today, however, it's like a bullet, buried deep into the flesh of our brotherhood. It's a bullet of doubt, a bullet of not knowing.

Outside the window, the city counts the seconds, as we sit there in silence.

One — two — three — four —

More words get to their feet.

They belong to Rube.

He says, "Are the dogs on today?"

"I think so, yeah. Saturday the eighth. Yep, that's today."

"You wanna go down?"

"Yeah, why not?" I smile. "We might see those cops again and have a laugh."

"Yeah, they're all right, those two."

I take a handful of my tip change and chuck some of it Rube's way.

"Thanks."

I put ten bucks in my jacket pocket. "No worries."

We put our shoes on and leave the house. We write a note saying we'll be back before dark, and place it on the kitchen table. It goes next to the *Herald*. That paper — it sits there, open at the employment section. It sits there like a war, and each small advertisement is another trench for a person to dive into. To hope and fight in.

We stare at it.

We pause.

We know.

Rube drinks some milk out of the carton, puts it back in the fridge, and we walk out, leaving the war on the table, with the note.

Outside, we walk.

Out the front door and beyond the gate.

We're in our usual gear. We're jeaned, flanno-ed, gymmied, and jacketed. Rube's jacket is corduroy. It's brown and old and ridiculous, but typically, he looks downright brilliant in it. Mine's my black spray jacket, and I'd say I look about okay. Or at least, I hope. Somewhere on the border of it anyway.

We walk, and the smell of street is raucous. It shoots through me and I enjoy it. The city buildings in the distance are holding up the sky, it seems. The sky is blue and bright, and the strides of Rube and I walk toward it. We used to languish when we walked, or sidle down the street like dogs that have just done something wrong. Now Rube walks upright, because he's on the attack.

We get to the track and it's about one o'clock.

"Look," I point. "It's Mrs. Craddock."

As expected, she's sitting in the stand, holding a hot dog in one hand and balancing a coldie and a cigarette in the other. The smoke smothers her and divides either side.

"Hi fellas," she calls to us, moving the cigarette to her lips. Or is she taking a chug on the beer? She has brown-gray hair, purple lipstick, a scrunched nose, and wears an old dress and thongs. She's big. A big woman.

"Hey Mrs. Craddock," we greet her. (It was the beer she was after, *then* a quick inhalation.) "How y' goin'?"

"Beautifully, thanks. Nothin' better than a day with the dogs."

"That's for sure." But I'm thinking, *Whatever y' say, love.* "Who do y' like in the next one?"

She grins.

Oh man. It's not pretty. Those falsies . . .

"Number two," she advises. "Peach Sunday."

Peach Sunday. Peach Sunday? What sort of person calls a greyhound Peach Sunday? They should get together with whoever called that other dog You Bastard.

"Can she gallop?" I ask.

"That's horses, love," Craddock answers. See how infuriating she is? Can she really think that *I* think I'm at the horse track? "And it's a he."

"Well?" Rube asks. "Is he a certainty?"

"Sure as I'm sittin' here."

"Well, she's sittin' here all right." Rube nudges me on our way. "All three hundred pounds of her."

We turn and bid her good-bye.

Me: "Bye, Mrs. Craddock."

Rube: "Yeah, see y' later. Thanks for the tip."

We look around. Our cop mates aren't here, so we have to hunt for someone else to put the bet on for us. It won't be hard. A voice finds us.

"Hey Wolves!"

It's Perry Cole, holding his customary beer, as well as a grin. "What are a couple of respectable young lads such as yourselves doin' down here?"

"Just puttin' a few on," Rube replies. "Can y' slap a bet on for us?"

"Of course."

"Race three, number two."

"Right."

He puts it on for us and we go down to the sunny part of the grandstand, where Perry sits in a big group. He introduces us, tells everyone what gunfighters we are (or Rube, at least), and we watch. There are some ugly guys and girls there, but some nice girls too. One of them is our age and pretty. Dark hair, cut short. Eyes of sky. She's skinny and she smiles at us, polite and shy.

"That's Stephanie," Perry tells us as he rattles through the names. Her face is tanned and sweet. Her neck and throat are smooth, and she wears a pale blue shirt, a bracelet, and old jeans. She's got gymmies on, like us. I notice her arms and her wrists and her hands and fingers. They're feminine and beautiful and delicate. No rings. Just the bracelet.

All the other people talk, behind us.

So where do y' live? I ask, inside. No words come out.

"So, where do y' live?" Rube asks her, but his voice is so different from the voice that I would have used. His is said to be said. Not said to be nice.

"Glebe."

257

"Nice area."

Me, I say nothing.

I only look at her and her lips and her straight white teeth when she speaks. I watch the breeze run its fingers through her hair. I watch it breathe onto her neck. I even watch the air go into her mouth. Into her lungs, and back out . . .

She and Rube talk about regular things. School. Home. Friends. What bands they've seen lately of which Rube has seen none. He just makes it up.

Me?

I would never lie to her.

I promise.

"Go!"

It's everyone yelling as the dogs get let out and take off around the track.

"Go Peach Sunday!"

Rube stands and yells with the rest of the people.

"Go Peaches! Go son!"

As he does so, I look at Stephanie. Peach Sunday doesn't concern me anymore, even when he wins by two lengths and Rube slaps me on the back, and Perry slaps us *both* on the back.

"Old Craddock's all right then, ay!" Rube shouts at me, and faintly, I smile. Stephanie smiles also, at both of us. We've just made sixty-five dollars. Our first real win at the track. Perry collects it for us.

We decide to stay ahead from there and we just hang around and watch for the rest of the afternoon, till

the shadows grow long and lean. When the crowd dis-
perses after the last race, Perry invites us to his place for
what he calls, "Food, drinks, and anything else you
might need."

"No thanks." It's Rube. "We've gotta get home."

At that moment, Steph talks to an older girl I assume
is her sister. They talk, then separate, and Steph is on
her own.

Walking out the gate, I see her and say to Rube,
"Shouldn't we walk with her or somethin'? You know,
to make sure she doesn't get clocked on the way home.
There are some good weirdos around here."

"We gotta be home before dark."

"Yeah, but —"

"Well, go if y' want," he urges me. "I'll tell Mum you'll
be in a bit later. You just stopped by a mate's place."

I stop.

"Come on," he says, "make up y' mind."

I pause, go one way, then the other. I decide.

I run across the road, and once I turn to see where
Rube is, he's gone. I can't find him anywhere. Steph's
walking up ahead. I catch up.

"Hey." Words. *More words*, I tell myself. *Gotta say
more words.* "Hey Steph, can I walk with you?" *To make
sure you get home all right*, I think, but I don't say it. It's
just not something I would say. I can only hope she
knows what I mean.

"Okay," she replies. "But isn't this out of your way?"

"Ah, not really."

It grows darker and there are no more words. It's just, I have no idea what to say, or what to talk about. The only thing that makes a sound is my heartbeat, stumbling through my body as we keep going. Our walk is slow. I look at her. She looks at me a few times too. Damn, she's beautiful. I see it under the streetlights — a world of sky in each eye, and the dark, short waves of hair and tanned skin.

It's cold.

God, she must be cold, and I take my jacket off and offer it to her. Still no words. Just my face, begging her to accept it. She does and she says, "Thanks."

At her gate, she asks, "You wanna come in? You can have something to drink."

"Oh nah," I explain. Quiet. Too quiet! "I have to get home. I wish I could though."

She smiles.

She smiles and takes the jacket off. When she hands it to me, I wish I could touch her fingers. I wish I could kiss her hand. I wish I could feel her lips.

"Thanks," she says again, and when she turns and walks toward her front door, I only stand and look at her. I take all of her in. Her hair, neck, shoulders. Her back. Her jeans and her legs, walking. Her hands again, the bracelet and her fingers. Then her last smile, when she says, "Hey Cameron."

"Yeah?"

"I might see y' tomorrow. I think I'll come down and have a look in the warehouse, even though I hate fights." She pauses a moment. "I hate betting at the dog track as well. I only go because the dogs are beautiful."

I stand there.

Still.

I wonder, *Can a Wolfe be beautiful?* However, "That's nice," is what I say. We connect. Her eyes pull mine into hers.

"So yeah," she says. "I'll try to make it there."

"Okay."

Then, "Hey, just out of interest," she asks. She considers something. "Is Rube as good a fighter as everyone says?"

I nod.

Just honestly.

"Yeah," I say. "He is."

"How 'bout you?"

"Me? I'm not much really. . . ."

There's one more smile and she says, "Might see you tomorrow then."

"All right," I reply. "I hope so."

There's a final turn and she's gone inside.

Once I'm alone, I stand a few more seconds and take off for home. I start running, from the adrenaline juice I taste in my throat.

Can a Wolfe be beautiful?

Can a Wolfe be beautiful?

I ask it as I run, with her image gathered in my mind. *I think Rube can be,* I answer, *when he's in the ring. He's handsome, yet ferocious, yet devastating, yet beautiful and handsome all over again.*

At home, I make it in time for dinner.

She's there, at the table with me. Stephanie. Steph. Eyes of sky. Sweet wrists and fingers, and waves of dark hair, and her love for the beautiful dogs at the track.

She might be there tomorrow.

She might be there.

She might be.

She might.

She.

I'm kidding, aren't I?

Cameron Wolfe.

Cameron Wolfe, and another girl who has shown just the slightest interest. And he loves her already. He's already prepared to fall all over her and beg her and vow to treat her right and do anything she wants. He's ready to give all of himself.

He's one boy, and surely, it is pain that looms, not bliss.

Or will this be different?

Can it be?

Will it be?

I don't know.

I anticipate and hope. I think about it all night. Even in bed, she's under my blanket with me.

Across the room, Rube's counting his money again.

Holding it out before him, he stares at it, like he's convincing himself of something.

I stare now as well, curious about what he sees.

"See this money," he says. "It's not three hundred and fifty dollars." He stares harder. "It's seven wins."

"Hey Rube?"

Nothing.

"Hey Rube? Rube?"

Tonight it's just her and me, under my blanket.

Visions echo.

They're played out on the ceiling, as hope grows inside me.

There are gold snippets of future in the darkness of the dark.

One last try:

"Hey Rube? Rube?"

Nothing.

All I have is the hope that I will fight well tomorrow and that she'll be there.

But she hates fights, *I tell myself.* So why would she come? *More questions.* Would she really come just to see me?

The visions are everywhere.

The answers are nowhere.

Yet, in the dead of night, in the listening dark, Rube says a very strange thing. Something I won't really understand until later.

He says, "Y' know, Cam, I've thought about it, and I think I like your money better than mine."

And I'm left lying there, in bed, thinking but not speaking. Just thinking.

CHAPTER 13

Sometimes I wish I had better fists on me. *Faster ones*, with faster arms and stronger shoulders. Usually I'm in bed when I think of that kind of thing, although today, I'm in the dressing room waiting for the call. I don't know. I just wish to be formidable. I wish I could walk through the crowd and climb into the ring to win, not just to fight.

"Cameron."

I wish I could look my opponent in the eye and tell him I'm going to kill him.

"Cameron."

I wish I could stand above him and tell him to get to his feet.

"Cameron!"

Finally, Rube has made it into my thoughts. He has hit me on the shoulder to burst through my mind. I still sit there, in my spray jacket, shivering. My gloves hang from my hands like dead weight, and I feel like falling to pieces.

"Are you fighting or what?" Rube shakes me.

She's out there, I think, and for once, I actually say it. To my brother. Quietly. "She's out there, Rube."

He looks at me closer, wondering who I'm talking about. "She is," I go on.

"Who?"

"That Steph, y' know the one?"

"Who?"

Oh, what's the point! I exclaim inside me.

Yet, I still speak softly. "Steph from the track."

"So what?" He's frustrated now, and close to picking me up and throwing me out into the crowd.

"So everything," I keep talking. I'm still vacant. Exhausted. "I saw her just a few minutes ago when I took a peek out the door."

Rube walks away. "Oh God almighty." He walks away and comes back. He's calm now. "Just get out there."

"Okay." But no movement.

Still calm. "Get out."

"All right," and I know that I must.

I stand up, the doors are kicked open, and I walk into the crowd. It's a crowd in which every person has the same face. It's her. Stephanie.

All is blur.

All confusion.

Perry, shouting.

The ref.

Keep it clean, fellas.

Fair fight.

Okay.

Do it.

Don't go down.

If you do go down, get up.

The bell, the fists, the fight.

It begins, and the first round is death.

The second round is the coffin.

The third is the funeral.

My opponent is not such a great fighter, but I'm not on today. I'm not up. I'm so scared of failing that I have accepted it. I've given in to it, almost as if I won't try because it will only make things worse.

"Get up!" screams Rube's distorted voice the first time I'm down. Somehow, I do it.

The second time, it's just the look in his eyes that makes me find my feet again. My legs ache and I stagger, over to the ropes. Hanging on. Hanging on.

The third time, I see her. I see her and it's only her. The rest of the crowd has disappeared and only Stephanie stands there, watching. The whole place is empty but for her. Her eyes are swimming with beauty and her stance makes me lunge for her, in an attempt for her to help me up.

"I only go because the dogs are beautiful," I hear her say.

What a strange thing to say, I think, then realize it's yesterday's voice that I hear. Today, she stands in silence, staring at me with solemn lips, closed up, as I struggle to my feet.

In the fourth round, I fight back. I rise up.

I navigate my head away from the other guy's fists and get in a few shots of my own. Blood has flooded my chest and stomach. It eats into my shorts.

Dog's blood.

A beautiful dog?

Who knows, because in the fifth round, I get knocked out, and it isn't just one where I can't get up. It's a knockout where I'm knocked cold, unconscious.

When I'm out, she fills me.

I see her and we're at the track, just us in the grandstand, and she kisses me. She comes close and she tastes so nice. It's unbearable. Me, with one gentle hand on her face and the other nervously gripping the collar of her shirt. Her with her lips on mine, and her hands gliding up my rib cage, bit by bit. Just gentle, so gentle.

Her lips.

Her hips.

Her pulse, inside mine.

So gentle, so gentle.

So

"Gentle," I hear Rube's voice. "Be gentle with him."

Damn, I'm awake.

Awake and ashamed.

After a while, I'm on my feet again, but I'm slumped between Rube and Bumper, who has kindly jumped into the ring to help us out. "You right, little fella?" he asks.

"Yeah," I lie. "I'm right," and Rube and Bumper help me out of the ring.

It's darker in here now and my sight is paralyzed. Tonight it's shame that flows down my side, as the fluorescent lights hit me. They scratch my eyes out. They blind me.

Once out of the ring, I stop. I have to.

"What?" Rube questions me. "What's up? C'mon, we gotta get you back in the room."

"No," I say. "I've gotta walk on my own."

Rube's eyes search inside me then and something happens. His hands drop and he nods at me with such intensity that I nod ever so slightly back. Feeling grabs me, turns through me, and I walk.

We all do.

I walk with Rube and Bumper on either side of me, and the crowd is silent. The blood is drying onto my skin. My legs move forward. Once more. Once more. *Just keep walking*, I tell myself. *Head up. Head up*, I chant, *but still concentrate on y' feet. Don't fall down.*

There is no applause.

Just people, watching.

Just Stephanie, out there somewhere, watching.

Just Rube's proud eyes, as he walks next to me . . .

"The door," he says to Perry, and Perry opens it, when we get there. On the other side, I fall down again, swallowing my blood and turning over to grin at the ceiling. It drops and squashes me, then rises up and does it again.

"Rube," I call out, but he's miles away. "Rube . . ." A shout now. "Rube, are y' there?"

"I'm here brother."

Brother.

It makes me smile.

I say, "Thanks Rube. Thanks."

"It's all right brother."

Again with the *brother*.

Another smile on my lips.

"Did I win?" I ask, because now, I can't feel anything. I'm one with the floor.

"Nah mate." He won't lie. "You got hurt pretty bad, ay."

"Did I?"

"You did."

Slowly, I regain edges of composure. I clean myself up and watch Rube's fight through a gap in the door. Bumper's in his corner in my absence, even though my brother doesn't need him. I see Stephanie, swaying with the rest of the crowd, just watching when Rube knocks down his man in the second. I see her smile and it's a beautiful smile. But it's not a grandstand smile. It's not a smile for me. I have drowned in those eyes. I have vanished in the sky. And there I am, remembering that she doesn't really like fights. . . .

The bout ends later in the round.

The girl ends two minutes after it.

She ends when Rube goes past and she says something to him. Rube nods. It makes me wonder. *Has she asked if Cameron's okay? Does she want to see me?*

The thing is, though, that I can tell. Her eyes cannot be for me.

Or can they?

Soon we'll know, because during the next fight, Rube goes out the back door, and listening, I can tell he's talking to her. He's talking to Stephanie.

I'm close. Too close, but I can't help it. I have to listen. It starts with Rube's voice.

"You wanna see if my brother's okay, do you?"

Silence.

"Well, do y'?"

"Is he all right?"

I'm in her voice for a brief moment, letting it cover me, smother me, until Rube sees things clearly. He says it hard.

"Y' don't care, isn't that right?"

"Of course I do!"

"Y' *don't.*" Rube's made up his mind. "Y' came for me, didn't you?" A gap. "*Did*n't you?"

"No, I —"

"See, there are smart girls out there somewhere, and they're not here. They're never round the back here with me, getting' it off against the wall because they think I'm tough and good and hard!" He's angry. "No way. They're at home, dreamin' of a Cameron! They're dreamin' of my brother!"

Her voice bruises me.

"Cameron's a loser."

Bruises me hard.

"Yeah, but," Rube goes on, "you know somethin'? He's a loser who walked you home yesterday when I couldn't have cared less. Hell, you could have been beat up or raped for all I cared." His voice batters her, I can feel it. "And there's Cameron, my brother, dyin' like hell to please you and treat you right." He moves her into a corner. "He would too, y' know. He'd bleed for you, and fight for you, without his fists. He'd take care of you and have respect for you and he'd love the hell out of you. You know that?"

It's quiet.

Rube, Steph, door, me.

"So if you wanna do it here with me," Rube jabs her again, "let's go. You're about worth me, but you're not worth him. You're not worth my brother. . . ."

He has swung his last verbal punch now and I feel them standing there. I picture it — Rube looking at her and Stephanie looking somewhere else. Anywhere but at Rube. Soon, I hear her footsteps. The last one sounds like something shattering.

Rube's alone.

He's on one side of the door.

I'm on the other.

To himself, he says, "Always for me." Some silence. "And for what? I'm not really even a . . ." He fades off.

I open the door. I see him.

I walk out and lean back against the wall with him.

I realize that I could have hated him or been jealous that Steph wanted him instead of me. I could have looked back on her question from last night with bitterness.

Is Rube as good a fighter as everyone says? she'd asked. Yet, I don't feel anything awful. All I can feel is a wish that I'd had the presence of mind to answer something different to her. I should have said, *A good fighter? I don't know — but he's good at being my brother.*

That's what I should have said.

"Hi Rube."

"Hi Cameron."

We lean against the wall and the sun is screaming out in pain on the horizon. The horizon swallows it slowly, eating it up whole. All the city faces it, including my brother and me.

Conversation.

I speak.

I ask, "Y' reckon there really is *a girl out there like the one y' mentioned? Waiting for me?"*

"Maybe."

Fire and blood are smeared across the distant sky. I watch it.

"Really, Rube?" I ask. "Y' reckon?"

"There has to be. . . . You might be dirty and down low, and not much of a winner, but . . ."

He doesn't finish his sentence. He just looks into the evening, and I can only speculate on what he might say, I hope it's something like "but you're big-hearted," or "but you're a gentleman."

Nothing, however, is said.

Maybe the words are the silence.

CHAPTER 14

When you lean against a wall and the sun's setting, sometimes you just stand there and watch. You taste blood but you don't move. Like I said, you let the silence speak. Then you go back inside.

"Twenty bucks tip money," Perry informs me, handing me a bag when everything's over.

"Huh," I retort. "Pity money."

"No," Perry warns me. He always looks like he's warning you. This time he's telling me to shut up and take the compliment.

"It's pride money," says Bumper. "Walkin' through the crowd like that. They appreciate that more than my win, more than Rube's win, more than all of 'em put together."

I take the money. "Thanks, Perry."

"You've got four more fights," he tells me. "Then your season's over, right? You deserve the break, I reckon." He shows Rube and me a sheet of paper that's a competition ladder. In his other hand he holds the draw. On the ladder, he points out where Rube is. "See, you came in three fights late, but you're still on top. You're the only one who hasn't lost a fight."

Rube points at the name sitting on second. "Who's Hitman Harry Jones?"

"You're fightin' him next week."

"He good?"

"You'll drop him easy."

"Oh."

"Look there, he's had two losses. One of 'em was against the bloke you fought tonight."

"Really?"

"Would I say it otherwise?"

"No."

"Well, shut up then." Perry grins. "The semifinals are comin' up in four more weeks." The grin leaves him. Immediately. Now he's serious. "However . . ."

"What?" Rube asks. "What?"

Perry pulls us both aside. He speaks slow and genuine. I've never heard him speak like this. "There's only one slight problem — it's in the last week of the regular comp."

Rube and I both look at the draw closely.

"See it?" Perry sticks a finger on Week Fourteen. "I've decided to be a bit of a bastard."

I see it.

So does Rube.

"Oh man," I say, because right there on the page of Week Fourteen in the lightweight division, it says *WOLFE vs. WOLFE.*

Perry tells us, "Sorry fellas, but I couldn't help it. There's just something about brothers fighting, and I wanted the last week before the semifinals to be memorable." He's still genuine. Just talking business.

"Remember, I said there was a slight chance this might happen. You said it wouldn't be a problem."

"You can't rig somethin'?" Rube asks. "You can't change it?"

"No, and I don't want to either. The only good thing is that it's gonna be here, at home."

A shrug. "Well, fair enough then." My brother looks at me. "You got a problem with it Cam?"

"Not really."

"Good," Perry finishes. "I knew I could count on y's."

When everything's packed up, Perry offers us our usual lift home. His voice hammers my mind, as I'm still in pretty bad shape from the beating I copped.

"Nah," Rube tells him. "Not tonight, ay. I reckon we might walk tonight." He goes for my opinion. "Cam?"

"Yeah, why not," even though I'm thinking, *Are you bloody crazy? My head looks like it's gone through a blender.* However, I say nothing more. I think I'll be happy to walk home with Rube tonight.

"No worries." Perry states his position. "Next week boys?"

"Certainly."

We walk out the back door with our gear and tonight there is no one waiting. There's no more Steph, no more anyone. There's only city and sky, and clouds that twirl in the growing darkness.

At home, I hide my battle-bruised face. I have a black eye, swollen cheekbone, and a torn, blood-rusted lip. I eat the pea soup in the sheltered corner of the lounge room.

The next few days fight their way past.

Rube lets his gruff grow a little.

Dad is on the employment trail, as usual.

Sarah goes to work and only goes around to her friend Kelly's place once or twice. She comes home sober and, on Wednesday, with overtime money jammed in her pocket.

Steve comes in once, to iron some shirts.

"Don't you have an iron?" Rube asks him.

"What does it look like?"

"It looks like you don't have an iron."

"Well, guess what, I don't."

"Well, maybe you should go and buy one, y' tighty."

"Who y' callin' tight, boy? How 'bout you go and have a shave. . . ."

"Can't y' afford an iron? This movin' out thing can't be too easy then."

"Damn right. It's not."

The thing is, though, that as they argue, both Steve and Rube are pretty much laughing. Sarah laughs from the kitchen and I smirk in my own juvenile way. This is the sort of thing we specialize in.

Mrs. Wolfe has actually taken the day off work.

What this means is that she has time to notice that there are cuts and bruises healing on my face. As I eat some cornflakes that afternoon, she corners me in the kitchen. I watch her watching me.

She calls out.

One word.

It's this:

"Rube!"

Not too loud. Not panicked. Just a confident strain of voice that expects nothing less than his quick arrival.

She asks, "Is it the boxing training?"

Rube sits down. "No."

"Or have you boys been fighting in the backyard again?"

He confesses a lie.

"Yeah." He's pretty quiet. "We have."

She only sighs and believes us, which is the worst thing. It's always bad when someone believes you when you know they shouldn't. You feel like screaming at them, telling them to stop, so you can live with yourself a little easier.

But you don't.

You don't want to disappoint them.

You can't face your own gutless self and explain that you're not worthy of their trust.

You can't accept that you're that low.

The thing is that we *have* been fighting in the yard, even if it's only practice for the real thing. I guess Rube hasn't exactly lied, but he hasn't told the truth either.

It's close.

I feel it.

I come so close to telling her all about it. Perry, the boxing, the money. Everything. The only thing stopping me now is the bowed head of my brother. Looking at him, I know he's heading somewhere. He's at the edge of something and I can't bring myself to snatch it from under his feet.

"Sorry Mum."

"Sorry Mum."

Sorry Mrs. Wolfe.

For everything.

We'll make you proud another day.

We have to.

We must.

"You know," she begins, "you fellas ought to be looking after each other." Her comment makes me realize that through the lies, the greatest irony is that we *are* looking out for each other. It's just that in the end, we're letting her down. That's what injures us.

"Any luck with work?" Steve asks Dad. I can hear it. They're in the lounge room.

"Nah, not really."

I expect them to begin the usual argument about getting the dole, but they don't. Steve leaves it alone, because he doesn't live here anymore. He only gets a fixed look on his face and says his good-byes. I can tell by his expression that he's thinking, *It'll never happen to me. I won't let it.*

On the Friday of that week, what seems like a typical morning turns out to be a very important one.

Rube and I are out for a run and it's nearly seven when we return. As always, we have our old jerseys, track pants, and gymmies on. The day wears a sky with boulder clouds and a bright blue horizon. At our gate, we arrive and Sarah's there. She asks, "Did y' see Dad while you were out? He's disappeared, ay."

"No," I reply, wondering what the big deal is. "Dad's been taking walks lately."

"Not this early."

Mum comes out.

"His suit's not there," she announces, and instantly, we all know. He's down there. He's waiting. He's gone down to get the dole.

"No."

Someone says it.

Again.

Against the hope that it isn't true.

"No way," and I realize that it's me who has spoken, because the morning-cold smoke has tumbled from my mouth with the words. "We can't let him." Not because we're ashamed of him. We're not. We just know that he's fought this for so long, and we know he sees it as the end of his dignity.

"Come on."

Now it's Rube who has spoken, and he tugs on my sleeve. He calls to Mum and Sarah that we'll be back soon, and we take off.

"Where we goin'?" I pant, but I know the answer, right up until we get to Steve's place. Out of breath from the sprint, we stand there, gather ourselves, then call out.

"Hey Steve! Steven Wolfe!"

People yell out for us to shut up, but soon enough, Steve appears on his apartment balcony in his underwear. His face says, *You bastards.* His voice says, "I thought it was you blokes." Then a shrill, unhappy shout: "What are y's doin' here? It's seven o'clock in the bloody morning!"

A neighbor shrieks, "What the hell's goin' on out there?"

"Well?" Steve demands.

"It's," Rube stutters. "It's Dad."

"What about him?"

"He's . . ." Damn, my voice is still panting. "He's down there." I'm shaking. "Getting the dole."

Steve's face shows relief. "Well, it's about time."

Yet, when Rube and I stare into him, he can tell. We're pleading with him. We're crying out. We're howling for help. We're screaming out that we need all of us. We need — "Ah, bloody hell!" Steve spits out the words. A minute later, he's with us, running in his old football training gear and his good athletic shoes.

"Can't y's run any faster?" he complains on the way, just to repay us for pulling him out of bed and humiliating him in front of his neighbors. He also says through clenched teeth, "I'll get you blokes for this, I promise y's."

Rube and I just keep running, and when we get back to our place, Mum and Sarah are dressed. They're ready. We all are. We walk.

After fifteen minutes, the employment service is in sight. At the doors, there sits a man, and the man is our father. He doesn't see us, but each one of us walks toward him. Together. Alone.

Mrs. Wolfe has pride on her face.

Sarah has tears in her eyes.

Steve has our father in his eyes, and finally, the realization that he would be equally as stubborn.

Rube has intensity clawed across him.

As for me, I look at my father, sitting there, alone, and I imagine his sense of failure. His black suit is a bit short at the ankles, exposing his worn-out socks beneath the pants.

When we get there, he looks up. He's a good-looking man, my father, although this morning, he's defeated. He's broken.

"Thought I'd get down here early," he says. "This is about the time I normally start work."

All of us stand around him.

In the end, it's Steve who speaks. He says, "Hi Dad."

Dad smiles. "Hi Steven."

That's all there is. No more words. Not like you might expect. That's all of it, except that we all know we won't let him do it. Dad knows it too.

He stands up and we resume the fight.

When we walk back, Rube stops at one point. I wait with him. We watch the others walk.

Rube speaks.

"See," he says. "That's Fighting Clifford Wolfe." He points. "That's Fighting Mrs. Wolfe and Fighting Sarah Wolfe. Hell, these days, that's even Fighting Steven Wolfe. And you're Fighting Cameron Wolfe."

"What about you?" I ask my brother.

"Me?" he wonders. "I've been given the name, but I don't know." He looks right at me and says truth. "I've got some fear of my own, Cam."

"Of what?"

What can he be afraid of?

"What will I do when a fight comes along that I might lose?"

So that's it.

Rube's a winner.

He doesn't want to be.

He wants to be a fighter first.

Like us.

To fight a fight he might lose.

I answer his question, to assure him.

"You'll fight anyway, just like us."

"Y' reckon?"

But neither of us knows, because a fight's worth nothing if you know from the start that you're going to win it. It's the ones in between that test you. They're the ones that bring questions with them.

Rube hasn't been in a fight yet. Not a real one.

"When it comes along, will I stand up?" he asks.

"I don't know," I admit.

He'd rather be a fighter a thousand times over among the Wolfe pack than be a winner once in the world.

"Tell me how to do it," he begs. "Tell me." But we both understand that some things can't be told or taught. A fighter can be a winner, but that doesn't make a winner a fighter.

"Hey Rube."

"Yeah."

"Why can't y' be happy bein' a winner?"

"What?"

"You heard me."

"I don't know." He goes over it. "Actually, I do know."

"Well?"

"Well, first, if you're a Wolfe, you should be able to fight. Second, there's only so long you can win for, because someone can always beat you." He draws a breath. "On the other hand, if you learn how to fight, you can fight forever, even when you get belted."

"Unless you give up."

"Yeah, but anyone can stop you being a winner. Only you yourself can make you stop fighting."

"I s'pose."

"Anyway . . ." Rube decides to finish it. "Fighting's harder."

CHAPTER 15

Like I've said earlier, there are four weeks now until I fight my brother. Fighting Ruben Wolfe. I wonder how it will be, and how it will feel. What will it be like to fight — not in our backyard, but in the ring, under all the lights, and with the crowd watching and cheering and waiting for the blood? Time will tell, I suppose, or at least, these pages will.

Dad's at the kitchen table, alone, but now, my father doesn't look so beaten down. He looks like he's back in it. He's been to the brink and come back. I guess when you lose your pride, even for just a moment, you realize how much it means to you. His eyes have some strength back in them. His curly hair is spiraling at his eyebrows.

Rube's quiet lately.

He spends a fair bit of time down in the basement, which, as you know, has been vacated by Steve. In the end, Mum offered it to everyone for their bedroom, but none of us wanted it. We said it's because it gets so cold down there, but really, I reckon the remaining wolves in our house feel like now's a time to stick together. I've felt it ever since Steve left. Not that I would say it out loud. I would never admit to Rube that I didn't take the basement because I'd get too lonely without him. Or that I'd miss our conversations and the way he always annoys me. Or, as disgraceful as it sounds, that I'd even miss the smell of his socks and the sound of his snoring.

Just last night, I tried waking him, because that snoring of his was dead-set detrimental to my health. Sleep deprivation, I'm telling you. That is, until it gets like a pendulum again, coaxing me into sleep. Huh. Hypnosis under the influence of Ruben Wolfe's snoring. It's hopeless, I know, but you get used to things. You feel weird without them, like you're not yourself anymore.

In any case, it's Mrs. Wolfe herself who has taken hold of the basement. She has a bit of an office down there and does the tax.

On Saturday night, though, I find Rube there instead, sitting on the desk, his feet resting on the chair. It's the night before his fight with Hitman Harry Jones. I pull the chair from his feet and sit on it.

"Y' right there?" He glares at me.

"I am, yeah. It's a pretty nice chair."

"Don't worry about my feet," he goes on. "They're danglin' now 'cause of you."

"Ah y' poor bloke."

"Got that right."

I swear it.

Brothers.

We're strange.

In here, he won't give me an inch, but out in the world, he'll defend me to the death. The frightening thing is that I'm the same. We all seem to be.

A pause yawns through the air, before Rube and I start speaking without looking at each other. Personally, I look at a blotch on the wall, wondering, *What is that? What the hell is it?* As for Rube, I can sense that he has lifted his feet to the desk and rests his chin on his knees. His eyes, I imagine, are fixed straight ahead, on the old cement stairs.

"Hitman Harry," I begin.

"Yeah."

"You reckon he's any good?"

"Maybe."

Then, right in the middle of it all, Rube says, "I'm gonna tell 'em." His statement brings with it no extra attention, no movement. No prospect of believing that he's thought out what he has said just now. It's been decided long ago.

The only problem is, I have no idea what he's talking about.

"Tell who what?" I inquire.

"Can you really be that thick?" He turns to me now, a savage look on his face. "Mum and Dad, y' yobbo."

"I'm not a yobbo."

I hate it when he calls me that. *Yobbo.* I think I hate it worse than *faggot.* It makes me feel like I'm eating a pie and drinking Carlton Cold and like I've got a beer gut the size of Everest.

"Anyway," he goes on impatiently, "I'm tellin' Mum and Dad about the boxing. I'm sick of the sneakin' round."

I stop.

Think it over in my mind.

"When y' gonna tell 'em?"

"Just before you and me fight."

"Are you crazy?"

"What's wrong with that?"

"They'll keep us from fighting and Perry'll kill us."

"No, they won't." He has a plan. "We'll just promise that it's the last time we'll ever fight each other." Is this part of Rube wanting a real fight? Telling Mum and Dad? Telling them the truth? "They can't stop us, anyway. They might as well see us for what we are."

What we are.

I repeat it, in my head.

What we are . . .

Then I ask it.

"What are we?"

And there's silence.

What are we?

What are we?

The weird thing about the question is that not long ago we knew exactly what we were. It was *who* we were that was the problem. We were vandals, backyard fighters, just boys. We knew what words like that meant, but the words Ruben and Cameron Wolfe were a mystery. We had no idea where we were going.

Or maybe that's wrong.

Maybe who you are *is* what you are.

I don't know.

I just know that right now, we want to be proud. For once. We want to take the struggle and rise above it. We want to frame it, live it, survive it. We want to put it in our mouths and taste it and never forget it, because it makes us strong.

Then Rube cuts me open.

He slits my doubt from throat to hip.

He repeats it and answers it. "What are we?" A brief laugh. "Who knows what they will see, but if they come and watch us fight, they'll know that we're brothers."

That's it!

That's what we are — maybe the only thing I *can* be sure of.

Brothers.

All the good things that involves. All the bad things.

I nod.

"So we'll tell 'em?" He's looking at me now. I see him.

"Yeah."

It's agreed, and I must confess that I myself get obsessed with the idea. I want to run up immediately and tell everyone. Just to let it out of me. Instead, I concentrate on what lies ahead before it. I have three fights of my own to survive, and I must watch Rube fight and the way his opponents fight him. I can't make the same mistakes they make. I've gotta go the distance, and for his sake, I have to give him a fight, not just another win.

To my own surprise, I win my next fight — a points decision.

Right after me, Rube puts the Hitman to bed midway through the fourth round.

The week after, I lose in the fifth, and the last fight before my meeting with Rube is a good one. It's at Maroubra, and compared with my first ever bout there, this time, I walk in and throw punches without hesitating. I'm not scared of being hit anymore. Maybe I've grown used to it. Or perhaps I know that the end is near for me. The guy I'm fighting doesn't come out for the last round. He's too wobbly, and I feel for him. I know how it feels to not want the last round. I know how it feels to concentrate hard on just standing, let alone even thinking about throwing punches. I know how it is for the fear to outweigh the physical pain.

Watching Rube fight later, I see something.

I find out why no one beats him, or why they don't even come close. It's because they don't *think* they can win. They don't believe they can do it, and they don't want it badly enough.

To survive him, I have to believe I can beat him.

It's easier said than done.

"Hey Cam?"

"It's about time."

"About time for what?"

"About time you started the talkin'."

"I've got somethin' important to say."

"Yeah?"

"We'll tell 'em tomorrow."

"Y' sure?"

"Yes. I'm sure."

"When?"

"After dinner."

"Where?"

"Kitchen."

"Okay."

"Good. Now shut up. I wanna get some sleep."

Later, when he starts snoring, I tell him.

"I'm gonna beat you." But personally, I'm not really too convinced.

CHAPTER 16

The money sits on the kitchen table and we all stare at it. Mum, Dad, Sarah, Rube, and me. It's all there. Notes, coins, the lot. Mum lifts Rube's pile up just slightly, to get an idea of how much there is.

"About eight hundred dollars all up," Rube tells her. "That's between Cameron and me."

Mum holds her head in her hands now. Thursday nights shouldn't be like this for her, and she stands and walks over to the sink.

"I think I'm going to be sick," she tells us, bent over.

Dad stands, goes over and holds her.

After about ten silent minutes, they return to the table. I swear, this kitchen table's seen about everything, I reckon. Everything big that's ever happened in this house.

"So how long's this been going on exactly?" Dad throws out the question.

"A while. Since about June."

"Is that right, Cameron?" Mum this time.

"Yeah, that's right." I can't even look at her.

However, Mrs. Wolfe looks at me. "So that's where all those bruises came from?"

I nod. "Yeah." I go on talking. "We did still fight in the backyard, but only for practice. When we started out, we told ourselves that we all needed the money. . . ."

"But?"

"But, I don't think it's ever been about the money."

Rube agrees and takes over. He says, "Y' know Mum, it's just that Cam and I saw what was happening here. We saw what was happening to us. To Dad, to you, to all of us. We were barely surviving, just keeping our heads above water, and . . ." He's getting feverish now. Desperate to tell it right. "We wanted to do something that would lift us up and make us okay again —"

"Even if it makes the rest of us ashamed?" Mum interrupts.

"Ashamed?" Rube boxes her through the eyes. "You wouldn't say that if you saw Cameron fighting, standing up, over and over again." He's nearly shouting. "You'd fall to your knees with pride. You'd tell people that he's your boy and he keeps fighting because that's the way you brought him up."

Mum stops.

She stares through the table.

She imagines it, but all she sees is the pain.

"How can you go through that?" she begs me. "How can you go through it, week after week?"

"How can *you*?" I ask her.

It works.

"And how can you?" I ask Dad.

The answer is this:

We keep getting up because that's what we do. Don't ask me if it's instinct, but we all do it. People everywhere do it. Especially people like us.

When it's nearly all over, I allow Rube to deliver the knockout blow. He does it. He says, "This week is Cameron's last fight." A deep breath. "The only thing is" — a pause — "he's fighting me. We're fighting each other."

Silence.

Total silence.

Then, in all honesty, it's taken quite well.

Only Sarah flinches.

Rube goes on. "After that I've got semifinals. Three more weeks at the most."

Both Mum and Dad seem to be handling it now, slightly. *What are they thinking?* I ask myself. Mainly, I think they feel like they've failed as parents, which is completely untrue. They deserve no blame, because this is something Rube and I did on our own. If we succeeded, it was us. If we failed — us. No blame on them. No blame on the world. We didn't want that, and we wouldn't tolerate it.

Now I crouch down next to my mother. I hug her and tell her, "I'm sorry, Mum. I'm so sorry."

Sorry.

Will that ever do?

Will it ever make her understand enough to forgive us?

"We promise," Rube still tries. "This is the last time Cameron and I will ever fight each other."

"Jeez, that's comforting." Sarah finally speaks. "You can't fight someone when he's dead."

Everyone looks at her and listens, but no one speaks.

It finishes.

A nervous quiet curls through the kitchen air, till only Rube and I sit there. Everyone else leaves. Sarah first, then Dad, then Mrs. Wolfe. Now we wait for the fight.

Living among the next few days, I continue in my determination to believe that I can beat him. I can't pull it off. The closest I come is believing that I *want* to beat him, in order to survive.

When we leave for the warehouse on Sunday night, Mr. and Mrs. Wolfe come with us. Dad makes us all pile into his panel van (with me cramped into the back).

The car takes off slowly.

I sweat.

I fear.

The fight.

My brother.

For my brother — for his own fight.

The whole way there, nothing is said, until we get out at the warehouse, when Dad says, "Don't kill each other."

"We won't."

It's organized in the dressing room that Perry will sit in Rube's corner. Bumper will be in mine. There's a good crowd.

I can hear it, and I see it, when I go into the *Visiting Fighters* dressing room. I don't look for Mum and Dad because I know they're out there, and I'm concentrating on what I have to do.

In the dirty dressing room, I sit for a while, and other fighters come and go. I walk around. I'm jumpy. This is the biggest fight of my life.

I'm fighting against my brother.

I'm also fighting *for* him. . . .

With a few minutes to go, I lose contact with everyone else. I lie down on the floor. With my eyes shut, my arms at my side. My gloves touch the tops of my legs. I don't see anyone. I don't hear anyone. I'm alone in my mind. There's tension all around me, pressed to the outline of my body. It gets beneath me and lifts me. . . .

I want it, I tell myself. *I want it more than him.*

Future scenes from the fight angle through my mind.

I see Rube trying to get at me.

I want it.

I see myself ducking and counterpunching.

More.

I see myself, standing, at the end. Standing at the end of a real fight. Not a win, or a loss, but a fight. I see Rube.

I want it more than him, I repeat, and I know that I do. I do want it more, because I have to. I've —

"It's time."

Bumper's near me now, and I jump to my feet and stare forward. I'm ready.

Perry's shouting voice registers, but only for a second. When Bumper pushes through the door, the crowd makes its usual noise. I see it, I feel it, but I can't hear it. I walk on, inside me. Inside the fight.

I climb the ropes.

I get rid of the jacket.

I don't see him, but I know he's there.

But I want it more.

Now.

The ref.

His words.

Silent.

Looking at my feet.

Anywhere but at Rube.

In the suffocating seconds between now and the fight, I wait. No practice punches, I'll need them all. It's fear and truth and future, all devouring me. It hunts through my blood and I'm a Wolfe. Cameron Wolfe.

I hear the bell.

With it, the crowd comes storming into my ears.

I walk forward and throw the first punch. I miss. Then Rube swings and gets me on the shoulder. There's no slow beginning, no warm-up period or watching time. I move in hard and get underneath. I hit him. Hard on the chin. It hurts him. I see it. I see it because I want it more and he is there to be hurt. He's there to be beaten and I'm the only one in the ring to do it.

It's three minutes per round.

That's all.

Fists and pain and staying upright.

Again, I feel my fist cut through my brother, only this time it rips into his stomach. In reply, a right hand lands on my left eye. We trade punches for nearly the whole round. There's no running, no circling. Just punches. Toward the end, Rube gashes me open. He gets me in the mouth, making my head swarm backward and the pulse in my throat go numb. My legs go, but the round's over. I walk straight to my corner.

I wait.

I want.

The fight is there, and I want Rube to know that he's in it as well. The second round has to convince him.

It begins hard again, with Rube miss-hitting two jabs. I follow, but miss with an uppercut. Rube gets annoyed. He tries to hook me, but it frees him up and I land the best punch of my life on his jaw, and . . .

He staggers.

He staggers, and I chase him to the neutral corner, throwing my fists into his face, and slitting him once over his eye. He finds composure and fights his way out. Nothing hard lands though, and somehow, I stay out of his way the entire round. Once more, I find him on the chin. A good shot. A real good shot, and the round is mine.

"You're in a fight," I tell him. It's all I say, and Rube looks into me.

He comes out even harder in the third, and he gets me on the ropes twice, but only a handful of punches reach their mark. His breathing is heavy and my own lungs are exhausted. When the bell goes, I fake a burst of energy and head straight for my stool. I glance over at Rube as Perry talks to him. It's the face of our mother when she gets up in the morning, ready for another double overtime shift. It's the face of Dad that day down at the employment service. It's the face of Steve, fighting in his own life and then for his father, simply saying, "Hi Dad." It's the face of Sarah, dragging washing off the line with me. It's my own face, right now.

"He's scared of losin'," Bumper tells me.

"Good."

In the fourth, Rube reacts.

He misses me just once, then opens me up several times. His left hand is especially cruel, pinning me into his corner. Only once do I get through him and clip his jaw again. It's the last time.

By the end of the round, I'm against the ropes, just about gone.

When the bell goes this time, I find my corner, oh, miles and miles away, and stagger toward it. I fall. Down. Into the arms of Bumper.

"Hey buddy," he tells me, but he's so far away. Why's he so far away? "I don't think you can go out for the last. I think you've had enough."

I realize.

"No way," I beg him.

The bell goes again and the referee calls us into the middle. One final handshake before the last round. It's always the same . . . until today.

My head is jolted back by what I see.

Is it real? I ask myself. *Is* . . . because there, in front of me, Rube is wearing only one boxing glove and his eyes circle inside mine. He's wearing one boxing glove, on his left hand, just like all those times in the back-yard. He's standing there, before me, and something very slight glimmers across his face. He's a Wolfe and I'm a Wolfe and I will never ever tell my brother that I love him. And he will never tell it to me.

No.

All we have is this. . . .

This is the only way.

This is us. This is us saying it, in the only way we can possibly do it.

It means something. It's about something.

I return.

To my corner.

With my teeth, I take off the left glove. I give it to Bumper, who accepts it in his right hand.

Mum and Dad are somewhere in the crowd, watching.

My pulse does a lap of the silence.

The ref calls something out.

Sight.

Is that what he yells?

No, it's "Fight," although . . .

Rube and I look at each other. He comes forward. So do I. The crowd erupts.

One fist covered. One fist naked.

That's all.

Rube throws first and takes me on the chin.

It's over. I'm hurt, I'm . . . but I throw a punch back, just missing. I cannot go down. Not tonight. Not now, when everything hinges on me staying on my feet.

I'm hit again, and this time the world has stopped. Opposite me, Rube's standing there, wearing a solitary boxing glove. Both his hands are at his side. Another silence gathers strength. It is broken, by Perry. His words are familiar.

"Finish him off!" he calls out.

Rube looks at him. He looks at me. He tells him.

"No."

I find them. Mum and Dad.

I collapse.

My brother catches me and holds me up.

Without knowing it, I'm crying. I'm weeping on my brother's throat as he holds me up.

Fighting Ruben Wolfe. He holds me up.

Fighting Ruben Wolfe. It hurts.

Fighting Ruben Wolfe. His fight inside.

Fighting Ruben Wolfe. Like the rest of us.

Fighting Ruben Wolfe. Not fighting him, no. It's something else. . . .

"Y' okay?" he asks me. It's a whisper.

I say nothing. I just cry on my brother's throat and let him hold me up. My hands feel nothing and my veins are on fire. My heart is heavy and hurting, and out there somewhere, I can imagine the pain of a beaten dog.

I find that nothing more has happened. The bell rings and it's over. We stand there.

"It's over," I say.

"I know," Rube smiles. I feel it.

Even in the following minutes, when scattered money falls into the ring, and when we walk back through the murmuring crowd, the moment carries on.

It carries me back to the dressing room with Rube at my side, as people stare at us and nod and reach out not for Rube or for me, but for this moment that is both of us. "That was some fight," some of them say, but they're wrong. It was more than that. It was Ruben Wolfe and me, and the blood of brothers in our veins.

In the dressing room, the feeling of it helps me get changed, and it waits with me for Rube. When he finds me, Perry arrives as well and sorts out the money, though we both know we'll split it tonight, down the middle. The money means nothing.

On our way out the back door, the crowd roars from another fight, and Perry stops us. I expect him to say something to Rube about not finishing me off, but he doesn't. Instead, with a smile and shake of his head, he says, "Not bad, lads. Not bad at all."

"Thanks," Rube answers, and we walk out.

Tonight, we're pretty quick to leave, mainly for our mother's sake. We meet back at the panel van.

Outside, the cold air slaps me.

We drive home, in silence again.

On our front porch, Mrs. Wolfe stops and gives us each a hug. She hugs our father as well. They both go in.

Standing outside, we still hear Sarah ask from the kitchen, "So, who won?"

We also hear the answer.

"Nobody."

It's Dad.

Mum calls out from inside. "Do you fellas want dinner? I'm heating it up right now!"

"What is it?" Rube answers, hopeful.

"The usual!"

Rube turns to me and says, "Bloody pea soup again. It's a dis-grace."

"Yeah," I agree, "but it's brilliant too."

"Yeah, I know."

I open the flyscreen door and walk into the kitchen. I check out what's going on, and the smell of everyday life fights its way into my nose.

"Hey Rube?"

We're on the front porch, eating pea soup in the dark.

"What?"

"You'll win that lightweight title in a few weeks, won't y'?"

"I'd say so, but I won't be doin' it again next year. I'll tell Perry soon enough." He laughs. "It was pretty good chop there for a while, wasn't it? Perry, the bouts, all of it."

I even laugh myself, for some reason. "Yeah, I guess."

Rube looks in disgust down at his soup. "This is bloody shockin' tonight." He lifts a spoonful and lets it drop back into the bowl.

A car drives past.

Miffy barks.

"We're comin'!" Rube shouts. He gets up. "Here, give us y' bowl."

He takes it inside and when he returns, we make our way off the porch, to get damn Miffy.

At the gate, I stop my brother.

I ask, "What'll y' do when the boxing's over?"

He answers without thinking. "I'm gonna hunt my life down and grab it."

Then we put our hoods on and walk out.

Street.

World.

Us.

GETTING
THE GIRL

For Scout
and
For Mum and Dad

CHAPTER 1

It was Rube's girl's idea to make the beer ice blocks, not mine.

Let's start with that.

It just happened to be me who lost out because of it.

See, I'd always thought that at some point I'd grow up, but it hadn't happened yet. It's just the way it was.

In all honesty, I'd wondered if there would ever come a time when Cameron Wolfe (that's me) would pull himself together. I'd seen glimpses of a different me. It was a different me because in those increments of time I thought I actually became a winner.

The truth, however, was painful.

It was a truth that told me with a scratching internal brutality that I was me, and that winning wasn't natural for me. It had to be fought for, in the echoes and trodden footprints of my mind. In a way, I had to scavenge for moments of alrightness.

I touched myself.

A bit.

Okay.

Okay.

A lot.

(There are people who've told me you shouldn't admit that sort of thing too early, on account of the fact that people might get offended. Well, all I can say to that is why the hell not? Why not tell the truth? Otherwise there's no bloody point really, is there?

Is there?)

It was just that I wanted to be touched by a girl someday. I wanted her to not look at me as if I was the filthy, torn, half-smiling, half-scowling underdog who was trying to impress her.

Her fingers.

In my mind, they were always soft, falling down my chest to my stomach. Her nails would be on my legs, just nice, handing shivers to my skin. I imagined it all the time, but refused to believe it was purely a matter of lust. The reason I can say this is that in my daydreams, the hands of the girl would always end up at my heart. Every time. I told myself that *that's* where I wanted her to touch me.

There was sex, of course.

Nakedness.

Wall to wall, in and out of my thoughts.

But when it was over it was her whispering voice I craved, and a human curled up in my arms. For me, though, it just wasn't a mouthful of reality. I was swallowing visions, and wallowing in my own mind, and feeling like I could happily drown inside a woman.

God, I wanted to.

I wanted to drown inside a woman in the feeling and drooling of the love I could give her. I wanted her pulse to crush me with its intensity. That's what I wanted. That's what I wanted myself to be.

Yet.

I wasn't.

The only mouthfuls I got were a glance here or there, and my own scattered hopes and visions.

' The beer ice blocks.

Of course.

I knew I was forgetting something.

It had been a warm day for winter, though the wind was still cold. The sun was warm, and kind of throbbing.

We were sitting in the backyard, listening to the Sunday afternoon football coverage, and quite frankly, I was looking at the legs, hips, face, and breasts of my brother's latest girlfriend.

The brother in question is Rube (Ruben Wolfe), and in the winter I'm talking about, he seemed to have a new girlfriend every few weeks or so. I could hear them sometimes when they were in our room — a call or shout or moan or even a whisper of ecstasy. I liked the latest girl from the start, I remember. Her name was nice. Octavia. She was a street performer, and also a nice person, compared with some of the scrubbers Rube had brought home.

We first met her down at the harbor one Saturday afternoon in late autumn. She was playing a harmonica so people would throw money into an old jacket that was sprawled out at her feet. There was a lot of money in it, and Rube and I watched her because she was damn good and could really make that harmonica howl. People would stand around sometimes and clap when she was done. Even Rube and I threw money in at one point, just after an old bloke with a walking stick and just before some Japanese tourists.

Rube looked at her.

She looked at him.

That was usually all it took, because that was Rube. My brother never really had to say or do anything. He just had to stand somewhere or scratch himself or even trip up a gutter and a girl would like him. It was just the way it was, and it was that way with Octavia.

"So where y' livin' these days?" Rube had asked her.

I remember the ocean green of her eyes rising then. "Down south, in Hurstville." He had her then already. I could tell. "You?"

And Rube had turned and pointed. "You know those crappy streets past Central Station?"

She nodded.

"Well, that's us." Only Rube could make those crappy streets sound like the best place on earth — and with those words, Rube and Octavia had begun.

One of the best things about her was that she actually acknowledged my existence. She didn't look at me as if I was an obstacle stuck between her and Rube. She would always say, "How's it goin', Cam?"

The truth is.

Rube never loved any of them.

He never cared about them.

He just wanted each one because she was next, and why not take the next thing if it was better than the last?

Needless to say, Rube and I aren't too much alike when it comes to women.

Still.

I'd always liked that Octavia.

I liked it when we went inside that day and opened the fridge to see three-day-old soup, a carrot, a green thing, and one VB beer can sitting inside. All three of us bent down and stared.

"Perfect."

It was Rube who said it, sarcastically.

"What *is* that?" Octavia asked.

"What?"

"That green thing."

"I wouldn't have a clue."

"An avocado?"

"Too big," I said.

"What the hell *is* it?" Octavia asked again.

"Who cares?" Rube butted in. He had his eye on the VB. Its label was the only green thing he was staring at.

"That's Dad's," I told him, still looking into the fridge. None of us moved.

"So?"

"So he went with Mum and Sarah to watch Steve's football game. He might want it when he comes home."

"Yeah, but he might also buy some on the way."

Octavia's breast brushed my shoulder when she turned and walked away. It felt so nice, it made me quiver.

Immediately, Rube reached in and grabbed the beer. "It's worth a shot," he stated. "The old man's in a good mood these days anyway."

He was right.

This time last year he was pretty miserable on account of having no work. This year he had plenty of work, and when he asked me to help on the odd Saturday or two, I helped him. So did Rube. My father's a plumber.

Each of us sat at the kitchen table.

Rube.

Octavia.

Me.

And the beer, sitting in the middle of the table, sweating.

"Well?"

Rube asked it.

"Well what?"

"Well what the hell are we gonna do with this beer, you stupid bastard?"

"Settle down, will y'."

We smiled, wryly.

Even Octavia smiled, because she'd grown used to the way Rube and I spoke to each other, or at least, the way Rube spoke to me.

"Do we split it three ways?" Rube continued. "Or just pass it round?"

That was when Octavia had her great idea.

"How 'bout we make it into ice blocks?"

"Is that some kind of sick joke?" Rube asked her.

"Of course not."

"Beer ice blocks?" Rube shrugged and considered it. "Well, I s'pose. It's warm enough, ay. Have we got any of those plastic ice block things? You know, with the stick?"

Octavia was already in the cupboards, and she found what she was after. "Pay dirt," she grinned (and she had a lovely mouth, with straight, white, sexy teeth).

"Right."

This was serious now.

Rube opened the beer and was about to pour it out, in equal amounts, of course.

Interruption.

Me.

"Shouldn't we wash 'em out or somethin'?"

"Why?"

"Well they've prob'ly been in that cupboard for ten years."

"So what?"

"So they're probably all moldy and mangy, and —"

"Can I just pour the goddamn beer!?"

We all laughed again, through the tension, and finally, painstakingly, Rube poured three equal portions of beer into the ice block containers. He fixed the stick on each of them so they were straight down.

"Right," he said. "Thank Christ for that," and he walked slowly to the fridge.

"In the freezer bit," I told him.

He stopped, mid-walk, turned slowly and carefully back round, and said, "Do you seriously think I'm pathetic enough to put beer which I just took *from* the fridge and poured into *ice* blocks back in just the fridge?"

"Y' never know."

He turned away again and kept walking. "Octavia, open the freezer, will y'."

She did it.

"Thanks, love."

"No worries."

Then it was just a matter of waiting for them to set.

We sat around in the kitchen for a while, until Octavia spoke, to Rube.

"You feel like doin' something?" she asked him. With most girls, that was my cue to leave. Octavia, though, I wasn't sure. I just cleared out anyway.

"Where y' goin'?" Rube asked me.

"Not sure."

I went out of the kitchen, took my jacket for later, and walked onto the front porch. Half out the door, I mentioned, "Maybe down the dog track. Maybe just out wanderin'."

"Fair enough."

"See y' later, Cam."

With a last look at Rube and a glance at Octavia, I could see desire in each of the eyes I met. Octavia had desire for Rube. Rube just had desire for a girl. Pretty simple, really.

"See y's later," I said, and walked out.

The flyscreen door slammed behind me.

My feet dragged.

I reached each arm into the jacket.

Warm sleeves.

Crumpled collar.

Hands in pockets.

Okay.

I walked.

Soon evening worked its way into the sky, and the city hunched itself down. I knew where I was going. Without knowing, without thinking, I knew. I was going to a girl's place. It was a girl I had met last year at the dog track.

She liked.

She liked.

Not me.

She liked Rube.

She'd even called me a loser once when she was talking to him, and I'd listened in as my brother smacked her down with words and shoved her away.

What I'd been doing lately was standing outside her house, across the road. I stood and stared and watched and hoped. And I left, after the curtains were drawn for a while. Her name was Stephanie.

That night, which I think of now as the beer ice block night, I stood and stared a bit longer than usual. I stood and imagined walking home with her and opening the door for her. I imagined it hard, till a reaching pain pulled me inside out.

I stood.

Soul on the outside.

Flesh within.

"Ah well."

It was a fair walk because she lived in Glebe and I lived closer to Central, on a small street with ragged gutters and the train line just beyond. I was used to it, though — both the distance and the street. In a way, I'm actually proud of where I come from. The small house. The craggy road. The Wolfe family.

Many minutes shuffled forward as I walked home, and when I saw my dad's panel van on our street, I even smiled.

Things had actually been okay for everyone lately.

Steve, my other brother.

Sarah, my sister.

Mrs. Wolfe — the resilient Mrs. Wolfe, my mother, who cleans houses and at the hospital for a living.

Rube.

Dad.

And me.

For some reason that night when I walked home, I felt peaceful. I felt happy for all of my family, because things really did seem to be going okay for them. All of them.

A train rushed past, and I felt like I could hear the whole city in it.

It came at me and then glided away.

Things always seem to glide away.

They come to you, stay a moment, then leave again.

That train seemed like a friend that day, and when it was gone, I felt like something in me tripped. I was alone on the street, and although I was still peaceful, the brief happiness left and a sadness tore me open very slowly and deliberately. City lights shone across the air, reaching their arms out to me, but I knew they'd never quite make it.

I composed myself and made my way onto the front porch. Inside they were talking about the ice blocks and the missing beer. I was actually looking forward to eating my share of it, even though I can never finish a full can or bottle of beer. (I just stop being thirsty, to which Rube once said, "So do I, mate, but I still keep drinkin' it.") In this case, the ice block idea was at least halfway interesting, so I was ready to go in and give it a shot.

"I was planning on drinking that beer when we got home."

I could hear my father talking just before I went inside. There was an element of bastardry in his voice as he continued. "And whose brilliant idea was it to make ice blocks out of *my* beer, sorry, my *last* beer, anyway? Who was it?"

There was a pause.

A long one.

Silent.

Then, finally, "Mine," came the answer, just as I walked into the house.

The only question is, who said it?

Was it Rube?

Octavia?

No.

It was me.

Don't ask me why, but I just didn't want Octavia to cop a bit of a battering (verbally, of course) from Clifford Wolfe, my father. The odds were that he'd be all nice to her about it, but still, it wasn't worth the risk. Much better for him to think it was me. He was used to me doing ridiculous things.

"Why aren't I surprised?" he asked, turning to face me. He was holding the ice blocks in question in his hands.

He smiled.

A good thing, trust me.

Then he laughed and said, "Well, Cameron, you won't mind if I eat yours then, will y'?"

"Of course not." You always say "of course not" in that situation because you figure out pretty quick that your old man's really asking, "Will I take the ice block or will I make you suffer in a hundred different other ways?" Naturally, you play it safe.

The ice blocks were handed out, and a small smile

was exchanged between Octavia and me, then Rube and me.

Rube held his ice block out to me. "Bite?" he asked, but I declined.

I left the room, hearing my father say, "Pretty good, actually."

The bastard.

"Where'd y' go before?" Rube asked me later in our room, after Octavia had left. Each of us lay on our bed, talking across the room.

"Just around a bit."

"Down Glebe way?"

I looked over. "What's that mean?"

"It means," Rube sighed, "that Octavia and I followed you once, just out of interest. We saw y' outside a house, starin' into the window. You're a bit of a lonely bastard aren't y'?"

Moments twisted and curled then, and off in the distance I could hear traffic, roaring almost silently. Far from all this. Far from Cameron and Ruben Wolfe discussing what in the hell I was doing outside the house of a girl who cared nothing for me.

I swallowed, breathed in, and answered my brother.

"Yeah," I said. "I guess I am."

There was nothing else I could say. Nothing to cover it up. There was only a slight moment of waiting, truth and feeling, then a crack, and I said more. "It's that Stephanie girl."

"The bitch," Rube spat.

"I know, but —"

"I know," Rube interrupted. "It makes no difference if she said she hated you or called you a loser. Y' feel what y' feel."

Y' feel what y' feel.

It was one of the truest things Rube had ever said, just before a quietness smothered the room.

From next-door's backyard we could hear a dog barking. It was Miffy, the pitiful Pomeranian we loved to hate, but still walked a few times a week anyway.

"Sounds like Miffy's a bit upset," Rube said after a while.

"Yeah," and I laughed a bit.

A bit of a lonely bastard. A bit of a lonely bastard.

Rube's statement reverberated inside me till his voice was like a hammer.

Later, when I got up and sat on the front porch and watched shadows of traffic filter past, I told myself it was okay to be like this, as long as I stayed hungry. It felt like something was arriving in me. It was something I couldn't see or know or understand. It was just there, mingling into my blood.

Very quickly, very suddenly, words fell through my mind. They landed on the floor of my thoughts, and in there, down there, I started to pick the words up. They were excerpts of truth gathered from inside me.

Even in the night, in bed, they woke me.

They painted themselves onto the ceiling.

They burned themselves onto the sheets of memory laid out in my mind.

When I woke up the next day, I wrote the words down, on a torn-up piece of paper. And to me, the world changed color that morning.

WORDS OF CAMERON

The city streets are lined with truth, and I walk through them. Sometimes, they *walk through* me. *Thoughts are like blood sometimes, when I think of women and sex and everything in between. I collect my thoughts as if they will stain me, murder me, and then resurrect me.*

I've stopped sometimes and felt the world turning, and I think there are hands that turn it.

I guess I think we turn the world ourselves, often making our hands and fingers dirty, and our wrists sore, from the work.

I feel like the world is a factory.

It's the factory of God's light and we just work here.

I clock onto the truth — that I'm small in terms of this world, but I'm awake.

Days and nights fight each other. The hours and minutes are the bruises, and as each day passes by, I know that I'm alone.

They say that no one really likes being alone, and I know that I am one of them. Having said that, I think there's something tough in it. Something stoic and strong and uncensored.

Another truth is that I am an animal.

A human animal.

With feral thoughts, and ragged furry hair that reaches for the sky.

God, how I want the skin of women! I want it on my lips and hands and fingers. How I want to taste her . . .

But then — then —

Beneath that.

That's not enough!

Yes, when that's done, I also want the everything that's her to fill up so much in front of me that it spills and shivers and gives, just like I'm prepared to do myself.

But for now, happiness throws stones.

It guards itself.

I wait.

CHAPTER 2

My oldest brother Steven Wolfe is what you'd call a hard bastard. He's successful. He's smart. He's determined.

The thing with Steve is that nothing will ever stop him. It's not only *in* him. It's on him, around him. You can smell it, sense it. His voice is hard and measured, and everything about him says, "You're not going to get in my way." When he talks to people, he's friendly enough, but the minute they try one on him, forget it. If someone tries to trample him, you'd put your house on it that he'll do twice the job on them. Steve never forgets.

Me on the other hand.

I'm not really like Steve in that way.

I kind of wander around a lot.

That's what I do.

Personally, I think it comes from not having many friends, or in fact, any friends at all, really.

There was a time when I really ached to be a part of a pack of friends. I wanted a bunch of guys I'd be prepared to bleed for. It never happened. When I was younger I had a mate called Greg and he was an okay guy. Actually, we did a lot together. Then we drifted apart. It happens to people all the time, I guess. No big deal. In a way, I'm part of the Wolfe pack, and that's enough. I know without doubt that I'd bleed for anyone in my family.

Anyplace.

Anytime.

My best mate is Rube.

Steve, on the other hand, has plenty of friends, but he wouldn't bleed for any of them, because he wouldn't trust them to bleed for him. In that way he's just as alone as me.

He's alone.

I'm alone.

There just happen to be people around him, that's all. (People meaning friends, of course.)

Anyway, the point of telling you about all this is that sometimes when I go out wandering at night I'll go up to Steve's apartment, which is about a kilometer from home. It's usually when I can't handle standing outside that girl's house, when the ache of it aches too much.

He's got a nice place, Steve, on the second floor, and he has a girl who lives there as well. Often she's not there because she works in a company that sends her on business trips and all that kind of thing. I always thought she was pretty nice, I s'pose, since she tolerated me when I went up to visit. Her name's Sal and she's got nice legs. That's a fact I can never escape.

"Hey Cam."

"Hey Steve."

That's what we say every time I go up and he's home.

It was no different the night after the beer ice block incident. I buzzed from downstairs. He called me up. We said what we always say.

The funny thing is that over time, we've become at least slightly better at talking to each other. The first time, we sat there and had black coffee and said nothing. We each just let our eyes swirl into the pools of coffee and let our voices be numb and silent. There was always a thought in me that maybe Steve held a sort of grudge against everyone in the Wolfe family because he seemed to be the only winner, in the world's eyes, anyway. It was like he might have good cause to be ashamed of us. I was never sure.

In recent times, since Steve decided to play one more year of football, we'd even gone to the local ground and kicked the ball around. (Or in truth, Steve had practice shots at goal and I returned them.) We'd go there and he'd turn the lights on, and even if it was extra cold and the earth was coated with frost and our lungs were trodden with winter air, we always stayed for quite a while. If it got too late, he even dropped me home.

He never asked how anyone was. Never. Steve was more specific.

"Is Mum still workin' herself into the ground?"

"Yeah."

"Dad got plenty of work?"

"Yeah."

"Sarah still goin' out, getting smashed, and comin' home reeking of club and smoke and cocktails?"

"Nah, she's off that now. Always workin' overtime shifts. She's okay."

"Rube still Mr. Excitement? One girl after another? One fight after another?"

"Nah, there's no one game enough to fight him anymore." Rube is without doubt one of the best fighters in this part of the city. He's proved it. Countless times. "You're right about the girls, though," I continued.

"Of course," he nodded, and that's when things always get a little edgy — when it comes to the question of me.

What could he possibly ask?

"Still got no mates, Cameron?"

"Still completely alone, Cameron?"

"Still wanderin' the streets?"

"Still got your hands at work under the sheets?"

No.

Every time, he avoids it, just like the night I'm talking about.

He asked, "And you?" A breath. "Survivin'?"

"Yeah," I nodded. "Always."

After that there was more silence, till I asked him who he was playing against this weekend.

As I told you earlier, Steve decided to have one last year of football. At the start of the season, he was begged to go back by his old team. They begged hard, and finally, he gave in, and they haven't lost a game yet. That was Steve.

That Monday night, I still had my words in my pocket, because I'd decided to carry them everywhere with me. They were still on that creased piece of paper, and often I would check that they were still there. For a moment, at Steve's table, I imagined myself telling him about it. I heard myself explaining how it made me feel like I was worth it, like I was just *okay*. But I said nothing. Absolutely nothing, even as I thought, *I guess that's what we all crave once in a while. Okayness. Alrightness.* It was a vision of looking inside a mirror and not wanting, not needing, because everything was there.

With the words in my hands, that was how I felt.

I nodded.

At the prospect of it.

"What?" Steve asked me.

"Nothing."

"Fair enough."

The phone rang.

Steve: "Hello."

The other end: "Yeah, it's me."

"Who the hell's *me*?"

It was Rube.

Steve knew it.

I knew it.

Even though I was a good distance from the phone, I could tell it was Rube, because he talks loud, especially on the phone.

"Is Cameron there?"

"Yeah."

"Are y's goin' up the oval?"

"Maybe," at which point Steve looked over and I nodded. "Yes, we are," he answered.

"I'll be up there in ten minutes."

"Right. Bye."

"Bye."

Secretly, I think I preferred it when it was only Steve and me who went. Rube was always brilliant, always starting something and mucking around, but with Steve and me, I enjoyed the quiet intensity of it. We might never have said a word — and I might have only kicked the ball back hard and straight, and let the dirt and smell of it thump onto my chest — but I loved the feeling of it, and the idea that I was part of something unspoken and true.

Not that I never had moments like that with Rube. I had plenty of great moments with Rube. I guess it's just that with Steve, you really have to earn things like that. You'd wait forever if you wanted one for free. Like I've said before, for other reasons, that's Steve.

On the way down to the ground floor a few minutes later, he said, "I'm sore as hell from yesterday's game. I got belted in the ribs about five times."

At Steve's games it was always the same. The other team always made sure he hit the ground especially hard. He always got up.

We stood on the street, waiting for Rube.

"Hey boys."

When he arrived, Rube was puffing gently from the run. His thick, curly, furry hair was too attractive for its own good, even though it was a lot shorter than it used to be. He was wearing only a jersey, sawn-off track pants, and gymmies. Smoke came from his mouth, from the cold.

We started walking, and Steve was his usual self. He wore the same pair of old jeans he always did at the oval and a flanno shirt. Athletic shoes. His eyes took aim, scanning the path, and his hair was short and wiry and tough-looking. He was tall and abrupt and exactly the kind of guy you wanted to be walking the streets with.

Especially in the city.

Especially in the dark.

Then there was me.

Maybe the best way to describe me that night was by looking again at my brothers. Both of them were in control. Rube, in a reckless, *no matter what happens, I'll be ready when it comes* kind of way. Steve, in a *there's nothing you can do that's going to hurt me* way.

My own face focused on many things, but never for too long, remaining eventually on my feet, as they traveled across the slightly slanted road. My hair was sticking up. It was curly and ruffled. I wore the same jersey as Rube (only mine was slightly more faded), old jeans, my spray jacket, and boots. I told myself that although I could never look the same as my brothers, I still had *something*.

I had the words in my pocket.

Maybe that was what I had.

That, and knowing that I've walked the city a thousand times on my own and that I could walk these streets with more feeling than anyone, as if I was walking through myself. I'm pretty sure that was what it was — more a feeling than a look.

At the oval Steve had shots at goal.

Rube had shots at goal.

I sent the ball back to them.

When Steve had a shot, the ball rose up high and kept climbing between the posts. It was clean, ranging, and when it came down, it rushed onto my chest with a complete, numbing force. Rube's ball, on the other hand, spun and spiraled, low and charging, but also went through the posts each time.

They kicked them from everywhere. In front. Far out. Even past the edges of the field.

"Hey Cam!" Rube yelled at one point. "Come out and have a shot!"

"Nah mate, I'll be right."

They made me, though. Twenty yards out, twenty yards to the left. I moved in with my heart shuddering. My feet stepped in, I kicked it, and the ball reached for the posts.

It curved.

Spun.

Then it collided with the right-hand post and slumped to the grass.

Silence.

Steve mentioned, "It was a good shot, Cameron," and the three of us stood there, in the wet, weeping grass.

It was quarter past eight then.

At eight-thirty, Rube left, and I'd had another seven shots.

At just past nine-thirty, Steve was still standing behind the posts, and I still hadn't got it through. Clumps of darkness grew heavier in the sky, and it was just Steve and me.

Each time my brother sent the ball back, I searched for a note of complaint in him, but it never came. When we were younger he might have called me useless. Hopeless. All he did that night, however, was kick the ball back and wait again.

When the ball finally fought its way up and fell through the posts, Steve caught it and stood there.

No smile.

No nod of the head, or any recognition.

Not yet.

Soon he walked with the ball under his arm, and when he was perhaps ten yards short of me, he gave me a certain look.

His eyes looked differently at me.

His expression was swollen.

Then.

I've never seen a person's face shatter like his did.

With pride.

HUNGER AND DESIRE ON A FRONT PORCH NIGHT

Tonight, I sit on the front porch as I write these words. The wind crawls up my sleeves and the pen wavers in my hand.

The city is cold and dark.

The streets are filled with numbness and the sky is sinking. Dark, dark sky.

Beside me, I look at the memory of twenty out and twenty left of the posts. I see a shattering face and the verge of something to become.

I tell me:

Let these words be footsteps, because I have a long way to travel. Let the words walk the dirty streets. Let them make their way across the crying grass. Let them stand and breathe and pant smoke in winter evenings. And when they're tired and have fallen down, let them buckle to their feet and arc around me, watchful.

I want these words to be actions.

Give them flesh and bones, I say to me, and eyes of hunger and desire, so they can write and fight me through the night.

CHAPTER 3

Faggot. Poofter. Wanker.

These are common words in my neighborhood when someone wants to *give you some*, tell you off, or just plain humiliate you. They'll also call you one of those things if you show some sign that you're in some way different from the regular, run-of-the-mill sort of guy who lives in this part of the city. You might also get it if you've annoyed someone in some inadvertent way and the person has nothing better to say. For all I know it's the same everywhere, but I can't really speak for anywhere else. The only place I know is this.

This city.

These streets.

Soon you'll know why I've mentioned it. . . .

On Thursday that week I decided I should go and get a haircut, which is always a pretty dangerous decision, especially when your hair sticks up as stubborn and chronic as mine. You just have to pray that it won't end in tragedy. You hope beyond all hope that the barber won't ignore all instructions and butcher your head to pieces. But it's a risk you have to take.

"Har-low, mate," the barber said when I entered the shop, deeper into the city. "Have a seat, I won't be long."

In the scungy waiting area there was quite a good range of magazines, though you could tell each one had been sitting there for the last few years, judging by the dates of issue. There was *Time*, *Rolling Stone*, some fishing thing, *Who Weekly*, some computer thing, *Black and White*, *Surfing Life*, and always a favorite, *Inside Sport*. Of course, the best thing about the *Inside Sport* magazine is not the sport, but the scantily clad woman who is planted on the cover. She is always firm and has desire in her eyes. Her swimsuit is nice and open, her legs long and tanned and elegant. She has breasts you can only imagine your hands touching and massaging. (Sorry, but it's true.) She has hips of extreme grace, a golden, flat stomach, and a neck you can only imagine yourself sucking on. Her lips are always full and hungry. The eyes say, "Take me."

You remind yourself that there are some pretty good articles in *Inside Sport*, but you know you're lying. Of course there *are* some good articles in the magazine, but that sure as hell isn't what makes you pick it up. It's always the woman. Always. Trust me on this one.

So, typically, I surveyed the area and made sure no one was looking when I picked up the *Inside Sport* magazine, opened it quickly, and pretended to scan the contents page for any good articles. I was (predictably) seeing which page the woman was on.

Seventy-six.

"Okay mate," the barber said.

"Me?"

"There's no one else waiting, is there?"

Yeah, but, I thought helplessly, *I haven't got to page seventy-six yet!*

It was futile.

The barber was ready, and if there's one man you don't keep waiting it's the guy about to cut your hair. He's all-powerful. In fact, he might as well be God. *That's* the kind of power he has. A few months at barber school and a man becomes the most important person in your life for ten or fifteen minutes. The golden rule: Don't give him a hard time or there'll be hell to pay.

Immediately, I threw the magazine back to the table, facedown so the barber wouldn't know right away what a pervert I am. He'd have to wait until later when he tidied the magazines.

Sitting in the chair (it sounds about as dangerous as the electric chair), I considered the whole woman on the cover situation.

"Short?" the barber asked me.

"Nah, not too short please, mate. I'm just tryin' to have it so it doesn't always stick up."

"Easier said than done, ay?"

"Yeah."

We exchanged a look of mutual friendliness and I felt much more at ease in the firing line of the scissors, the chair, and the barber.

He started cutting and like I said a minute ago, I reviewed the woman on the cover situation. My theory on this subject was and still is that I obviously desire the physicality of a woman. Yet, I honestly believe that *that* part of my desire for a girl is somewhere on the surface of my soul, whereas further and much deeper inside is the fiercer desire to please her, treat her right, and be immersed by the spirit of her.

I honestly believe that.

Honestly.

Still, I had to stop thinking about it and talk to the barber. That's another rule of the barbershop. If you talk to the man and get him to like you, maybe he won't screw it up. That's what you hope for anyway. It doesn't mean you'll have instant success, but it might help, so you try it. There are no guarantees in the world of barbershops. It's a gamble no matter which way you look at it. I had to start talking, and fast.

"So how's business?" I asked, as the barber cut his way through the thickness of my hair.

"Aah, you know, mate." He stopped, and smiled at me in the mirror. "Here 'n' there. Keepin' my head above water. That's the main thing."

We talked for quite a while after that, and the barber told me how long he'd been working in the city and how much people have changed. I agreed with everything he said, with a dangerous nod of my head or a quiet "Yeah, that sounds about right." He was a pretty nice guy, to tell you the truth. Very big. Quite hairy. A husky voice.

I asked if he lived upstairs from the shop and he said, "Yep, for the last twenty-five years." That was when I pitied him a little, because I imagined him never going anywhere or doing anything. Just cutting hair. Eating a dinner alone. Maybe microwave dinners (though his dinners couldn't be much worse than the ones Mrs. Wolfe cooked, God bless her).

"Do you mind me askin' if you ever got married?" I asked him.

"Of course I don't mind," he answered. "I had a wife but she died a few years ago. I go down the cemetery every weekend, but I don't put flowers down. I don't talk." He sighed a bit and he was very sincere. Truly. "I like to think I did enough of that when she was alive, you know?"

I nodded.

"It's no good once a person's dead. You gotta do it when you're together, still living."

He'd stopped cutting for a few moments now, so I could continue nodding without risk. I asked, "So what do you do when you're standin' there, at the grave?"

He smiled. "I just remember, that's all."

That's nice, I thought, but I didn't say it. I only smiled at the man behind me in the mirror. I had a vision of the large hairy man standing there at the cemetery, knowing that he gave everything he could. I also imagined myself there with him, on a dark gray day. Him in his white barber's coat. Me in the usual. Jeans. Flanno. Spray jacket.

"Okay?" he turned and said to me in the vision.

"Okay?" he said in the shop.

I woke back into reality and said, "Yeah, thanks a lot, it's good," even though I knew it would be standing up within forty-eight hours. I was happy, though, but not only for the haircut. The conversation too.

With my hair congregating around my feet, I paid twelve dollars and said, "Thanks a lot. It was nice talking to you."

"Same here," and the large hairy barber smiled and I felt guilty about the magazine. I could only hope he would understand the different layers of my soul. After all, he was a barber. Barbers are supposed to have the answers to running the country, along with taxi drivers and obnoxious radio commentators. I thanked him again and said good-bye.

Once outside, it was still mid-afternoon, so *Why not?* I thought. *I might as well head over to Glebe.*

Needless to say, I got there and stood outside the girl's house.

Stephanie.

It was as good a place as any to watch the sun collapse behind the city, and after a while I sat down against a wall and thought again about the barber.

The importance of it was that he and I were really doing similar things, only in reverse order. He was remembering. I was anticipating. (Hopeful, almost ludicrous anticipation, I admit.)

Once it was dark, I decided I'd better get home for dinner. It was leftover steak, I think, with vegetables boiled into oblivion.

I got up.

I slipped my hands into my pockets.

Then I looked, hoped, and walked, in that order.

Pathetic, I know, but it was my life, I guess. No point denying it.

It turned out to be later than I thought when I finally left, and I decided to get the bus back to my own neighborhood.

At the bus stop there was a handful of people waiting. There was a man with a briefcase, a chain-smoking woman, a guy who looked like a laborer or carpenter, and a couple who leaned on each other and kissed a while as they waited.

I couldn't help it.

I watched.

Not obviously, of course. Just a quick look here and there.

Damn.

I got caught.

"What are *you* lookin' at?" The guy spat his words at me. "Don't you have anything better to do?"

Nothing.

That was my reply.

Absolutely nothing.

"Well?"

Then the girl got stuck into me as well.

"Why don't y' go and stare at someone else, y' weirdo." She had blond hair, green eyes shrunken in under the streetlight, and a voice like a blunt knife. She beat me with it. "Y' wanker."

Typical.

You get called that name so many times around here, but this time it hurt. I guess it hurt because it was a girl. I don't know. In a way, it was kind of depressing that this was what we'd come to. We can't even wait for a bus in peace.

I know, I know. I should have barked back at them, nice and hard, but I didn't. I couldn't. Some Wolfe, ay. Some wild dog I turned out to be. All I did was steal one last look, to see if they were about to level some final fragments of abuse at me.

The guy was also blond. Not tall or short. He wore dark pants, boots, a black jacket, and a sneer.

Meanwhile, the briefcase man checked his watch. The chain smoker lit up another. The laborer shifted his weight from one foot to the other.

Nothing more was said, but when the bus came, everyone pushed on and I was last.

"Sorry."

When I got on and tried to pay, the driver told me that fares had just gone up and I didn't have enough money for a ticket.

I got off, smiled ruefully, and stood there.

The bus was pretty empty — the final insult.

As I started walking, I watched it pull away and shove itself along the street. Many thoughts staggered through me, including:

* How late I'd be for dinner.
* Whether or not anyone would ask where I'd been.

* Whether Dad wanted Rube and me to work with him on Saturday.
* If the girl named Stephanie would ever come out and see me (if she knew I was there at all).
* How much longer it would take for Rube to get rid of Octavia.
* If Steve clung to the memory of the look we'd exchanged on Monday night as often as I did.
* How my sister Sarah was doing lately. (We hadn't spoken for a while.)
* Whether or not Mrs. Wolfe was ever disappointed in me or knew that I had turned out such a lone figure.
* And how the barber was feeling above his shop.

I also realized as I walked, then began to run, that I didn't even have any bad feelings toward the couple who'd abused me. I knew I should have, but I didn't. Sometimes I think I need a bit more mongrel in me.

THE CEMETERY

There's a cemetery in my mind and I can see my own grave, on a blue-sky day with cotton clouds and angry sun.

People pass by that grave.

They speak and turn and wilt under the heat of the horizon and the scattered voice of death.

I can see fear churning in their hearts, as they build fences around what they say and believe, and what they tell the people around them. Only certain things make it out, onto the heated grass.

I write and hope — to stand in this vision long enough to see a shadow emerge over my grave.

No flowers.

No spoken words.

Only a person.

Remembering.

CHAPTER 4

"This dog's an absolute embarrassment," said Rube, and I knew that some things would never change. They would only slip away and return.

After the whole bus stop issue, I got home, and after dinner, Rube and I were taking Miffy, our neighbor's midget dog, for his usual walk. As always, we wore our hoods over our heads so no one could recognize us, because in the words of Rube, the sight of Miffy was an absolute shocker.

"When Keith gets another dog," he suggested, "we'll tell him to get a Rottweiler. Or a Doberman. Or at least something we can be seen in public with."

We stopped at an intersection.

Rube bent down to Miffy.

In an over-friendly voice, he said, "Aren't you an ugly little bastard, Miffy, ay? Aren't you? Yes you are. You are, you know," and the dog licked its lips and panted quite happily really. If only he had some idea that Rube was giving him a good mouthful. We crossed the street.

My feet dragged.

Rube's feet ambled.

Miffy pranced, and his chain jingled next to him, in time with his breathing.

Looking down at him, I realized he had the body of a rodent and the fur of something that can only be called stupendous. Like he'd gone a thousand rounds with a spin dryer. The problem was, we happened to love that dog, in spite of everything. Even that night, when we got home, I gave him the piece of steak Sarah couldn't finish at dinner. Unfortunately, it was a bit too tough for Miffy's pitiful little teeth and he nearly choked on it.

"Bloody hell, Cam," Rube laughed. "What are y' tryin' to do to the poor little bastard? He's gaggin' on it."

"I thought it'd be all right."

"All right, my arse. Look at him." He pointed. "Look at him!"

"What should I do, then?"

Rube had an idea. "Maybe you oughta get it out of his mouth, chew it up a bit, and *then* give it to him."

"*What?*" I looked at him. "You want me to put *that* in my mouth?"

"That's right."

"Maybe *you* should."

"No way."

So basically, we pretty much let Miffy choke a bit. In the end it didn't sound all that serious anyway.

"It'll build his character," Rube suggested. "Nothin' like a good choking to toughen a dog up." We both watched intently as Miffy eventually finished off the steak.

When he was done and we were sure he hadn't choked himself to death, we took him home.

"We should just throw him over the fence," Rube said, but we both knew we never would. There's a big difference between watching a dog half-choke and throwing him over the fence. Besides, our neighbor Keith would be pretty unthrilled with us. He could be a bit unpleasant, Keith, especially when it came to that dog of his. You wouldn't think such a hard man would own such a fluffy kind of dog, but I'm sure he probably just blamed it on his wife.

"It's the wife's dog," I can imagine him telling the boys at the pub. "I'm just lucky I've got those two shit-head boys next door to walk him — their old lady makes 'em do it." He could be a hard man, Keith, but okay nonetheless.

Speaking of hard men, it turned out that Dad did want our help on the upcoming Saturday. He pays us quite generously now, and he's always pretty happy. A while back, like I've said before, when he struggled to get work, he was pretty miserable, but these days it was good to work with him. Sometimes we went and got fish 'n' chips for lunch, and we played cards on top of Dad's small, dirty red cooler, but only as long as we all worked our guts out. Cliff Wolfe was a fan of working your guts out, and to be fair, so were Rube and I. We were also fans of fish 'n' chips and cards, even if it was usually the old man who won. Either he won or the game was taking too long and he cut it short. Some things can't be helped.

What I haven't mentioned is that Rube also had another job. He left school last year and got an apprenticeship with a builder, despite getting an abysmal result on his final exams.

I remember when he got them delivered.

He opened the envelope next to the slanted, slurred front gate of our house.

"How'd y' go?" I asked.

"Well Cam," he smiled, as if he was thoroughly pleased with himself. "I can sum it up in two words. The first word is *completely*. The second word is *shithouse*."

And yet, he got a job.

Straightaway.

Typical Rube.

He didn't need to work with the old man on Saturdays, but for some reason, he did. Maybe it was an act of respect. Dad asked, so Rube said yes. Maybe he didn't want anyone to think he was lazy. I don't know.

Either way, we were working with ol' Cliff that weekend, and he woke us nice and early. It was still dark.

We were waiting for Dad to get out of the bathroom (which he's always likely to leave in a pretty horrendous state, smell-wise), when Rube and I decided we'd get the cards out early.

As Rube dealt the cards at the kitchen table, I recalled what happened a few weeks earlier, when we had a game during breakfast. It wasn't a bad idea, but I managed to spill my cornflakes all over the deck because I was still half-asleep. Even this week there was still a dried corn-flake glued to a card I threw onto the out pile.

Rube picked it up.

Examined it.

"Huh."

Me: "I know."

"You're pitiful."

"I know." I could only agree.

The toilet flushed, the water ran, and Dad came out of the bathroom.

"We go?"

We nodded and gathered up the cards.

At the job, Rube and I dug hard and talked and laughed. I'll admit that Rube's always good for a bit of a laugh. He was telling me a story about an old girlfriend of his who always munched on his ears.

"In the end I had to buy her some bloody chewie. Otherwise I wouldn't have my ears anymore."

Octavia, I thought.

I wondered what story he would have about her in a few weeks' time, when it was dead and gone and thrown out. Her searching eyes, ruffled hair, and human legs and nice feet. I wondered what quirks of hers he'd have to talk about. Maybe she insisted on him touching her leg in a movie, or liked turning her fingers in his hand. I didn't know.

It was quick.

I spoke.

"Rube?"

"What?"

He stopped digging and looked at me.

"How much longer for you and Octavia?"

"A week. Maybe two."

There was nothing for me to do but continue digging then, and the day wandered past.

At lunch, the fish was greasy and great.

The chips were sprayed with salt and drenched in vinegar.

When we ate, Dad looked at the paper, Rube took the TV guide, and I started writing more words in my head. No more cards today.

That night, Mrs. Wolfe asked me how everything was going at school, and I returned to my earlier thoughts that week of whether or not she'd had cause lately to be disappointed in me. I told her everything was all right. For a moment, I debated whether I should tell someone about the words I'd started writing down, but I couldn't. In a way, I felt ashamed, even though my writing was the one thing that whispered okayness in my ear. I didn't speak about it, to anyone.

We cleaned up together, before dinner's leftovers had a chance to get stagnant, and she told me about the book she was reading called *My Brother Jack*. She said it was about two brothers and how one of them rose up but still regretted the way he lived and the way he was.

"You'll rise up one day," were her second-to-last words. "But don't be too hard on yourself," were her last.

When she left and I was standing alone in the

kitchen, I saw that Mrs. Wolfe was brilliant. Not smart-brilliant, or any particular kind of brilliant. Just brilliant, because she was herself and even the wrinkles around her aging eyes were the shaded color of kindness. That was what made her brilliant.

"Hey Cameron." My sister Sarah came to me later on. "You feel like goin' out to Steve's game tomorrow?"

"Okay," I replied. I had nothing better to do.

"Good."

On Sunday, Steve would be playing his usual game of football, but at a different ground from the local, out more Maroubra way. It was only Sarah and me who went to watch. We went up to his apartment and he drove us out there.

Something big happened at that game.

THE COLOR OF KINDNESS

I've thought once in a while about the color of kindness, and I realize that its shades and contrasts are not painted onto a person. They're worn in.

Have you ever stood in your kitchen and felt like falling to your knees?

I don't know.

There are very few things that I know for sure.

I know that when I eat fish and chips, my fingers and throat get greasy. The gorgeous ugliness of it slithers to my stomach, but it's all forgiven when my old man smiles at me, and I wouldn't trade that grease for anything.

When I look in the mirror, I see the color of awkwardness and uncertainty and longing.

If there was an expert amongst these pages, they'd say that I just want to belong somewhere.

But the truth is, I'm not sure I want to belong.

Not like everyone else.

That's what scares me.

CHAPTER 5

On the way up to Steve's, I wondered what the hell my sister Sarah was going to do with her life. She walked next to me, and most men who walked past us watched her. Many of them turned around once they'd gone past and took a second look at her body. It seemed that to them, that's all she was. The thought of it made me a little sick (not that I can talk), and I hoped she would never end up actually being that life.

"Friggin' perverts," she said.

Which gave me hope.

The thing is, I think we're all perverts. All men. All women. All disgruntled little bastards like me. It's funny to think of my father as a pervert, or my mother. But somewhere, in the crevices of their souls, I'm sure they've slipped sometimes, or even dived in. As for me, I feel like I live in there at times. Maybe we all do. Maybe if there's any beauty in my life, it's the climbing out.

Like always, Steve was pretty quick to come down once we arrived at his apartment. He was on the balcony, raised his head, and next thing, he was with us, keys in hand. Steve's never been late for a single thing in his life.

He chucked his gear in the boot and we left.

We took Cleveland Street, which is always a bit choked, even on Sundays, and the radio was quiet as Steve drove. People cut him off and buses pulled out in front of him, but nothing moved him. He never blew the horn or yelled. To Steve, such things were irrelevant.

It was good for me to be at the ground at Maroubra that day. It was good to watch Steve and his ways. Just like the words I'd been writing made me feel and see things differently, it also gave me a greater curiosity. I wanted to see the way people moved and spoke and the reactions they were given. Steve was a good person to take notice of.

There was a rope fenced around the field and from where Sarah and I stood, I could see Steve approach the other members of his team. Every one of them looked his way and said something very briefly. Only one or two spoke with him longer. He stood at the edge of them and I could tell he wasn't close with them. With any of them. Yet, they liked him. They respected him. If he wanted it, he could have laughed with them and been the one that everyone listened to.

But it meant nothing there.

Not to Steve.

In the game, though, when he said he wanted the ball, he would get it. When something big was needed, Steve would do it. In the easy games the others would shine, but when things were hard, Steve was there, even if it was on his own.

They got ready and there was a lot of shouting and carrying on from the dressing sheds and both teams ran out. Steve was the captain of his team, and like I thought he would, he spoke a lot more on the field. Never yelling. I could just always see him mentioning something to another player or telling him what he had to do. Each one listened.

It was three o'clock when the game started.

The crowd was pretty big, with most of them drinking beer or eating meat pies or both. Many of them shouted things out, often losing food or spit from their mouths.

As was often the case, there was a brawl in the first few minutes, which Steve stayed right out of. There was a guy who leaped up and hit him around the throat, and everyone ran in. Punches collided with skin, and fists were cut up on teeth.

Steve only got up and walked away.

He crouched down.

He spat.

Then he got up, took the penalty, and ran twice as hard.

They called his name incessantly.

"Wolfe. Watch Wolfe."

They would send a few guys to take care of him every time, making sure to hurt him.

Each time Steve returned to his feet and kept going.

It made Sarah and me smile, as Steve sliced through them a few times and set up other people to score. By halftime, his team was well in front. It was late in the second half when the importance of the day occurred.

The sky was a heavy gray and it was about to rain.

People were huddling now, in the cold.

A slippery wind was sliding across the air.

Kids kicked a ball and chased it behind us, with tomato sauce glued to the corners of their mouths, and scabs on their knees.

Steve was lining up a shot at goal from as far out on the field as you could get, right where the opposition supporters stood.

They mocked him.

Swore at him.

Told him he was useless.

As he moved in to kick the goal, a can of beer was thrown at his head. Beer flew out of it and the can slapped my brother on the side of his face.

He stopped.

Mid-step.

He froze.

In no rush, he bent down, picked up the can, and studied it. He turned to the group where it came from, who were quiet almost immediately, and without looking at them again, he gently placed the can on the ground, out of the way, and lined the kick up again.

The crowd watched as Steve moved in and kicked the ball.

It rose up and soared through the posts, and Steve turned to face the people at his side. He stared at them for a few seconds, then returned to the game, leaving the beer can, half-full, half-empty, and half-hearted as it lay abandoned next to the sideline.

As I watched the end of the incident, I couldn't help but notice that Steve's stare wasn't angry in any way. If anything, it was amused. He could have done anything he wanted. He could have said anything. He could have spat at them or hurled the can right back at them.

But that was something *they* could have done just as easily.

There was no way they could have walked in again, taken the shot, put it straight through the middle, and then stared as if to say, "Well? Have you got anything else for me?"

That was how he beat them.

That was how he won.

He did the only thing they weren't capable of themselves.

When I realized that, I couldn't help but laugh, which made Sarah do the same, and we were the only people laughing in the whole ground. For everyone else, the game went on.

The game went on, the rain held off, and Steve's team won by a country mile.

When it was over, he said his good-byes and that maybe he'd go for a drink with the other players, though everyone knew he wouldn't. We were going home.

There was more silence in the car than anything else, and I don't know about Steve or Sarah, but I couldn't stop thinking about the thrown beer can. I kept seeing the ball soar through the posts and the content stare on Steve's face. Even when Sarah reached for the dashboard and sang with the radio, it was the memory of that stare that spoke loudest through my mind. His face was the same now as he drove, and in some strange way, I think Steve was also thinking about it. I was even expecting him to smile, but he never did.

Instead, we were all pretty quiet, until Steve dropped us home.

"Thanks," Sarah said.

"No worries. Thanks for coming."

As I was about to get out of the car myself, Steve stopped me.

He stopped me with, "Cam?"

"Yeah?"

He looked into the mirror and I could see his eyes as he talked to me.

"Just hang on a minute."

This had never happened before, so I was unsure of what to expect. Would he tell me what the stare had meant, or how it felt to make those people look so stupid? Would he give me a guide on how to be a winner?

Of course not.

Or, at least, not like that.

His eyes were soft and honest as he spoke and it was strange for me to be feeling this way about Steven Wolfe.

He said, "When I was your age, there were these four other blokes who beat me up. They took me round the back of a building and beat me up for some reason I'll never know." He stopped a moment and he wasn't emotional in any way. He wasn't telling me some sob story about how other kids hated him and this was why he'd turned out the way he did. He was just telling me something. "When I was lyin' there, all crumpled up, I vowed that each one of them was going to get his share of what they all did to me. I went over it in my mind and thought about what I wanted to do. Every morning, every night; and when I was ready, I went to them, one by one, and beat the absolute crap out of them. By the time I'd got to three of them, the last one tried to make peace." The eyes sharpened a little, remembering. "I bashed him too, even better than the other three."

He stopped.

He stopped talking and I waited for more, until I realized that was it, and I nodded to my brother.

At the eyes in the mirror.

For a moment, I wondered, *Why is he telling me this?*

He didn't look proud or happy. Maybe just that same expression of contentment as before. Or maybe he was just glad he'd told somebody, because it sure didn't seem like he'd tell a whole load of people what he'd just told me. I couldn't be sure. As usual.

Finally, when I got out of the car, I wondered if anyone knew my brother. I wondered if Sal knew him.

I just knew that Steve was talking to me that day and it felt all right.

No, it felt good.

When he left, I waved to him but he was already halfway up the street. In the house, Octavia was sitting in our kitchen.

Rube wasn't.

They were as good as over.

She looked beautiful.

ALLEY BOYS

There must be thousands of alleys in this city.

Dark alleys everywhere.

In many of them, people have fought, cutting each other down and placing punches and kicks to bodies that have already fallen. . . .

But what about the alleys in a person?

In a boy?

In a human?

How many times have I beaten myself down? I wonder. How many times have I lain there, in one of those alleys, between buildings that shiver and houses who slouch, their hands fixed in their pockets, doing nothing?

Tonight, I run through those alleys.

Past wounded cars.

Down grimly lit stairways.

Till I'm there.

I feel it.

Know it.

I see myself, lying there, at the bottom of the deepest, darkest alley. A slight breeze wades across the floor of it. It whispers to the rubbish, then picks it all up and moves it along.

Get up, I tell me.

Get up.

Slowly, I do. I make myself realize that it's okay to be Cameron Wolfe, and desire reaches through me again.

I realize that there's no one else in these alleyways, to beat me down or help me up.

There's only me.

CHAPTER 6

Three words:

God damn Miffy.

I wasn't really in the mood for walking him, especially when I had to wait around quite a while for Rube.

At first, I sat in the kitchen with Octavia.

She didn't look too impressed with things, considering she and Rube were supposed to be going out that afternoon. It must have slipped Rube's mind. At least, that was what I told her. Me, though? I knew. Rube was away from her on purpose. I'd seen him do this before.

Come in late.

Argue.

Tell them he doesn't need this garbage.

It was a pretty good technique for Rube. He didn't mind being the villain.

There were leftovers on offer, but Octavia didn't stay for them. I walked out with her and we remained on the front porch a while, talking, and even managing to laugh now and then. Next door, I think Miffy could hear us and was expecting his walk. He sounded agitated at first, then started going off his nut.

"I'll just go get him," I said, and quickly went next door to pick up the little bastard.

When we got back, I noticed Octavia was shivering.

As she stroked the dog, I took off my jacket and offered it to her. She accepted it, and soon after she said, "It's warm, Cam." She looked just past me. "It's the warmest I've felt for a while. . . ."

In a way, I hoped she wasn't just talking about the jacket, but it was better not to think that way. When you think like that, you end up standing outside people's houses, waiting for something that never comes.

She gave it back when we walked down to the gate and I opened it for her.

The moon was stuck to the sky and Octavia said, "There's no point coming back really, is there?"

"Why?" I replied.

"Don't why me, Cameron." She looked away and glanced back. "Don't worry about it." Even when she leaned onto the gate with her hands and her voice became unsteady, Octavia looked great, and I don't mean that in a dirty kind of way. I just mean that I liked her. I felt sorry for her, and for what Rube was doing to her. Her eyes smiled at me, for just a moment. One of those hurt smiles a person gives you to let you know they're okay, even though they're far from it.

After that, she left.

When she was just past the gate, I asked, "Octavia?"

She turned around.

"Y' gonna come back?"

"Maybe," she smiled. "One day."

She walked along our street and it was cold and brutal and beautiful. For a few seconds, I hated my brother Rube for what he was doing to her.

Also, watching her walk slowly up our street, I remembered what Rube had said about Octavia and him following me one day when I walked over to Glebe and stood outside Stephanie's house. I could clearly see the image of them looking at me. Looking at me looking. She must have thought I was pathetic. A bit of a lonely bastard, as Rube put it. Maybe now, as she walked up the street, she knew how I felt.

Somehow, though, I understood that it was thoughts of Rube that filled her. Not thoughts of me. Maybe she was thinking of his hands on her, the thrill of it. Maybe it was laughter she remembered, or the words of a conversation. I would never know. I sat down again and Miffy jumped on my lap. As I watched Octavia, Miffy watched me, and when the girl had disappeared completely, the dog was giving me a certain look.

"What?" I asked him, but of course, he didn't answer. The dog looked like he'd genuinely caught me out, but soon enough, he returned to his usual disgusting self, yawning in my face. "Your breath smells like a cesspool," I said, and we waited for Rube.

He came in late for dinner and the old man gave him a good serve for it, as well as for leaving Octavia out to dry. I made sure to keep out of it. All I did was hang around with Miffy until Rube came out.

It was absolutely bloody freezing now and I wasn't in the mood.

The air was cold enough for us to wear our hoods indefinitely, and to watch the smoke pour from our mouths when we breathed.

Smoke came from Miffy's mouth too, especially when he had a bit of a coughing fit. That was when we quickened the pace for home.

Later, we watched TV.

I looked over at my brother. He could sense it.

"What?" he said.

I was on the couch and Rube was in the worn-through chair.

"Is Octavia gone?"

He looked.

First away. Then back at me.

Yes.

That was the answer and Rube knew he didn't have to say it.

"There a new one?"

Again, he didn't have to answer.

"What's her name?"

He waited a while, then said it. "Julia . . . but relax, Cam — I haven't done anything yet."

I nodded.

I nodded and swallowed and I wished hard that it didn't have to be this way, for Octavia. I couldn't have cared less about Rube at this point. I thought only of the poor girl, and I thought of a time a few years ago when Sarah got dumped by this one particular guy. I remembered how shattered she was, especially when she found out there was another girl.

Rube and I hated the guy who did that.

We wanted to kill him.

Rube especially.

Now that guy was Rube.

For a moment, I nearly mentioned it, but all I did was sit there stupidly and look at Rube's face, side-on. There was no remorse in him. Almost no trace of thought about what he was doing.

Julia.

I could only wonder what she'd be like.

The only problem for Rube was that Octavia wanted to find things out for sure, so she came over again during the week.

They went out to the yard, and after a few minutes, she came back through the house on her own. When she saw me, she said, "I'll see you, Cameron," and again, she gave me that courageous smile — the one I saw the other night. Only this time, her green eyes were soaked more definitely, the water rising higher, only just managing not to fall out. She gathered herself and we stood in the hall and she said one last time, "I'll see you around."

"No you won't," and I smiled back at her. We both knew that people didn't see Cameron Wolfe — at least not unless they walked through the streets of the city a lot.

This time, when she left, she told me not to come out, but secretly, I stood on the front porch and watched her disappear.

"I'm sorry," I whispered.

I figured that was the last time I'd ever see Rube's girl Octavia.

I was wrong.

WALK ON

At times I've wondered harder than usual about the girl in Glebe, where I constantly wait in the guttered city street. I wonder if she ever sees me.

I wonder if she sees me, knows me, or even likes the fact that I stand outside her house, or sit, waiting in vain. I wonder when I walk away if she might be pulling the curtain just slightly aside to watch me leaving.

God, I imagine it so hard.

So hard that it claws me.

Yet, I never turn around.

I just keep walking on because that's what I do. I never speak or shout or show anyone I'm there. I never allow my hand to form a fist and knock on the wood of her frightening front door.

Me?

I just walk on and never turn around.

And do you know why?

It's because I'm afraid she won't be there, watching for me.

When I walk on without looking, at least there's still some hope.

CHAPTER 7

Julia was, of course, an absolute scrubber. There's not a whole lot more I can say about her. A scrubber (in case you don't know) is a girl who might be described as kind of slutty or festy, yet still without being a complete prostitute or anything like that. She chews gum a lot. She might drink excessively and smoke for show. She'll call you a faggot, poofter, or wanker with a lovely smirk on her face. She'll wear tight-arse jeans and good cleavage and she won't care too much if her headlights are on. Jewelry: moderate to heavy, maybe with a nose ring or eyebrow ring for rebellious originality. Then there's the makeup. At times it's *bucketed* on, especially if there's a bit of acne involved on her face, although more often than not, a scrubber isn't too bad-looking at all. She just has a tendency to make herself ugly, by what she says and what she does.

And Julia?

What can I say?

She was beautiful. She was blond.

And she was a scrubber and a half.

"So this is Cameron," she said when she first saw me. She was chewing that low-sugar gum that dentists highly recommend.

"Hey," I said, and Rube winked at me. I knew what the wink meant. Something like, *Not bad, huh?* or, *You wouldn't knock her back, would y'?* or even simply, *Pretty good handfuls, ay?* The bastard.

As you can imagine, I got out of there pretty quick smart, because that girl annoyed the crap out of me very bloody fast. My only hope was that Rube wouldn't take her to see me staring at that Stephanie girl's house. Octavia, I could handle, because she at least had a bit of class about her. A bit of niceness. But not this one. She'd most likely call me a bit of a lonely bastard as well. Or maybe she'd say something like, "Get a life," or repeat something Rube had previously said, hoping his charisma would rub off on her. No way. I wouldn't give her a chance. Not this one (even though *Christ*, I thought at one stage, *take a look at her.* She had an *Inside Sport* body if ever I'd seen one).

But no.

I'd made up my mind.

Rather than hang around them like a bad smell, I decided to go to the movies and hang around like a bad smell there instead.

On a cold, windy Saturday, when Dad didn't need me, I saw three movies on the one day, before going over to Glebe a while, and then home. In the night, I went down to our basement and wrote for a while, feeling everything that was me shift and turn inside.

I was in bed for quite a while when Rube came in and slumped down on his own bed across from me. When I got up to turn off the light, he said, "Well Cam?"

"Well what?"

"What are your thoughts?"

"On what?"

"On Julia."

"Well," I began, but I didn't want to congratulate him on her, and I didn't want to interfere either. The injured darkness of the room swayed and stumbled and I said, "She's okay, I guess."

"Okay!?" He raised his voice excitedly. "She's pretty bloody brilliant if you ask me."

"But I didn't ask you, did I?" I stated. "You asked *me* and I told you the answer."

"Smart-arse."

I laughed.

"Are you tryin' to start somethin'?"

"Of course not."

"Well you better bloody not . . ."

Rube's voice trailed off and he fell asleep, letting the night throb around me, alone.

I lay there, not sleeping for hours — thinking about the cover model on the magazine at the barber, then an exotic supermodel I saw on an ad at the movies. In my mind, I was with them. In them. Alone. For a while I even thought of Julia, but that was too much. I mean, there's perversion and there's perversion. Even for me.

In the morning, the previous night's conversation between Rube and me was forgotten. He ate slabs of bacon in the kitchen before going out again, while I stayed in because I had work due in at school next day.

Of course, I knew Rube was with Julia, and the pattern continued.

About two weeks went by, and everything was normal. Normal routine.

Dad was working hard, plumbing.

Mrs. Wolfe was the same, cleaning people's houses and doing a few cleaning shifts at the hospital.

Sarah did some overtime.

Steve kept winning at football, working in his office job, and living in his apartment with Sal.

Rube went out with Julia.

And I still wrote my words, sometimes in our bedroom, sometimes in the basement. I also went over to Glebe quite a few times, more out of habit now than anything else.

Soon, though, a day came that changed everything.

It . . . I don't know how to explain it.

It all seemed so normal, but slightly off-center at the same time.

I walked the city streets, as usual.

I made my way over to the suburb of Glebe, without even thinking about where I was walking.

I went there, sat there, stood there, waited there, even begged there for something, anything to happen.

It was a Thursday, and in the dying moments of day, when the last rays of light stood up to be killed in the sky, I could feel someone behind me, just to the side. I could feel a presence, a shadow, standing just obscured behind a tree.

I turned around.

I looked.

"Rube?" I asked. "That you, Rube?"

But it wasn't Rube.

I was sitting down against the small brick fence when I saw the person step into the last remnants of light, and walk slowly toward me. It was Octavia.

It was Octavia and she walked over and sat next to me.

"Hi Cameron," she said.

"Hi Octavia." I was shocked.

Silence bent down then, just for a moment, and whispered to each of us.

My heart threw itself to my throat.

Then, down.

Down.

She looked into the window I'd been staring at. Stephanie's window.

"Nothing?" she asked, and I knew what she meant.

"No, not tonight," I answered.

"Any night?"

I couldn't help it.

I promise you, I couldn't. . . .

A huge stupid tear rose up and fell out of my eye. It stammered down my face to my mouth and I could taste it. I could taste the saltiness of it, on my lips.

"Cameron?"

I looked at her.

"You okay?" she asked.

And all I did from there was tell her the truth.

I said, "She's not comin' out tonight, or any other night, and there's nothing I can do about it." I was even moved to quote Rube. "Y' feel what y' feel, and that girl doesn't feel a thing for me. That's all there is to it. . . ." I looked away, at the dying sky, attempting to pull myself together.

I began wondering exactly why I'd chosen this Glebe girl as the one I wanted to please, to drown in.

"Cam?" asked Octavia.

"Cam?"

She kept wanting me to look at her, but I still wasn't ready. Instead, I stood up and stared into the house. The lights went on. The curtains were drawn, and the girl, as always, was nowhere to be seen.

Yet, there was a girl next to me, who'd stood up now as well, and we were both beside the brick fence. She looked at me and made me look back. She asked one more time.

"Cam?"

Finally, I answered, quietly, timidly. "Yeah?"

And Octavia's face cried out to me in the silent city night as she asked, "Would you come and stand outside my house instead?"

THE CHARCOAL SKY

Sometimes you go to the wrong place, but the right way comes and finds you. It might make you trip over it or speak to it. Or it might come to you when a day is stripped apart by night and ask you to take its hand and forget this wrong place, this illusion where you stand.

I think of the mess in my mind and the girl who walked through it to stand before me and let her voice come close.

I remember brick walls.

There are moments when you can only stand and stare, watching the world forget you as you remove yourself from it — when you overcome it and cease to exist as the person you were.

It calls your name, but you're gone.

You hear nothing. See nothing.

You've gone somewhere else. You've gone somewhere to find a different definition of yourself, and it's a place where nothing else can touch you. Nothing else can swing on your thoughts. It's only yourself, flat against the charcoal sky, for one moment.

Then flat on the earth again, where the world doesn't recognize you anymore. Your name is what it always was. You look and sound like you always did, yet you're not the same, and when a city wind begins to call out, its voice doesn't only hit the edges.

It connects.

It blows into you, rather than in spite of you.

Sometimes you feel like it's calling out for you.

CHAPTER 8

She broke into me.

It was that simple.

Her words reached into me, grabbed my spirit by the heart, and reefed it from my body.

It was the words and the voice, and Octavia and me. And my spirit, on the silent, shadow-stricken street. I could only watch her, as slowly, she collected my hand and placed it gently in hers.

I took all of her in.

It was cold and her smoky breath flowed from her mouth. She smiled and her hair kept falling over her face, so beautiful and true. She suddenly had the most human eyes I'd ever seen, and the slight movements of her mouth whispered without the words. I could feel her pulse in my hand, beating gently onto my skin. Her shoulders were slight, and she stood with me on the city street that was slowly flooding with darkness. Her hand was holding on to me. She was waiting.

Silent howls howled through me.

The streetlights flickered on.

I remained still. Completely still, looking at her. Looking at the truth of her, standing before me.

I wanted to pour myself out and let my words spill onto the footpath, but I said nothing. This girl had just asked me the most brilliant question in the world and I was completely speechless.

"Yes," I wanted to say. I wanted to shout it and pick her up and hold her and say, "Yes. Yes. I'll come and stand outside your house anytime," but I didn't say anything. My voice found its way into my mouth but it never made it out. It always stumbled somewhere, then became lost, or was swallowed again.

The moment was cut open. It fell in pieces all around me, and I had no idea what would happen next, whether it would come from Octavia or me. I wanted to crouch down and pick up every piece of it and put it in my pockets. In a way, somewhere close to me, I could hear the voice of my spirit, telling me what to say, or what to do, but I couldn't understand it. The silence around me was too strong. It overwhelmed me, until I noticed her fingers wrapping tighter in mine for just a moment.

Then gone.

Slowly, she let her hand come loose, and it was over.

My hand fell back and gently slapped my side from the impact of her letting go.

She looked into me and then away.

Was she hurt? Did she expect me to speak? Did she want me to hold her hand again? Did she want me to pull her into me?

Questions lunged at me, but still I didn't get close enough to doing anything. I simply stood there like a hapless, hopeless fool, waiting for something to change.

In the end it was Octavia's voice that stamped out the burning silence of the night.

A quiet, courageous voice.

She said, "Just . . ." She hesitated. "Just think about it, Cam," and after a moment of thought and a last glance into me, she turned and walked away.

I watched.

Her legs.

Her feet, walking.

Her hair, echoing down her back in the dark.

I also remembered her voice, and the question, and the feeling I felt rising up through me. It shouted in me and warmed me and chilled me and threw itself down inside me. Why didn't I say anything?

Why didn't you say anything? I abused myself.

I could hear her footsteps now.

They lifted and scratched just slightly as she walked away in the direction of the train station.

"Cameron."

A voice called to me.

"Cameron!"

I remember clearly that my hands were in my pockets, and when I looked over to my right, I swear I could make out the figure of my spirit, also standing against the brick fence, also with its hands in its pockets. It looked at me. It stared. It said more words.

"What the hell are you doing?" it asked me.

"What?"

"What do you mean *what*? Aren't you going after her?"

"I can't." I looked down, at my old shoes and the jaded bottom sleeves of my jeans. I just looked and spoke. "It's too late now anyway."

My spirit came closer. "Bloody hell, boy!" The words were brutal. They made me look up and stare, to find the face connected to the voice. "You stand and wait outside some girl's place who couldn't care less, and when something real arrives, you fall apart! What kind of person *are* you?"

It shut up then.

The voice ended abruptly.

What it wanted to say was said, and we resumed standing against the fence, with our hands in our pockets, and silence feeding on our mouths.

A minute passed, and another. Time scratched itself through my thoughts, like the sound of Octavia's feet.

Finally, I moved.

It was after about fifteen minutes.

I took a final stare at the house, knowing it was probably the last time I would ever see it, and I began walking toward Redfern Station, under the electric wires, and through the cold of the street. The leaded windows of houses glimmered when the streetlights rushed at them, and I could hear my feet lifting and then clawing down onto the road as I started running. Behind me somewhere, I could hear the footsteps and breathing of my spirit. I wanted to beat it to the station. I had to.

I ran.

I let the cold air splash into my lungs as I thought the name *Octavia*, over and over. I ran till my arms ached as hard as my legs and my head throbbed with the blood rushing into it.

"Octavia," I said.

To myself.

I kept running.

Past the university.

Past the abandoned shops.

Past a few guys who looked like they might try to rob me.

"Come on," I told myself when I thought I was slowing down, and I looked hard into the distance to see the legs and footsteps of Octavia.

When I made it to the station there were hordes of people pouring through the gates and I managed to slip through between a guy with a suitcase and a woman holding flowers. I went to the Illawarra line and sprinted down the escalator, past all the suits, the briefcases, and the different day-old perfumes and hair spray.

I made it to the bottom, nearly tripping.

Look at this bloody crowd! I thought, but slowly I edged my way along the platform. When the train arrived all the people crammed and crushed and shook their heads when I got in their way. There was even a pretty bad smell like someone's underarm sweat. It licked me in the face, but still I looked and rushed through the crowd.

"Get out of the way," someone snarled, and I was left with no other choice.

I got on the train.

I got on and stood in the packed middle compartment, right next to a guy with a mustache who was obviously the owner of the putrid underarm sweat. We both held on to the greasy metal pole until both the train and I got moving.

"Excuse me," I said. "Sorry," and I made my way through the carriage downstairs. I figured I'd do all the lower levels of the train first and come back on the upper levels. This was the only train going to Hurstville. She had to be on it.

She wasn't in the carriage I got in on, or the next.

I opened the doors between each carriage and went through, with the cold tunnel air coughing around me before I entered the next carriage. Once I nearly slammed the door in my spirit's face as it closed in on me.

"There!"

I heard its voice point her out to me in the crowd of humans locked up in the suburban train.

I saw her just after the train rattled and burst out of the tunnel and into the paler darkness of the night. She was standing, just like I'd been standing a few carriages back, but facing the other way. From the lower level of the train, I could see her legs.

Footstep.

Footstep.

I edged my way closer and made it to the stairs and started climbing them.

Soon I could see all of her.

She stood and looked out the smeared window of the train. I wondered what thoughts she was thinking.

I was close, and I could see her neck and the movement of her breathing. I saw her fingers holding the pole as the train stuttered and the lights flooded and blinked.

Octavia, I said inside.

My spirit shoved me forward.

"Go on," it said, but it didn't dare me, order me, or demand anything anymore. It was just telling me what was right, and what I needed to do.

"All right," I whispered.

I walked closer and stood behind her.

Her flannel shirt.

The skin of her neck.

The ruffled streams of hair landing on her back.

Her shoulder . . .

I reached out and touched her.

She turned around and I looked into her and a feeling lurched in me. God, she looked beautiful. I heard my voice. It said, "I'll stand outside your house, Octavia." I even smiled. "I'll come and stand there tomorrow."

That was when she closed her eyes for a moment and smiled back.

She smiled and said, "That'd be good, Cam." The voice was quiet.

I moved closer and grabbed hold of her shirt at her stomach and held on to her, relieved.

At the next stop, I told her I'd better get out.

"See you tomorrow?" she asked.

I nodded.

The train doors opened and I got out. When they closed I had no idea what station I was at, but as the train pulled and dragged itself along, I walked with it, still looking into her through the window.

When the train was gone I stood there, eventually realizing how cold it was on the platform.

Something struck me.

My spirit.

It was gone.

I searched everywhere for it, until I realized.

It didn't get off the train with me. It was still in the carriage, with Octavia.

TRACKS

A crowded train drags itself through me.

I own it now. I live inside the carriages, letting them carry me home.

If I stay inside long enough, the train slowly empties, until it's just her and me standing inside it, under the flickering fluorescent lights and above the metallic shifting of the wheels, rolling over the tracks.

The train breathes.

It speaks.

Its voice is made up of memory and the words of now.

Sparks flick and fall from above.

We stand.

I hold her by the shirt.

My spirit's at my shoulder, whispering.

Even when I get out of the train, I find myself running alongside it, bargaining with fatigue, and making sure I'll always remember it.

Finally, it goes too fast. It shivers in front of my eyes and fades, and I bend down, amongst the words. I allow my hands to fall to my knees. I suck the air hard. I can't breathe it quick enough, it tastes that good.

CHAPTER 9

"Oi," Rube said to me when I made it in that night. "What the hell happened to you? You're a bit late, aren't y'?"

"I know," I nodded.

"There's soup in the pot," Mrs. Wolfe cut in.

I lifted the lid off it, which is usually the worst thing you can ever do. It clears the kitchen, though, which was pretty useful that night, considering. I wasn't really in the mood to be answering questions, especially from Rube. What was I going to tell him? "Ah, you know, mate. I was just out with your old girlfriend. You don't mind, do y'?" No way.

The soup took a few minutes and I sat and ate it alone.

As I ate, I started coming to terms with what had happened. I mean, it's not every day something like *that* happens to you, and when it does, you can't help but struggle to believe it.

Her voice kept arriving in me.

"Cameron?"

"Cameron?"

After hearing it a few times, I turned around to find Sarah talking to me as well.

"You okay?" she asked.

I smiled at her. "Of course," and we washed up.

Later, Rube and I went over and collected Miffy, walking him till he started wheezing again.

"He sounds bloody terrible. Maybe he's got the flu or somethin'," Rube suggested. "Or the clap."

"What's the clap?"

"I'm not sure. I think it's some kind of sex disease."

"Well I don't think he's got that."

When we took him back over to Keith he said Miffy got fur balls a lot, which made sense, since that dog seemed to be made up of ninety percent fur; a couple percent flesh; a few percent bones; and one or two percent barking, whingeing, and carrying on. Mostly fur, though. Worse than a cat.

We gave him a last pat and left.

On our front porch I asked Rube how the Julia girl was going.

"Scrubber," I imagined him announcing, but knew he wouldn't.

"Ah, not bad, y' know," he replied. "She's not the best but she's not the worst either. No complaints really." It didn't take long for a girl to go from brilliant to run-of-the-mill with Rube.

"Fair enough."

For a moment, I almost asked how Octavia rated, but I wasn't interested in her the way Rube was, so there was no point. It wasn't important. For me, it was the way that thoughts of her could keep finding me that was important. I just couldn't stop thinking about her, as I convinced myself about everything that had happened.

Her appearance on the street in Glebe.

Her question.

The train.

All of it.

We sat there a while on the worn-out couch Dad put out there a few summers ago and watched the traffic amble by.

"What are youse starin' at?" a scrubberish sort of girl snapped at us as she idled past on the footpath.

"Nothin'," Rube answered, and we could only laugh a while as she swore at us for no apparent reason and continued walking.

My thoughts turned inward.

In each passing moment, Octavia found a way into me. Even when Rube started talking again, I was back on the train, pushing my way through the humans, the sweat, and the suits.

"Are we workin' with Dad this Saturday?" Rube stamped out my thoughts.

"I'm pretty sure we are," I said, and Rube got up and went inside. I stayed on the porch a fair while longer. I thought about the next night, and standing outside Octavia's house.

I didn't sleep that night.

The sheets stuck to me and I turned and got tangled in them. At one point, I even got up and just sat in the kitchen. It was past two in the morning then, and when Mrs. Wolfe got up to go to the toilet, she came to see who was there.

"Hey," I whispered.

"What are you doing?" she asked.

"I couldn't sleep."

"Well, go back to bed soon, all right?"

I sat there a while longer, with the talkback radio show talking and arguing with itself at the kitchen table. Octavia filled me that whole night. It made me wonder if she was sitting in her own kitchen, thinking of me.

Maybe.

Maybe not.

Either way, I was going there the next day, and the hours were disappearing slower than I thought possible.

I returned to bed and waited. When the sun came up, I got up with it, and gradually, the day passed me by. School was the usual concoction of jokes, complete bastards, shoves, and a laugh here and there.

For a few anxious seconds in the afternoon, I wasn't sure what Octavia's last name was and feared I might not be able to look her up in the phone book. I was relieved when I remembered. It was Ash. Octavia Ash. When I got the address, I looked the street up on the map and found it to be about a ten-minute walk from the station, as long as I didn't get lost.

Maybe for comfort, I jumped the fence and gave Miffy a pat for a while. In a way, I was nervous. Nervous as hell. I thought of everything that might go wrong. Train derailment. Not being able to find the right house. Standing outside the *wrong* house. I covered all of it in my mind as I patted the ball of fluff that had rolled over and somehow smiled as I rubbed his stomach.

"Wish me luck, Miffy," I said softly as I got up to leave, but all he did was prop himself up and give me a look of *Don't you stop patting me, you lazy bastard.* I jumped the fence anyway, though, and went through the house. I left a note saying I might go to Steve's that night so no one would worry too much. (The odds were that I might end up there in any case.)

I was wearing the sort of thing I always wear. Old jeans, a jersey, my black spray jacket, and my old shoes. Before I left, I went to the bathroom and tried to keep my hair from sticking up, but that's like trying to defy gravity. My hair sticks up no matter what. Thick like dog's fur, and always slightly messy. There's just never a lot I can do about it. *Besides*, I thought, *I should just try to be like I was yesterday. If I was good enough yesterday I should be good enough today.*

It was settled. I was going.

I let the front door slam shut behind me and the fly-screen rattle. It was as if each door was kicking me out of the old life I'd lived in that house. I was being thrown out into the world, new. The broken, leaning gate creaked open, let me out, and I gently placed it shut. I was gone, and from down the street, maybe fifty yards away, I looked back for a second at the house where I lived. It wasn't the same anymore. It never would be. I kept walking.

The traffic on the street waded past me, and at one point, when it all got blocked, a passenger from a cab spat out the window and it landed near my feet.

"Christ," the guy said. "Sorry, mate."

All I did was look at him and say, "No worries." I couldn't afford to be distracted. Not today. I'd picked up the scent of a different life, and nothing was going to get me off it. I would hunt it down. I would find it, taste it, devour it. The guy could have spat in my face and I would have wiped it off and kept walking.

There would be no distractions.

No regrets.

It was still afternoon when I made it down to Central Station, bought my ticket, and headed for the underground. Platform Twenty-five.

Standing there, I waited at the back of the platform till I felt the cold wind of the train pushing through the tunnel. It surrounded my ears until the roar entered me and slowed to a dull, limping sigh.

It was an old train.

A scabby one.

In the last carriage, downstairs, there was an old man with a radio, listening to jazz music. He said hello to me (a very rare event on any form of public transport), and I knew that things would have to go right today. I felt like I'd earned it.

My thoughts veered with the train.

My heart held itself back.

When Hurstville came, I stood up and made my way out, and to my amazement, I found Octavia's street without any problems. Usually when it comes to directions I'm an absolute shocker.

I looked at each house, trying to guess which one was number thirteen Howell Street.

When I made it, I found the house to be nearly as small as where I lived, and red brick. It was getting dark, and I stood there, waiting and hoping, hands in pockets. There was a fence and a gate, and a close-cut lawn with a path. I began wondering if she'd come out.

People came from the station.

They walked past me.

Finally, when the same darkness as the previous day overcame the street, I turned away from the house and faced the road, half-sitting, half-leaning on the fence. A few minutes later, she came.

I could barely hear the front door open or her footsteps coming toward me, but there was no mistaking the feeling of her behind me when she stopped and stood within reaching distance. I shiver even now as I remember the feeling of her cool hands on my neck, and the touch of her voice on my skin.

"Hi Cameron," she said, and I turned around to face her. "Thanks for coming."

"It's okay," I spoke. My voice was dry and cracked open.

I smiled then, I remember, and my heart swam in its own blood. There was no holding back anymore. In my mind, I had gone over moments like this a thousand times, and now that I was truly in one, there was no way I could blow it. I wouldn't allow myself.

I went along the fence and into the gate, and when I made it over to Octavia, I picked up her hand and held it in mine. I raised it to my mouth and kissed it. I kissed her fingers and her wrist as gently as my clumsy lips could.

Her eyes widened.

The expression on her face came that little bit closer.

Her mouth merged into a smile.

"Come on," she said, leading me out the gate. "We don't have long tonight," and we moved onto the path.

We walked down the street to an old park, where I searched myself for things to say.

Nothing came.

All I could think of was utter crap like the weather and all that sort of thing, but I wasn't going to reduce myself to that. She still smiled at me, though, telling me silently that it was okay not to talk. It was okay not to win her over with stories or compliments or anything else I could say just to say *something*. She only walked and smiled, happier in silence.

In the park, we sat for a long time.

I offered her my jacket and helped her put it on, but after that, there was nothing.

No words.

No anything.

I don't know what else I expected, because I had absolutely no idea how to confront this. I had no idea how to act around a girl, because to me, what she wanted was completely shrouded in mystery. I didn't really have a clue. All I knew was that I wanted her. That was the simple part. But actually knowing what to do? How in the hell could I ever come close to coping with that? Can you tell me?

My problem came, I think, from being inside aloneness for so long. I always watched girls from afar, hardly getting close enough to smell them. Of course I *wanted* them, but even though I was miserable about not actually having them, it was also kind of a relief. There was no pressure. No discomfort. In a way, it was easier just to imagine what it would be like, rather than confront the reality of it. I could create ideal situations, and ways that I would act to win them over.

You can do anything when it's not real.

When it *is* real, nothing breaks your fall. Nothing gets between you and the ground, and that night, in the park, I had never felt so real. I'd never felt so lacking in control. It seemed to be the way it was, and the way it always would be.

Before, life was about getting girls (or hoping to).

Not about getting to know them, or actually *getting* what they were about.

Now, it was much different.

Now, it was about *one* girl, and working out what to do.

I thought for a while, trying to find the elusive breakthrough of what to say. Thoughts pinned me down, leaving me there, to think about it. In the end, I tried convincing myself that everything would turn out. Nothing turns on its own, though.

All right, I told myself, trying to pull myself together. I even started listing the things I'd actually done right.

I'd chased her down on the train the day before.

I'd spoken to her and said I'd stand outside her house.

God, I'd even kissed her hand.

But now I had to talk, and I had nothing to say.

Why don't you have anything to say, you stupid bastard? I asked myself.

I begged inside me.

Several times.

The disappointment in myself was bitter as I sat on a splinter-infested park bench with her, wondering what to do next.

At one point I opened my mouth, but nothing came out.

In the end, I could only look at her and say, "I'm sorry, Octavia. I'm sorry I'm so bloody useless."

She shook her head, and I saw that she was disagreeing with me.

She said quietly, "You don't have to talk at all, Cameron." She looked into me. "You'd never have to say a thing and I'd still know you're big-hearted."

That was when the night burst open and the sky fell down, in slabs, around me.

GETTING THE GIRL

I think about it hard — about silence and getting the girl.
   Getting.
   Getting.
   When you're young and dirty, everything's about getting your hands on a girl . . . or at least, that's what people say. It may not be what they think, but it's what they tell you.
   For me, though, it feels like more than that. I want to hear her, and know her.
   I want to understand.
   What to do.
   What to say.
   I don't want to stand in naked silence, pathetically unaware of how to be. I want to cut myself free. I want to shake myself away from the silence, and I want it now.
   Yet, I think, as usual, I'll have to wait.
   And you never know.
   Maybe one day I'll understand.
   One day I'll get the girl.
   One day I might even get the world . . . but I doubt it.

CHAPTER 10

Sarah knew.

She could tell by looking when I came in that night, she reckoned. She told me right away, when I tried to slip past her on my way down the hall to Rube's and my room.

It was funny.

Unbelievable.

How could she be so sure — so sure that when I came in, she could stop me and shove her hand to my heart and say with a grin and a whisper, "Tell me, Cameron. What's the name of the girl who can make your heart beat this fast?"

I grinned back, shocked and shy, amazed.

"No one," I denied.

"Huh," and a short laugh.

Huh.

That was all she said, as she took her hand off me and turned away, still smiling.

"Good for you, Cameron." That was what she said as she walked away. She faced me, one last time. "You deserve it. You really do, I mean it."

She left me to stand there, remembering what happened right after the slabs of sky fell down around me.

For a while, Octavia and I remained on the bench, as the air grew colder. Only when she started shivering did we stand up and walk back to her house. At one point, her fingers touched mine, and she held on just faintly.

Before she went in, she said, "I'll be down the harbor on Sunday, if you feel like coming. I'll be there around noon."

"Okay," I replied, already imagining myself standing there, watching her play the harmonica with people throwing money onto her jacket. Bright blue sky. Climbing clouds. The hands of the sun, reaching down. I could see all of it.

"And Cameron?" she asked.

I returned from my vision.

"I'll wait for you." She let her eyes hit the ground and arrive again, in mine. "You know what I mean?"

I nodded, slowly.

She would wait for me, to talk, and to be with her the way I could be. I guess we could only hope it would just be a matter of time.

"Thanks," I said, and rather than let me watch her go inside, Octavia stayed at the gate and waved each time I turned around for one last glimpse of her. With every turn, I whispered, "Bye Octavia," until I was around the corner, on my own again.

Memories of the ride home are shaded by the haziness of a train ride at night. The clacking of the train rolling and turning over the tracks still rides through me. It gives me a vision of myself sitting there, traveling back to where I came from, but a place that would no longer be the same.

It was strange how Sarah could sense it immediately.

She could see the change in me straight away, in the way I existed in our house. Maybe I moved or spoke differently, I didn't know. I *was* different, though.

I had my words.

I had Octavia.

In a way, it seemed like I wasn't pleading with myself anymore. I wasn't begging for those scraps of alrightness. I just told myself to be patient, because, finally, I was standing somewhere close to where I wanted to be. I'd fought for this, and now I was nearly there.

Much later in the night, Rube came home and collapsed like always into bed.

Shoes still on.

Shirt half-undone.

There was a slight smell of beer, smoke, and his usual cheap cologne that he didn't need because the girls fell over him anyway.

Loud breathing. Smiling sleep.

It was typical Rube. Typical Friday night.

He also left the light on, as always, so I had to get up and switch it off.

We both knew good and well that Dad would be waking us in the morning when it was still dark. I also knew that Rube would get up, and he'd look rough and tired and yet still pretty damn good. He had a way of doing that, my brother, which annoyed the absolute hell out of me.

As I lay there, across from him, I wondered what he would say when he found out about Octavia and me. I went through a whole list of possibilities, because Rube was likely to say anything, depending on what was happening at the time, what had previously happened, and what was going to happen next. Some of the things I thought of were:

He'd slap me hard across the back of the head and say, "What the hell are y' thinking, Cam?" Another slap. "Y' don't do that sort of thing with y' brother's old girlfriend!" Another slap, and one more, just in case.

Then again, he might just shrug. Nothing. No words, no anger, no mood, no smile, no laugh.

Or he might pat me on the back and say, "Well Cam, it's about time you pulled y' finger out."

Or maybe he'd be speechless.

No.

No chance.

Rube was never speechless.

If there was nothing he could think of saying, he'd most likely look at me and exclaim, "Octavia!? Really!?"

I'd nod.

"Really!?"

"Yeah."

"Well that's just bloody brilliant, that is!"

The situations merged through me as I fell down slowly into sleep. My dreams collected everything up

401

until a hard hand shoved me awake at quarter past six the next morning.

The old man.

Clifford Wolfe.

"Time to get up," said his voice, through the darkness. "Wake that lazy bastard too." He jerked his thumb over at Rube, but I could tell he was smiling. With Dad, Rube, and me, calling each other bastards was a term of endearment.

The job was right on the coast, at Bronte.

Rube and I pretty much dug under the house all day, listening to the radio.

For lunch, we all walked down to the beach and Dad got the obligatory fish 'n' chips. When we were done, Rube and I went down to the shoreline to get the grease off our hands.

"Friggin' freezin'," Rube warned me about the water, but still he pooled it in his hands and threw it on his face and through his thick, sandy hair.

Along the shore, there were shells washed up.

I started shuffling through them and picking up the best ones to keep.

Rube looked over.

"What are y' doin'?" he asked.

"Just collectin' a few shells."

He looked at me in disbelief. "Are you a bloody poofter or somethin'?"

I glanced at the shells in my hands. "What's wrong with it?"

"Christ!" he laughed. "You are, aren't y'?"

I only looked over and laughed back, then picked up a shell that was clean and smooth and had a gentle tiger pattern on it. In the center there was a small hole, for looking through.

"Look at this one," I said, holding it out to him.

"Not bad," Rube admitted, and as we stared over the ocean, my brother said, "You're okay, Cameron."

All I could do was stare a few seconds longer before we turned back. The old man had already given us an "Oi" to get us back to work. We walked over the sand and back up the street. Later that day, Rube told me some things. About Octavia.

It started innocently enough, with me asking how many girlfriends he reckoned he'd had.

"I wouldn't know," he answered me. "I never counted 'em. Maybe twelve, thirteen."

For a while, there was only the sound of the digging, but I could tell my brother, like me, was going over the girls in his head, touching each girl with the fingers of his mind.

In the middle of it, I had to ask him.

I said, "Rube?"

"Shut up — I'm tryin' to concentrate."

I ignored him and kept going. I'd started now and I wasn't going to stop. I asked, "Why'd you get rid of Octavia?"

Rube stopped digging, and I could tell he was debating what to say in his mind. He gave me the answer. "To tell you the truth, Cam. *She* quit *me.* That night when she came back I was expecting her to cry and carry on like some of the others." He shook his head now. "But I was wrong. She just came and really gave it to me. She said I wasn't worth the effort." He shrugged a moment, then spoke again. "The funny thing was, when she left, she looked so brilliant, I almost felt like running after her." For the first time then, he met me in the eyes. "That's never happened before. It was like, I don't know, Cam. I think it was the first time I felt like I'd lost something good."

I nodded and stayed silent, and even started digging a bit prematurely. I thought about loss and gain and everything in between. And naturally, I forced myself to forget about it.

What confused me most was how Rube could still be so calm about it. If it were me in his shoes, the agony of someone like Octavia breaking up with me would have left me in strips and pieces on the ground. It would have broken me.

But that was me.

For Rube, the next best thing came along, so he took it, and I guess there was nothing wrong with that. The only problem for Rube now, it seemed, was that the Julia girl came with some excess baggage. She'd come at a price.

"Apparently she was still with some other bloke when she started up with me," he stated matter-of-factly. "Some honcho from out Canterbury way."

"Honcho?" I asked. "What the hell's a honcho?"

Rube leaned on his shovel. "You know all those guys out there — gangs, nicknames, chains. All that crap." He smiled a moment, maybe looking forward to the challenge. "And apparently this guy's after killin' *me* for his girl losing interest in him. It's not like I did anything wrong, for Jesus' sake. It's not like the girl told me she was already taken."

"Just be careful," I told him. Once again, he could tell by the tone of my voice that I wasn't a big fan of this Julia girl. He asked me straight out.

He said, "You don't like her, do y'?"

I shook my head.

"Why not?"

You hurt Octavia to get her, I thought, but I said, "I don't know. I've just got a bad feeling about this one, that's all."

"Don't worry about me," Rube responded. He looked over and gave me his usual grin — the one that always says everything will be all right. "I'll survive."

As it turned out, I kept just the one shell from the beach. It was the one with the tiger pattern. At home, I held it against the light from our bedroom window. I already knew what I'd do with it.

It was in my pocket the next day when I walked down to Central and caught the train over to Circular Quay. The harbor water was a rich blue, with the ferries trudging over it, cutting it, then allowing it to settle. On the docks, there were people everywhere, and plenty of buskers. The good, the brilliant, and the hopeless. It took a while, but I finally saw her. I saw Octavia on the walkway to the Rocks, and I could see the people milling around her, drawn to the powerful voice of her mouth organ.

I arrived when she was just finishing a song and people were putting money into her old jacket, which was spread out on the ground. She smiled at them and said thanks, and most of the people moved slowly on.

Without noticing I was there, she went straight into another song, and again, a crowd began to gather around her. This time it wasn't quite as big. The sun surrounded her wavy hair, and I watched intently as her lips slid across the instrument. I looked at her neck, her soft flannel shirt, and stole visions of her hips and her legs through gaps in the crowd. In the song, I could hear her words, "It's okay, Cameron, I can wait." I also heard her calling me big-hearted, and hesitantly at first, then without thinking, I moved to the crowd and made my way through it.

Breathing, stopping, and then crouching, I was the closest person in the world to Octavia Ash. She played her harmonica, and before her, I was kneeling down.

She saw me and I could see the smile overcome her lips.

My pulse quickened.

It burned in my throat as slowly, I reached into my pocket, pulled out the tiger shell, and placed it gently onto the jacket where all the money was strewn.

I placed it there and the sun hit it, and just as I was about to turn around to make my way back through the crowd, the music stopped. In the middle of the song it was cut short.

The world was silent and I turned again to look up at a girl who stood completely still above me.

She crouched down, placed her harmonica amongst the money, and picked up the shell.

She held it in her hand.

She pulled it to her lips.

She kissed it, softly.

Then, with her right hand, she pulled me toward her by my jacket and kissed me. Her breath went into me, and the softness, warmness, wetness, and openness of her mouth covered me, as a sound from outside us burst through my ears. For a moment, I wondered what it was, but fell completely into Octavia again as she poured through me. We both kneeled, and my hands held onto her hips. Her mouth kept reaching for mine, touching me. Connecting. Her right hand was on my face now, holding me, keeping me close.

The roaring sound continued around us, forming walls to make this a world within the rest of the world. Suddenly I knew what it was. The sound was clear and clean, and magnificent.

It was the sound of humans clapping.

CLAPPING HANDS

What is it about the sound of clapping hands?
It's only skin against slapping skin, so why can it

407

make a tide turn in you? Why can it break on top of you and lift you up at the same time?

Maybe it's because it's one of the most noble things humans do with their hands.

I mean, think about it.

Humans make fists with their hands.

They use them to fight, to steal things, to hurt each other.

When people clap, it's one of the few times they stand together and applaud other people.

I think they're there to keep things. They hold moments together, to remember.

CHAPTER 11

"It's the best thing anyone's ever given me," she said, holding it up and looking at me through the hole. She kissed me again, lightly on the mouth and once on my neck. She whispered in my ear. "Thanks, Cameron." I loved her lips, especially when the sun hit them and she smiled at me. I'd never seen her smile like that when she was with Rube, and hoped it was a smile she'd never been able to give to anyone else alive. I couldn't help it.

The people were gone now and we collected up the money from Octavia's jacket. It was just over fifty-six dollars. In my left jacket pocket, I still held all my words, including what I'd just written when she'd returned to playing. My fingers held them tightly, guarding them.

"Let's go," she said, and we started walking along the water toward the bridge. Shadows of cloud lurked in the water, like holes the sun forgot about. The girl next to me still looked at the shell, and my heartbeat felt like fingers climbing over my ribs. Even when it slowed, there was still a force to it. I liked it.

Under the bridge, we sat down against the wall, Octavia with her legs outstretched, me with my knees held up to my throat. I glanced over at her and noticed the way the light touched her skin and handled the hair that fell into her face. It was the color of honey. She had salty green eyes — the color of the harbor on an over-cast day — and she had tanned skin and a straight-teeth smile that got crowded on the right side when she opened her mouth further. (I'd never noticed that pre-viously.) She had a smooth neck and the shins of her legs wore a few bruises. Nice knees and hips. I liked girls' hips, but I liked Octavia's especially. I . . .

It was there again.

Between us.

The silence.

There was only the sound of water throwing itself against the walls of the harbor, until finally, I looked over at Octavia and said quietly, "I just wanted to . . ."

Pause.

A long pause.

She wanted to speak, I could sense it. I noticed it in the pleading of her eyes, and the slight movement of her lips. She was dying to say something but held back. I finished the sentence.

"I just wanted to say . . ." I cleared my throat, but it remained cracked. "Thanks."

"For what?"

I hesitated slightly. ". . . For wanting me."

She looked over and placed her eyes in mine for just the briefest of seconds. Her fingers touched my wrist and made their way down to hold my own fingers in hers. She then said something very deliberately.

She smiled a moment and calmly said, "I like your hair, Cameron. I like how it sticks up no matter how hard you try to keep it down. It's the one thing you can't hide." She swallowed. "But the rest of you is hidden. It's hidden behind your measured walk, the crushed collar of your jacket, and your awkward, nervous smile. You can kill me with that smile if you want."

I looked over.

"Do you know that?" she asked again, almost accusingly.

"No."

"Well it's true, but . . ."

"What?"

"Can't you see?" She squeezed my hand. "I want more than that." A tough kind of smile fought its way to her face. "I just want to know you a bit, Cameron, that's all."

Again, I noticed the sound of the water.

Rising.

Bashing against the wall before diving back down.

Finally, I nodded. I decided.

There was only one way to do this and now I had it.

I stood up and walked to the water.

I turned around.

The bridge towered over me and I started talking as I crouched down maybe ten yards away and looked into her.

Words flew from my mouth.

"My name's Cameron. I've always said that I wanted to drown inside a girl, inside her spirit, but I've never even come close — I've barely even touched a girl. I don't have friends. I live in the shadow of both my brothers — one for his single-minded focus on success, the other for his brilliance, rough smile, and ability to make people like him. I hope my sister won't just be another slab of flesh that some guy just picks up and throws a few dollars at to buy cheap lipstick but don't forget the beer. I work with my father on weekends and my hands get dirty and blistered. I get thoughts in my head of movies with sex scenes and about girls from school, model girls, a female teacher or two, girls in ads, girls on calendars, girls on TV shows who turn letters, girls in uniforms or corporate suits who sit on the train reading thick books with perfume smothered on their throats and perfect makeup. I walk around the city a lot and when I do, it feels like the soul of home. I love my brother Rube but I hate what he does to girls, especially when they're real girls like you who should have known better than to go out with him in the first place. I idolize Mrs. Wolfe because she keeps us together and works like hell. She works harder than she should ever have to, and one day I want to do something brilliant for her like put her in first class on a plane to wherever she wants. . . ." I remembered to breathe but forgot what I was going to say next.

I stopped talking and stood up, because my legs were getting sore from the crouching down. Slowly, I walked toward Octavia Ash, whose bruised shins were now held up by her folded arms.

"I —"

Again, I stopped, as I walked to her and crouched down in front of her. I could feel the blood collect again in my legs.

"What?" she asked. "What is it?"

For a few seconds I wondered if I should do it or not, but before I allowed myself not to, I reached into the pocket of my jacket and pulled out clumps of paper and held them out to her, as if I were offering her everything I owned. On the paper were the words.

"These are mine," I said, placing them in her outstretched hand. "Open them and read them. They'll tell you who I am."

She did as I asked, opening the small piece of writing that was my first. The only thing is, she read only the start of them. She handed the paper back to me and asked, "Would you read them to me, Cameron?"

My thoughts kneeled down.

The breeze wandered between us and I sat next to her again and began reading the words I wrote back in Chapter One of this story.

"*The city streets are lined with truth, and I walk through them. Sometimes,* they *walk through* me. . . ." I read the page slow and true, exactly how it felt to me, as if it were oozing from me, and I said the last part just a touch louder. "*Yes, when that's done, I also want the everything that's her to fill up so much in front of me that it spills and shivers and gives, just like I'm prepared to do myself. But for now, happiness throws stones. It guards itself. I wait.*"

When I was finished, a final silence gripped us both and the sound of the paper folding up again sounded like something crashing. A look of feeling clutched at her face, holding it.

She waited a while, before gently speaking. "You've never touched a girl before?"

"No."

"Not till me?"

"No."

"Could you do me a favor?" she asked.

I nodded, looking at her.

"Could you hold my hand?"

Feeling every part of it, I took Octavia's hand, and she came closer and rested her head on my shoulder. She put her leg over mine and hooked her foot under my ankle, linking us.

"I never thought I'd show anyone my words," I said quietly.

"They're beautiful." She spoke softly in my ear.

"They make me okay. . . ."

Soon after, she moved in front of me, crossed her legs, and faced me, making me read everything I'd written so far. When it was over, she moved my hands across her stomach to hold her on her hips.

She said, "You can drown inside me anytime, Cameron," and she put her lips on mine again and let herself flow through the inside of my mouth. The pages were still in my hands, pressed against her as I held her hips, and I could feel her on top of me, breathing me in.

After a while, we got up and Octavia turned to me. She asked a serious question.

She leaned toward me and said, "You feel like getting high?"

"High?" I asked.

"Yeah." She smiled in a dangerous, self-mocking way, and I only began to understand why when we headed back toward the middle of the city, to the tower.

We entered the lift and it took us right to the top, with some English golf pro–looking types, and a family on a Sunday outing. One of the kids kept stepping on my foot.

"Little bastard," I felt like saying. If I had been with Rube I probably would have, but with Octavia, I only looked at her and implied it. She nodded back as if to say, "Exactly."

Once up there, we walked around the whole floor and I couldn't help but look for my own house, imagining what was happening there, and hoping, even praying, that everything was going okay. That extended to include everyone down there, as far as I could see, and as I always do when I pray to a God I wouldn't have a clue about, I stood there, lightly beating at my heart, without even thinking.

Especially this girl, though, I prayed. *Let her be okay, God. All right? All right God?*

That was when Octavia noticed my fist lightly touching my heart. There was no answer from God. There was a question from the girl.

She asked, "What are you doing?" I could feel the curiosity of her eyes on my face. "Cameron?"

I stayed focused on the city sprawled out beneath us. "Just sort of prayin', y' know?"

"For what?"

"Just that things will be okay." I stopped, continued. Almost laughed. "And I haven't been in a church for nearly seven years. . . ."

We stayed up there for over an hour, walking around to see the whole city from this high up.

"I come up here a fair bit," she told me. "I like the height." She even climbed to the carpeted step at the window and stood there, leaning forward onto the glass. "You comin' up?" she asked, and I'll be honest — I tried, but no matter how much I wanted to lean forward onto that glass, I couldn't. I kept feeling like I was going to fall through.

So I sat there.

Only for a few seconds.

When she came back down she could see I wasn't doing too well.

"I wanted to," I said.

"Don't worry, Cam."

The thing was, I knew there was something I had to ask, and I did it. I even promised myself that this would be the last time I asked a question like this.

I said, "Octavia?" I kept hearing her telling me that she came up here all the time. I heard it when I spoke the words, "Did you bring Rube up here too?"

Slowly, she nodded.

"But he leaned on the glass," I answered my own question. "Didn't he?"

Again, she nodded. "Yeah."

I don't know why, but it seemed important. It *was* important. I felt like a failure because my older brother leaned on the glass and I couldn't. It made me feel hopeless in some way. Like I wasn't even half the guy he was.

All because he leaned on glass and I couldn't.

All because he had the neck and I didn't.

All because . . .

"That doesn't mean anything." She shot down my thoughts. "Not to me." She thought for a moment and faced me. "He leaned on the window, but he never made me feel like you do. He never stood outside my house. He never gave me any truth, the way you have with your pages there. He never gave me something he couldn't give to anyone else." She struggled not to explain it, but to actually say it. "The few times I've been with you, I feel like I'm kind of outside myself, you know?" She finished me. "I don't want Rube. I don't want anyone else." Her eyes ate me, quietly. "I want you."

I looked.

Down.

At my shoes, then back up, at Octavia Ash.

I went to say, "Thanks," but she stopped me by pushing her fingers up to my mouth.

"Always remember that," she spoke. "All right?"

I nodded.

"Say it."

"All right," I said, and her cool hands touched me on my neck, my shoulder, my face.

SOMETIMES YOU GET THE GIRL — SOMETIMES THE GIRL GETS YOU

Inside me, I'm high up, leaning forward onto glass.

It cracks.

It comes apart and falls open.

Momentum pushes me out and I'm being dragged to earth at a speed beyond my imagination.

I see the width of the world.

The farther I fall, the faster it turns, and around me, I see visions of everyone and everything I know. There's Rube and Steve, Sarah, Dad and Mrs. Wolfe, Keith and Miffy, and Julia the Scrubber, looking seductive. Even the barber's there, chopping hair that litters down around me.

I think only one thing.

Where's Octavia?

As I get closer to the bottom, I notice that it's water I'm falling into. It's salty-green and smooth, until . . .

I'm driven through the surface and go deeper. I'm surrounded.

I'm drowning, I think. I'm drowning.

But I'm smiling too.

CHAPTER 12

When I got home that Sunday night, Rube and I did the usual deed of walking Miffy. The hound was in even worse shape than usual. The coughing sounded deeper, like it was coming from his lungs.

When we got back I asked Keith if he was going to take him to the vet.

"I don't think this is fur balls," I said.

Keith's reply was pretty short and simple. "Yeah, I think I'd better. He looks shockin'."

"Worse."

"Ah, he's been like this before," he explained, more out of hope than anything else. "It's never been anything too serious."

"Well let us know what happens, okay?"

"Yeah, bye mate."

I thought for a moment about the dog. Miffy. I guess no matter how much Rube and I complained about him, we knew we'd sort of miss him if something happened to him. It's funny how there are things in this world that do nothing but annoy you, but you know you'd miss them when they're gone. Miffy, the Pomeranian wonderdog, was one such thing.

Later, when I was sitting in the lounge room with

Rube, I missed many opportunities to tell him about Octavia and me.

Now, I told myself. *Now!*

No words ever came out though, and we just sat there.

The next night I went up and paid Steve a visit. It had been a while since I'd been to see him, and in a way, I missed him. It's hard to pinpoint exactly what it was, but I'd grown to like Steve's company a lot, even though very little was ever said. Sure, we spoke more than we used to, but it still wasn't much.

When I got there only Sal was home.

"He should be here any minute," she said, in a not-too-thrilled voice. "You want something to eat? Drink?"

"Nah, I'll be right."

She didn't make me feel too welcome that night, like she just wasn't up to tolerating me this time around. Her expression seemed to throw words down to me. Words like:

Loser.

Dirty little bastard.

I'm sure that at some point, a while ago, before Steve and I gathered an understanding of each other, he probably told Sal what a couple of loserous bastards he was the brother of. He'd always looked down on Rube and me when we all lived together. We did stupid things, I admit it: stealing road signs, fighting, gambling at the dog track . . . It wasn't quite Steve's scene.

When he came in, about ten minutes later, he actually smiled and said, "Hey, I haven't seen you for a while!" For a moment, I smiled back and thought he was talking to me, before realizing it was Sal he was talking to. She'd been doing a lot of interstate work lately. He walked over and kissed her. Then he noticed his brother sitting on the couch.

"Hey Cam."

"Hi Steve."

I could see they wanted to be alone, so I waited a few seconds and stood up. The kitchen light surrounded them in the dimly lit lounge room.

"Hey, I'll come back some other time," I said too fast. I made sure to get the hell out of there. Sal was giving me the best *piss off* look I'd ever seen.

"No."

I was just about out the door when the word booted itself into my back. I turned around and Steve was standing behind me. His face was serious as he spoke the rest of the words.

"You don't have to go, Cam."

All I did was look at my brother and say, "Don't worry," and I turned and left without thinking too much about it. I had other places to go now anyway.

It was still fairly early, so I decided to run to the station and get a train down to Hurstville. In the train's window I saw my reflection — my hair was getting longer again and standing up wild and rough. It was black. Pitch-black in the window, and for the first time, I kind of liked it. Swaying with the train, I looked inside me.

Octavia's street was wrapped in darkness. The lights from the houses were like torchlights. If I closed my eyes tight and opened them again, it looked like the houses were stumbling around in the dark, finding their way. At any moment I expected them to fade. Sometimes human shadows crossed through them, as I waited, just outside her front gate.

For a while, I imagined myself walking to the front door and knocking, but I stayed patient. For some reason, it didn't seem right to go in. Not yet. I was dying for her to come out, make no mistake about that. Yet I knew that if I had to leave again without even a glimpse of her, I would. If I could do it for a girl who cared nothing for me, I could do it for Octavia.

In that one stolen second, I considered the Glebe girl. She entered my mind like a burglar, then vanished again, taking nothing. It was like the humiliation of the past had been taken instantly from my back and left somewhere on the ground. I wondered for a moment how I could stand outside her house so many times. I even laughed. At myself. She was erased completely a few minutes later when Octavia moved the kitchen curtain aside, and came out to meet me.

The first thing I noticed, before any words hit the air, was the shell. It was tied to a piece of string and was hanging around her neck.

"It looks good," I nodded, and I reached out and held it in my right hand.

"It does," she agreed.

We went to the same park as the first night I came, but this time we didn't sit on the splintered bench. This time we walked over the dewy grass and ended up stopping by an old tree.

"Here," I said, and I gave Octavia the words I wrote the previous night in bed. "They're yours."

She read them and kissed the paper and held on to me for quite a while. I told her I loved the howling sound of her harmonica. That seemed to be the limit of my courage that night. I had to get back home, so I couldn't stay too long. It was just nice to see her and touch her and give her the words.

When we made it back to the gate, I kissed her hand and left.

"See you this weekend?" she asked.

"Definitely."

"I'll call you," she said, and I was on my way.

At my place, when I returned, I was shocked to find Steve on our front porch, waiting for me.

"I was wondering how long I'd have to sit here," he fired when I showed up. "I've been here an hour."

I walked closer. "And? Why'd you come?"

"Come on," he said, standing up. "Let's go back up to my place."

"I'll just go in and —"

"I already told 'em."

Steve's car was parked farther along the street, and after getting in, there were very few words spoken in the car. I turned the radio up but don't remember the song.

"So what's this all about?" I asked. I looked at him but Steve's eyes were firmly on the road. For a while I was wondering if he'd even heard my question. He let his eyes examine me for a second or two, but he said nothing. He was still waiting.

When we got out of the car, he said, "I want you to meet someone." He slammed the door. "Or actually, I want her to meet you."

We walked up the stairs and into his apartment. It was empty.

"Looks like she's in the shower," he mentioned. He stood and made coffee and put a cup down in front of me. It still swirled, taking my reflection with it. Taking me down.

For a moment, I thought we were about to go through our usual routine of questions and answers about everyone back at home, but I could see him deciding not to do it. He'd been at our place earlier and found out for himself. It wasn't in Steve's nature to manufacture conversation.

I hadn't been to watch him at football for a while, so I asked how it was going. He was in the middle of explaining it when Sal came out of the bathroom, still drying her hair.

"Hey," she said to me.

I nodded, giving her half a smile.

That was when Steve stood up and looked at me, then at her. I knew right then that at some point, like I'd suspected, he did tell her about Rube and me. I'd imagined it on the park bench in Hurstville for some reason, and I could hear the quiet tone of Steve's intense voice practically disowning his brothers. Now he was rewriting it, or at least trying to make it right.

"Stand up," he told me.

I did.

He said, "Sal." She looked at me. I looked at her, as Steve kept talking. "This is my brother Cameron."

We shook hands.

My boyish, rough hand.

Her smooth and clean hand, which smelled of perfumed soap. Soap I imagined you'd get in hotel rooms I'd never get to visit.

She recognized me through the eyes and I was Cameron now, not just that loser brother of Steve.

On the way back home sometime after that, Steve and I talked a while, but only about small things. In the middle of it, I cut him short. I said, with knifelike words, "When you first told Sal about Rube and me you said we were losers. You told her you were ashamed of us, didn't you?" My voice was still calm and not even the slightest bit accusing, though I was trying as hard as I could.

"No." He denied it when the car came to a stop outside our house.

"No?" I could see the shame in his eyes, and for the first time ever, I could see it was shame he held for himself.

"No," he confirmed, and he looked at me with something that resembled anger now, almost like he couldn't stomach it. "Not you and Rube," he explained, and his face looked injured. "Just you."

God.

God, I thought, and my mouth was open. It was as if Steve had reached into me and pulled out my pulse. My heart was in his hands, and he was staring down at it, as if he too, could see it.

Beating.

Thrusting itself down, then standing up again. Almost bleeding down his forearms.

I said nothing about the truth Steve had just let loose.

All I did was undo my seat belt, take my heart, and get out of that car as fast as I could.

Steve followed but it was too late. I heard his footsteps coming after me when I was walking onto our porch. Words fell down between his feet.

"Cam!" he called out. "Cameron!" I was nearly inside when I heard his voice cry out. "I'm sorry. I was . . ." He made his voice go louder. "Cam, I was wrong!"

I got behind the door and shut it, then turned to look back out.

Steve's figure was shadowed onto the front window. It was silent and still, plastered to the light.

"I was wrong."

He said it again, though this time his voice was weaker.

A minute shuddered past.

I broke.

Walking slowly to the front door, I opened it and saw my brother on the other side of the flyscreen.

I waited, then, "Forget about it," I said. "It doesn't matter."

I was still hurt, but like I said, it didn't matter. I'd been hurt before and I'd be hurt again. Steve must have wished he'd never tried showing Sal that I wasn't the loser she thought I was. All he'd succeeded in doing was proving that not only had he once thought I *was* a lost cause, but that I was the *only* one.

Soon, though, I was stabbed.

A feeling shook through me and cut me loose. All my thoughts were off the chain, until one solitary sentence arrived and wouldn't leave me.

The words and Octavia.

That was the sentence.

It wavered in me.

It saved me, and almost whispering, I said to Steve, "Don't worry, brother. I don't need you to tell Sal that I'm not a loser." We were still separated by the flyscreen. "I don't need you to say it to *me* either. I know what I am. I know what I see. Maybe one day I'll tell you a little more about me, but for now, I guess we'll just have to wait and see what happens. I'm nowhere near what I'm going to be, and . . ." I could feel something in me. Something I've always felt. I paused and caught his eyes. I leaped into them through the door and held him down. "You ever hear a dog cry, Steve? You know, howling so loud, it's almost unbearable?" He nodded. "I reckon they howl like that because they're so hungry it hurts, and that's what I feel in me every day of my life. I'm so hungry to be somethin' — to be *somebody*. You hear me?" He did. "I'm not lyin' down ever. Not for you. Not for anyone." I ended it. "I'm hungry, Steve."

Sometimes I think they're the best words I've ever said.

"I'm hungry."

And after that, I shut the door.

I didn't slam it.

You don't shoot a dog when it's already dead.

WHEN DOGS CRY

I saw a dog cry once.

It was one of those nights when the wind tries to tear the ground along with it, and a storm stirs itself amongst the sky. Lightning roared and thunder cracked above me.

The street was empty but for the dog, first walking the dangerous, desolate city floor, silently clicking over it with his paws and claws. He looked hungry, and desperate, until he simply stood there, and began.

He reached deep, and his fur stood on end, climbing ferociously up. From his heart, from everything in his instinct, he began to howl.

He howled above the howling thunder. He howled above the howling lightning, and beyond the howling wind.

With his head claiming the endless sky, he howled hunger and I felt it rise through me.

It was my *hunger.*

My *pride.*

And I smiled.

Even now, I smile, and I feel it in my eyes, because hunger's a powerful thing.

CHAPTER 13

The phone was ringing. Wednesday night. Just past seven o'clock.

"Hello?"

"Ruben Wolfe?"

"No, it's Cameron here."

"Tell you what," the voice went on, laced with friendly malice. "Could you get him for me?"

"Yeah, who's callin'?"

"No one."

"No one?"

"Listen, mate. Just get y' brother on the phone or we'll beat the crap out of you as well."

I was taken aback. I pulled the phone away, then returned it to my ear. "I'll get him. Hang on a minute."

Rube was in our room with Julia the Scrubber. I knocked on the door and went in.

"What?" said Rube. He wasn't happy to see me, and neither was Julia. She adjusted her clothing.

I took another step into the room. "Someone on the phone."

"For me?" Rube asked.

I nodded.

"Well who is it?"

430

"Do I look like y' bloody secretary? Just get up and answer the phone."

He looked strangely at me, got up grudgingly, and walked out, which left me in the room with Julia the Scrubber, alone.

Julia the Scrubber: "Hi Cam."

Me: "Hi Julia."

Julia the Scrubber, smiling and moving closer: "Rube's been tellin' me you're not too much in love with me."

Me, inching away: "Well I guess he can tell you whatever he wants."

Julia the Scrubber, sensing my complete lack of interest: "Is it true?"

Me: "Well, I don't know, to be honest. It isn't really any of my business what Rube does . . . but I know for sure that whoever's on that phone wants to kill him, and I've got some idea it's because of you."

Julia the Scrubber, laughing: "Rube's a big boy. He can take care of himself."

Me: "That's true, but he's also my brother, and there's no way I'd let him bleed alone."

Julia the Scrubber: "How very noble of you."

Rube came back in, saying, "I don't know what you're talkin' about, Cam. There's no one on the phone."

"I'm tellin' you," I said, pulling Rube out into the hallway. Once we got there, I whispered at him. "There was a guy there, Rube, and he sounded like he wanted to kill you. So when the phone rings again, get up and answer it."

The phone did ring again and this time Rube came running out of the room and got it. Again, they hung up on him. By the third time, Rube barked into the phone. "How 'bout you start talkin'? If you want Ruben Wolfe, you've got him. So talk!"

There was no response from the other end, and the phone didn't ring again that night, but after Julia left, I could see that Rube was a little pensive. He was about as worried as Ruben Wolfe gets, because he knew without doubt now, like I did, that something was coming. In our room, he looked at me. In the exchanging of our eyes, he was telling me a fight was looming.

He sat on his bed.

"I guess that bad feeling you had was right," he began. "About Julia. It's definitely that last bloke she had." It wasn't like Rube to be scared, because we both knew he could take care of himself. He was one of the most liked but most feared people in our neighborhood. The only trouble now was that nothing was certain. It was a feeling, that's all, and I could sense Rube was feeling it as well. I could smell it.

"Did you ask what's-her-name about him?"

"Julia?"

"Yeah."

"She reckons he isn't the brightest spark, and that he's got way too much time and a lot of friends. She was with him for about a year."

"And she just up and ditched him?"

Rube looked over. "That would about cover it."

"For you? He must be a real ugly bastard if she quit him for *you*."

"Don't get smart," he half warned. ". . . I'd consider gettin' after him, but you always end up worse when you do that. That's when they come back for y' with half their bloody neighborhood behind 'em."

We were quiet for a while, both thinking about it.

"If somethin' comes up," I finally said, "I'll be there, okay?"

Rube nodded. "Thanks, brother."

The phone rang the next night as well, and the next.

On the third call of Friday night, Rube picked up the phone and shouted, "What!?"

He then grew quiet.

"Yeah." A pause. "Yeah, sorry about that." He looked over at me and shrugged his shoulders. "I'll get him." He took the receiver away and covered the mouthpiece. "It's for you." He held it out to me, thinking. What was he thinking?

"Hello?"

"It's me," she said. Her voice reached through the phone and took me. "You working tomorrow?"

"Till about four-thirty."

She thought for a moment. "Maybe," she said, "we can do something when you get back. I know an old movie house. I think they're playing *Raging Bull*." Her words were soft but intense. The voice was excitement. The voice was shivers.

I smiled. I couldn't help it. "For sure."

"I'll come over just after four-thirty."

"Good, I'll see you then."

"I have to go." She almost cut me off, and she didn't say good-bye. She said, "I'm watching the clock," and she was gone.

When I hung up, Rube asked what I knew he would.

"Who was that?" He bit into an apple. "She sounded familiar."

I moved closer and sat at the kitchen table and swallowed. I concentrated on breathing. This was it. This was it and I had to say it. "Remember Octavia?"

Nothing was said.

The tap dripped.

It exploded into the sink.

Rube was halfway through another bite when he realized what I was saying.

His head tilted. He swallowed the piece of apple and made the calculation, while I was thinking, *Oh no, what the hell's about to happen here?*

Something happened.

It happened when Rube went and tightened the tap, turned back around, and said, "Well Cam . . ." He laughed.

Was that a good laugh or a bad one? Good laugh, bad laugh? Good laugh, bad laugh? I couldn't decide. I waited.

"What?" I asked. I couldn't stand it anymore.

"Tell me."

Nervously, I started telling him about what happened. I told him about standing outside the house in Glebe. About Octavia showing up. About the train and going there, and the shell, and —

"It's all right, Cam," he said, but I wasn't sure about the expression on his face. "That Octavia," and he shook his head now. "You'll treat her like a goddess, won't y' Cam?"

I smiled, but didn't bare my teeth. This seemed too easy.

He repeated the question. "Won't y' Cam?" because we both knew the answer.

This time, I couldn't hide the smile, even though I was still uneasy about Rube's response. He *seemed* happy enough, but in all honesty, Rube was never the type to let you wonder what he was thinking. He laughed a little and I decided that was a good thing, and we stayed together in the kitchen, just as Sarah came in.

"What's going on?" she asked. "What's all this smilin'? It looks like the end of a Scooby bloody Doo episode in here."

Rube clapped his hands. "Wait till you hear this," he nearly shouted. I don't know — he appeared to be trying too hard. "Remember Octavia?"

"Of course."

"Well." He was more subdued now. "Looks like you'll be seein' a bit more of her again because —"

"I knew it!" Sarah went through him. She pointed at me. "I knew there was a girl, you little bastard, and *you* wouldn't tell me anything!" I'd never seen Sarah grin like this. "Wait!" she said, and maybe thirty seconds later, she came back with her Polaroid camera and took an instant shot of Rube and me, both leaning against the sink.

"Smile again, will y's," she said, and we did.

We crowded around to watch the picture form, and soon I could make out the rough gatherings of Rube's hair and the outline of my face. The apple was still balancing in Rube's hand and we were standing there, leaning, both in old jeans, Rube in a flanno work shirt, me in my old spray jacket. It appeared to be so right, both our faces imprinted with smiles.

Appeared . . .

Sarah pulled the photo closer to her.

"I love this picture," she said, without a moment's thought. "It looks like brothers."

What brothers should be, I thought, and we all continued looking at it, as the tap still dripped down, exploding more quietly now, into the sink.

"Give us a look at that," Rube said, and he snatched the photo from Sarah's hand. Immediately, I could tell. Somehow I knew.

The way he did it.

The way his eyes zeroed in on the photo.

I knew my brother was about to ruin everything.

In the last few minutes, it had been coming, and now it was here. A quiet anger about the situation had reached him completely now. He'd decided that he didn't like this at all. Octavia and Cameron — to Rube, it wasn't right. It didn't sound right. It didn't feel right. In his eyes, I could see it now. He was about to end it, on gut feeling.

He smiled, but suddenly it wasn't genuine anymore. It was sarcastic as he said, "Yes sister, this sure is a great shot you've produced here." He showed it to her as if he'd taken it himself. "It's such a great shot of me and young Scraps here, isn't it?"

Sarah was confused. "Scraps?" she asked, just as I felt my insides collapse.

"Sure," my brother laughed, still focused on the photo. I could only just hear his words above the anxiety that boxed me in the ears. "Sure sister," he explained. "Scraps — I find the girls and Cam picks up the scraps. . . ."

I remember Sarah looking over at me then.

With a few sentences, Rube had destroyed me. Weeks later, I found out why he *really* did it, but for now, it seemed like he'd done it only because he was capable — because he was the guy who got the girls in this house, not me. Not Cameron. And especially not with a girl who was once with him.

Defeat opened the kitchen floor at my feet, raising its hands up to pull me down. *Stay calm*, I told myself as I watched Sarah pull the photo back from Rube's hands. A wounded look scattered slowly and painfully across her face, and when she looked back at me, I felt my anger gathering itself together. When it was all there, I climbed up from the defeat and stood before my brother, face-to-face.

I read his expression. It shaped up to me.

"You're a real bastard," I said. It didn't sound like me, though. I didn't normally have this much aggression in me. "You know that?"

"Well just remember that you pick up the scraps of a bastard," he answered. "If it wasn't for me you'd have nothing," and that was it. It was all I needed. I leaped at my brother and tore him down to the floor. In the background I could hear the shrieks of Sarah. I couldn't even understand her for the electricity in my ears, and too quickly, I could see the plates and cups and forks from the table crash silently to the kitchen floor. Straightaway, I was on my back. Rube, the faster, the stronger, had me pinned. Next I saw his fist, close up. It met my face right beneath my eye and everything shook. I thought the ceiling was splitting apart, and just when it all joined up and found its right place again, it burst open as my brother threw his fist into my face many times. His knees burned through my shoulders. His eyes tore into me. And his hair showered into his face as I fell limp and took it now without feeling anything.

"Stop it!" I heard Sarah screaming now. She'd gone out and come running back into the kitchen with a bucket of water. She threw it down just as Rube got off me. The freezing water splashed over me, covering me like a nice, icy blanket. "Bastard!" she yelled and threw the bucket at Rube. He shrugged it off and walked out.

Just before exiting the room, he pointed his finger at me.

"What the hell's *wrong* with you, anyway?" he said callously. "You couldn't find anything of your own, could y'?" He laughed. "Jesus! You don't pick up the girls y' brother once had. It's low! It's screwed up, you bloody freak!" He laughed hard and angry and awful. "How 'bout I give y' Julia's number when we're done? Would y' like that?" He left then, finally, slamming the front door behind him.

And me?

I was spread out on the kitchen floor.

Bruised. Soaked.

Beaten.

I closed my eyes and opened them again. The whole thing seemed surreal.

Did that really happen? I asked myself, but then the swelling on my face proved it to me, aching and turning over my skin. The disbelief and shock held me down — I'd always been worried about telling him, and now my worst fears had been realized. They were free to trample me.

Slowly, I looked all around.

The kitchen floor was covered with water, broken crockery, and other assorted scraps.

MARKUS ZUSAK

PIECES

Sometimes there only seem to be clouds.

Tonight, the clouds hang above me, sulking in the sky. They watch me write the words. I don't even think they bother to read them.

I imagine myself in a room, where some shattered pieces are strewn on the floor, in front of me.

As I walk toward them, I have no idea what they are, so I approach with trepidation. They seem to be a puzzle, all torn up and thrown apart. They look injured.

I crouch down and begin putting them together, finding each scrap that surrounds my feet.

Gradually, I see the picture form as I put it all together.

Gradually, I see.

These pieces on the ground.

Are made of me.

CHAPTER 14

I didn't go out with Octavia the next night.

She showed up right at the time she said she would, but when she saw my face, she knew immediately what had happened. I had a bruise that swelled blue around my eye and slid across my cheekbone. When she came onto the porch, I remember seeing her eyes back away from me. It didn't take long for her body to follow.

There was no hello.

No niceties.

I only stood and wanted to touch her hand, and the girl said, "Is that . . . ?"

Is that.

All I could do was nod my head in agreement with the question that was cut in half. It was an attempt to ignore the pain of it. *Is that from Rube?* is what she'd really meant to say.

Watching her feet.

I recall it so clearly — watching as her feet backed down the steps, carrying her toward the gate.

She said, "I'm sorry, Cam." Her words winced. "I'm so sorry — I should have known." The pain she felt at coming between my brother and me was obvious. It was wringing itself out through her expression. Her face dripped to the ground. What she didn't know was that it wasn't just her that came between Rube and me the previous night. It was everything that was different about us. It was Rube being the winner and me not settling to be the underdog anymore. It was the way he treated girls against the way I *wanted* to treat them. It was me facing the reality that I had lived my whole life not in Rube's shadow, but behind it, not even able to touch it. Yes, it felt like everything.

"Please," I called out then, afraid that it sounded like a yelp. "Octavia, don't go."

But she did.

She shook herself from the gate and walked onto the street. Half a walk. Half a run. There was panic in every footstep, and the sound of each one seemed to erase everything else that had happened before. Her face had been so full of sacrifice. In an instant she was willing to give up whatever she wanted, or what the two of us wanted, for the sake of Rube and me. She left so fast, and my reactions were simply too slow.

Can it be so quick? I asked myself. *Can everything burn down so fast? Can she just tread past me because of Rube?*

The truth of it kept rolling over me. It was like a virus, arriving with more strength with each passing thought of it. I replayed it at least a hundred times within a few minutes. Her words, her face. And the savage sound of her soft, falling footsteps.

How could it be so fast? I asked again, but there were no answers. A week ago she wanted every piece of me.

She loved me even for my failures, like not being able to lean on the glass windows in the tower. She loved the shell and my words. All those things were gone now.

I'd envisioned so many things for this night.

A cold street with us walking through it, warm.

An empty movie cinema, but for us.

Laughing.

Talking.

Sitting in the underground waiting for Octavia's train home.

Counting the trains as they pulled in, waited, then pulled back out — we'd be too happy for her to get on a train and go home. I'd sit there, proud that I could make Octavia Ash this happy. . . .

It all brushed past me with the icy breeze that lifted itself to our front porch and swept across my face.

A few minutes later, in *real* reality, the door slammed behind me and Rube walked out. We looked at each other a moment, but nothing was said. All day at work, he and I had said nothing to each other. On account of my face, Dad knew we'd fought, but he stayed out of it. We'd fought before and got over it, but this time I wasn't so sure.

As I sat there in the darkness of the porch, Rube only continued down the steps and onto the street, just like Octavia. When he was gone, I realized that neither of them had looked back at me.

The night was cold, but for a long time, I stayed there, enjoying it in a depressed sort of way. The wind grew stronger and slapped me in the face and even my jacket pockets were soaked with bitter coldness.

It was the first night I'd ever gone out with a girl — and I never even made it off the front porch.

Eventually, I went back inside.

I watched TV with Mr. and Mrs. Wolfe but I saw and heard nothing. When they laughed at something, it shocked me.

Soon after, I went into Rube's and my room and sat against the wall, under the window. In the dark. It's unfortunate to admit, but some tears burned their way down my face. When there was a knock at the door, I didn't even bother wiping them off.

I said nothing.

Another knock, but this time, Sarah walked in and hit the light. I let the pain of it ignite in my eyes.

"You didn't go out?" she asked.

Slowly, I shook my head.

"Why not?"

"She saw my face." My voice was numb. "And she knew Rube and I had fought."

"And that's it? She just left?"

"She ran," I pointed out.

"I see. . . ."

There was a while of no talking then, but Sarah sat down at the opposite end of the room from me. We only sat there, staring, and I must admit that it was kind of nice to have some company. When she got up, she came over and offered me a hand.

"Come on," she said. "Let me show you something."

Cautiously, I took it and stood up, following her out of the room, down the hall, and into her own room.

"Shut the door," she said.

I did as I was told.

She lifted her mattress and pulled out a big spiral booklet. Some Polaroids fell out. I noticed the one with Rube and me in the kitchen, right before the fight.

"Sit down."

Again, I did as I was told, and before my eyes, I saw the secret life of Sarah Wolfe, my sister. She turned pages and on each sheet, there was a sketch or a drawing, or a fully realized charcoal-colored work. There were sketches of our house, our family, our street. There were mothers dragging kids along at the supermarket, people boarding trains, cars lined up like dominoes on Elizabeth Street, and leftovers heating up in the kitchen.

She gave me the book and I kept turning the pages, looking down in awe at the strength and feeling in the drawings.

There was Dad getting out of his panel van after work.

Mrs. Wolfe sleeping on the couch one night, exhausted.

An anonymous person struggling down the street in the rain.

Page after page.

445

It took me a few minutes to be able to speak.

"They're brilliant," I said.

"Just keep going," she nodded. "Go to page thirty-eight."

I turned all the pages until I found the right one.

Standing on that page, was me. I was standing there in colored charcoal, in a blue suit, with a red tie, black shoes. My face was dirty but my head was high, and of course, my hair was a shocker — all tangled and rough and reaching for the sky. Most importantly, though, I was wearing a pair of red boxing gloves.

Cameron Wolfe.

In a blue suit and boxing gloves . . .

"I love it," I said to my sister.

"Yes," she said, "but do you know what it means, Cameron?" Any form of a smile left her face. She was serious. "Should I tell you what it means?"

"The suit and the gloves?"

"Yes."

I looked straight at her. "Tell me."

She answered. "Well, first of all, you're dirty. That's what you've always considered yourself to be — dirty, small, not worth much." She pointed now to the suit. "The suit tells us that you've had enough of that. You want so badly to be better that it hurts . . . am I right?"

Dumbly, I nodded.

"Then, the gloves." She was strong, and so sure. "The gloves show that you'll always fight to get there, to be that person." Now she became even more determined, and her words ran at me. Into me. "But I'll tell you something, Cam — if you still want that girl and leave things as they are . . . if you just let that girl walk away, I'll rub those gloves off altogether and disfigure your hands. I'll even make it look like you're about to cut them off." Her last words were spoken harshly. "You got it?"

Silently, I agreed.

"Do you still want her?" she said.

"Of course." There was no other answer.

"Well don't," she continued, "let Rube, or anyone else tell you what to do or what to be. Don't worry about what everyone else wants, just so their own miserable lives can be easier. Do what *you* want, Cam. Understand?"

For the last time, I nodded.

"Now shut the door behind you." This time she smiled.

I walked to the door but turned around halfway and returned to my sister. I leaned down quickly and kissed her cheek, then walked back out.

"Hey Cam," she called, just before I was gone. I turned back. "And keep writing too. . . ."

I stepped closer. "How did . . . ?"

I gave up and nodded, and walked back up the hall.

MARKUS ZUSAK

THE HALLWAY

If there are alleys inside me, there must also be hallways.

I take a walk inside, treading past rooms and closets, to find a dark hallway where I've never been before. There's no door, so I walk right in, find a string, and pull on it, to produce the adequate light.

The hallway glows now, but dimly enough to not hurt my eyes.

Slowly, I look from side to side as I walk, and I understand that this is a hallway of underdogs.

Plastered to the walls are the images of Sarah Wolfe, my sister. They're the photos and drawings from her notebook — the people on the street, my mother and father, the ones struggling with their shopping. They're all people fighting their way through their lives.

I study each one on my way through.

They keep me, and I keep them.

. . . At the end of the hallway, there's a light. It's a lot brighter than what's in here, but it blinks. It even seems to be limping in its attempt to get my attention.

I keep walking, toward that limping light. I vow to remember each person I've just seen, each image of the hallway.

The light awaits me, and I approach it uncertain.

CHAPTER 15

After everything that had happened, there was no chance of sleeping that night. I considered getting myself down to Octavia's place, but decided to wait out the hours and find her the next day down at the harbor.

There was an old movie on TV.

I watched it until I staggered to bed and dropped in.

Earlier, I wrote some words and tucked them under my mattress, and lying in bed, they seemed to crawl out and step over me as I stared at the ceiling.

It was late when Rube came in, tired and clumsy. He tripped over his shoes after he swept them off his feet, and briefly, before he went to bed, he came and stood over me. With my eyes closed, I could feel the presence of my brother.

Keep your eyes shut, I told myself. I came close to saying something to him, but I remembered the kitchen and the fight, and the words and the fists. A hatred climbed into bed with me, whispering that I should be still and silent and wait for the intruder to leave.

The intruder.

It hurt to think of my brother like that, but in one glorious moment, he had ripped apart the first chance I ever had.

To touch a girl.

To be with a girl . . .

"Hey Scraps," I imagined him saying, but he said nothing.

He only stood there.

Even now, I wonder what he was thinking at that moment.

Was he contemplating throwing his hand down to wake me, to call me brother and say he was sorry? Or did he want to ask me why I couldn't find a girl of my own? Did he want to plead with me to stop being his shadow?

I'll never know, because the moment passed and never came up again. It ended when his feet dragged him over to his own bed and he fell down, on top of the sheets. It seemed fitting that night that Rube rarely covered himself in bed. He didn't need the warmth, whereas I froze if I wasn't covered up to my nose, lying there with just my snout sticking up for air.

The hours dragged themselves by, and when Rube began to snore it felt like insult being lent to injury. The sound tore open the night, as I lay there with visions swimming and circling in my head. It was mostly Octavia, but images of Rube and Steve and Sarah also made their way inside me. I kept seeing the drawing Sarah showed me — the blue suit and the boxing gloves. For some reason, the visions of Steve also bothered me. I kept hearing the words he'd spoken — it was funny how my two brothers were so capable of hurting me, and how my sister was the one who could see something in me to believe in. All this time, she'd been watching, and I guess, if it wasn't for her, I wouldn't have resolved that night to find Octavia the next day, and to face Steve one last time.

In the morning, I decided Steve would be first.

Around ten, I walked up to his apartment. I didn't have to ring the buzzer because he and Sal were up on the balcony. He didn't call me up. Instead, he disappeared and came down to meet me. It was a gesture, I guess. He was coming to me.

He opened his mouth to speak, but I beat him.

"Where you on at today?" My voice was friendly. Giving.

Steve looked up at the balcony, but he didn't answer my question. He said, "What are you doing here?" I could tell he was shocked that I'd come, to face him in daylight. "If I were you, I'd never speak to me again." He looked away. "If I were you, I'd hate me forever."

"But I'm *not* you," I said. "I can't beat up a group of guys one by one. I can't kick a goal after beer's been thrown at my head — hell, I can't even kick one *without* the beer. But I *can* stand here, in front of you. I can look you in your eyes when you never expected to see me again. I can survive anything you do or say to me."

The breeze took a breath.

It paused — stopped completely — and Steve spoke. "Okay."

For a last moment, I looked at him, then left. I moved out from under the balconies and called up to

Sal, "I'll see y' later," then turned back to Steve. "I might come up tomorrow or later in the week. Maybe we can go up to the oval."

"Sounds good," he replied, and we went our own ways.

That was the first part done. Now for Octavia.

I went by train to the harbor, and when I stepped out onto the platform, I felt like nothing today would stop me. All my thoughts leaned now toward the girl, and from the railing, I looked for the crowd of people that would be gathered around her, watching, listening, and taking in the music that flowed from her.

She wasn't there, though.

The place that was hers was completely empty. Not even other buskers went there, because it seemed Octavia had ownership of it. The stretch toward the Harbour Bridge was only that — a stretch, a path. There was no music, and no people.

I ran down there and stood alone at the exact place, hit hard by the silence that surrounded me. For a few minutes, I looked wildly around, trying to find something, anything that would lead me to a scent of the girl.

Nothing.

I even asked some people if they'd seen a harmonica player.

They said there was one over on the other side, near the Opera House, and barely remembering to thank them, I took off. I ran around to the other side, past the ferry entrance, the ticket offices, and the boulevard of too-expensive cafés and restaurants.

Finally, near the Opera House steps, I could hear the sound of a harmonica and I hoped.

There! I thought, but when I rounded the corner, there was an old man, sitting down, playing. No Octavia.

My hopes struggled forward.

They fell crooked as I moved in a staggered circle, looking and attempting to find her. I began walking the city, and soon realized that I'd be walking all afternoon. My feet took me through the entire city center, but all I found were those mime people, pen sellers for the Royal Blind Society, and the odd didgeridoo player. The girl was nowhere.

With aching legs and feet, I eventually boarded a train for Hurstville and walked back down to Octavia's place. God, it was such a parody of the first time I'd walked down there. The nerves were even more intense now, but the reality was awful. It was almost obscene, because last time, I knew she wanted me. Deep down, I knew. This time though, if she was in there, I couldn't be sure if she would come out. And even if she did, would it be to tell me to go home, go away, go anywhere as long as it was away from her?

It was late afternoon when I made it there and started the vigil.

Soon, an hour was gone and so was the light.

The streetlights scratched themselves on.

There was no Octavia.

There was no girl.

There was only me, Cameron Wolfe, standing in front of a house where Octavia Ash happened to live. At one point, there was movement near the light that hid behind the front door, but no one came out.

You better go, I told myself, but not before I stayed one last minute and reminded myself of what this all meant. The cruelty of it walked past, digging its shoulder into me along the way. *The cruelty*, I thought, because here I was again, standing outside a girl's house who didn't want me — and this time it was worse, much worse, because she'd even asked me to stand there. Only twenty-four hours ago, she'd still wanted me, and now, it was all finished. I was still alone. I was still standing there, and now it wasn't just a walk from home. Now I had to come a lot further to stand amongst the same failure, to feel the same aloneness and humiliation.

When I left, I looked back, and there was no one looking out the window or brushing a curtain aside to watch me leave. There was nothing but the empty street and me.

The next night was the same.

Then, the next, and the next.

I resolved to stand there every night until Octavia came out, no matter how long it took.

It became routine, like waking up and putting on your pants. My routine was getting up, walking to school, and contemplating all of it as I stared at graffitied desks and wandered through the lonely halls of each building. I noticed how much laughter there was at school. It came to me suddenly, like echoes, like paint. Like paint splayed over me, coloring me a sickly human color. I would do what had to be done there, then head down to Octavia's, stand for two hours, and come home. Dinner was next, and walking Miffy, alone. Rube stopped walking him with me after the fight.

It was rare for me to see Rube at all that week.

The only time we spoke was when the phone started ringing again.

"It's the Phonecaller," I'd tell him. I never hung around to listen to what was said, and most times the phone was left dead. I could see Rube getting more and more frustrated, and I quietly felt glad that his womanizing had made his life at least a little uncomfortable.

As for the vigils down in Hurstville, the door finally opened on Friday night, but it wasn't Octavia who came out. It was a woman who had clearly given Octavia the shape of her face, and her eyes and lips. She walked slowly, almost sadly toward me.

There was kindness in her eyes and I recall the sincerity in her voice.

When she was close enough, she said, "You're Cameron, aren't you?"

I nodded. "Yes, Mrs. Ash, I am." I kept my head up and made sure to look at her. *Keep proud*, I thought.

"I thought it was best to come out and tell you that Octavia's not here tonight — she's gone to stay at a friend's place for the weekend." I could tell it pained her slightly to have to speak to me like this. "You should go home."

"Okay."

I said the word but I didn't mean it.

Nothing was okay, and I didn't want to go home.

Before I walked away, I turned and asked, "The whole weekend?"

Mrs. Ash nodded. "Take tomorrow night off — you deserve a rest." Her eyes swayed momentarily. "And Cameron?"

"Yes?"

"For what it's worth, I'm sorry, okay?"

That was when I simply stood there. I didn't want her pity. I wanted to spit at it. Throw it off me. Kill it. Yet all I managed to do was stand there a few seconds more and walk away.

I'll be back Sunday, I said to myself when I turned off the street, and I wondered if the girl truly was at a friend's place.

"You haven't given up, have you?" Sarah asked me the next night, and I told her about the conversation with Mrs. Ash. We were in her room. Her photos and some other small drawings were sitting on the desk.

"Don't worry," I reassured her. "I'll be back there tomorrow night."

"Good."

Like clockwork, I was there again the next night, and then every evening during the week. I stood there for up to two hours. Sometimes longer. A few times, it looked like rain, but it didn't come until a week and a half later. I stood there and splinters of rain soon turned to nails. I remained standing there, soaked, and that was what finally drew the girl out the front door and onto the porch.

"Cameron!?" she cried out, and I begged for her next words to be, "Come inside, come inside," but they weren't.

She came down toward the gate and the rain clamped down on her hair and dribbled down her face. Her voice was hard and loud, and it trapped me amongst the rain.

"Cameron, get out of here!" It was almost a shriek. Her green eyes were desperate and full of warm water, ready to mix with the ice that seemed to be bucketing from the sky. It didn't even take a minute for her to be completely wet and she was so beautiful, it nearly made me choke. "Go!" she shouted again. "Go home!" She closed her eyes in pain and turned, to go back inside.

She was nearly at the front door when I found my voice. It made its way over my beating heart and into my mouth.

"Why!?" I called to her. She turned to face me as I went on. "Why are you doing this to me!?" I swallowed, and met her face. "You rescued me from this once. Why are you putting me through it again?"

Hurt, she moved to the edge of the steps, raised her head, and punctured me.

She said, "Well maybe it's time you started rescuing yourself!"

It rained — harder and louder — and we stood there, each alone, as the words defeated both of us. Octavia was wounded and wet, and slowly, completely soaked with sorrow, she turned and went back inside. I remained at the gate, crushed by the heaviness of her words and the rain.

In the train on the way home, no one sat next to me because I was so wet.

There was so much of me, drooling all over the seat and onto the floor, sitting in a pool of defeat. At Central, I pulled my ticket out of my pocket, but all that was left of it was a soggy lump of paper. It would never go through the machine.

A collector was in the booth. She was a relatively old lady with some facial hair, and she was chewing gum. When I approached her, I held out the pathetic clump in my hand.

"*That's* your ticket?" she inquired.

"That's right," I answered morosely.

She studied me for a second or two but decided to let me through. "One of those days, huh?"

"Shocker," I answered, and she winked at me on my way past.

"Don't worry, love," she chewed. "Things can only get better from here." To that, I said nothing. I only listened as my soaked shoes squeaked on the dirty tile floor, and I imagined the trail of wet footprints stretching out behind me. It felt like those foot-prints stretched back forever.

IF HER SOUL SHOULD LEAK

I'm running, with wet feet.

There's a girl up ahead.

She doesn't move fast, but no matter how hard I run, I can't catch up with her. My feet become heavier and more sodden with every step. I want to call out, but some-how I know she won't hear.

Even as other people pass by, I want to tell them. I want to say it —

I love that girl.

But I don't.

Eventually, she turns a corner and by the time I make it around, she's gone.

Defeated, I lean back to the cold, hard bricks, and I understand that there are many things I haven't seen or felt or known.

At this moment, there's only one thing I know for sure.

It's about the girl, and it's this.

If her soul ever leaks, I want it to land on me.

CHAPTER 16

It rained nonstop for a week, and amongst all the water, an event occurred that had the potential to turn everything on its head.

A tragedy.

A debacle.

And you guessed it, it involves Miffy, the wonder-dog, the little bastard, the ball of fluff who's always managed to elbow his way into our lives.

What happened was this:

The poor little guy just up and died on us.

It was Thursday afternoon and torrential rain poured itself down, battering the streets and rooftops. Someone was smashing their fist into our front door.

"Hang on!" I yelled. I was glumly eating toast in the lounge room.

I opened the door and there was a small balding man on his knees, completely drenched.

"Keith?" I asked.

He looked up at me. I dropped the toast. Rube was behind me now, asking, "What's goin' on?"

Keith's face was covered in sorrow. Dribbles of rain ambled down his face as he slowly picked himself up. He fixed his eyes on our kitchen window and said it, with pain rinsing through his voice.

"Miffy." He almost went to pieces again. "He's dead. In the backyard."

Rube and I looked at each other.

We ran out the back and clambered over the fence as the back door slammed behind us. Halfway over the fence, I saw it. There was a soggy ball of fluff lying motionless amongst the grass.

No, I thought, as I landed on the other side. Disbelief held me down inside my footsteps, making my body heavy but my thoughts wild.

Rube also hit the ground. His feet slapped down into the sodden grass, and where my footsteps ended, his began.

I kneeled down in the pouring rain.

The dog was dead.

I touched him.

The dog was dead.

I turned to Rube, who was kneeling next to me. For the moment, our differences were cast aside.

The dog was dead.

We sat there a while, completely silent as the rain fell like needles onto our soaked bodies. The fluffy brown fur of Miffy the pain-in-the-arse Pomeranian was being dented by the rain, but it was still soft, and clammy. Both Rube and I stroked him. A few stray tears even sprang into my eyes. I recalled all the times we walked him at night with smoke climbing from our lungs and with laughter in our voices. I heard us complaining about him, ridiculing him, but deep down, caring for him. *Even loving him*, I thought.

Rube's face was devastated.

"Poor little bastard," he said. His voice clung strangely to his mouth.

I wanted to say something but was completely speechless. I'd always known this day would come, but I didn't imagine it like this. Not pouring rain. Not a pathetic frozen lump of fur, or a feeling as despondent as the one I felt at this exact moment.

Rube picked him up and carried him under the shelter of Keith's back veranda.

The dog was dead.

Even once the rain stopped, the feeling inside me didn't subside. We kept patting him. Rube even apologized to him, probably for all the verbal abuse he'd leveled at him almost every time he saw him.

"Sorry," he said, and I had to check who he was talking to.

Keith arrived after a while, but it was mainly Rube and me who stayed. For about an hour or so, we sat with him.

"He's getting stiff," I pointed out at one stage.

"I know," Rube replied, and I'd be lying if I didn't say a smirk didn't cross our faces. It was the situation, I guess. We were cold, soaking wet, and hungry, and in a way, this was Miffy's final revenge on us — guilt. Or was it a sacrifice, to bring us back together?

Here we were, just about frozen in our neighbor's backyard, patting a dog that was getting stiffer and stiffer by the minute, all because we'd consistently insulted him and then had the audacity to love him.

"Well forget this," Rube finally said. He gave Miffy a last pat and told the truth with a wavering voice. He said, "Miffy — you were undoubtedly a pathetic individual. I hated you, loved you, and wore a hood on my head so no one saw me with you. It's been a pleasure." He gave him a final pat, on the dog's head. "Now, I'm leavin'," he pointed out. "Just because you had the nerve to die under your clothesline in the middle of what was practically a hurricane, I'm not about to get pneumonia because of it. So good-bye — and let's pray the next dog Keith and his wife decide to get is actually a *dog* and not a ferret, rat, or rodent in disguise. Good-bye."

He walked away, into the darkness of the backyard, but as he climbed the fence, he turned and gave Miffy one last look. One last good-bye. Then he was gone. For a moment, I realized that this was more than he'd given me when I sat on the porch that night after Octavia ran from me. He sure as hell didn't look back at *me*. But then, to be fair, I wasn't dead.

I hung around a little while longer, and when Keith's wife came home from work she was quite distressed about what I was beginning to call "The Miffy Incident." She kept repeating one thing. "We'll get him cremated. We've gotta get that dog cremated." Apparently, Miffy was a gift from her dead mother, who insisted that all corpses, including her own, had to be burned. "Gotta get that dog cremated," she went on, but rarely did she even look at him. Strangely enough, I had the feeling it was Rube and me who loved that dog the most — a dog whose ashes would most likely end up on top of the TV or video, or in the liquor cabinet for safekeeping.

Soon, I said my last good-bye, running my hand over the stiff body and silky fur, still a little shocked by all of it.

I went home and told everyone the news of the cremation. Needless to say, everyone was amazed, especially Rube. Or maybe amazed isn't quite the right word for my brother's reaction. Appalled was more like it.

"Cremate him!?" he shouted. He couldn't believe it. "Did you see that dog!? Did you see how bloody soggy he was!? They'll have to dry him out first or else he'll never even burn! He'll just smolder! They'll have to get the blow-dryer out!"

I couldn't help but laugh. Trust Rube to still make me laugh despite my hating his guts at that point in time.

It was the blow-dryer, I think.

I kept imagining Keith standing over the poor mongrel with the blow-dryer on full speed and his wife calling out from the back door:

"Is he dry yet, love? Can we chuck him in the fire?"

"No, not yet darlin'!" he'd reply. "I'll need about another ten minutes, I reckon. I just can't get this damn tail dry!" Miffy had one of the bushiest tails in the history of the world. Trust me.

We found out the next day that there'd be a small ceremony on Saturday afternoon at four. The dog was being burned on Friday.

Naturally, as the walkers of Miffy, we were invited next door for the funeral. But it didn't stop there. Keith also decided he wanted to scatter Miffy's ashes in the backyard that was his domain. He asked if we'd like to be the ones who emptied them. "You know," he said. "Since you spent the most time with him."

"Really?" I asked.

"Well, to be honest," he shifted on the spot a little. "The wife wasn't too keen on the idea, but I put my foot down. I said, *No, those boys deserve it and that's it, Norma.*" He laughed and said, "My wife referred to you as the two dirty bastards from next door."

Old bitch, I thought.

"Old bitch," Rube said, but luckily, Keith didn't hear.

On Saturday, Dad, Rube, and I finished work at two so we could get home in time for the big funeral, and by four o'clock it was Rube, Sarah, and me who went next door. We all climbed the fence.

Keith brought Miffy out in a wooden box, and the sun was shining, the breeze was curling, and Keith's wife was sneering at Rube and me.

Old bitch, I thought again, and you guessed it, Rube actually said it, as a whisper only he, Sarah, and I could hear. It made us all laugh, though I tried to resist. The wife didn't look too happy.

Keith held the box.

He gave a futile speech about how wonderful Miffy was. How loyal. How beautiful. "And how pitiful," Rube whispered again, to which I had to bite the inside of my mouth to keep from laughing. A small burst actually made it out, and Keith's wife wasn't too impressed.

Bloody Rube, I thought. Even when I hated him he could make me laugh. Even when I despised everything he stood for and had done to me, he could make me laugh by giving Miffy a good mouthful.

The thing was, though, it was fitting for it to be like this. There was no point in us standing there claiming how much we loved the dog and all that kind of thing. That would only show how much we *didn't* love him. We expressed love for this dog by:

1. Putting him down.
2. Deliberately provoking him.
3. Hurling verbal abuse at him.
4. Discussing whether or not we should throw him over the fence.
5. Giving him meat that was a borderline decision on whether or not he could adequately chew it.
6. Heckling him to make him bark.
7. Pretending we didn't know him in public.
8. Making jokes at his funeral.

9. Comparing him to a rat, ferret, and any other creature resembling a rodent.
10. Knowing without showing that we cared for him.

The problem with this funeral was that Keith was
going on and on, and his wife kept insisting on attempting to cry. Eventually, when everyone was bored
senseless and almost expecting a hymn to be sung,
Keith asked a vital question. In hindsight, I'm sure he
wished like hell he didn't ask it at all.

He said, "Anyone else got something to say?"

Silence.

Pure silence.

Then Rube.

Keith was just about to hand me the wooden box
that contained the last dregs of Miffy the dog when
Rube said, "Actually, yes. I have something to say."

No, Rube, I thought desperately. *Please. Don't do it.*

But he did.

As Keith handed me the box, Rube made his
announcement. In a loud, clear voice, he said, "Miffy —
we will always remember you." His head was held high.
Proud. "You were strictly the most ridiculous animal on
the face of the earth. But we loved you."

He looked over at Sarah and smiled — but not
for long.

Definitely not for long, because before we even had
time to think, Keith's wife exploded. She came tearing

across at us. She was onto me in a second and she started wrestling me for the bloody box!

"Give us that, y' little bastard," she hissed.

"What did *I* do?" I asked despairingly, and within an instant, there was a war going on with Miffy in the center of it. Rube's hands were on the box now as well, and with Miffy and me in the middle, he and Norma were going at it. Sarah took some great action shots of the two of them fighting.

"Give us that," Norma was spitting, but Rube didn't give in. There was no way. They struggled on, Norma with all her might, and Rube in a relaxed, amused way.

In the end, it was Keith who ended it.

He stepped into the middle of the fray and shouted, "Norma! Norma! Stop being stupid!"

She let go and so did Rube. The only person now with their hands on the box was me, and I couldn't help but laugh at this ludicrous situation. To be honest, I think Norma was still upset about an incident I haven't previously mentioned. It was something that happened two years ago. It was the incident that got us walking Miffy to begin with, when Rube and I and a few other fellas were playing football in our yard. Old Miffy got all excited because of all the noise and the ball constantly hitting the fence. He barked until he had a mild heart attack, and to make up for it, Mrs. Wolfe made us pay the vet's bill and take him for walks at least twice a week.

That was the beginning of Miffy and us. The *true* beginning, and although we whinged and carried on about him, we did grow to love him.

In the backyard funeral scene, however, Norma wasn't having any of it. She was still seething. She only calmed down a few minutes later, when we were ready to empty Miffy out into the breeze and the backyard.

"Okay Cameron," Keith nodded. "It's time."

He made me stand up on an old lawn chair and I opened the box.

"Good-bye Miffy," he said, and I turned the box upside down, expecting Miffy to come pouring out.

The only problem was, he didn't. He was stuck in there.

"Bloody hell!" Rube exclaimed. "Trust Miffy to be all bloody sticky!"

Keith's wife looked slightly aggravated, to say the least. Actually, I think ropeable would be a more appropriate word.

All I could do was start shaking the box, but still the ashes didn't come out.

"Put your finger in it and stir it round a bit," Sarah suggested.

Norma looked at her. "You're not gettin' smart now too, are y' girly?"

"No way," Sarah replied honestly. Good idea. You wouldn't want to upset this lady at this point in time. She looked about ready to strangle someone.

I turned the box back over and cringed before rummaging my hand through the ashes.

The next time I tried emptying it, there was success. Miffy was set free. As Sarah took the photo, the wind picked up the ashes and scattered them over the yard and into Keith's other neighbor's yard.

"Oh no," Keith said, scratching his head. "I knew I should have told next door to take their washing off the line. . . ."

His neighbors would be wearing Miffy on their clothes for at least the next couple of days.

PAUSE OF DEATH

I pause a moment and thoughts of death climb onto me. They hang from my shoulders and breathe in my face, and I get to thinking about religion and heaven and hell.

Or to be honest, I think of hell.

There's nothing worse than thinking that that's exactly *where you're going when eternity comes for you.*

That's where I usually think I'm going.

Sometimes I take comfort in the fact that most people I know are probably going to hell too. I even tell myself that if all my family are going to hell I'd rather go with them than enter heaven. I mean, I'd feel sort of guilty. There they'd be, burning through eternity, while I'm eating peaches and most likely patting pitiful Pomeranians like Miffy up in heaven.

I don't know.

I don't.

Really.

I'm pretty much just hoping to live decent. I hope that's enough.

CHAPTER 17

The question now is, what the hell happened next? Every time I think about the whole death of Miffy saga, the story gets obscured in my mind. I have to concentrate to get it right.

The sound.

That's always how I remember — the sound of Rube in the basement, punching the bag that hung in there. He was preparing for the Phonecaller, who was still calling on a three nights per week basis. Rube would stay down there for a long time each night, and when he entered our bedroom, I could see some blood leaking across his knuckles.

If our differences were set aside for Miffy's sake, they returned almost immediately after. In death, Miffy had only brought us together momentarily. He'd failed. There was an outward indifference that Rube constantly sent me in the eyes, if he looked at me at all. The only time he spoke to me was by staring out the window and talking more to himself than to me.

"That friggin' Julia," he said one night.

It was a cold Tuesday evening at the start of August when Rube got what seemed like the usual call. This time, though, it was Julia. She told him she'd gone back to the previous bloke — the Phonecaller. Apparently, he'd begged her to go back and she did. She also warned Rube that he was still after him, to which Rube offered to get it over with immediately, in the backyard, if necessary. . . .

The scrubber was gone, but she'd left a legacy.

As he stood at the window and spoke of these things, I remembered once telling him I'd be there if he needed me. "Thanks brother." That's what he'd told me back then, but now I wasn't so sure. I wasn't sure if he would even *want* help from me, and I didn't know if I had the strength to give it to him. I could only watch him at the window, as he enjoyed the hardness of his hands, and the blood that crept from them.

I stopped going to Octavia's place altogether.

"Maybe it's time you started rescuing yourself," I kept hearing her say, though I could also see the pain on her face. I told myself at times that she didn't mean it; that she didn't want me to stop coming and standing there. She only did it because she thought it was the right thing to do. The irony was that she thought she was keeping Rube and me together by staying away, but as it currently stood, I'd lost both of them.

Days and nights collected up and slipped by, and Rube continued his routine of answering the empty phone calls and blasting the bag in the basement. In a way, I could only feel sorry for someone who wanted to take him on. Even if there were more than one, at least a few of them would get hurt, because Rube had speed and strength and no hesitation.

One night when the phone rang I answered it and asked the guy on the other end to hang on. "My brother wants to talk to you," I said. "I mean, this is getting ridiculous. You call three times a week. You say nothing. I'm starting to think you actually *like* my brother rather than want to kill him — otherwise you'd just beat him up and be done with it. So hang on. Just a minute."

I went down to the basement.

"What is it?"

Rube didn't usually sweat much, but after a good hour on the bag, he was drenched.

"It's him," I said.

He walked up the cold cement steps and practically mauled the phone when he picked it up.

"Now listen," he growled. "I'll be waiting down near the old train yard at eight o'clock tomorrow night. You know where that is? . . . Yeah, that's the one. If you want, come and get me. If not, stop ringin' me — you're a pain in the arse." There was a longer silence. Rube was listening. "Good," he spoke again. "Just you and me, alone." Again, he listened. "That's right — no help, no tricks, and then it's over. Good-bye." He slammed the phone down and I could see he was already fighting in his mind.

"So it's on?" I asked.

"Apparently so," and he went to shut the basement door. "Thank Christ for that."

Then the phone rang. Again.

Rube picked it up, and immediately, I could tell it was his mate again. Rube wasn't happy.

"What is it this time?" He shot the words through the phone. "You can't!?" He was getting more irritated by the second. "Now listen, mate — you're the one who wants to kill *me*, so make up your mind about when you feel like doin' it. What about tonight, or right now? No? Well how about Friday? Could you check your calendar and make sure you've got nothing else on?" He waited. "Y' sure now? Positive? You won't be ringin' in a minute or two attempting to reschedule? No? So Friday night sounds like a good time to kill me? Good. Same place, same time. *Friday.* Good."

Again, he hung up, forcefully. He shook his head but laughed. "It's an absolute circus with this bloke."

He started eating some bread and got ready to go out. I guess with Julia gone, there were more girls on the horizon. For a moment, I nearly asked if he wanted me to come along on Friday, but I guess he would have viewed that as *scraps* behavior — following him around.

Anyway, I thought. *He got himself into this.* He'd finally stumbled onto the wrong girl, and maybe he was going to pay. Sure, I also told myself that I'd been wrong in the past, because Rube had often escaped dangerous situations for no other reason than the fact that he was Ruben Wolfe and Ruben Wolfe could handle anything.

With his fists.

With his wayward charm.

Any way he could.

This time, though, I couldn't be sure. It was different. I guess we'd discover the outcome on Friday night.

There were a few days till then, and I spent most of my time thinking about the confrontation, and Octavia. Always Octavia. I considered writing her a letter or calling her, but I couldn't bring myself to do it. Sarah said I should keep trying.

"You haven't cut my hands off in that picture, have you?" I asked her on Thursday night.

She only shook her head, almost forlornly. "No, Cam — I think you've fought hard enough. At least for the time being."

All that was left was Friday night.

Rube got ready in our room at about seven-thirty, putting on his oldest jeans, his work flanno, and boots, which he did up nice and tight. He stared into the mirror, telling himself what to do. Eyeing himself off.

Just before he left, we looked at each other.

What was there to say? Good luck? I hope you get the crap beaten out of you? You want me to come?

No.

It was all silence, and he left.

On his way out, he announced that he was going to a friend's place, shut the door hard, and went out onto the street. Even from the kitchen window, I could tell he was hyped up and hardened. The cold night air seemed to get out of his way as he walked through it.

Now it was decision time.

Was I going after him or not?

The minutes passed and finally I resolved to go. I knew it was wrong, but I couldn't help it, even after everything that had happened. The kitchen. Losing Octavia. I still couldn't get past the fact that Rube was my brother and that trouble was looming in his direction. I moved quickly back to our room, threw on my boots and spray jacket, and headed out.

It was close to eight when I got there, to the old train yard. I could see Rube waiting down by the fence, and I took a different street and a side alley. That way, I doubled back and stood closer, waiting. From near the edge of the alley, I could still see him standing there, but he couldn't really see me. All I could do now was wait.

The yard was full of wrecked train carriages, standing around in the dark. Their windows were smashed, and stolen words were written across them like scars. The fence was tall and made of wire, cordoning off the yard from the street. Rube was leaning against it with his back.

For a moment, I wondered why he didn't bring friends, just in case. There were plenty of people around here who would gladly fight for him and could fight well. Maybe Rube decided this was his own doing and he would face it alone.

Thoughts passed.

Minutes passed.

Some voices started loitering around the street and soon their shadows turned into humans. There were three of them. I could see Rube straighten up as they went past me, not even noticing I was there.

They moved closer and adrenaline shot me down.

This was it.

DEEP BREATHS

My breath is made of smoke.

It crouches down.

Right after it comes from my mouth.

It crouches down, holds on a moment, and is swallowed by the air.

I stand in the darkness, in the perpetual shadow. My eyes feel like they glow. My furry, furious hair knots upward for the stars. Thoughts scratch me. My life itches me, and I prepare.

To step out.

To rip the shadows from the ground and hoist the darkness from the air.

I look at my hands, my feet.

Deep breaths.

Breathe depths.

Solemnly, I nod, to myself.

Make a step.

Take a threat.

Not far away, there's one last fight, one last struggle.

There's something here, in this place — a smell. It's all that's awful, all that's precious, raw, and real.

When I walk out and face it, I notice what it is.

This place smells.

Like brothers.

CHAPTER 18

I waited for the sound of it.

The jabs of words and the left hook of the fight's beginning.

But nothing came.

The footsteps of the three figures turned into another small alley, and again, Rube was alone down at the fence. He leaned backward again, moving back and forth into the wire.

He's late, I could see him thinking. He looked at his wrist, even though he never wears a watch.

By half-past eight I decided I should get going. As I moved away, I scuffed the ground and Rube looked up and saw me, or at least an edge of me.

"Oi!" he called, and he came toward me. I froze. "What are y' doin' here, Cam?"

I shoved my hands in my pockets. "I don't know."

We met under a streetlight that poured over the street. It was the only light on it.

"He's late," my brother said. A long time elapsed before I answered.

"Maybe *we* should have it out instead."

"What?"

"You heard me."

Rube scanned the street for any more people but it

was still deserted. He looked back at me and said, "Have what out?"

"You and me and Octavia and the kitchen and Scraps — how's that for a start?" I said the words quickly. Instantly.

"I don't have time for that tonight, Cam."

"Fair enough," and I started walking off. My feet scraped the road. "When you and me are important enough, let me know."

A fair way up the street, I heard him call out.

"Cameron!"

I turned. "What?"

"Get back here."

And I walked back to my brother and said it all. We stood under the streetlight that showered over us. My words were fists and I threw them at my brother. There was no hesitation. "Why'd y' have to do it, Rube? Tell me. Why did you have to ruin my first chance — my first chance ever?" The combination of words lunged at my brother, hitting him in the face.

He took them well and came back. "I don't know, okay!"

"Yes you do."

The light seemed even brighter now. No place to hide.

"All right," he said angrily, conceding. He looked at the ground, as though he were reading it, checking the sentences over before he said them. "I just — bloody hell, Cam — I didn't want you to have her."

"That's it?" I was incensed. "Why the hell not!?"

"Because . . ." He shifted feet. "You'd treat her so sickeningly bloody good, Cam, and I'd have to look at her as she compared us and thought about what a bastard *I* am. Okay?" My brother's eyes sank into mine. "That good enough for y'?"

I let the realization of that kick in. It took a while. Eventually, when I went to speak, Rube beat me to it. He said, "I didn't know she'd get the hell out of there so fast either. How could I know that, Cam? . . . Do you think I haven't been walkin' round hating myself? Of course I have."

We stood there.

Should I have pitied him, or hated him?

So long went by and finally, I realized it was me who had to break the silence. Everything was changing, on a quiet back street, with no one but ourselves to watch.

I said, "You were always the one, Rube. You always got the girls." I looked him flatly in the face. "But not one of those girls ever got *you*. They got your filthy good looks, your hands, and everything else you wear, but they never got you. You're too busy taking to give anything. . . ."

An even more penetrating silence arrived then, and I knew it was time to leave.

Rube remained a few paces away from me, shocked by what he'd heard, or actually, not that he'd heard it, but that someone else had told him exactly what he'd been trying to tell himself for a long time but refused to hear.

Just before I left, I said, "You weren't only my brother, Rube — you were my best friend."

He nodded then, and I could see emotion welling in his eyes.

"I'll see y' then."

"Yeah," he spoke quietly. "I'll see y' later," and I walked off. Not triumphant or successful. Just satisfied that what needed to be done was finished.

At the top of the street, I called back one last time.

"Y' comin' home?"

Rube shook his head. "No, I'm waitin' a bit longer."

With that, I turned back onto the street that belonged to the world — the one leading to the train yard seemed removed, like it was its own entity. As I walked, I imagined the shadow of Rube, still leaning against the fence, waiting. One of his feet would be up against the wire and his breath would be going smoky in the winter air.

When I made it home, I didn't do too much at all. I thought about our conversation and started reading a book for school. Not one word made it inside me.

The night went on and I resolved to wait up for Rube. I fell asleep on the couch a few times, and when everyone else went to bed they woke me and told me to go as well. I wanted to keep hating him, but as the hours went by, a strange determination kept growing inside. No matter how much I hated him, I was determined to see Rube come walking through the front door. Don't ask me why, but I needed to see it.

I wanted to see his face.

Unmarked.

Unbruised.

I wanted to hear his voice tell me to get up as he went past.

But that night, my brother Rube didn't come home.

It was just past midnight when I woke up with a silent start. My eyes opened and the yellow light from the lounge room sliced me through the eyes.

I was hit twice by one thought.

Rube.

Rube.

His name was repeated in me as I scissored off the couch and walked slowly into our room. I was hoping against hope that he would be in there, sprawled out across his bed. The darkness of the hall captured me. The creaking floorboards gave me away. Then, as the door crept open, I sent my eyes into the room, ahead of me. It was empty.

I turned the light on and shivered. It blinded me and I realized. I was going back out, to the night.

In the lounge room, I pulled my shoes on as quietly as possible, slipped my jacket back on, and headed for the kitchen, toward the front door. A pale light from the moon was numb in the sky. I was out in the uncertain coldness of the street.

A bad feeling intensified in my stomach.

It made its way to my throat.

Soon, as I walked fast to the old train yard, I could feel it gathering on its way through me. There were drunk people who made me edge out onto the road. Cars sped toward me with the brightness of their lights, then passed and faded away.

My hands sweated inside my jacket pockets. My feet were cold inside the warmth of my shoes.

"Hey boy," a voice slung out to me. I avoided it. I pushed past the guy who said it and broke into a run and had the street leading to the train yard in sight.

When I made it there, I could feel my heartbeat's hands, ripping me open.

The street.

Was empty.

It was empty and dark except for the widening light of the moon that seemed to spray down on each forgotten corner of the city. I could smell something. Fear.

I could taste it now.

It tasted like blood in my mouth, and I could feel it slide through me and open me up when I saw him. . . .

There was a figure sitting down, crooked, against the fence.

Something told me Rube didn't sit like that.

I called his name, but I could barely hear it. There was a giant pounding in my ears that kept everything else out.

Again, I called, "Rube!?"

The closer I got, the more I knew it was him. My brother was slumped against the fence and I could see the blood flooding his jacket, his jeans, and the front of his old flanno.

His hands gripped the fence.

The look on his face was something I'd never seen on him before.

I knew what it was because I was feeling it myself.

It was the fear.

It was fear, and Ruben Wolfe had never been afraid of anything or anyone in his life, until now. Now he was sitting alone in the city and I knew that one person alone couldn't have done this to him. I imagined them holding him down and taking turns. His face almost made its way into a smile when he saw me, and like a breeze through the silence, he said to me blankly:

"Hey Cam. Thanks for comin'."

The pulse in my ears subsided and I crouched down to my brother.

I could tell he'd dragged himself to this position on the fence. There was a small trail of blood smeared to a rusty color on the cement. It looked like he'd climbed two yards when it was too much and he couldn't go on. I had never seen Ruben Wolfe defeated.

"Well," he shuddered, "I guess they got me good, huh? You must be glad. . . ."

I ignored his comment. I had to get him home. He was shivering uncontrollably. "Can you get up?"

He smiled again. "Of course."

Rube still had that smile perched on his lips when he staggered up the fence and collapsed. I caught him and held him up. He slipped through me and fell facedown, holding on to the road.

The city was swollen. The sky was still numb.

Ruben Wolfe was facedown on the road with his brother standing there, helpless and afraid, next to him.

"You've gotta help me, Cam," he said. "I can't move." He pleaded with me. "I can't move."

I turned him over and saw the concussion that surrounded him. There wasn't as much blood as I'd originally thought, but his face was brutalized by the night sky that fell on him and made him real.

I dragged him back to the fence, propped him up, and lifted him. Again, he nearly collapsed, and when we started walking, I knew he wasn't going to make it.

"I'm sorry, Cam," he whispered. "I'm sorry."

"We'll just get y' home, ay."

"No," he said, hanging on to me. "Not sorry for *this* — sorry for everything." His expression swallowed me.

"Okay," I said. "We're okay."

That was when relief seemed to wash over him and he fell to the ground. Maybe that was the sweetest punch — and the final defeat. "We're okay, huh?" I had never heard a person so happy in this condition.

We'd traveled only about five yards from the fence.

I rested for a minute as my brother continued lying on his back. . . .

As the moon was smothered by a cloud, I slid my arms beneath my brother's back and legs and picked him up. I was holding Rube in my arms and carried him up the deserted street.

On the way home, my arms ached and I think Rube fell unconscious, but I couldn't rest. I couldn't put him down. I had to make it home.

People watched us.

Rube's tough curly hair hung down toward the ground.

Some extra blood landed on the footpath. It dripped from Rube onto me and then onto the path.

It was Rube's blood.

It was my blood.

Wolfes' blood.

There was a hurt somewhere far down inside me, but I walked on. I had to. I knew that if I stopped carrying him it would be harder to keep going.

"Is he all right?" a young party-going sort of guy asked. I could only nod and continue walking. I wouldn't stop until Rube was in his bed and I was standing over him, protecting him from the night, and from the dreams that would wake him in the hours until morning.

The last turn onto our street finally came and I lifted him in one last effort.

He moaned.

"Come on, Rube," I said. "We're gonna make it," and when I think about it now, I don't understand how I made it that far. He was my brother. Yes, that was it. He was my brother.

At our gate, I used one of Rube's feet to free the latch and walked up the porch steps.

"The door," I said, louder than I'd wanted to, and after putting him down on the porch, I opened the flyscreen, got my key in, and turned back to face him. My brother. *My brother Rube*, I thought, and my eyes ached.

As I walked back toward him, my arms throbbed, and my spine climbed my back. When I picked him up again, we nearly fell together into the wall.

On the way through the house, I managed to jam one of Rube's knees into a door frame, and by the time I got us into our room, Sarah was standing there, sleepy-eyed until terror strangled her face.

"What the hell —"

"Quiet," I said. "Just help me."

She stripped the blanket off Rube's bed and I placed him down on it. My arms were on fire as I took his jacket and flanno off, leaving him in his jeans and boots.

He was cut up and badly bruised. A few ribs were swollen and one of his eyes was pitch-black. Even his knuckles were bleeding. *He got a few good ones in*, I thought, but all of that meant nothing now.

We stood there. Sarah looked from Rube to me, recognizing his blood on the arms of my jacket. She cried.

The light was off now but the hall light was on.

GETTING THE GIRL

We could feel someone else arrive and I knew it was Mrs. Wolfe. Without even looking, I could picture the hurt expression on her face.

"He'll be okay," I managed to say, but she didn't leave. She came toward us as Rube's voice fought its way next to me.

His hand came out from under the blanket and held on to mine.

"Thanks," he said. "Thanks, brother."

The pale light hit me from the window. My heart howled.

THE EYES HAVE IT

I see myself standing on a city street, where a flood of people crowds toward me. Somehow, I manage to stay still, and I soon realize that all of these people are faceless. A blankness shrouds their eyes and they have no expression at all.

It's only when I begin to walk, through the gaps, against the flow, that I notice that some of the faces have actually kept their form.

At one point, I see Sarah, finding her own way through, and at another, I see my father, and Mrs. Wolfe, walking together, holding hands.

A long way off, I see Octavia.

I don't see her face, because she's going in the same direction as me. I see only her hair, and her neck and shoulders through the crowd.

Of course, like before, my first instinct is to go after her — but immediately, I stop. I stop and look to my right and see my reflection, even though there's no mirror or glass to speak of. There's only a concrete wall, but I'm able to see myself.

I see my eyes.

They're eyes of hunger and desire.

They tell me:

Don't move from here — not yet.

They ask me:

Are you okay, Cameron?

I think about it and take a good look at me. I look at my boyish arms, my dirty fingers, and wanting face. I look at the eyes, and I see the hunger and desire, growing and feeding, determined to make me worthwhile, to be somebody, *on my own.*

And I nod.

I can move on now, because here, at this moment, no matter how fragile it might be, I can feel okayness growing inside me.

The funny thing is that okayness *is not a real word. It's not in the dictionary.*

But it's in me.

CHAPTER 19

I'll give it to him.

Rube actually got up the next morning and went to work with Dad and me. He was bruised and still prone to constant bleeding, but he still showed up and worked as hard as he could. I don't think there are many people who could take a beating like that and get up the next day and work.

That was Rube.

There isn't anything else I can say to explain it.

Everyone woke up in the morning when he and Dad argued, but once it was over, that was it. Mrs. Wolfe asked, or actually, begged Rube to stay in at night more often, and there was no way he'd be arguing with that. He agreed completely and we filed out to the car and left. In the car, I could smell him — there was disinfectant on all his cuts.

It was mid-afternoon when Rube finally asked about some of the hazier details of the previous night.

"So how far was it, Cam?" His words came and stood in front of me. They wanted the truth.

I stopped work. "How far what?"

"You know." He caught himself in my eyes. "How far did you carry me last night?"

"A fair way."

"All the way?"

I nodded.

"I'm sorry," he went to say, but we both knew it wasn't needed.

"Forget about it," I said.

The rest of the afternoon passed by pretty quickly. I watched Rube work at times and knew that somehow he'd be all right. He was just that type. If he was alive, he'd be all right.

"What are y' lookin' at?" he asked me later, when he saw me watching him and wondering about it.

"Nothin'."

We even afforded a laugh, especially me, because I decided I had to stop being caught when I was watching people. Watching people isn't really a bad habit in my opinion. It's the getting caught I need to cut out.

When we got home, there was a present waiting for me, on my desk in Rube's and my room. It was an old gray typewriter with black keys. I stopped and looked at it from a few steps away.

"You like it?" came a voice from behind. "I saw it in a secondhand shop and had to buy it." She smiled and touched the back of my arm. "It's yours, Cam."

I walked to it and touched it. My fingers ran along the keys and I felt it under me.

"Thank you." I turned around and faced her. "Thanks, Sarah. It's beautiful."

Later on, Sarah was on the phone for a while, talking

to Steve. His semifinal was on the next day and everyone decided on going. What I didn't count on was Steve coming down to our place later that night.

I was on the front porch when his car pulled up and he walked toward me. He stood there.

"Hi Cam."

"Hi Steve."

I stood up and we both watched each other. I remembered the last time we'd spoken down here. Tonight, though, Steve's face was shattered, like it was at the oval, way back at the start of winter.

"I heard what happened last night," he began. "Sarah told me on the phone."

"You came to see Rube?" I asked. "He's in bed, but I'd say he's still awake." I went to open the door, but Steve didn't go in.

He stayed in front of me and didn't move.

"What?" I asked. "What?"

His voice was abrupt, but quiet. "I didn't come here to see Rube — I came to see you." He adjusted his eyes slightly. More respectful. "Sarah told me you carried him home from the old train yard. . . ."

"It wasn't anything —"

"No. Don't lie, Cam. It *was* something." He stood above me, but it was only a physical thing now. A matter of height. "It was something, all right?"

I agreed with him. "All right."

Steve stood there.

I stood there.

493

The silence collected between us, and we smiled at each other.

He went inside a bit later but didn't stay long. He came and said good-bye not long after I went in to write on the typewriter. No words came.

In truth, I think the typewriter scared me, because I wanted to write perfectly on it. I was still staring at it just after ten o'clock.

Soon, I thought. *The words will come soon. . . .*

The weeks traveled and winter was drawing to a close. Steve won his grand final. Rube and I were brothers again, though things had changed now forever. He healed up nicely and was still far too handsome for his own good. If anything, his scars would make him even more desirable.

Dad didn't need us at work too much, and one Saturday afternoon, I was curious about Octavia Ash. I still wanted her badly, and on many occasions I'd imagined us being together. I hoped she felt the same. There were no days or nights without her, and on the last Saturday of winter, I went down to the harbor to see if she was there. I hoped she was, mainly because I didn't want her to still be hiding from me. I wanted her to stay as she was, whether she wanted me or not. The harbor belonged to her, and I would have hated myself if I took that away from her.

I boarded a train at Central and made it in quick time to Circular Quay.

From the platform, I saw the people.

They were crowded around the girl with the harmonica, and a familiar feeling showed its face in me again. *Octavia Ash*, I thought, and I went down there, to watch from far away, and maybe hear just a few musical glimpses that came from her mouth. *One more chance*, I thought.

I caught a bus to Bronte in the afternoon and looked for another shell. I didn't find one like the first one. I didn't even try. The one I found was slightly broken, but it was beautiful nonetheless. It had soft ripples and a tanned color that was worn into it. That night, I told Rube what I'd be doing with it the next day. He didn't object. In fact, I think he was glad. He wanted it.

"Y' don't mind?" I asked.

He shook his head. "No — I'll even come with you if y' want."

It didn't matter anymore. There was no animosity. Not even any thought that Octavia and Rube had ever been together. That felt so long ago now. We were different people. Octavia never *had* been with Rube — not in *this* life. Not in the life that began the night I carried my brother home.

"So do you mind?" he asked again.

"What?"

"If I come with y'?"

I thought about it and it felt right.

"No worries," I said.

The next day arrived and we caught the train. On the platform at Circular Quay, I took the shell from my pocket and we made our way down.

"Good luck," said Rube. He stayed back and waited.

The crowd was there.

The girl was there, and today, I didn't hesitate.

I walked through the crowd and stood before her, then crouched down. When the music stopped, I kissed the shell and gently placed it in the jacket, stood back, and looked into her. "I'm Cameron Wolfe," I said. My eyes blurred but I kept talking. "And I miss you. . . ."

The words registered and for a moment, Octavia and I stood there, silent, along with the crowd.

"Well?" some old lady asked, just as I noticed that Octavia was still wearing the necklace she'd made out of the previous shell. Maybe there was some hope. . . .

I wanted to hear her voice. I wanted her to say that she already had a shell like that but that she'd take it anyway. And I wanted to see her smile — the straight line of teeth that crowded at the edges.

None of that came, though.

We only stood.

"I'll wait by the water," I spoke quietly. "If you want to come over when you're finished, I'll be there. If not, it's all right," and I walked away, back through the crowd. A silence stretched itself out until the music arrived like a knot. When I crouched at the water, I could still hear it, and I knew I'd done enough, whether she came to me later or not. I'd done enough.

I'd forgotten all about Rube, but it wasn't long until he was behind me.

"Cam?"

"Hey Rube."

"It went okay?"

"I think so."

As he crouched down, his hands played with his pockets. We both stared at the water, and I could tell Rube was falling apart, just slightly. He looked on and said, "I'll go in a second, but first I have to tell you somethin'. . . ." He looked at me now. We were in each other's eyes.

"Rube?" I asked.

The water of the harbor rose up and dived down.

"See," he said. "All my life I sort of expected you to look up to me, y' know?" The expression on his face only just held on.

I nodded.

"But now I know," he went on. "Now I know."

I waited but nothing came. I asked. "Know what?"

He stared into me and his voice shook as he said, "That I look up to you. . . ."

His words circled me and went in. They got beneath my skin and I knew there was no way back out. They were in there for always, and so was this moment, between Ruben Wolfe and me.

We crouched there, and when we finally stood up and turned to face the world, I could feel something climbing through me. I could feel it on its hands and knees inside me, rising up, rising up — and I smiled.

I smiled, thinking, *the hunger*, because I knew it all too well.

The hunger.

The desire.

Then, slowly, as we walked on, I felt the beauty of it, and I could taste it, like words inside my mouth.

THE EDGES OF WORDS

I sit here by the water, writing only in my mind.

At home, the typewriter waits.

At my side, a girl sits silently, and I'm thankful, because, in the end, I realize I didn't get this girl, in every way that that means —

I found her.

And I want to keep finding her, for as long as we allow.

. . . The water looks at us, and I think now, of the edges of words, the loyalty of blood and the music of girls. I think of the hands of brothers, and of hungry dogs that howl through the night.

There are so many moments to remember, and sometimes I think that maybe we're not really people at all. Maybe moments are what we are.

Moments of weakness, of strength.

Moments of rescue, of everything.

I see people walking through the city and wonder where they've been, and what the moments of their lives have done to them. If they're anything like me, their moments have held them up and shot them down.

Sometimes I just survive.

But sometimes I stand on the rooftop of my existence, arms stretched out, begging for more.

That's when the stories show up in me.

They find me all the time.

They're made of footsteps not only to the girl, but to me. They're made of hunger and desire and trying to live decent.

The only trouble is, I don't know which of those stories comes first.

Maybe they all just merge into one.

We'll see, I guess.

I'll let you know when I decide.

THIS BOOK WAS DESIGNED BY STEVE SCOTT
AND ELIZABETH B. PARISI.
THE TEXT WAS SET IN MINION PRO,
A TYPEFACE IN THE MINION FAMILY, UPDATED IN 2000,
DESIGNED BY ROBERT SLIMBACH.
THE BOOK WAS PRINTED AND BOUND AT
R. R. DONNELLEY IN CRAWFORDSVILLE, INDIANA.
PRODUCTION WAS SUPERVISED BY CHERYL WEISMAN,
AND MANUFACTURING WAS SUPERVISED BY ADAM CRUZ.